ALL HER
LITTLE SECRETS

ALL HER
LITTLE SECRETS

WANDA M. MORRIS

THORNDIKE PRESS
A part of Gale, a Cengage Company

Copyright © 2021 by Wanda M. Morris.
Thorndike Press, a part of Gale, a Cengage Company.

LIBRARY OF CONGRESS CIP DATA ON FILE.
CATALOGUING IN PUBLICATION FOR THIS BOOK
IS AVAILABLE FROM THE LIBRARY OF CONGRESS.

ISBN-13: 978-1-4328-9592-1 (hardcover alk. paper)

Published in 2022 by arrangement with William Morrow Paperbacks, an imprint of HarperCollins Publishers

Printed in Mexico
Print Number: 01   Print Year: 2022

To my parents,
Mabel, who taught me the power and joy
of the written word,
And
Herman, a fighter to the end.
And for
Fred, Cynthia, and Ural.

When elephants fight, the only thing that suffers is the grass.

— African proverb

Chillicothe, Georgia, August 1979

The three of us — me, my brother, Sam, and Vera or Miss Vee as everyone in Chillicothe called her — looked like a little trio of vagabonds as we stood in the Greyhound Bus Station, which, in Chillicothe, meant a lean-to bus port in the parking lot of the Piggly Wiggly. By God's grace, we'd survived summer's blazing days and humid nights, the fire ant stings and mosquito welts, and all the side-of-the-mouth whispers that floated around town. *What happened? What did those young 'uns do? Why is Ellie Littlejohn really leaving town?* Even though I was headed to Virginia on a full-ride scholarship to boarding school, it didn't stop some people around town from talking in hushed tones and asking meddlesome questions.

The morning sun sizzled across the black asphalt parking lot scattered with a few dented cars and an old Ford pickup. But we were the only ones waiting for the 7:15 bus headed north. I wore a tie-dyed T-shirt and a pair of jeans Vera had cut off at the knees when they got too short. She hadn't gotten to the jeans Sam was wearing because they were about two inches above his ankles. His yellow T-shirt still bore the cherry Popsicle stain from the day before. And from the looks of it, he hadn't combed his hair, either.

I held tight to the old brown cardboard suitcase Vera had borrowed from her friend Miss Toney. I didn't have much, but everything I owned was neatly packed inside it, including a sturdy winter coat, two pairs of new shoes, and a few toiletries courtesy of Vera passing around the hat among her friends and the congregation at the Full Gospel Baptist Church.

In my other hand, I held a paper bag with three pieces of fried chicken, a couple of biscuits, and an ample slice of sweet potato pie. There was no extra money for McDonald's or Burger King along the way. Vera's cousin Birdie drove us to the station and stood against her '68 black-and-gold Impala a few feet away, waiting for us to say our good-byes. I was a frazzled bag of nervous energy at the thought of traveling so far away from the only place I'd ever known. I was leaving Sam and Vera, the only people I loved.

But I had to go.

I was tall for my age, so Vera had to reach up to fuss with the thick ponytail on top of my head. "Now, Ellie, you mind your lessons at school. Remember, you have to work twice as hard as them white kids, even though you just as smart. Aim high. Take no blessing for granted." She patted the ponytail for good measure. "You write me as often as you want. I put some stamps in your suitcase. Everything gon' be fine."

Vera, a thick light-skinned woman with deep dimples that framed a large gap-toothed smile, always spoke with such authority. Like everything she said was right or true. She flashed that smile at me.

"Yes, ma'am."

Sam hung at Vera's side kicking the rubber toe of his canvas sneaker against the asphalt. Even though he did what he called "cool stuff" like smoking cigarettes and stealing candy from the grocery store, at that moment, he looked exactly like what he was, a small and frightened ten-year-old boy. I sat my suitcase down and placed my lunch bag on top of it. I grabbed his hand and pulled him off, out of Vera's earshot.

"No more smoking cigarettes while I'm

11

gone, okay?" I said.

"I ain't touched no cigarettes since Miss Vee caught me. I'm not going through that again." Sam rolled his eyes.

I giggled. "And you can't be stealing from the grocery store, okay? That was cute when you were little but you're too big for that stuff. You can get into really big trouble, especially if Miss Vee finds out." He frowned and looked away.

"I just don't understand why you got to leave. Why can't you go to school here?" Sam asked.

I plucked a piece of lint from Sam's little Afro. "I told you. It's a different kind of school. You study there *and* live there. And don't worry. You'll be safe now. There's nobody around to hurt you anymore."

I reached down and hugged him so tight if he had been any smaller, I might have snapped him in two. A few seconds later, he wriggled from my grip and ran off to Birdie's car. I knew he was crying and didn't want me to see.

The Greyhound bus pulled to a stop in front of us with a long loud hiss. "Here it is," Vera said. "Now you got enough money in your bag for a taxicab once you get in Virginia. I know that school got telephones so don't pretend like they don't. You call

12

me as soon as you get there. Call collect, you hear me?"

I smiled. "Yes, ma'am."

Vera leaned her large frame in and hugged me and the waterfall between us started. Vera wasn't much on crying, but anyone standing in that parking lot would have thought the opposite. She finally let me go and pulled a couple tissues from her skirt pocket. She wiped my face and handed the tissue to me.

I stared at Vera. "I'm scared."

She wrapped an arm around my waist. "I know you are, honey bunny. But it's all gonna work out just fine. Your momma was right about one thing. You ain't but four-teen, but you too big for this place. This town ain't equipped to hold somebody as smart and strong as you. Now, get on that bus and don't come back until the good Lord sends you back. Now go."

The driver trotted down the stairs of the bus and smiled at us. He took my suitcase and tucked it underneath in the luggage compartment.

Vera gave me another hug. "Go on now."

I climbed the stairs of the bus into the stifling scent of disinfectant and human sweat. *I'm a big girl. I can handle this.*

I walked past a pregnant lady with two

13

little kids snuggled underneath each of her arms, an old man and woman sitting side by side talking, before I took a window seat near the middle of the bus. I located my little ragtag family out in the parking lot. Sammy, Vera, and Birdie stood beside the car waving up at me. I watched them, Vera smiling and Miss Birdie blowing kisses, as the bus pulled out of the lot and onto the street. And then I cried for a solid hour, straight across the Georgia–South Carolina state line.

■ ■ ■ ■

PART 1
THE ELEPHANTS

■ ■ ■ ■

CHAPTER 1

Six forty-five in the morning was far too early for keeping secrets.

But Michael and I are lawyers and that's what lawyers do. We keep secrets. Attorney-client privilege, confidential work product, ethical rules, all the ten-dollar terms we use to describe the ways we harbor information from prying eyes.

I hustled through the parking garage, a veritable wind tunnel on a cold blustery January morning, and inside the lobby of Houghton Transportation Company. Houghton management proudly announced its corporate prosperity and success to visitors with an entryway of gleaming chandeliers, polished steel, and veined marble floors. Inside this sleek glass and metal cage, we raced around for ten- and twelve-hour days in our hamster wheels of closed-door meetings, videoconference calls, and potluck lunches in the breakroom.

It was so early, the security guard hadn't even shown up for his post at the front desk. *Good. No clumsy banter.* The only sound in the lobby was the click-click of my red suede Louboutin pumps skittering across the marbled floor to the elevator bank. I pressed the call button for the twentieth floor. I don't drink coffee, but I wished I had brought a travel mug of tea or a bottle of water with me to wash away the brain fog. Morning meetings weren't unusual for us. But this one was particularly early and I'm not partial to sunrise secrets.

As the elevator rose, I closed my eyes for a moment and leaned into the wall. Michael is the executive vice president and general counsel, and I work under him as assistant general counsel in the Legal Department. Michael was cryptic in his call the night before, maybe because someone else was nearby: *Let's meet in my office in the morning. 6:45.* I didn't press him. He did the same thing last week, a late-night meeting that lasted over an hour. Only we didn't talk about work. We didn't even have sex.

That time, he wanted me to sympathetically listen while he complained about his wife. My better judgment told me I needed to end this. So many years. So much time wasted.

Michael was gorgeous with chiseled features, deep blue eyes, and the tall trim stature of a Kennedy from Cape Cod. If anyone had seen us together as a couple, we would have made quite the sight, me with all my tall, cocoa-hued coily mane and jiggly midsection against his slim buttoned-down WASP frame.

I've stood five feet, eight inches — six feet, in the right heels — since I was in the seventh grade. Men are either intimidated by me or challenged to climb and conquer "Mt. Ellice." Honestly, I think men are attracted to the darker side they see in me. *What makes her tick?* they ask themselves. But Michael was different, or at least that's what I told myself. He matched me in every way — height, intellect, and humor. He was my equal except for that pesky little business of a wife and two kids. I was stupid for sleeping with this man. Vera and her friends had a saying: *Never get your honey where you make your money.*

I should have gone somewhere different after leaving Dillon & Beck, the law firm where we used to work, but he made me a generous offer and I followed him here. And nothing had changed, despite all his promises of a new beginning and a different work-life balance as in-house counsel.

Maybe one day I'll get my shit together and go find the job, and the life, that I deserve.

The elevator pinged and the doors slid open onto the executive suite. Everything on this floor was plush, soft and expensive, unlike the utilitarian, budget-friendly accommodations two floors below in the Legal Department. I paced past the darkened offices of the CEO's sycophants, more commonly referred to as the Executive Committee, before I reached Michael's suite. Everything was dark here, too. If he dragged me up here at this ungodly hour and forgot about our meeting, I'd be royally pissed.

The company's reserve lighting system created a menacing tangle of shapes and shadows in the anteoffice. A small pit-a-pat of fear slid through me as I flipped the light switch. His assistant's desk was neat and orderly, just the way she always left it.

I tapped lightly on his door. "Michael, it's me. Ellice."

No answer.

My skin prickled. I opened the door and flipped on the lights.

The bright crimson spray of blood was everywhere. Shock raced through me like a torpedo before landing in a hard knot at the pit of my stomach. My knees buckled as a tidal wave of nausea washed over me, like I would be sick and fade into black at any moment. But I didn't panic. I didn't utter a sound.

The star-shaped hole in Michael's right temple was ragged and grisly, like someone had tried to open his skull with a sledgehammer instead of a bullet. Blood had oozed in erratic streams along the side of his face, creating diminutive red rivers in the wrinkles along his jawline, before pooling at the end of his chin and trickling onto his starched white oxford shirt. The air hung thick with the acrid, copper scent of blood. And the hum of the fluorescent lights, the only sound in the room, was like a thousand bumblebees.

An instant later, my mind clicked, as if someone else were inside my head, directing me.

Run. Just go.

I turned my eyes away from Michael's lifeless body and the gun beside him. I hated myself for what I was thinking. Amid all this carnage, my first thoughts were to run, to leave without calling for help.

No one knows I'm here.

I slowly inched away from his body, careful not to touch anything. The few shreds of conscience I had left warned me that to leave would be reprehensible.

21

I prayed to God for forgiveness, turned off the lights, and quietly closed the office door behind me.

This would be the last secret between Michael and me.

CHAPTER 2

What the hell had I just done?

I rushed off the elevator onto the eighteenth floor, inside the Legal Department. My body buzzed like someone had slapped me, leaving the sting to rumble underneath my skin. My thoughts were on fire. Blood. Death. This was Chillicothe all over again. And I did what I always did. I ran. My earliest memory is of running. My brother, Sam, hadn't been born yet. My mother, Martha, had me by my hand and we were running, my little legs beating fast to keep up with her. It was nighttime. Cold outside. And she kept telling me to hurry. I don't know who or what we were running from. I started to cry but she told me if I cried, she would have to leave me behind. So I ran.

I didn't hit the override switch for the reserve lighting; the dim spotlights were enough. I needed the cloak of darkness to cover my shame. I darted through a maze of soft-walled cubicles in the center of the floor that housed the support staff. Attorney offices, tight but windowed, formed a perimeter around the maze. Even though we didn't bill our hours like people did in a law firm, most people in the department still kept law firm hours — start late, work late. With any luck, it would be over an hour before people would start to trickle in.

Seven A.M. on this floor was like a fire station after a three-alarm call — offices and cubicles empty, things left scattered and unsettled. Each of us, working late into the evening until, realizing there were kids to pick up or dry cleaners to hit before closing, left our desks, files, papers disheveled, waiting exactly as we'd left them the night before.

I made it to my office from the executive suite without anyone seeing me. *Thank God.* No one really sees me around this company anyway. They see what I want them to see. Smart. Tempered. Ellice Littlejohn, the consummate professional. My legal advice spot-on. Impeccably dressed, a funny quip when needed. I'm the one they admire and respect. That's who they see.

I stood inside the cramped, drafty space that doubled as my office. I'm the only Black person in the Legal Department. I'm not saying one had anything to do with the other, but if an employee's office space reflects their value to the company, Houghton didn't think much of me. I used to dream of becoming the chief legal officer or even the CEO of a Fortune 500. I was supposed to have it all by now — a doting husband, two point five bright and gifted kids, and a successful career that others envied — but now, those things were well out of my reach. I was closer to menopause than marriage material.

And all the stupid decisions I'd made before led me to this small gray freezer of an office, the lone Black lawyer working with other lawyers half my age, the majority of whom I didn't like. Their pompous, know-it-all attitudes made it hard for me to settle in and feel like a real part of the "Houghton family," as executive management liked to refer to the company. Michael always paid me so well, I learned to ignore it.

The inklings of a headache nibbled at my left temple. I tossed my coat and bags in one of the guest chairs, scooted around to the business side of my desk and pulled a small portable heater from behind a stack of folders. I set the knob on "High" and listened to the scratchy hum of the fan blades for a few seconds before collapsing into my chair. Having portable heaters in your office was a violation of company policy. But I'd be damned if I gave up my heater before Building Services installed a better HVAC system on this floor.

Now, there was a dead man two floors above me and if anyone knew I had been sleeping with him, it would be another disaster. I closed my eyes. A jagged bloody hole in his head. A gun on the floor beside him. My eyes popped open. *Suicide?* It didn't make sense, although Michael had complained about his wife recently. Maybe something more happened between them. Maybe she found out about us. What would I do now? I would keep my ass in this chair, keep a low profile, and let someone else bring me the awful news about Michael. The farther away from this, the better.

God forgive me. All I had to do was call for help. Surely calling for help wouldn't be enough for anyone to dig through my background. Or would it? Yes. I'd made the right decision to leave his office. He was dead. My sticking around to answer a flurry of questions from the police wouldn't bring him back. And then, in an instant, sadness engulfed me. Michael deserved better.

I stared out at the pink-orange blush of

dawn crawling across the city. Long fingers of white clouds slowly inched across the sky. With its constant construction, Atlanta's skyline had shorn its squat brick buildings for the gleaming high-rise look of New York City or Chicago. A southern mecca for business and industry. The New South. I was still staring out the window when the lights popped on across the floor. My pulse quickened. Someone else was here. I knew there were no security cameras in the executive suite. Michael had told me. Still, I couldn't help but think: *Had anyone seen me leaving the twentieth floor?*

I watched the door and perked up to listen for more sounds. The walls in the Legal Department had the soundproof capacity of toilet paper. But things went silent. I needed to look busy in case someone passed by my office, so I flipped on my computer and stared into the screen. After a few seconds, the company logo of a fast-moving gray truck and tag line popped on the screen. *Houghton Transportation — where you're family and family comes first!*

"Hey! Morning, sunshine!"

I jumped. Rudy Clifton, one of the senior lawyers in the Legal Department, was leaning in my doorway with a Starbucks coffee cup in his hand and a wide pearly smile.

27

Even though Rudy reported to me, he never had any qualms about walking into my office uninvited and most times without knocking. I tolerated it only because he brought in good work product and good gossip. Rudy and I had worked on several legal panels together over the years and became good friends. When he got laid off from his law firm, I immediately hired him to work at Houghton six months after Michael hired me. He repaid that favor with unwavering loyalty, one of the few people I trusted at Houghton.

"Why are you here so early?" I heard my fragile nerves popping through the cracks in my voice.

"Good morning to you, too." He grimaced. Rudy was handsome and hunky in a college-frat-boy sort of way with his two-day stubble and a mop of dark wavy hair. "Those little people that live in my house — they woke up at four o'clock this morning crying for bottles. Couldn't get back to sleep. What dragged you in this early?"

I hesitated for a few seconds, skirting through my brain for some deflection. I feigned a smile. "Haven't you heard? I sleep here now since the settlement fell apart in the Robbins litigation."

"Good luck." Rudy laughed. "Oh snap,

you wanna hear the latest?" Rudy, still wearing his overcoat, glanced over his shoulder before slipping inside my office.

"Please, Rudy. No gossip this early, okay?" I rubbed a thumb into my left temple. Morning traffic and sirens echoed up from the ground below.

"I heard Jonathan's having an affair. Guess who the lucky lady is?"

I sighed deeply and settled in. I knew he wouldn't rest until he could unload the latest nugget he'd uncovered. Rudy was King of the Gossip Mill. His friendly nature and the ability to talk to anyone made people tell him their deepest, darkest secrets. And then, he told me. Under any other circumstances, I might have indulged him and pretended to be interested.

"C'mon. Guess."

I shook my head and shrugged.

"Willow . . . Willow Sommerville. HR VP."

I signed into my computer and pretended to read something from the monitor. "Oh."

"*Oh!* Is that all you have to say?"

Rudy got his kicks from being the first to pass along a fresh, tender piece of gossip, and I could tell I had disappointed him greatly.

"What's up?" Rudy said, inspecting me like a pair of Michelin tires on a used car.

"You okay?"

"Just a little tired, I guess."

"You sure?" He raised an eyebrow. Rudy had picked up on a scent. "I know you're my boss, but you're my buddy, too. You good?"

"I'm good." I stood from my chair and grabbed my mug, like I was about to head to the breakroom, a subtle cue for him to leave my office. "Seriously, I'm fine. Just a little out of sorts. Didn't sleep well last night." Before I could usher Rudy out of my office, Anita, my administrative assistant, poked her chubby face inside the office door. *Damn!* I couldn't catch a break.

Anita, a short stout woman with a graying poodle perm, either bought her clothes one size too small or decided she wasn't buying new ones that fit. "Hey, did you guys see the ambulance downstairs?" she said.

Oh God. I glanced at my watch. It wasn't even eight o'clock. Someone had discovered Michael's body already.

Rudy's eyes grew wide. "Ambulance?"

"Yeah. There's an ambulance and a ton of police cars in front of the building. Jimmy, down at the security desk, said something happened up on Twenty. But he didn't have any details. At least, that's what he told me," Anita said, the last sentence spiked by the skepticism in her voice.

Rudy and I dashed over to my window and stared down onto the street below. The entire block of Peachtree Street was a blur of red and blue lights. Traffic was snarled all the way up to Seventeenth Street. A few impatient drivers honked their horns in the mounting backup of cars, as if that ever does any good in Atlanta traffic. A heavy sense of dread settled in my chest. I backed away from the window.

"Are you serious?" Rudy said, asking no one in particular. "I'll be right back."

Anita and I watched him hustle from my office and down the hall. I knew he was off in search of his sources to shake them down for information. I already knew what his sources knew.

"What d'ya think happened up there?" Anita said, removing her coat.

I didn't respond. The lingering headache tightened its vise across my forehead. *Calm down.* I had to keep my wits about me now. Soon enough, everyone in the office, lawyers and admins alike, would be scampering between their offices and cubicles, leaving breadcrumbs of gossip and guesswork along the way. That's the way it worked around Houghton. It was protocol for big events in the department that no one wanted to discuss openly like layoffs, demotions, or, in this case, an executive officer's suicide.

Fifteen minutes later, Rudy walked into my office with a grim face and closed the door. "Michael committed suicide."

"Who told you that?" My skin began to buzz again. *Had anyone seen me leaving the twentieth floor?*

"Don't ask. But suicide?" Rudy shook his head. "That doesn't make sense. What healthy, well-adjusted guy gets dressed for work, packs a gun in his briefcase, and says to himself, 'Okay, I'll eat my gun here at my desk right after I finish reading the *Wall Street Journal*'?"

"Please don't talk like that." I pushed around a couple folders on my desk to quell my nerves.

Rudy slumped into the chair in front of my desk. "I'm just sayin' people don't usually commit suicide at their job, unless it's a workplace shooting, in which case they try to take a few others out with them. It's a private act."

I swiveled my chair and stared out at the fully blossomed winter sunrise now bathing the downtown skyline. Private acts. I thought about my own life. Decades pass and I think I've processed the horror, but somehow it still ebbs and flows. A few seconds later, memories from Chillicothe bubbled to the surface too — an old utility shed, a little boy's tears, and a cavern of fear.

People around here didn't see the real me.

As expected, I had a hard time concentrating on work. After Rudy left, at least three other people poked their head inside my office asking, *Did you hear what happened up on Twenty?* Michael was dead and, slowly, bits and pieces about his death trickled out like the drip-drip of a leaky faucet, laced with the spin and embellishment of every person who shared the dreadful news of Michael's suicide. Michael was depressed. Michael had tried to kill himself before. Michael accidentally shot himself. All of it was so far from the truth and what I knew about him.

I'd had enough. I decided to go down to the lobby for a cup of tea and some clarity. The flashing lights and sirens of the morning's activity had settled down to the normal din of passing traffic outside and the white noise of people milling about inside the lobby, nodding sadly at one another, speculating about why such a nice guy would do such a horrible thing.

I rounded the corner out of Starbucks

when I spotted Hardy King, the director of Corporate Security. Hardy made two of me and I'm not petite. His crumpled suit jacket and shirt had long since surrendered to the girth of his oversize gut, giving him the appearance of a hastily made bed with a pillow tossed in the center of it. Hardy was originally from New Jersey. No southern accent. I didn't have one either. I ditched my accent fifteen minutes after stepping foot on the grounds of Coventry Academy Prep when a girl giggled after I raised my hand during orientation to say I wanted to *axe* a question. She made a chopping motion and said I probably shouldn't hurt the teacher. I learned the proper way to say the word *ask* and never made another diction mistake again. My first lesson in code-switching.

Hardy threw both arms around me in a big bear hug. Hardy hugged everyone. "You heard?"

"Yeah."

"How you doing? What about the rest of the folks in Legal?" Hardy had served as a witness in a few cases and knew everyone in the Legal Department. Most people in the company considered Hardy a schmuck, an overpaid driver for Nate and other executives on the twentieth floor. But, like Rudy, he was a nice guy, always helpful and had the scoop on whatever was going on inside the company. He was also a widower with no kids. I figured he was probably lonely, so I always felt a little sorry for him.

"I think we're all in shock. It doesn't make sense."

Hardy shook his head sadly. "Yeah, Mikey was one of the good guys."

I was nervous but I had to ask. "Who found him?"

"His assistant. She's a mess now too. For good reason. It wasn't a pretty scene. We had to send her home."

"Oh." Michael's bloody body flashed through my mind again.

Hardy looked at me, all sad and pitiful with the corners of his mouth folded down. "Did he say anything to make you think he'd do something like this?"

"No. That's why everyone's in shock. Michael hated guns. I didn't think he even owned one."

"Really?"

Two women passed by us laughing about something. They weren't particularly loud, but their jovial behavior seemed out of place in the lobby today. Hardy and I watched them until they were out of earshot.

"Did he leave a note?"

Hardy scratched his graying buzz cut. "Nothing."

A part of me was glad he didn't. Whatever demons Michael wrestled with should remain his own. Less fodder for the gossip herd to feed on. For a fleeting moment, I wondered what part I might have played in his death. Had this been his way out of a bad marriage and a lackluster affair?

"I guess it might not matter now, but was there anything going on in Legal? Some big case you guys were trying that was getting to him? Stressing him out?"

"No. I'm telling you, he was fine."

"This is crazy stuff." Hardy shook his head slowly. "And I think the media is gonna have a field day with all this. Don't forget about the folks outside."

I turned toward the lobby windows facing out onto Peachtree Street. A small group of protesters were carrying placards: HOUGHTON HATES BLACKS AND UNFAIR TREATMENT, UNFAIR HIRING AND DON'T SPEND YOUR $$ WITH HOUGHTON.

"The protesters have been out there for months now," Hardy said. "I can't imagine they'll let up now that the news cameras are around."

"Three months to be exact, but you have to admit, there aren't many people around this company that look like me."

Hardy nodded understandingly. "Yeah, that needs to stop too."

The protests began a few weeks after several Black and Latinx applicants filed an EEOC charge alleging they were denied employment at Houghton despite their qualifications. A few weeks after, several Black employees in Operations joined and alleged they were denied management promotions. The company was bracing for a lawsuit. Over the weeks leading up to the holidays, the protesting crowds had grown smaller. There weren't more than a handful now. But Hardy made a good point. Racial discrimination allegations and an executive officer's suicide could be a recipe for a PR nightmare.

"You don't think the two are connected?" I asked.

Hardy shrugged. "It won't matter if the news guys can spin it the right way. Either way, this is not a good time for Houghton."

CHAPTER 3

A few hours later, I stepped off the elevator onto the twentieth floor, *again,* this time tightly gripping a notepad and pen. I had been summoned to Nate Ashe's executive suite. I'd never been to the CEO's office — until now. Michael had made a string of broken promises to give me executive exposure, opportunities to "stretch my wings" and get me promoted into a business role in the company. Lately, whenever I complained of not attending meetings with the executives or getting on the agenda for executive presentations, he told me he was protecting me, and I should thank him.

Our little "friends with benefits" situation had run its course and still had left me empty-handed.

It was here, on the twentieth floor, that Houghton's executives decided the career fates of director-level employees like me, hungry for the next rung of the corporate ladder. Here, we were relegated to HR folders of résumés and performance reviews that were scrutinized and picked apart by the Executive Committee. And when things didn't work out, this was where decisions were made about who got fired. Had they found out about me and Michael? Would this be a repeat of what happened at the law firm?

Whatever the reason for my being here, it couldn't be good.

After my tight gray quarters, a couple floors below, I stepped inside Nate's office like Dorothy wandering into the Technicolor sparkle of Oz. The CEO sat behind a massive custom-leather-wrapped desk without a scrap of paper on it. His plush high-back wing chairs gave the stiff guest chairs in my office a run for their money. Two entire walls of floor-to-ceiling windows offered a mesmerizing view of Ansley and Piedmont Parks, with the skyscrapers of Buckhead's financial district off in the distance. Modern art with whip splashes of bright color adorned the remaining walls, giving the entire room an air of New York's Museum of Modern Art.

"Hi. You wanted to see me?" I asked.

"Hey, Ellice! C'mon in. You want a water, a Coke-Cola?" Nate asked in his easy southern drawl.

"No, thank you."

"Let's sit over there where we'll be more comfortable." Nate pointed toward the vintage Egg chair and leather sofa on the other side of the room. Everything about him was warm and friendly. His soothing southern tone, the froth of silver-white hair and neatly trimmed mustache, the Armani suit, and the slightest hint of a paunch made him very statesmanlike. He could have easily been groomed to be a senator from the great state of Georgia, kindly yielding the floor to his congressional colleagues. Instead, he reigned as the CEO, a wise paternal figure, guiding his family-owned company.

I stood for a moment admiring a picture hanging over the sofa. The painting, a striking depiction of an African elephant charging through trees and foliage, stood out from the other art in his office.

"You like that painting, huh?" Nate said.

"I do."

"It was a gift from a friend. He had it commissioned by an artist in Mexico. Did you know that Indians, Persians, and Carthaginians used elephants as tanks in ancient war battles?"

"I didn't."

Nate walked around his desk and stood beside me. "Elephants are some of the most intelligent creatures on Earth." He cocked his head and folded his arms across his chest, admiring the picture as if he had painted it himself. "They're powerful, too, not just because of their size, but because they have a commitment to family, the ability to stick together that is unlike any other animal species aside from humans. They even grieve the loss of their kin just like humans. Reminds me of us here at Houghton . . . charging forward, sticking together, taking care of our own. There's power in that."

The family thing again.

"Have you ever been on safari?" I asked, trying to edge him off the topic of family.

"Not unless you call huntin' deer and wild rabbit up in the Blue Ridge Mountains a safari." Nate laughed.

I gave a half smile. So Nate was another crusty old white guy, living out his colonial fantasies by shooting up some poor animals out in the wilderness for sport.

"C'mon, Ellice," he said, dropping onto the sofa beneath the painting. "Let's take a load off."

I sat in the chair across from him. Nate was pleasant enough. Even so, I was cautious. Before this conversation, I would have bet my mortgage payment that Nate couldn't pick me out of a precinct lineup.

A few seconds later, Willow Somerville strolled into Nate's office without a knock or an announcement. "Good afternoon, Ellice," she said in a sugar-and-syrup southern accent that reminded me of mint juleps and ladies catching the vapors on plantation porches. She wore a bloodred St. John knit sheath and looked the quintessential modern-day southern belle — blond and bone-thin. The rumor mill went into overdrive right after Nate plucked her, a relatively new and unknown middle manager, and appointed her head of HR for the entire organization. She took a seat beside Nate on the sofa, sitting on the edge, feet tucked together like a beauty pageant contestant waiting her turn to give her speech for solving world peace. The two of them were giving me what Vera used to call "a shit-eating grin." A smile of the insincere.

Something was up. My guess: HR was here to act as a witness to my termination. Somehow, they found out about me and Michael. Now Michael was dead, and I would be fired. Fear slinked down my spine.

Nate was the first to speak. "I thought it might be a good idea to have Willow join us." Willow nodded, the same uncomfortable grin still planted across her face. All I could think was, *Where will I go now?* I'd followed Michael here to Houghton three years ago after the fiasco at the law firm.

Nate stared out the window for a beat, then turned back to me. "I don't have to tell you how hard Michael's death has hit us. Something awful like this doesn't leave anybody unscathed, least of all the folks who worked with him. It's been a bear up here, too." I could feel my left eye twitch. I gazed down at my notepad.

Nate continued, "Board members are calling and asking for details I can't give 'em. Sayles was family, but they're more concerned about how it all looks. It's irksome. The worst thing in the world is a board member with too much time on his hands, huh?" I looked back at him and smiled at his joke.

Nate smoothed his mustache, his brows pinched together in confusion. The room went silent. If he was going to fire me, I wished he would just get on with it already. I glanced at Willow. For the first time since entering the office, her expression changed. She gave a side-eye of concern at Nate.

"Now, where was I?" Nate said.

Willow glanced at me, then back at Nate.

"I believe you were just about to discuss the changes in the Legal Department," she said.

"Yes . . . oh yes!" Nate piped up. "That's right. Ellice, I want you to head up the Legal Department. I'd like you to replace Michael as Houghton's executive vice president and general counsel."

My jaw went slack with surprise.

"You'll be an easy approval for the board of directors," Nate continued, "And don't worry. I'll make sure we maintain Michael's precedent for paying you handsomely. We'll give you a thirty-five percent pay raise. You'll get bonus, car allowance, club memberships. All the perks that go along with the job. Isn't that right, Willow?"

"Absolutely!" she replied.

I couldn't breathe. My quick and dirty math meant this raise would put me in a stratospheric pay range for attorneys and executives at Houghton. Here was the promotion I'd been craving, along with a huge salary to boot.

I just didn't expect it to come about this way.

"But why . . . I mean . . . why me?" I could hear my voice quivering slightly. "I just assumed Walter Graves or one of the other attorneys who've been here longer would be —"

44

Nate beamed. "Why not? You're certainly qualified. I know you would have been Michael's first pick. Did he ever tell you the story behind his hiring you?"

"Uh, I'm not sure I know what story you're referring to." I couldn't imagine Michael sharing the details of our relationship or how I came to work for him here at the company. Michael was pretty private. We both were.

"Michael was convinced you were the right person to work under him in the Legal Department. He said you were smart, and you didn't mind a lil' hard work. Hell, Michael all but told me he'd quit if I didn't give him authorization for a salary variance to hire you."

"I didn't know that." Michael had never told me that story and it made me feel even guiltier now.

"He was right, too. You're a smart lawyer and those are the best kind!" Nate grinned and winked.

"Thank you."

"And people respect you too. I like that. It takes a lot to navigate your way around an organization like Houghton." Nate eyed me for a moment. "So tell me a lil' bit 'bout yourself."

I looked at Willow. She snapped to, as if

45

she had finally found something of real interest in this meeting. "Oh . . . well, I imagine the things you'd want to know about me you already know," I said. "Georgetown undergrad, Yale Law. Worked at Dillon & Beck before coming to Houghton and —"

Nate brushed his hands through the air. "You're right. I already know that stuff. That's the stuff you've done. I want to know who you *are.*"

"I guess I'm just one of the many hard-working souls you have in the Legal Department." I softly chuckled. I knew this was the part of the conversation where I was supposed to relax and toss about polite banter. Share a story about the kids I didn't have and the tennis I didn't play. Instead, I sat across from him, my brain on a two-minute delay trying to figure out why I was being offered a spot in the executive suite.

Nate smiled. "Now, I'm sure there's more behind all that educational pedigree. Where'd you grow up?"

"Here in Atlanta." I told the same lie I'd been telling since I left Chillicothe. It didn't matter anyway. Chillicothe, Georgia, was so small that most people hadn't heard of it or if they did, they usually confused it with the city of the same name in southern Ohio.

Nate leaned forward on the sofa, his ocean-blue eyes anchored on me. "Married? Kids?"

"No." *God, just let this be over so I can get out of here.* Willow was still planted on the sofa like a well-dressed mannequin, offering nothing to the conversation.

"A beautiful woman like you?" Nate smiled. "Any other family?"

"No. I'm an only child." Better not to mention my family, or what was left of it.

"I see."

"How about you? Are you from Atlanta?" I already knew the answer but asked anyway just to move things along.

"Yep. Born and bred." Nate leaned back on the sofa. "You know, Ellice, I think you could be exactly what this company needs right now. A strong, smart lawyer who can shake off the cobwebs on some of the folks around here. Isn't that right, Willow?"

"I couldn't agree more, Nate." Willow never looked up as she brushed her hand across the hem of her sheath, as if she were flicking away invisible crumbs from her lap.

Nate winked again. "Look, I won't lie. The fact that you're Black is like brown gravy on a biscuit." He chuckled, amused by his own joke.

The company never did any diversity

47

training and now it was showing. Willow's eyes flitted in my direction before she cleared her throat and cast a raised eyebrow at Nate.

That's what this was all about. This wasn't about recognizing me as a valuable asset to the company. This was about me being a *colored asset* they could prop up in front of people to keep the protesters off Houghton's doorstep.

Nate either pretended not to notice Willow's signal or missed it altogether because he talked right through it. "Yep, a Black lady like you is just what we need up here," he said.

"W-w-well," I stammered. "I appreciate the vote of confidence but I'm not sure I . . . I mean . . . it's so soon after —"

"Look, I get it. Michael just died and you think it's too soon to talk about replacing him. Trust me, it's not. We have a responsibility to this company, to the Houghton family."

Even though I'd long craved a role in the executive suite, I didn't want *this* one. Not this way. I opened my mouth to offer a more forceful objection, but Nate raised his hand.

"Hear me out. The board is acting like a bunch of nervous Nellies. All concerned about the optics of this thing. But I'm more concerned with continuing the good work Michael started." Nate leaned forward. "Michael was a good guy. A really good guy. Straight shooter with good moral fiber. I think the best we can do to respect his memory is to keep the company moving forward the way he did. I know he thought very highly of you. I think you'd be the perfect lawyer to replace him. Besides, this is the kind of opportunity that'll do wonders for your career."

I couldn't argue with him on that last point. But Nate was offering me the job full out, not even on an interim basis. It was highly unusual for the company to appoint someone to the executive suite without the usual "dog and pony" show of hiring a search firm, floating names, and interviewing candidates.

But then, it was highly unusual that the general counsel would commit suicide in his office.

Nate stood from the sofa, eased over to the window, and peered out for a beat. He turned back to me. "Listen, I hate the circumstances that brought us to this point. But we need to keep making the right decisions for the right reasons. And I think you're the best person to help us do that. I know this is coming at ya pretty fast and I don't expect an answer right now. Take a little time to think it over."

"Um . . . okay, I will. Thanks." I rose from the chair, finally, grateful to be leaving.

I headed for the elevators with a sense of remorse so strong it made me wince. I shouldn't want this job. Michael died in the very office Nate was now offering me. I tried to mentally grasp the idea of working in the executive suite. As usual, I would be "the only one" on the twentieth floor, just like I'd been in the Legal Department. The lone Black person, expected to speak on behalf of Black folks everywhere, the one expected to represent the success or failure of every Black woman who worked in corporate America. Logically, I knew this wasn't true, but it didn't stop me from feeling that way. It was a burden I'd borne since Coventry Academy Prep.

But becoming an executive was the job I had dreamed of for years. And I had a hard time not smiling to myself whenever I pondered how I might finally be on the right track for a change. As Vera used to say, everything happens for a reason and there just might be a reason that I was tapped for this position.

CHAPTER 4

An hour later, I sat at my desk, the portable heater blowing a lukewarm current, hardly enough to conquer the bone-chilling air in my office. I was about ten degrees away from pulling out the blanket I kept in my bottom drawer. The surreal insanity of the morning's events sliced through my brain: discovering *and leaving* Michael's dead body and the offer to replace him as Houghton's general counsel.

Anita tapped lightly before quietly easing her head inside my office door. "Security just called up. There's a Detective Bradford here to see you?"

"A detective?" I sat straight up in my chair. "To see *me*?"

"Yeah. So what's up?" she said, stepping inside my office, all wide-eyed and expectant, as if we were two preteens about to discuss a middle-school boy crush. "Why would the police want to talk to you?"

I rested my chin in my hand. "I'm not sure we'll ever know the answer to that question."

"Huh?" Anita stared back at me, perplexed.

"Maybe if you go get him, we could both find out. What do you think?"

She snickered. "Oh, right. Sorry," she said before scurrying off. Anita was pleasant enough, but she leaned on the nosy side. Generally, I don't care for nosy people, but she worked harder than any of the other admins on the floor and she had a good sense of humor, which made this place bearable.

I slumped back in my chair and massaged my temple. *Oh God, where's Sam and what the hell has he screwed up now?* I hate the police. Maybe it was my southern upbringing or my own up-close-and-personal experience with law enforcement that made me leery of any guy with a badge and a gun. And now, Sam had dragged them right to my office door. I tried to imagine what kind of trouble he'd fallen into this time. Gambling. Burglary. Car theft.

A few minutes later, Anita returned to my office with a thirtyish honey-colored Black woman in tow. Her svelte figure, pixie haircut, and stylish good looks made her look like a J.Crew model — not someone

52

who would go around shooting bad guys. I pegged her for a runner by her long, lean, nearly-zero-body-fat appearance. I made a mental note to find a gym to join on the weekend. Anita slipped out, closing the door behind her.

"Ms. Littlejohn. I'm Detective Shelly Bradford. I'd like to speak with you about Mr. Sayles's death." Her voice was smooth, professional, no southern accent. She flashed a small badge that I barely looked at as I wrestled with the nervous flutters in my stomach.

So this wasn't about Sam.

But maybe it was worse.

I motioned the detective to one of the stiff guest chairs in front of my desk. She sat, crossed her legs, and surveyed my cramped office with an air that hovered somewhere between curiosity and disdain. She reminded me of the girls I went to school with at Coventry Academy, pretty in their own upper-crust way.

"I understand you worked for Mr. Sayles, correct?"

"Yes, I do — I did."

"His assistant told us you and Mr. Sayles typically met early most mornings." The detective fell silent, as if searching for some telltale tic of incrimination. I didn't flinch.

"Did you meet with him this morning?"

"No." I wasn't lying. Technically, we hadn't. But if Michael committed suicide, why was she in my office asking me a bunch of questions? Maybe someone did see me leaving the twentieth floor. A slow throb pulsed through the center of my left temple.

The detective scrutinized me for a few seconds. "Did you sign in or use your ID badge like everyone else who works here?"

My palms started to slick with sweat. "I lost my badge a few days ago and no one was at the security desk when I arrived."

"Security wasn't on duty when you arrived? What time was that?"

The throb in my temple pulsed full and strong. "Early. Maybe seven or a little after." *Just chill.* All this could be behind me in a matter of minutes. The only thing she had to go on was that I entered the building. I knew firsthand there were no security cameras on the twentieth floor, so she had nothing to ping me for being up there or anywhere near Michael's office.

The detective nodded, pursed her lips, and searched my tight quarters with a more discerning eye this time. The silence between us was uncomfortable, but her pregnant pause was wasted on me. I'm a lawyer. We invented the pregnant pause.

"When was the last time you met with Mr. Sayles?"

"Last week."

"An early morning meeting?"

"No." Another lie. More flutters.

"Did anyone else meet with the two of you last week?"

"No."

"May I ask what the two of you discussed?"

"Just the company's legal matters. Nothing out of the ordinary. Why are you investigating his death if he committed suicide?"

"Just routine," she said casually. She scanned the folders sitting across my desk. More power to her if she could read upside down and didn't grow bored with the crap I was working on lately. "Do you know if Mr. Sayles had any disagreements with anyone here in the Legal Department or maybe one of his colleagues in the executive suite?"

"Uh, no. I can't think of anyone," I said quietly. This was more than routine. She knew something.

"I heard he might have had some personal problems. You know anything about that? Maybe problems with his family, money problems?"

"No! Absolutely not . . ." I caught myself. I was so sick of people dragging out this

55

line as a justification for a man who was obviously in some serious pain. Other people in the department had said the same thing. "I just mean, that kind of speculation couldn't be further from the truth. Michael was well respected around here and in the legal community."

Bradford smiled. "I see. How long have you worked for Houghton?"

"Three years." Guilt started to burn welts into my conscience. Maybe this time, I should have stayed and explained things.

"Always for Mr. Sayles?"

"Yes." This time, the detective stared for a beat longer than was comfortable for either of us. Perhaps I'd been too forceful in protesting her theories about Michael.

"Well, if you remember anything that you think might be helpful to my investigation, I hope you'll call me." She stood and handed me a business card.

"Sure."

"By the way, do you know who will be replacing Mr. Sayles as general counsel?"

"Um . . . I . . . I'm not sure." Not exactly a lie since I hadn't formally accepted the job yet.

"Thanks for your time."

"Of course." I sat mute, watching the back of her camel-hair coat float out of my office door. Why was a detective asking *routine* questions about Michael's suicide and why was she asking *me*? Detective Shelly Bradford had just moved to the top of my list of people not to trust.

"What's going on?" Anita said as she bustled back into my office.

"Just the police asking routine questions. Can you grab the door on your way out? I need to get back to work."

"Everything okay?"

"Yep. Thanks." Everything was not okay. I fell back into my chair. A heavy cheerless sky blanketed the city and threatened dismal weather. Appropriate, too, since the detective's questions left me feeling vulnerable.

A few hazy frames of memory fluttered to the surface — a slim blue metallic knitting needle, a dirty gray tarp, mud-brown water rising against a rugged riverbank. Thoughts rushed in so fast I couldn't tuck them back into the cubbyholes of my mind. All of them blurred with the sight of Michael's bloody body. All the deadly images spliced together, playing on a silent loop in my head like short vignettes of death. The more I tried to shake it loose, the more intertwined the past became with the present. I blinked. Chillicothe. I blinked again. Atlanta. Blink. Chillicothe.

Chillicothe, Georgia, April 1978

The Georgia spring wind blew across Periwinkle Lane and our tattered neighborhood of shotgun houses and weed-covered yards with the promise of trouble. A brooding disturbance in the air made plain when Willie Jay Groover pulled his police cruiser up to Earthalene Jackson's four-room shack across the street.

Nothing good was coming to the Jackson household.

Willie Jay Groover was the kind of man people in town talked about, but not in a good way. He was a wall-eyed man with dirty blond hair, angular features, and knuckles like walnuts. He always reminded me of a cottonmouth snake if it could walk on two legs: long and lanky with slow deliberate movements but ready to pounce without warning. Willie Jay was a human wrecking ball that crushed flesh and spirit.

58

As he climbed out of the patrol car, people slowly crept from behind their screen doors onto their weathered porches like timid children easing up to a freakish carnival sideshow. Some perched themselves along the curb to watch things unfold. Miss Birdie, the Jacksons' next-door neighbor, sat alongside her cousin Miss Vera in a couple red vinyl kitchen chairs they'd dragged onto the porch. Both women stopped talking midsentence and moved to the front steps at the sight of the patrol car.

Sam and I sat quietly on the front stoop. My mother, Martha, leaned out the front window. "Who called the cops?" Her shrill voice sliced through the air. "What's going on over at Earthalene's?" Martha Littlejohn was probably ninety pounds dripping wet, a small, brown wisp of a woman you could topple over by blowing too hard on her, thanks to her steadfast diet of Thunderbird wine and Golden Flake corn chips. Martha had a habit of talking too fast and chattering on about nothing.

Willie Jay, dressed in a blue police uniform, strutted up Earthalene's front porch steps and banged on her screen door with the side of his fist. And so, the show began. He slowly turned and scanned all of us now watching. Ms. Jackson's front porch was his open-air stage and he held every curious eye on the block. Whatever happened at Ms. Jackson's house would be a beneficial lesson for his raggedy little audience, a live and up-front deterrent to anyone who thought about running up against him in the future. Everyone within earshot watched and waited. Willie Jay banged again, rattling the old wood screen door.

"Mario Jackson, get out here. *Now!*"

Silence floated across the neighborhood. Willie Jay banged again. Finally, Miss Jackson appeared and stood at the door, not bothering to open it. She was a thin brown woman, dressed in a pink flowered housecoat with pin curlers in her hair. "Yes? Can I help you?" she asked, as casually as if she were waiting on a customer at the Piggly Wiggly where she worked.

"Where's your boy, Mario? Tell him to get out here."

"Mario ain't here and I don't know where he is." Her voice more defiant this time.

Willie Jay rested a crusty palm on the gun at his waist holster. "You sure about that?"

Miss Jackson sucked her teeth and rolled her eyes. "I done told you, he ain't here."

Just as she was about to close the door, a second police car rolled up. Sheriff Butch Coogler stepped out. He spit a slick brown circle of chewing tobacco on the ground and hiked up his pants. Coogler was a short, fleshy man who barely reached past Willie Jay's breast pocket. You almost never saw one without the other — Coogler made sure of that. He waddled up the front steps of the house. The two men stood on the porch peering through Miss Jackson's screen door.

"I told y'all, Mario ain't here. I ain't got time for this." She turned her back and started to walk away when Willie Jay gave a hard tug on the screen door, the cheap latch giving way.

Ms. Jackson shrieked. "Hey! You can't just barge in my house!"

"I'll just take a look for myself," Willie Jay said as he barreled inside. It was like Ms. Jackson was invisible the way he stormed past her.

Miss Vera hustled down Birdie's front stairs. "He can't go in there. He can't just bust in there like that."

Coogler sheepishly looked over his shoulder as Vera approached. "Now hold on, Miss Vee. This here is a police matter."

She ignored him and forged her way past Coogler and inside the house. Coogler glanced over his shoulder again at the rest of us across the neighborhood before he took a few tentative steps inside the house

61

behind Vera.

A few minutes later, Willie Jay rushed out of the house. Mario Jackson stumbled out in handcuffs, Willie Jay holding him by the scruff of his neck. His T-shirt was torn in a couple places and his jeans were disheveled. The side of his face bore a bright red mark. We didn't even have to guess to know what happened after the two men stepped inside that house.

"I didn't do nothing," Mario yelled. "I told y'all crackas, I didn't do nothing!"

Coogler followed behind them. Vera and Miss Jackson came out last with Miss Jackson sobbing in Vera's arms. Willie Jay threw the teenager in the back of the patrol car with such brutal force, Mario's head hit the top of the door opening, causing him to wail in pain. His scream sent an electric spark of fear through me. A hard knot rose up in my chest at the sight of Mario being manhandled and tossed into the patrol car like a child's discarded toy. Willie Jay stormed around the car, jumped inside, and sped off, leaving Coogler behind. The short, thick man stood in the middle of three Black women nervously trying to explain that Earthalene could pick up her son at the station after they finished questioning him.

A couple minutes later, I watched Birdie

spring into action, backing her old Impala out of her driveway and into the front of her neighbor's house. Earthalene, still wearing her housecoat and pin curlers, hopped inside the waiting car with Miss Vera. All three women sped off, hanging on the tail of Coogler's patrol car.

Three hours later, the women returned home with Mario. He was missing two teeth and one of his eyes was crusted shut with blood. All because old lady Nessie from across the tracks told the police she *thought* she saw Mario throwing rocks at the windows of an abandoned building.

Two weeks later, Earthalene and Mario Jackson packed up everything they owned into her brother's van and moved somewhere up north. That same day, Martha Littlejohn shocked everyone on Periwinkle Lane by announcing that she was getting married — to Willie Jay Groover.

CHAPTER 5

It had been a day straight out of hell. If I drank, this would have been the perfect excuse to drown myself in a wine bottle. My feet hurt, I was hungry, and I was miserable at the thought of spending the end of a day like today alone. It was almost eight o'clock at night by the time I dragged myself to the front door of my condo in Vinings, a conservative section of Atlanta with lots of old white wealth and a few folks, just a few, who decided to buck the tradition and add some melanin to the neighborhood. Every day, I drove past a historical marker indicating the spot where General William Tecumseh Sherman's Union troops marched toward Atlanta to shut down the Confederate soldiers. To this day, some die-hard fans of the Civil War still reenact the Battle of Kennesaw Mountain less than thirty minutes from that marker.

The faint soothing sounds of a Ravel

piano concerto drifted from Mr. Foster's condo across the hall. I didn't know any of my neighbors except for Mr. Foster, a widower with a penchant for making small talk at the door. By now, he was probably tucked in his favorite chair in the living room listening to his record albums. He abhorred CDs and the one time I tried to explain the convenience of streaming services like Spotify and Pandora to him, he brushed it off saying those things were money-grabbing follies. Maybe he was onto something. Vinyl was making a comeback. Sometimes, I wished I had grown up with a father like Mr. Foster. Some elegant man with good taste and an eye for social standing. Someone to pass along fatherly advice and wisdom while we chatted in a Zagat-rated restaurant over dry-aged porterhouse steaks. *Silly.*

I dropped my tote bag and keys in the foyer, slipped off my shoes and coat, and crossed through my condo, a huge open-concept kitchen-dining-living room. Viking appliances, dining room seating for eight, three large bedrooms, all exquisitely decorated. My sanctum. Every square foot of my home was like a barometer of how far I'd come from the squalor of that dilapidated shotgun house back in Chillicothe,

Georgia.

I stepped into the kitchen, clicked on the burner under the teapot, and stood staring into the dancing blue flame. I glanced down at my cell phone. Three voice mails from Grace and another two from Lana. Grace, Lana, and I were roommates at Georgetown University. A few seconds later, the phone buzzed in my hand. An incoming call from Grace again. I didn't have the energy to talk to her tonight, but I answered anyway.

"Hey, Grace." I tried to sound normal.

"Ellice, are you okay? Lana and I have been trying to reach you all day. I heard something on the news about a lawyer at Houghton who committed suicide in his office. Did you know him?"

"Yeah, I knew him. He was my boss."

"Oh, my heavens. What the hell was going on over there? Why did he commit suicide?" I expected this question. Of the three of us, Grace had no filter.

"I don't know. He didn't leave a note."

"I'm so sorry. I keep telling you, you guys work too hard. At least I know you do. We haven't seen you in a couple months. How are you doing?"

"I'm fine."

"Girl, you *can't* be fine. You work for a man who just killed himself. Isn't that the same guy you worked with at the law firm?"

"Look, Grace —"

"Weren't you two kinda close?" Something about her question tugged at me. Had I talked about Michael too much over the years? I never confided to Grace or Lana about my romantic involvement with Michael. It makes for awkward Sunday brunch conversation since married women typically don't encourage single women to sleep with another woman's husband. "Do you want some company? I can swing by your place."

"Thanks, but no. It's been a long day. I think I'm just gonna take a shower and head to bed."

"Okay . . . if you're sure. Let's get together this weekend. Just you and me. We'll leave Lana to hang on her own. Then we won't have to listen to her complain about her husband. Besides, he can't be as bad as she makes him out to be or else she would have left him and all his money a long time ago. Right?" Grace giggled into the phone.

"Yeah. Listen, Grace, it's been a hellish day."

"Okay, you get some rest. I'll call you this weekend. Don't leave me hangin'."

I gave a weak chuckle. "I won't. Good night."

Our little triumvirate — Lana, Grace, and

Ellice — was still hanging on from college. Of the three of us, Lana was the one always trying to patch us up from the dings and bruises we suffered navigating life, dusting us off and sending us back out into the world. Grace was the one always trying to get us to do Jell-O shots and detoxifying spa wraps, like we were taking our last gasps of youth before stepping into that otherness called middle age. If I were in trouble, Lana would bring a casserole to my house and help me find a good lawyer. Grace would bring a gallon of bleach, a tarp, and a couple shovels.

Years ago, whenever the three of us got together, we were like some teen girl group, full of energy and limitless potential to do something great in the world. But things changed over the years, as they always do. Now, it was shameful how I always bailed on them. These days, when I was free, they weren't because they were occupied with family stuff like kids' basketball games and wedding anniversaries. Most times they wanted to get together for a couples' date, dragging along some milquetoast friend of one of their husbands as my date for the evening. Lately, when they invited me to hang out, I begged off with the usual "gotta work" excuses, and then curled up on the sofa with the latest issue of *O Magazine* or actual work from the office.

For the first time in a long time, I felt completely alone in my home. Even though Michael didn't live here, somehow I'd managed to fill this place with his presence: the kind of coffee he drank, his favorite magazines, a spot in the closet for a couple of his shirts and clean underwear. Truthfully, I was never interested in a happily-ever-after with Michael or any man for that matter. A lot of single men my age come with too much baggage — bitter ex-wives and jealous kids — or else they're passive-aggressive about the baggage I bring along, like a higher salary than theirs. For me, Michael was someone to knock the edge off the hormonal urges and, supposedly, mentor my career. Sometimes I could be an opportunistic bitch, and other times I could be a lonely middle-aged woman seeking companionship that was not mine to have. Thus far, only half my plan worked out: I finally got the promotion. I was still alone.

I grabbed dinner from the pantry — a party-size bag of Lay's barbecue potato chips — and ate them straight from the bag while waiting for the teakettle to boil. A few minutes later, I headed off to the bedroom with a cup of chamomile tea and dinner tucked under my arm.

The first thing I noticed in the room was Michael's duffel bag beside my closet door. I set my dinner on the bedside table and picked up the bag. I ran my fingers along the strap and fought back tears. I didn't love this man, so why was I crying?

Maybe he did mean something to me.

Or maybe I cried over my heinous behavior at leaving his body without calling for help.

I unzipped the bag. Inside, a cylinder of Mitchum deodorant, a couple pairs of boxer briefs, and a white polo shirt. And there, lurking in the bottom of the bag, was a flyer for a gun shop called Tri-County Outfitters. My heart sank. How did I not see this coming? And why would he tell me to meet him at the office if he was planning to kill himself? Did he *want* me to find his body?

I dropped the bag and flyer and slid down onto the bed. I slipped my cell phone into the docking station and opened up my music. I hit play for an old Curtis Mayfield song, "You're So Good to Me." Mayfield's soft falsetto vocals floated through my bedroom like lyrical dust settling on memories of me and Michael.

Embracing me this way . . . kiss my lips for taste . . . I can never get over, get over you.

As I sat on the bed, I stared at the empty spot beside me. His side. Michael had lain in this bed just a few nights ago. I placed my head on his pillow and inhaled, seeking the soft clean mint of his aftershave, the tangy smell of his sweat. When Michael touched me, it was like I didn't have childhood scars or cellulite or an emerging midsection paunch. All my insecurities about those things simply melted away when I was with him. What was supposed to be a bit of harmless fun between two consenting adults was starting to cut deep.

And for the first time since I left Michael's bloody body in that office, I wept. I lay on his side of the bed and cried with Curtis Mayfield still singing in the background . . .

I can never get over, get over you.

CHAPTER 6

The next morning was bright but bitter cold. The kind of deceptively sunny day that would make you run off and leave your coat at home if you didn't check the weather first. I drove into the office with a goose-bumpy premonition sense of dread. I couldn't explain it, but I could definitely feel it. I thought about calling in sick, but I knew it might raise more questions. *Why would Ellice be so broken up over Michael's death that she couldn't come to work?* or *What's she hiding?* But what if that detective showed up again with more questions and suspicions?

I'm a big girl. I can handle this. I'm Ellice Littlejohn. Cool under pressure. Houghton had yet to get under my skin.

The few fitful hours of sleep I'd had the night before made me fuzzy and unfocused, like my brain was wading through clam chowder. I must have gone through a hundred iterations of why Michael *wouldn't* kill himself. I knew him better than anyone else at Houghton. Suicide made absolutely no sense at all. Not the Michael Sayles I knew. But then again, he had a wife and two kids he'd managed to keep in the dark about our relationship. The likelihood was pretty high he could keep a secret or two from me as well.

I half listened to the radio banging out Stevie Wonder's "Don't You Worry 'Bout a Thing." The song ended and the DJ handed things over to a soft-spoken news anchor with the morning headlines: *Yesterday morning, Michael Sayles, chief legal officer of Houghton Transportation, was found dead in his office of an apparent suicide.* In a final blow, the anchor rambled off the additional commentary about the recent protests at Houghton, as if the two were related. Hardy was right. The media would link every bad thing about Houghton to Michael's suicide. I clicked off the radio. I couldn't bear to listen to another insensitive news report about Michael.

As I pulled into the parking garage, I noticed more protesters out front. Their numbers had nearly doubled since the day before and they were louder, too. Serious-looking brown faces like mine chanting,

"Houghton hates Blacks . . . ! Houghton hates Blacks!" An uncomfortably repetitious ditty that could get stuck in your ear and nestled in your mind. A few passing cars honked their horns in support of the protesters as they drove by. The same guilty wash of shame flooded over me just like it did months ago when the protests began. Traitor. Turncoat. I collected a hefty paycheck every month from a company that rarely hired other people who looked like me. What would any of the protesters think if they knew I quietly worked at a place where they believed they were not welcome? Was I doing my part to help the tribe or taking ill-gotten gain from a corporate bigot?

Inside, the lobby echoed with a second day of frenzy in the aftermath of Michael's death. Extra security guards in too-tight uniforms lurked around the lobby along with a couple of dour-faced police officers I recognized from the day before. Hardy and his security team did a pretty good job of holding the media circus outside the building, but there was little they could do with the unusual number of Houghton's employees meandering and gawking out the window at the protesters and reporters.

I tried to jostle my way through a group of people leering out the window and blocking my path. "Excuse me," I said quietly, before nudging a short bald guy who ignored me. I finally found a clear shot to the security desk and offered a friendly nod to the anxious-looking guard before signing into the logbook.

"Good morning, Ms. Littlejohn. You still haven't found your security badge, huh?"

"Hey, Jimmy. I can't find it anywhere. I guess I'll have to wear the badge of shame again today."

"I don't know if you heard, they're making us tighten up things around here," he said. "You know, after what happened yesterday. They don't want the newspeople getting in. They won't let us cover for folks no more. You gotta get yourself a new badge if it doesn't turn up soon. Sorry."

"I understand."

He offered a sympathetic smile filled with a cluster of crooked teeth as he handed me a peel-and-stick temporary name tag. "By the way, the fourth elevator's out again. It might be a wait for your ride up."

"Thanks." I picked up the name tag and headed for the elevators, bypassing the wooden scaffolding and caution tape surrounding the broken elevator.

A couple minutes later, I stepped into the Legal Department. An unnatural calm hung in the air. The usual morning noises of clicking keyboards, copy machines humming, and people lightly chattering was gone, replaced by the quiet, heavy pall of Michael's death. Word of his suicide had consumed the entire company, especially the Legal Department staff for the past twenty-four hours. People were genuinely overwhelmed by the loss. A few of the admins even cried the day before.

As the weight of the tragedy settled in, people either worked quietly in their offices or stood around talking in muted little clumps. I quickened my pace when I spotted a small cluster of paralegals standing outside my office door. One of them, Penny Dolan, Walter Graves's paralegal, stood alongside two other paralegals. Rudy and I called her "Pinkie Do Little" because she had a remarkable skill for getting out of work or doing anything that required her to stay past five o'clock. She watched me approach my office with her arms folded. She flipped her hair across the back of her latest 100 percent polyester outlet mall purchase. "Congratulations, Ellice." No smile. All snark.

"Excuse me?"

She rolled her eyes and walked off from the small group.

I looked at the others. "What was that about?"

The other women scurried off like a couple cockroaches exposed by the flip of a kitchen light. Sometimes, I wished there were another Black woman who worked in the department. Just anyone else who could pull me from the edge when I wanted to jump down the throat of one of these witches. Rudy and Hardy were supportive, but it wasn't the same.

I entered my office and closed the door behind me. I took off my coat and hung it on the hook on the back of the door before I sat down at my computer and clicked it on. I started in on the emails. The first one:

INTERNAL COMMUNICATION

Date: Wednesday, January 4
To: The Houghton Transportation Family
From: Nate Ashe, Chairman & CEO
Cc: Executive Committee

It is with a heavy heart that I announce the unexpected passing of Michael Sayles, Executive Vice President & General Counsel. Michael was a tireless leader in our organization. His uncompromising ethics and intellectual prowess led the Houghton family through a number of challenges and successes. His presence will be terribly missed.

I am pleased to announce that Ellice Littlejohn has accepted the promotion to replace Michael as Executive Vice President and General Counsel. Ellice is an honors graduate of Georgetown University and Yale Law School. She has been a stellar legal business partner since joining the Houghton family three years ago. Her unwavering commitment to the Houghton family will be a tremendous asset to us all. Please join me in congratulating Ellice on this momentous achievement.

What the hell?!

I was so stunned by Nate's email that I read it twice to make sure I wasn't mistaken. I hadn't accepted the offer. We agreed that I would think about it. Why would he make such an announcement?

I picked up the phone. "Hi, Sarah. It's Ellice. I was —"

"Congratulations, Ellice," she said, giggling into the phone.

"Uh . . . yeah . . . thanks. I'm calling to see if Nate has a few minutes. I need to speak with him. It's rather urgent."

"Well, if you wanna come up now, it

shouldn't be a problem. He doesn't have a meeting for another hour."

"Thanks."

A flood of sunlight saturated Nate's office with a light and airy feel. Vibrant hues in the artwork seemed to leap from the walls, bouncing off every reflective surface in the room. And the elephant in the picture above his sofa looked as if it would charge right off the wall and into the center of the room.

Nothing was as it seemed.

"Ellice, c'mon in, darlin'. Can I get ya some coffee, juice?"

"No, thank you. I wanted to talk to about the email you sent this morning. Well . . . I guess I thought you would give me a few days to think about the offer. I mean —"

"Now about that." Nate leaned back in his chair with a wide smile and placed his feet on his desk. "I really wish we had the benefit of time. But, darlin', Houghton has a full plate. We need a top lawyer in place ASAP. Willow always tells me I don't have enough women on the Executive Committee."

"I understand that. But —"

"Well, what is it? It can't be the money. What's your hesitation?"

I stared at Nate for a beat. I was trying to

be respectful and find the right words. "It's a huge task. I just thought I would have a bit of time to think it over."

"Knock, knock. I don't mean to interrupt." I turned to find Willow standing in the door of Nate's office. "Congratulations, Ellice!"

"Willow, I'm glad you're here. Ellice seems a little reticent about taking the job."

Her eyebrows arched in surprise. Willow looked at me and back at Nate before she strutted into the office and stood beside me. "Ellice, you weren't thinking of turning us down, were you?" she said, her voice an octave higher than normal, asking as if my saying no would be a personal affront to her.

"I guess I just hadn't expected all this so soon. Michael just died *yesterday.* I don't think people have really had time to grieve the loss and now we're announcing his replacement. I just think all this is moving a little too fast."

"Well, the company has to continue to operate seamlessly, more so now," Nate said.

Willow smiled and gently tapped my arm. "As an HR professional, I can tell you, you don't want to pass up a career move like this. And whether we asked you to serve in an interim capacity or as the permanent replacement, we still need someone in charge. We just thought by moving this along, things could go back to normal as soon as possible."

Nate removed his feet from his desk and stood. "Listen, from what I hear around the company, you're the real brains in the Legal Department. Michael just hogged up all the sunshine for it. I know he would have wanted it this way."

"It's just . . . I guess I assumed . . ." Suddenly, I was at a loss for words. They had made all sorts of assumptions that I would take the job because they tossed it to me with a big bag of money. How do I explain that maybe I *had* planned to take the job, but it would have been nice to pretend like I had a say in my own career? Hell, I hadn't even figured out whether I wanted to work in the same office where someone *died.* I didn't believe in ghosts or bad juju, but it was still worth thinking about.

Nate smiled at me. "Take a chance on us up here on Twenty. I think you're going to enjoy the executive suite."

Maybe I was being foolish to even think about squandering such a huge opportunity. All my doubts were just that — doubts. Surely I was smart enough to navigate my way up on this floor. Besides, I was tired of

81

watching people half my age and with a quarter of my intellect get promoted. It was my turn now. But I wasn't stupid, either. I knew this promotion was more about squashing the protests in front of the building. Houghton needed a Black person in their upper ranks. Maybe in the end, we could both get what we really wanted: Houghton could shore up its horrendous reputation and I could use my position to finally convince the company to hire more people of color.

The two of them stood staring at me, optimistic smiles neatly planted on their faces. I smiled back. "I think I'm going to enjoy it, too."

"Well now, it's a great day for the Executive Committee," Willow said, clasping her hands in front of her chest. "As I've told Nate before, a company like Houghton could always use another smart woman in its executive ranks."

Nate chuckled. "See, Ellice. What did I tell ya?"

It felt like all this had been planned long before Nate offered me the job yesterday. But how could that be? Who knew Michael would have committed suicide?

"Listen, I have a couple things I want you to make a priority," Nate said. "Some unfinished business left over from Sayles." Nate stared out the window for longer than a quick glance. Maybe he was having second thoughts, pangs of guilt about the warp speed at which things were moving. Everyone moving on as if Michael had meant nothing to us, as if his death were just a passing blip on the company's radar screen.

A moment later, Nate broke his stare from the window. "I'm sorry, where were we?"

I cleared my throat. "You mentioned Michael had some unfinished business you wanted me to handle."

"Hmm . . ." Nate sat down again and leaned back in his chair. The three of us sat in silence for a beat. "Let me think." Nate rubbed his brow. Willow gave him a worried look. "Oh yes. Yes, I remember now. We're getting ready for the executive retreat in two weeks. I'll need your help getting some of the reports ready."

"Sure."

Willow eased the hair of her bob cut behind an ear. "Nate, did you want to mention the cocktail party this weekend for the board?"

"Ah yes, I'm glad you brought that up. I don't know why I didn't think of it sooner. Ellice, I've invited the board members and a few other folks to join me at a lil' club we frequent down near Savannah. It's pretty informal, just a way for me to connect with the board on a social level. With Michael's death and all, I need to do a little hand-holding. Ya know what I mean? And what better way to do that than to have them meet the new GC? I want you to join us. It'd be a nice surprise for them."

"Well . . . I would love to but —"

"I won't take no for an answer. It'll give me a chance to show you off." Nate quickly rose and walked around his desk. He threw his arm around my shoulder. "You can take the company jet down Saturday morning and you'll be back in Atlanta, tucked in your jammies before bedtime Saturday night. You won't even have to stay overnight. We fly out of Brown Airfield. I'll have Sarah get you all the details. I think everyone's gonna love you."

"Thanks, Nate, for the invitation. I'll look forward to it," I said, ever the good soldier. My weekends were supposed to be for me. The time I needed to replenish my well so I could face another Monday and the burden of being the lone "drop of brown gravy." I maneuvered myself from under Nate's arm. "I'd better get going."

On the way out, I nodded politely at Sarah, a short, wiry woman in her sixties who ran Nate's office with executive precision.

"Oh, Ellice, darlin', hang on for a second! I have something for you," Sarah said as she dropped a large ring of keys into her desk drawer. "You might want to start perusing these." She reached underneath her desk and handed me several oversize sample books.

"What's this?"

"Upholstery samples, flooring samples — you know, all the stuff Building Services needs to get your new office in order, sweetie. Now, there's flooring, furniture, and even artwork samples if you wanna hang something pretty on the walls."

"Oh."

Sarah grinned sheepishly. "Congratulations. Now, sweetie, take a look at those samples and I'll have the decorator call Anita to get some time on your calendar to go ova a few things."

"Okay . . . thank you."

Sarah turned her attention toward a buzzing telephone and waved good-bye as she picked up the receiver.

Struggling under the weight of the sample books, I started to feel a little heady with how things were coming together. But maybe, for a change, things were working in my favor, despite the unfathomable way this all came about.

"Whoa! Let me help you there, Legal Lady." Hardy laughed and hustled over. He grabbed a few of the sample books. "What's all this?"

"Apparently things to help me furnish my new office." We walked to the elevator bank together.

"What new office?"

"So you didn't read your emails this morning. I'm replacing Michael as GC."

"Hey! Congratulations!"

"Well, thanks."

We reached the elevators and Hardy pressed the call button. "You don't seem very happy."

"It's not that. It's . . . it's all happening pretty fast."

"Hmm . . . I get that. Maybe you can put in a good word for me, though. Max says he's trying to get me promoted to a role on the Executive Committee, too. Vice president of Security. He says HR is dragging their feet, but it should come through any day now."

"That's great. Colleagues."

"So you going out tonight to celebrate your big promotion?"

"I don't know if I feel like celebrating.

Michael's funeral is the day after tomorrow."

"I heard."

The elevator pinged and we stepped on. I pushed the button for Eighteen. "It feels so weird and surreal, you know?"

"Tell me about it. The place isn't the same without him. I feel really bad for his wife. Losing a spouse, that's tough," Hardy said. "Right after my Junie died, those were some of the roughest days of my life." Hardy's voice was soft, distant. I decided against interrupting him. I had absolutely nothing to offer in the way of empathetic words. I'd never shared anything about my personal life with anyone here at work and I wasn't going to start with this conversation. Everybody else at Houghton considered themselves family. But they weren't *my* family.

We stepped off the elevator and headed toward my office. Hardy continued, "Nobody loved me like that woman. Nobody. Not even my own mother . . ." His voice trailed off.

"I'm sorry. What happened?" I said.

"Cancer. Ovarian. In the end, it spread everywhere." He went silent for a moment. "I'll tell ya one thing," he said, his voice now booming again. "I would have lost my mind if it hadn't been for Nate. He might

87

be the CEO, but he was right there with me through it all. He said I was family and he treated me like it, too. At the end, he was right beside me at the hospital. There's nothing I wouldn't do for that guy."

"I'm sorry about your wife."

"Thanks. Anyway, I really think you're gonna like working for Nate. He's the best."

We arrived at my office. "Thanks for the help."

"Anytime." Hardy sat the sample books in one of my guest chairs and surveyed my tight office. "Looks like that new office is gonna be an upgrade."

"Just tell me the HVAC system works better up there than down here and we're good." We laughed.

"Listen, you need anything, you just holler." Hardy ambled off.

I dropped the remaining clunky books in the guest chair, plopped into my chair, and clicked on the heater under my desk. Moving up to the executive suite would be more than I'd ever taken on before and my doubts were larger than my confidence. Could I pull off the task of running an entire department? Did I *really* want to replace Michael and sit in the very same office where he died? Vera would have called this my "God sense" trying to warn me. I dismissed it all as nervous jitters. I would be the first Black executive vice president at Houghton.

To hell with nervous jitters.

CHAPTER 7

I hate funerals.

Three days after Michael's death, I trembled as I climbed the front steps of the First Presbyterian Church of Buckhead, a small frame structure rapidly filling to capacity. News trucks were perched along the street, almost as many as the first day after his death. Grizzled and fresh-faced reporters alike stood in front of bulky video cameras and the cameramen shouldering them, speaking into microphones and pointing at the mourners. Why the sudden media interest again?

Everyone filed into the church, heads bowed, stiff-lipped and solemn. Most people headed to the front row to offer a hug and personal condolences to Anna, Michael's wife. I couldn't face her. I quietly slinked along the side wall before taking a seat several rows behind Michael's family. I spotted Hardy across the aisle from me, along with the attorneys and staff from the Legal Department sprinkled in among the mourners. Despite the large crowd, only an occasional sniffle or cough broke the somber silence.

If would-be gawkers thought they'd attend, looking for the vicious evidence of Michael's demise, Anna had other plans. No open casket with Michael's body pumped full of formaldehyde, slathered in camouflage crème and lip tint. *Thank God.* At the front of the church, an oversize picture of Michael was propped on an easel. He was tanned, windswept, and smiling as he steered a sailboat. An easy and carefree shot that bumped up against the uncomfortable solitude of the sanctuary.

And the respectful solemnity of a Presbyterian service was not lost on me either. Every funeral I'd attended before this was a full-out Southern Baptist "homegoing" service, replete with wailing women screaming, *Why, Jesus?,* a hard-charging raspy-voiced preacher whose eulogy lasted well over an hour, and open caskets that weren't closed until the choir's final verse of "I'll Fly Away."

Michael's two college-aged kids sat on either side of their mother, the three of them painted in a stoic canvas of familial grief

91

along with Michael's parents, who appeared to be in their eighties, stooped over and fragile looking. I imagined Michael's death had provided enough personal devastation to bring his parents to the precipice of their own deaths. He was the bedrock of their family, and with him gone so unexpectedly, they were all wading into new territory without an emotional compass to guide them. Vera used to call the time right after a loved one dies the "bewitching season" — that surreal wedge of time when everyone searches for a new normal but the void is too deep and too raw, leaving you in emotional limbo.

I stared at Anna in the front row, draped in a black wool suit, her face drawn and pale, the hollow look of a woman emptied by despair. For a minute, I found it hard to believe she was the same woman who stood beside Michael at dinner parties and laughed at his jokes, no matter how many times she'd heard them before. She was my polar opposite, the dream of every American male WASP, from her pale complexion and blond chignon wound at her nape, to her petite figure maintained through what I'm sure was a zealous avoidance of carbs and a steady diet of Pilates and Barre classes.

Rudy and his wife, Kelly, came in a few

minutes later. Kelly and I exchanged a cordial hug before they sat beside me, Rudy in the center. This was our usual seating arrangement at all work events that Kelly attended, lest she risk becoming a human fence over which Rudy and I would banter. They made an attractive couple. Kelly was Barbie-doll cute to Rudy's tall Ken-doll handsome. But she was also a no-nonsense Jersey girl, too. Not like the fake, phony kind I went to school with at Coventry, either. Sometimes I wished I could hang out with the two of them more, but I tried to be mindful of appearing to play favorites among the legal staff. It was bad enough that Rudy usually spent half the day in my office gossiping.

Rudy nudged me. "So where are your new colleagues?" he whispered.

"What?"

"You see anybody else in here from the twentieth floor?"

I scanned the church. No sign of Nate, Willow, or anyone else who worked in the executive suite. "Hmm . . . the detective who came to my office the other day asked me if Michael had any disagreements with the people he worked with."

"It must have been a hell of a disagreement if you can't spend an hour at the funeral service of someone you call 'Houghton family.' I'm just sayin'." Rudy was right. I scoped the church again. Even Michael's former assistant was missing in action.

A minute later, Rudy leaned over again and whispered in my ear, "Did you hear the latest about Michael?"

"What?" I asked, perking up nervously.

"I heard Michael was having an affair."

My stomach wrapped itself in a tight little knot and my ears muffled, like my head had suddenly plunged deep underwater. Maybe it was my subconscious attempt *not* to hear what I was hearing. "What are you talking about? Who told you that?"

"One of the admins on Twenty. She said she heard he tried to break it off and the woman killed him, staged the office to look like a suicide."

"That's crazy!" A woman sitting in front of me whipped her head around, giving me a stabbing glance. I dropped my voice back to a whisper. "I mean, the police said it was a suicide. They would know better than some admin on Twenty. Did she say who the woman was?"

"Nah."

"Well, then, it's just stupid speculation. Geez, you're worse than a blabbering old woman," I said, shaking my head and motioning him to be quiet.

"Yeah, I'm not sure whether it's true or not. Michael always struck me as the salt-of-the-earth, straight-arrow type. Anyway, with his work hours who *could* he be having an affair with?"

"It's not true," I said, shaking my head vigorously. "Stop talking like that. We're at his memorial for God's sake." I toyed with the handle of my purse and stared straight ahead.

A few minutes later, Rudy nudged me once more. This time, he nodded his chin toward a stranger sitting across the aisle from us. "Who's that?"

I followed Rudy's chin across the aisle. A serious-looking Black man with a shaven head, dressed in an expensive charcoal suit, peered back in my direction. Something about his demeanor gave an aura of formality, all business.

I looked back at Rudy and shrugged.

"I don't know him, either. He looks out of place here," Rudy said softly.

"What? You think he looks out of place because he's a Black man at Michael's funeral?"

"I'm just saying. You and I both know there's maybe a handful of Black men who work at Houghton. I've never seen him there or at any of Michael's parties."

"Are you trying to tell me that you know everyone in this church except that one man?"

"I'm not saying that, either."

"Michael did have a life outside of work. Maybe he's a personal friend."

Rudy shook his head slowly. "Hmm . . . I don't know. There's something about him . . ."

Kelly threw us a stern expression and whispered, "You two might want to tamp down all the yapping. The pastor is about to pray." Rudy and I passed a couple guilty looks at each other before bowing our heads.

But Rudy had piqued my curiosity. I glanced back at the man again. I could see him scanning the room as if doing some sort of mental intake. Rudy was right. He did look out of place.

The pastor cleared his throat at the podium and the solemn crowd shuffled quietly before settling in for his eulogy. He began with laudatory words about Michael's devotion to his family and his uncompromising work ethic. I gazed at the picture of Michael and forced my thoughts on the things I hated about the two of us, things that would thwart my crying at his funeral. Things like the secrecy and all the broken promises to get me promoted. I'd been so incredibly stupid to waste my time with him. Heartache fell over me like a wet blanket across a fire, heavy and suffocating. It didn't matter that I sat behind his grieving wife and children, or that I sat shoulder to shoulder with one of my direct reports who tattled of rumors about Michael having an affair with an as yet unnamed woman.

We stood outside the church. Michael's kids and his parents looked beyond the news cameras and slowly piled into a black stretch limo where they would be shuttled off to a private graveside service. I caught Anna's eye just before she climbed inside. She hesitated a beat, and her piercing gaze stopped me in my tracks. For a moment, we stood staring at each other. Did she know? I remember Vera used to say not every husband is truthful with his wife, but every wife knows the truth about her husband. *You just know,* she would say.

I watched Michael's small grieving family, neatly bundled up and heading off into the cold winter morning for a private good-bye. I stood in the curl of exhaust smoke from the limo's tailpipe, staring at the sleek black car as it pulled away from the church. The wind blustered across my face. No private good-bye for me. No one to hold my hand and tell me everything would be okay in time. No one to share the bewitching season. I blinked back tears.

I would find my own way. I always did.

I watched the newspeople start to dismantle and shove their camera equipment back into their vans. I took a deep breath before I glanced across the street. I did a double take when I spotted a face I hadn't expected to see. I darted my eyes away and quickly hustled toward Rudy and Kelly at the front of the church.

"Hey, Rudy, you might be right about the man inside the church, the one you said looked out of place."

"Yeah?"

"Don't look now, but the woman he's talking to? Attractive Black woman, gray coat, long legs. She's the detective who came to my office."

Rudy peered across the street. "Okay, now it makes sense."

"What makes sense?"

"They're here to see who else is here. Or who isn't." Rudy raised an eyebrow at me. "Kelly's brother is a cop. Sometimes they do that."

Detective Bradford caught my eye and

poked an elbow into the charcoal-suited man before they both walked over to us.

"Hello, Ms. Littlejohn," Detective Bradford said. Smooth. Cool. Pixie cut perfect. I gazed at her and wondered if I had ever been so self-assured when I was in my thirties or at any point in my life. "Let me introduce you to my partner, Detective Charles Burke." Burke gave a small nod, his hands planted deep in his pockets, with no intent to engage in the normal pleasantries of an introduction. Rudy gave me an *I-told-you-so* sort of look.

"Apparently you were right," Detective Bradford said. "Judging from the attendance at this funeral, a lot of people admired Mr. Sayles."

"Yes," I nodded.

"Any word on who will replace him?" Bradford asked. She caught me off guard for a moment. I hesitated, as if I were being exposed, like some big secret was leaking out. Her questions were always so pointed. Maybe it was just the nature of her being a cop. But somehow, as at our first meeting, I felt a little off-kilter in her presence.

I gave a quick glimpse at Rudy and Kelly. "I'll be the new general counsel."

Bradford raised an eyebrow and smiled. "Congratulations."

"Thank you."

"Well, I hope I can count on you to assist me in my investigation. You might be interested to know the coroner ruled Mr. Sayles's death a homicide. Apparently someone killed him and staged his death to look like a suicide."

Someone killed him.

My knees buckled slightly. The detective's words repeated over and over again like an earworm winding its way through my head. *The coroner ruled Mr. Sayles's death a homicide.* And right there, in front of the First Presbyterian Church of Buckhead, I sensed a shift. Like the first small tug at a loose thread that unravels a tapestry. A troubling bend in the arc of my life. And all I wanted to do was leave, to quietly run away from everything like I did before.

Chillicothe, Georgia, August 1979
The day had lumbered, laden with the sweltering summer heat. The humidity hung thickly and sealed the entire town in a blanket of sweat and listlessness. People sat out on their porches, fanning themselves, shooing flies, and talking about how long it had been since the last rainfall. By eight o'clock at night, the temperature had barely dipped below ninety.

I stood on Martha's front porch peeking through a hole in the cheap screen door, silently praying that Miss Vera was right about this entire plan. This was the last piece of the puzzle to put into place before I headed to Virginia. I could see Martha sprawled across that lumpy brown sofa in the living room. She wore a pair of dirty seersucker shorts and a blue *Happy Days* T-shirt, her dingy bra strap peeking from under the sleeve. Vera's large frame hovered over her like a human dirigible. The two women were both Black, but they couldn't have been more different: Vera, large and formidable; Martha, small and weak.

"I told you get outta my house," Martha said, slurring her words. On nights like this one, when her "demons," as she called them, chased after her, her conversation was slower and rambling. "I don't want to hear nothin' you got to say."

"You gonna listen to me tonight."

Martha didn't respond. Neither of them spoke and I held my breath, waiting. The cicadas chirped noisily underneath the warped planks of the porch, highlighting the unbearable silence between the two women. I was terrified that Vera might give up and change her mind about talking to her.

"Martha, you listening?"

Martha blinked a few times as she righted herself on the sofa. She used to make me and Sam walk around without making a sound on nights like this because she said any little noise made her head hurt.

Vera was far from being quiet. "Are you listening to me, Martha?"

She frowned up at Vera for a second then rubbed her forehead. "I need a cigarette. Sammy? SAMMY, bring me my cigarettes!"

"He ain't here," Vera said softly. "He's back at my place. Ellie told me you not gonna let her go off to that private school. Why would you block this girl's chances for making something outta herself?"

"No," Martha said with a scowl. It seemed like Martha was always mad at Miss Vera since Sam and I started spending so much time at Miss Vera's house. But things were always so much better there. "I said no. Them my kids. Who you think you is coming in my house and telling me what to do with my kids?" Martha stood from the sofa on wobbly legs. She might have fallen face first into the floor if Vera's girth hadn't broken her fall. "I ain't got no money for something like that. She can stay here and go to school. What, she *too good* for the schools here in town?"

I rested my head against the doorframe, fighting back tears. They went silent again. I peeped back inside the screen. It was hard to see what she was doing at first. Then, I realized Martha was digging through the sofa cushion for a cigarette.

"Listen here, Martha, Ellie is smart. That school will pay for her books and food and everything. Now, me and Birdie and some other folks, we took up some money. We got enough to get her up there to the school."

Martha perked up. "What money?"

"We took up a collection. The church helped out, too. Now, you her momma and it ain't right for me to just send her off without getting your blessing. But if I have to, I will. So you all good with this, right?"

Martha peered toward the screen door and spotted me staring inside. "Ellice Renee Littlejohn." — her tone was bitter and fermented on her tongue — "Get in here!"

My stomach tumbled. I only hoped Vera would step in between us if Martha tried to slap me or snatch me by my hair. The screen door slowly creaked, announcing my arrival inside the house. The room smelled like stale beer, probably spilled on a rug somewhere. I hadn't been at the house for the past few days. That meant no one was around to clean it up.

I didn't move beyond the door entry. "Ma'am?" I never called Martha "Mama" or any other iteration of Mother. It was always "Martha" or "Ma'am."

"Get over here," Martha said.

I looked at Vera. She nodded her consent before I eased toward the sofa.

Martha scanned me from head to toe before she met my eyes. "You my child." Martha's words slid one into the other, the Thunderbird wine fully in control of her tongue. "*My* child. You understand me? You do what I say do." She pounded a finger into her chest to emphasize her authority.

I fought back tears as I spied Vera again. Vera offered a fragile smile. "Tell her about the school, Ellie, go on, honey."

Vera and Martha waited for me to talk. Any other time I discussed the scholarship with breathless abandon. But this time, I opened my mouth to tell Martha about it and the words wouldn't come out. I swallowed hard and took a deep breath. "Like I've told you before, it's a school up north like Miss Vee said. They only take you if you can pass a test and I passed the test. The school will pay for every—"

"I told you, you ain't going nowhere. Why you spend so much time at Vera's anyway? She ain't even your kin. You need to come back home and stay with me," Martha said. She spotted half a cigarette on the floor beside the coffee table and grabbed it like she was afraid Vera or I might steal it first. She scooped up the matches nearby and lit it. She then took a long drag, tilted her head back, and blew smoke toward the ceiling as if it were an offering to the gods. The room quickly filled with the pungent burnt smell of tobacco. "You and Sammy need to be with me. I know we had that little hiccup a few weeks back but Vera fixed things. Right, Vera? Everything will be better now." She reached for my hand and I flinched. With Martha, I could never be sure whether her touch would hurt or heal, whether her words would cut or console.

Martha sank back into the sofa and took another long drag before she blew the smoke out the side of her mouth. I stood frozen, suffocating in the small hot space. And then, Martha did what she always did on nights like this. She started to cry, openly weeping. I didn't know whether to move or stay put. Vera didn't move, so I didn't either.

"That's enough, Martha Littlejohn. I'm sending this girl on to Virginia. I tried to do right by you, but we are done with this. You hear me? Ellie is gonna get outta this dead-ass town and make something of herself whether you want her to or not. She's leaving on the 7:15 bus tomorrow morning. It's up to you if you wanna say good-bye proper when she leaves. Your choice."

Martha stopped crying and wiped her face with the back of her hand. I hoped she would say something nice, but instead she stared down at the coffee table, scattered with an overflowing ashtray full of Newport cigarette butts, an empty Thunderbird wine bottle, and the *Tolliver County Register* newspaper.

Martha never took her eyes off the table as she started to speak, so soft I almost didn't hear her at first. "You know my momma died when I was little? I told you that before. Everybody I ever loved has left me."

Martha was born in Rome, Georgia, a "little town full of nothing" she used to say. Her mother had died when she was seven years old and she was passed around among a host of relatives and charitable neighbors who took her in until she was fifteen and finally ran away with a twenty-seven-year-old man who brought her to Chillicothe, then left her six months pregnant with me. She'd told me the story so often I could recite it as if it were my own.

Martha continued, "All I ever wanted to do was give you and Sammy a home. Someplace that was yours. Now *you* leaving me, too."

I sat down on the arm of the sofa next to her. "I'm not leaving you," I said. "I'm just going off to school. I can come home on holidays and summers."

Martha stared at me. Time dragged, as if on hands and knees. She took another slow dramatic pull on her cigarette and blew a long cloud of smoke in my face and finally spoke: "You have caused me nothing but heartache since you came into this world."

It wasn't my first time hearing this from her, but still I had to fight back the sting of tears. I had never figured out how to make Martha happy. Maybe leaving Chillicothe would make her happy and she just didn't know it yet. Maybe she would finally be happy when I was gone.

"Nah, I can tell you won't be back. You always thought you was better than this," she said, waving her hand through the air. "Like you too good for Chillicothe. Like you better than me or something."

Her words cut deep this time. It was as if she were poking her finger at me, accusing me of the crime of wanting something better. I reached down and put my hand on her shoulder. "I'll be back."

Martha jerked her shoulder away and ground her cigarette butt in the ashtray. She stood from the sofa, as straight as a lead pencil. Everything about her changed in an instant. She raised her head and stared back at the screen door for a moment, like she'd reached the end of the conversation and had come to a decision. I wasn't used to seeing this kind of resolve in her. Maybe I was lucky and she was going to go along with Vera's plan. I waited for her to hug me and if she did, I would make up for flinching earlier. I'd hug her so tight if she reached out this time.

She didn't. Instead, Martha gave me a hateful side-eye and strolled off to the kitchen. The last words I heard her utter before I left Chillicothe: "Make sure you don't slam my goddamn door behind you when you leave."

CHAPTER 8

Saturday morning, I boarded the Houghton corporate jet, a Gulfstream 550, all hand-crafted leather interior propelled by a couple of Rolls-Royce turbo engines. Another executive perk. I was the only passenger, traveling alone to Nate's party in Savannah, Georgia. Everyone else from the executive suite had flown in the night before. Me, traveling on this plane alone — to a party no less — seemed like such a wasteful endeavor. And the thought of spending part of my weekend with work colleagues was about as enticing as a root canal on a hard-to-reach molar. I hated events like this. But I learned by my third-year law school internship, invitations to partners' lake homes and law firm charity golf tournaments were not optional. These were work events just as much as attending a 7:30 A.M. breakfast meeting.

The flight attendant, a lean guy with a

goatee and spiky hair, tried to make small talk. I wasn't really in the mood for chitchat and he finally picked up the hint. All I wanted to do was get to Savannah, survive the irritation of yuck-yucking it up with a bunch of people I didn't know, get back on this plane, and head home.

Forty-five minutes later, I landed in Savannah where a driver and a private car at the airport whisked me off to the Altamonte Club, just outside Savannah on Tybee Island. I did my research and I didn't like what I found. The Altamonte was established as a men's social club at the turn of the last century. Women were allowed inside only if they were accompanied by their husbands. No Jews. No Blacks. No Catholics. Essentially, no "Others." The club deity finally decided to join the twentieth century in 1996 when they admitted their first Black member. From what I could tell, he was still the only member of color. Going to a party inside a place like this made me question the people I now called my colleagues.

Another forty-five minutes later, we reached the grounds of the Altamonte. Nate's "lil' club," as he called it, was sprawling. Two-hundred-year-old southern live oak trees draped in Spanish moss lined the

111

winding driveway to the club. Their gnarled and twisted branches had hidden my runaway slave ancestors and cast shadows to cool the sunburnt heads of Confederate soldiers alike. A tortured past that shamefully connected all of us in the South.

The car eased past horse stables and tennis courts before finally cruising to a stop in front of a huge water fountain and sago palm trees flanking a massive white stucco building with terra-cotta roof tiles. I took a few deep breaths, willing myself not to act like a goofy-eyed tourist on her first trip off the farm.

It seemed cruel — almost blasphemous — to attend a cocktail party the day after Michael's funeral. Michael was murdered. His body hadn't been in the ground a full twenty-four hours yet. His fellow executives couldn't even bother to attend his funeral but were now laughing and gallivanting about like he never existed. What happened to all that Houghton family BS?

My new colleagues joined Detective Bradford on that list of people I didn't trust.

I touched up my lipstick, plumped my hair — a fresh silk press — and slid out of the town car. I brushed the front of my black crepe halter dress one last time. *Shoulders back. Head up. Showtime.*

I entered through a large marbled foyer that opened onto a huge great room swathed in a wall of windows, a picture-perfect frame for the sparkling blue water of the Atlantic Ocean. Soft music drifted from a small jazz trio stationed in a corner of the room. The club brimmed with people, including board members, executives, and even a couple US senators. I spotted a Fox News commentator, too, one of the more ardent supporters of making America great again for some folks. Men stood about pompous and barrel-chested, bragging about their golf games. Their reed-thin wives huddled together nearby in strapless sundresses and Tory Burch sandals, their faces full of Botox and unmet desires.

I quickly scanned the room, as I always do at events like this, looking for guest faces like mine, counting the number of women, brown folks, anyone else who might be an "Other" like me. I was it. As usual. Nate's party was a glimpse inside a lavish cross section of the world that reminded me of Coventry Academy: wealth that went beyond the imagination; people who eyed me like a party novelty; and just like Coventry, I was "the one." The good one. The safe one.

Everyone mingled about, sipping Moët &

Chandon, chatting and laughing as the wait-staff, *all* Black, served gravlax and caviar blinis from silver trays. Nate was already working the room like the silver-haired politician he could have been, patting people on the back and bending over in laughter, even teasing one of the board members about his tennis swing.

"There she is!" A booming voice echoed through the foyer behind me. I spun around and Hardy was already in motion, throwing both arms around me, swallowing me in a big bear hug.

"Oh, hey, Hardy," I said, struggling against his flabby frame. He was sweating and, for a brief moment, I was slightly repulsed by his grip.

"A party the day after Michael's funeral?" I said. "Don't you think it's a little soon for something like this when one of the company's executives was *murdered*?"

"Hell, yeah, but do you think I'm going to tell the CEO when and where he can throw a party? I'm just here to make sure nobody touches a precious hair on the well-heeled heads of all these inebriated folks." We both laughed.

"Point taken."

"Hey, you want something to drink? Let me get you a glass of wine or something."

"No, I'm fine."

Hardy plucked a few bruschetta from a passing tray and popped at least two of them in his mouth at the same time. "So you heard about Michael?"

"Yeah. Have you talked to the police? Do they have any leads?" I asked.

"I don't think so. That detective told me the only thing they have to go on is that it had to be somebody with access to the building. Brilliant, huh? But I think you were right about Mikey not liking guns. I think that's what tipped the police off that they had a homicide and not a suicide."

"That's a lot of trouble for someone to go through. They wanted Michael dead without anyone asking questions." I thought about Michael's duffel bag at my house. Why would he have a flyer for a gun shop if he didn't like guns and he didn't kill himself?

"Unfortunately, Nate doesn't want security cameras in the executive suite, so we don't have any footage from Twenty."

"Why doesn't he want cameras on the twentieth floor?"

Hardy shook his head. "Something about everybody being family you can trust. Not a great idea for security protocol, if you ask me — the guy in charge of security. Like I said before, he's the CEO. The big guy speaks, I just do as I'm told."

Hardy polished off the last remnants of his bruschetta and swallowed. "One of my guys said Mikey was working pretty hard lately. Said he came into the office last Saturday *and* Sunday to work."

"He did?" I tried to think back to last weekend. It seemed like a lifetime ago. He'd spent the night at my place Friday night, but he didn't mention going into the office the next day. It was New Year's weekend. I just assumed he was going home to be with his family.

Hardy continued, "I know he and Jonathan had their heads together over the past couple weeks. I tried to ask Jonathan about it but . . ." An older Black man passed by with a tray of chicken satay. I smiled and motioned *no thanks* to the server. Hardy took three off the tray.

"But what?"

"Let's just say Jonathan was less than helpful." Hardy popped a skewer into his mouth.

"What does that mean?"

"Said he and Mikey were working on some big deal, but he couldn't go into it with me. That it was confidential work stuff." Hardy downed another skewer. "But can I ask you something?"

"Sure." I looked around the room and scanned the door, a habit mostly. The same way I never liked to sit with my back to the door.

"What's going to happen with the protesters and the EEOC stuff?"

"They're lawyered up so most likely a lawsuit unless we can come to an agreement and settle. Why?"

"I heard a few of the folks on Twenty talking about it. Not everybody sees it the same way you do."

"What do you mean?"

Before he could answer, Jonathan Everett sauntered up to us as if he were trailing a voice-over announcing his arrival. Jonathan was the "yin" to Hardy's "yang." As Houghton's chief financial officer, he always commanded attention with his "cash is king" vibe, salt-and-pepper stubble, and horn-rimmed glasses. He had an annoying habit of always looking down at his Rolex, in the hopes that other people would too. He constantly threw around words like *deep dive* and *the optics* of a situation to make people think he was smart. A lot of women in the company found him attractive. I didn't see it.

"Congratulations, Ellice," Jonathan said.

"Thanks."

"Excuse me. I gotta go make a phone call. Ellice, let me know if you need anything else," Hardy said with an annoyed expression before he rolled his eyes at Jonathan and hustled off. Jonathan neither acknowledged Hardy's presence nor batted an eye at his departure. Odd.

"So . . . you getting all settled in?" Jonathan asked.

"I am." I slid my hands inside the pockets of my dress. "I'm looking forward to working on Twenty."

"We're looking forward to it too. Now, I hope you're not planning to run a department of *no* like your predecessor. We're expecting big things out of you."

A department of no? What the hell? Maybe the rumors were true about this guy being a jerk. Before I could respond, Nate walked up from behind me and shoved a champagne flute in my hand, despite the fact that I don't drink.

"Hey, sorry to interrupt you two. Ellice, come with me. I want you to meet some folks." Judging from Nate's unusually loose manner and the pungent smell of bourbon on his breath, he had started partying long before I arrived. He swiftly ushered me through the room with promises to the people we passed that we'd be back later for formal introductions.

"I want you to meet these two board members in particular. They can be a little stodgy, and I want them to think as highly of you as I do."

We stepped out onto the deck where a smattering of guests mingled about. The southern Georgia temperature was warmer, a refreshing change from the frigid Atlanta winter weather. The deck spanned the entire length of the building and seemed to beckon the soft tumble of waves and sea foam dancing against the beach below. The ocean air gave me a rush and, under ordinary circumstances, I might have relaxed a bit to enjoy the atmosphere. But this was a work event and, despite the enticing surroundings, work was work.

Nate escorted me over to a couple of graying men huddled together in quiet conversation.

"Gentlemen," Nate said. "I'd like to introduce you to our new chief legal officer, Ellice Littlejohn."

Both men immediately rose to their feet. Old school. I liked that.

"Ellice, I'd like you to meet Newt Harris and Denmark . . . Denmark . . ."

"Ealy. Denmark Ealy." The man shook his head and smiled at Nate. "Pace yourself on

119

the Jack Daniels, huh?"

All three men laughed. "Sorry about that, Denny," Nate said. "These two fellas are board members on the Finance Committee." I smiled and offered my firmest grip.

Nate patted one of the men on the back and politely excused himself. The older of the two men nodded and gazed at me with a frozen, uncomfortable smile. His receding hairline revealed a haphazard pattern of age spots and a kidney-shaped mole he probably needed to keep an eye on. The other man looked so weirded out, I thought he would piss his pants or have a heart attack right in front of me. We stood there facing one another, all three of us quiet. I noticed their identical lapel pins, a red heart sitting across two intersecting gold flags.

I tried to knock off the awkwardness of the moment with a stab at small talk. "That's an unusual pin you're wearing. What does it mean?"

The older man gave a stiff smile that barely flexed a muscle in his face and gently patted the pin. "Oh, just a little club we belong to. So, Ellice Littlejohn . . . now what kind of name is that?"

"Excuse me?" I said.

"Littlejohn? I mean it's not very common. What kind of name is that? Where d'ya come from with a name like that?"

Was this guy serious? I glanced around the deck, stunned and offended at the same time. Half the Black people I know can't trace their lineage past their great-grandparents. *Who are my people?* My people are his ancestors' chattel. "Well, I haven't done my Ancestry.com research, but I suspect my name comes about much like yours. From our shared ancestors, huh? I would love to hear about where your ancestors immigrated from, but maybe we can do that another time. Would you excuse me for a moment?"

He blinked, stunned to silence. I sat my champagne flute on a nearby table and headed back inside.

His question was another example of the "polite racism" of the New South, much like the way Black people in Atlanta coexisted around Confederate soldier statues and venues containing the words *plantation* and *Dixie.* The expectation was that such things were harmless symbols of white heritage. They weren't. They were relics of slavery and a secessionist society that stirred hurtful messages of racism. And now, a board member wanted to know where my family's slave owners were from. I wanted to hustle to the nearest exit and a plane back home. I'd pay for the damned ticket myself and they could keep their corporate jet.

I stepped back inside the party, where Nate was holding court with Willow and a couple other board members. He caught my eye, tinkled his glass with his Auburn University class ring, and cleared his throat.

"Everyone, let me have your attention," Nate said. I stopped in my tracks.

A hush fell over the room as people lowered their voices. "Some of you have already met Ellice Littlejohn, our new general counsel. For those of you who haven't, I hope you'll take the opportunity to introduce yourselves. Ellice is a brilliant lawyer who will help us navigate Houghton into new heights of success. I am proud she has accepted the offer to lead us in all matters legal. Here's to Ellice."

"To Ellice!" everyone said in unison.

People cheered and clinked their glasses in a pretentious little chime, as if I had done something extraordinary. I could feel my face warm. I wasn't sure whether it was the embarrassment or a hot flash.

For the rest of the party, I tried to make the best of things. But there was a disturbing undercurrent that ran through the crowd, as if people were anxious, nervous even. A few people tried to engage with me. But most of them stood off, staring at me or ignoring me altogether. I was a big girl. I could tell they didn't want me here. The feeling was mutual.

Office gatherings like this, the need to be "on," can be so exhausting. Smiling and pretending to enjoy the stilted conversations and awaiting the threat that someone might tell a wildly inappropriate joke with everyone looking at me for reassurance that it was okay to laugh. Once at a legal conference, I stood alongside Michael and a group of male lawyers. One of the men, red-faced and potbellied, had stood in the circle complaining about one of the female presenters during an earlier panel presentation and said, "I couldn't tell whether she was just passionate about class action lawsuits or she was on her period." They are all roared in laughter. I left the group. Michael followed behind me, trying to explain that's just the way guys talk. That boys-will-be-boys bullshit. It was like I was invisible to them.

I scanned the room again. The so-called New South wasn't very different from the "Old South" — me and the waitstaff, the only people of color. Surely, this couldn't be normal in the twenty-first century. I caught the eye of one of the waiters, a Black woman, about my age, dressed in black slacks and shirt, white apron, and a pair of dark Skechers speckled with the stains of a dozen parties before this one. Her eyes were vacant and cold, as she served patê and lamb pops on a silver tray. *There but for the grace of God go I.* Deep down, I knew I could be the one in the white apron passing trays if I had been born a few years earlier or if I had never escaped Chillicothe. She extended the tray in my direction. I gave a warm smile and nodded at her. A habit mostly. My small way of saying, *I might mingle with them, but I'm still down with my tribe.* She returned my warm greeting with the same stone face she gave every other guest at the party. Obviously, she wasn't buying my I'm-part-of-the-tribe crap. Or maybe she'd worked too many of these kinds of parties, witness to the excesses and trivialities of its guests — both Black and white — and she was just too tired to care about making me feel better about me.

I chalked this party up to another example of my being "too Black" for one group of people here and "not Black enough" for the other. I left the party in search of the bathroom to take a respite. I crossed the foyer and walked down the hall where I heard the voices of men arguing. The men were holed up in a room across the hall from the bathroom. I stood outside the door for a moment.

"I gave him one fucking job to do and he screwed that up!"

Jonathan?

The other voice, southern, twangy: "Can we talk about Libertad for a minute? I don't think Libertad should be a part of this. It's too risky. Everything could be exposed."

Jonathan responded, "I tried to tell Nate this was all a bad idea. I'll have to fix it myself. And take off that fucking pin!"

Their voices lowered. I tiptoed inside the bathroom and closed the door to a crack. And I waited. A moment later, Jonathan stormed from the room with Max Lumpkin, the executive vice president of Operations, in tow behind him.

I stood in front of the Altamonte Club waiting for the car service to shuttle me back to the airport. All I wanted was a shower and my own bed. The next time Nate invited me to one of these creepy, racially *non* diverse parties at his old boys' club, I would have an ironclad excuse for not attending at the ready.

A couple minutes later Maxwell Lumpkin strolled up beside me. Max was in his midsixties, a short, mousy sort of man with a passable comb-over and the extraordinary ability to blend into the wall of any room he entered. I hadn't even realized he was at the party until I saw him following Jonathan. He wore a suit jacket and sported the same lapel pin as the board members. Not surprising since Max looked like he could easily belong to the same lily-white country club as those dusty old board members.

"Hey, Max. I didn't know you were flying back tonight."

"Yeah, I've got church in the morning." Max's voice carried the kind of short staccato southern accent that reminded me of a calloused thumb plucking a banjo.

We stood there, the splashing water fountain the only sound between us. Max finally broke the awkward silence.

"Look, Ellice, I'll be straight with you. I liked Michael. He was a smart guy, but I'll admit I don't know much about you. A company like Houghton can throw a lot at you, which means it takes a lot to be up for the task. I'm sure you're a fine person, but I won't sacrifice the safety of Houghton's employees for novice advice."

I was so shocked I couldn't speak. It was

one of those moments where saying the perfectly right comment to put him in his place was beyond my grasp and would only come to me hours later. My first inclination was to rattle off my résumé to convince him I was perfectly capable of doing my job, that I belonged in the executive suite too. But I knew he'd already made up his mind about me. All the code words from Max's comments came in loud and clear. Translation: *Michael was a white male like me. He was smart. I don't think you are smart even though I don't know a thing about you. I will not send work to you if I don't have to.* Racist? Maybe. Ignorant? Definitely.

The two of us flew back to Atlanta on the corporate jet — me sitting in the front, him in the back — in total silence.

CHAPTER 9

The slow, peaceful current of the Chatta-
hoochee River swept me away without an
ounce of effort or concern. My rowboat
drifted farther from the shore as I dipped
my fingers over the side into the water. A
small splash echoed across the river. The
ripples of water from my fingers fanned
across the surface. Beautiful white swans
drifted pass me. It was like they were smiling at me, if that were possible. I couldn't
remember how long I'd been in the boat,
but I wished I could float like that forever.
And just when I thought this slow river ride
couldn't get any better, I began to rise from
the boat, a slow weightless rise over the lake.
I was enthralled by my ability to lift myself
so high. Higher. Higher. Suddenly, without
warning, I started to plunge toward the
river. The surface of the water racing toward
me. I yelled for Sam to help me. But he
didn't answer. A knot of fear rose up in my

chest. I hit the murky black water with a hard force that took my breath away. I couldn't scream. I couldn't breathe. As I struggled against the muddy river coffin, faint soft bells tinkled in my ears. The bells grew louder. I opened my eyes, almost gasping for air.

Daylight beamed through my bedroom window.

My doorbell.

Someone was at my door. I sat up in bed and glanced at the clock: 8:17 A.M. *Who the hell was laying on my doorbell at eight o'clock on a Sunday morning?!* I shook loose the dream and scampered out of bed.

I opened the door. "Grace? What are you doing here?"

"I knew if I called, you'd blow me off. El-lice Littlejohn, you've been hiding from me." Grace was a petite, fair-skinned Black woman with a dotted map of red freckles across her entire face. Even after we moved into our forties, she still sported the same fresh-faced glow and ponytail she'd worn since the day I met her freshman year at Georgetown.

She was dressed in a bright red coat, jeans, and a pair of suede booties that slipped her the extra inches her DNA had neglected.

I smiled and leaned in for a hug. She was

right. Whenever I was dealing with something awful, I didn't call up my girlfriends and "talk" through my problems. I climbed inside myself and took shelter in all my things — my condo, my work, my pain.

"What is going on with you? You've been avoiding my calls after somebody came inside your office building and killed your boss. I heard on the news that he didn't kill himself. He was murdered. And don't bullshit me."

"I guess it's just been kinda crazy." Grace stepped inside and I closed the door behind her. Like everyone else, I told Grace the same lies — no troublemaking brother, no illicit lover. All she knew was that Aunt Vera raised me. Graduating from a prestigious prep school like Coventry had given me the perfect cover to start my new life as Ellice Littlejohn, orphan and only child from Atlanta, Georgia.

"Elliiiice." She dragged out the end of my name like she knew I was lying. Fifteen minutes into a conversation with Grace and you could tell she could have been the first Black female president. The charismatic personality, her ability to learn fast and think quickly on her feet were the things I loved most about her. But second semester freshman year, she met Jarrett Sampson.

He was a sophomore and star point guard for the Georgetown Hoyas. He told her he could give her a life better than the one she imagined for herself. She foolishly believed him. After getting recruited into the NBA straight out of college, Jarrett bought Grace the biggest diamond ring I'd ever seen in my life, and the rest is bourgeois Black history. They lived in a sprawling gated community on the southwest side of Atlanta, where a lot of Black-moneyed folks settled. He retired from the Atlanta Hawks and now owned one of the most successful Lexus dealerships in the Southeast. But Grace had grown bored with being Jarrett's arm candy and, six years ago, she attended and graduated from Emory Law School. She never practiced law, but at the right point in a cocktail party conversation, she can work in the fact that she's a lawyer.

Grace removed her coat and slung it across the arm of the sofa. She stood in front of me and cocked her head. "Ellice, what's really going on?"

"Okay, okay. I was going to tell you. I was promoted to replace my boss."

"What?! Oh my God. That's fantastic. I mean the promotion, not your boss's death, of course. So, you're the general counsel?"

"Yeah, but it's weird. The way it all came about."

"Weird, how?"

"The CEO offers me the job the same day Michael was murdered and announces my promotion the very next day. He didn't even give me a chance to accept or turn it down."

"Don't most companies announce an interim replacement? Make sure nothing falls through the cracks?"

"Yeah. But this wasn't like that. I know this sounds crazy, but it's almost like they had it all planned out that I would take this job when Michael died."

"Yeah, that's called succession planning. Every smart company has a succession plan. You're the corporate lawyer. You should know this."

"Hmm . . . Michael never mentioned my being in the succession plan. There are other lawyers who've been there longer, have more experience and stuff. It's all just a little too convenient. I don't know. Maybe I'm reading too much into it. Whatever. I'm now the executive vice president and general counsel for Houghton Transportation. They had a party down in Savannah yesterday to introduce me to the board members."

"Nice."

I started to head toward the kitchen. "You

want some coffee or a cup of tea?"

"Forget about that. Go get dressed. Let's go celebrate! We're going to brunch and then shopping. You need to get your mind off all this death and dying stuff."

For the first time since Michael's death, I was actually enjoying myself. Grace convinced me that celebrating my big promotion meant I should eat whatever I wanted. I could go back to counting carbs and calories tomorrow. We cackled over omelettes and bottomless mimosas for Grace and virgin Bloody Marys for me while Grace caught me up on all the gossip about people we knew. I don't drink because that's what Martha did and I never wanted to do what she did or be what she was. After, we strolled through the Shops of Buckhead, a swanky knock-off of California's Rodeo Drive with upscale boutiques and shops.

"How's your aunt Vera?"

I blew a deep sigh. "Same. I feel so bad, too. I need to do right by her."

"What does that mean?"

"She always told me she never wanted to go in a nursing home. And what did I do?"

"Ell, you have nothing to feel bad about. Beachwood is the best in Atlanta. My father-in-law was there before he passed.

Girl, with the hours you work, you can't take care of her."

"I know, but still . . ." I went quiet wondering what Vera was doing at that moment. Maybe I'd go by and visit when I left Grace. I'd take her some magazines or some mints, the things that always brightened her spirits.

"So, I didn't want to bring this up again, but what's going on with the murder investigation?" Grace said.

"I don't know. The police aren't really sharing a lot of information."

"Did the guy . . . Michael, right? Did he have any enemies?"

Grace had turned things all serious again. I just wanted to go back to laughing and gossiping about people we knew. I wanted to keep giggling like we did in college. I didn't want to deal with my real life.

I sauntered up to the window of an über-expensive store called the Port. "What do you think of that blue dress? The one with the belt."

"Hmm . . . nice. I like that pantsuit, though. So was he married? The police always suspect the spouse first."

"Yeah, he was married."

"Didn't you say this was the same guy you worked with at the firm a few years back?"

I continued staring in the store window.

"Mm-hmm."

"So were you guys tight?"

I could feel her eyes examining me. She was digging around again, but I guess it came from a good place. She was my best friend. Still, I never broke my stare from the window. "You think that shade of blue is too bright for me? I'm not in my twenties, you know."

"You don't have to be twenty to wear bright colors. And you're not slick. You're acting the same way you acted back in school when you were messing around with that biology TA sophomore year."

I finally swung around to face her. "Are we gonna shop or talk about my questionable taste in men?"

Grace's eyes narrowed. "Were you sleeping with your boss?"

"I thought you said we came here to get my mind off all that death and dying stuff."

Grace gave me a *yeah, whatever* kind of look but said nothing.

"You're right, I can pull off that color. Hell, Beyoncé's mama wears whatever she wants and she's in her sixties! I'm going in to try it on."

Grace shook her head and followed me in the store.

"Good afternoon." The salesclerk offered

135

a curt greeting along with a plastic smile of bright red lipstick and porcelain veneers. I watched her give a quick glance to the security guard standing near the door.

"Good afternoon," Grace and I said in unison.

The store was one of those places with sparse racks of clothes that hung from chains in the ceiling and round glass tables flaunting sparkly orbs of jewelry and accessories. Grace and I began to stroll through the store. I wasn't even halfway through a rack when I noticed the security guard moving in behind Grace as she picked through earrings on a table.

"Hey, what do you think of these?" Grace held up a pair of crystal globe earrings. I nodded my agreement at her. She turned a serious face to the security guard, who stood so close to her she could have leaned over and pecked him on the lips. "What do *you* think?" she asked him. He flushed red with embarrassment and eased away. She glanced back at me and silently mouthed the words *Fuck him.*

I grinned and picked up a blouse. I noticed the salesclerk in my peripheral vision as she eased from behind the counter. Even though we were the only customers in the store, she still hadn't offered to help us with anything.

"That blue dress in the window, do you have it in a size twelve?" I asked.

"That dress is Alexander McQueen and it's twenty-seven hundred dollars."

I looked at Grace then back at the sales-clerk. "That's not the answer to my question, but thanks for volunteering that information. Size twelve, please."

"I'm not sure that particular designer makes clothing in anything above a size ten."

"Maybe you should go check, huh?"

She grimaced and hustled off to the back of the store. I watched her walk off. I eyed the security guard again. He gave me a sheepish expression, then slinked off.

"Oh God," Grace said. "Is she serious?"

"I know." I shook my head in disgust. "I think I just got dissed twice — I'm Black and fat. This city is what, like fifty percent Black? The cradle of the civil rights movement. Let's just go. Let that heffa sell that rag to someone else."

We walked out the store and stood on the sidewalk silent for a beat. Racism is exhausting and embarrassing, even in front of your best friend, who's also Black. It's as if there's a stealth undercurrent of unwarranted assumptions, petty slights, and dismissals always ready to pop up and reinforce the idea that people of color aren't good enough, they aren't welcome. The reality was that I earned enough money in one day to pay a week of her wages. But still, she felt entitled enough to conclude that I couldn't afford to buy a dress she was paid by the hour to sell.

"So how was the party yesterday?" Grace asked, shifting the conversation.

"You mean the one they had the *day after* their colleague's funeral?" I shook my head at the poor timing of the party. "Fine, I guess."

"You guess?"

We strolled down the street again, but I'd lost my interest in window shopping after our little reception at the Port. "Well, for starters, it was a work function, so anything resembling *fun* was in very limited supply there."

Grace snickered.

"But it was something else. They have this party exactly one day after Michael's funeral and not one of them attended. Maybe it was my imagination. I don't know. It was a vibe I caught while I was there."

"Like what?"

"Well, as usual, I was the *only one,* if you don't count the waitstaff. But more than that, it was like a few people there had these staged phony facades while the majority of them shot daggers at me."

"But you've said before we don't have a lot of *cousins* at Houghton."

"True. But something about this party was different. Some of the people acted like I was the first Black person they'd ever been in the same room with. You remember that scene in the movie *Get Out,* where the brother walks into the garden party and all the white people fawn all over him all weird and everything? Yeah, it was kinda like that, except the folks weren't fawning over me and they weren't as sophisticated. And the VP of Operations, Maxwell Lumpkin, essentially told me he wouldn't send work to me. *His* vibe came through loud and clear."

"Oooh . . . he sounds delightful. Ell, how did you manage to find the one company in *all* of Atlanta without Black people in the upper ranks?"

"You'd be surprised how few Black people there are in the executive ranks of major companies. It's getting better, but we still have a long way to go."

"Okay, so what's up with all the protests against Houghton that they show on the news?"

"That's what made me take the job. Maybe now that I'm there, I can help change all that. I have a plan to work with HR, help them get some initiatives and policies in place to hire more of our cousins."

"Good luck. I just think the hate up in there must run pretty deep if they've managed to keep their executive suite lily white in a city with a Black mayor for the past forty years and one of them is named Keisha."

I laughed out loud. "You might have a point there. Michael used to assure me that the company was working on it, but being family-owned and all, it was taking more time than usual." I stopped talking. I never liked to talk too much about Michael to Grace. We stood at the corner waiting for the traffic light to change.

"Can I ask you something and you promise not to get mad?" Grace said.

"Oh God, what?"

"Why would you follow your boss over to a company with an abysmal record for hiring minorities and then continue to stay there after someone killed that boss?"

Grace's question was a good one, but I deflected again. "Did I mention the thirty-five percent raise?"

Grace tilted her head and gave me a lopsided *girl-please* kind of smirk, fully aware of what I was doing. "Ell, you were sleeping with Michael, weren't you?"

The light changed and we stepped off the curb. I hooked my arm inside hers. "Come on. Let's go find a store that doesn't mind taking green cash from Black people."

CHAPTER 10

The promotion to head up the Legal Department was like almost every other thing in my life — a cruel irony of blessings. I finally get the job I've craved, and it comes at the cost of a man's life, a man I was sleeping with. I finally reach a pinnacle in my career, but I didn't have a say in it. God was speaking to me in some kind of way. I just wished I understood what He was saying.

Grace and I parted ways after shopping and I headed to the only person with whom I shared everything, good and bad. I went to visit Vera. Depending on the kind of day she was having, she might not understand my good news. But just being around her was always plenty enough for me.

Twenty minutes later, I pulled into the visitors' lot of the Beachwood Assisted Care Facility. Inside the bright lobby, the heavy pungent smell of Pine-Sol spiraled through the air and attacked my nostrils. But the place didn't smell like pee or worse, which sometimes hung in the air of other nursing homes. By all recommendations, this facility was the best in Atlanta, but I always second-guessed my decision to place Vera here.

I smiled over the ledge of the front desk. A pretty young woman, twentysomething, with mustard-colored cornrows glanced up and smiled back.

"Oh, hey, Miss Littlejohn."

"Hi, Quineisha. How's my girl today?" I said while signing the visitors' log.

"She had a really good day. She had a good appetite, too — ate all her breakfast."

"That's good to hear."

The elevator pinged and I rode to the third floor. This level bustled with activity, starting with a couple of residents sitting in wheelchairs in the TV room watching *The Golden Girls* about eighty decibels too high. I smiled at them before I rounded the corner of the hallway and strolled up to a doorplate marked VERA HENDERSON. Inside, the saxophone-infused theme song from an episode of *Sanford and Son* blared through the room. Vera was planted deep in the brown leather Barcalounger beside her bed asleep, a *Redbook* magazine open and perched on top of her head like a tent. *Her straw hat again.* I gently removed the magazine, bent over, and kissed her on the top of her head. She smiled, eyes still closed, as if enjoying the last remnants of an amusing dream.

"Hey, sleepyhead."

Vera slowly opened her eyes and gave a drowsy smile. "Hey, sugar."

She didn't recognize me. Either Quineisha lied or Vera's good day had slipped away after her morning breakfast. "Turn off that idiot box and sit with me for a spell."

I hit the remote control.

She fidgeted in her chair for a few seconds, struggling to lift her frail frame. "Where is that doggone thing?"

I took off my coat. "Can I get something for you, Vee?"

"My hat. I can't find my hat. That sun beating down something awful. You seen my straw hat around here?"

"No, but I don't think you need it right now. We're indoors."

"Oh." Vera looked around quizzically and then back at me. Her eyes blinked a few times and fell to her lap.

When I was growing up, Vera was what folks called a "red-bone." Men lusted after her. Women did too. But she used to say she had "next to no time" for either. Whenever I think of Vera back in Chillicothe, I always remember her laughing. The kind of laugh that churned from a well deep inside her, before rumbling and gushing her infectious spirit onto everyone around her.

She rolled into Georgia back in 1967 on the Crescent City Line straight out of the Louisiana bayou. As she used to say, *The white man blinked and I broke free.* I was never completely sure what that meant, but I knew there had been some sort of trouble back in the bayou. She said she settled in Georgia instead of heading to Chicago where she had family because "they" would have looked for her up there. I never got any details about who was looking for her or why, and Vera considered it disrespectful of children to question their elders. Whatever happened, it was bad enough to make her pass on the Great Negro Migration north in favor of inferior Jim Crow facilities and a town so small it barely ranked a spot on a Rand-McNally road atlas.

Now, decades and a dozen illnesses later, the thick auburn ponytail she used to wear at the back of her head had transformed into two long gray braids that fell over her shoulders. Her soft yellow skin was now a dull copper color, ashen and clinging to thin fragile bone. But her broad, gap-toothed smile was still without rival.

She chattered on about Chillicothe as if decades hadn't stepped between her and the small town she remembered, the days when her friends Miss Toney and Bank-robber would come by and sit on her porch, tsk-tsking over some poor soul's untimely death. Vera's cousin Birdie might stop by, too, with an apple pie or German chocolate cake. That old farmhouse was raucous with the sound of people laughing and "swapping lies," as Vera used to say, and Otis Redding or Aretha Franklin drifting from the big black radio on the windowsill. I knew how much Vera missed her home, a modest house that sat on twenty-five acres of farmland that she inherited from a "gentleman friend," as she used to call him. Even though I hated Chillicothe, sitting at Vera's bedside listening to her stories about the place was like a balm for my anxious soul.

A few minutes later, I was half listening until she uttered my mother's name.

"I saw that no-count Martha Littlejohn today at the Piggly Wiggly," Vera said.

I gave Vera my full attention, afraid of what past sins or secrets she might utter in a moment like this. What awfulness might she unearth to a nurse or attendant she mistook for me? And if she did, would they take her seriously or chalk it up to her brain's dysfunction?

Vera continued, "She hightailed it outta that store, too, when I told her not to come around my house no more. Ellie and Sammy mine now. Anyway, she got to moving." Vera gave a woo-hoo kind of chuckle like she had won the battle between them. I sank back into the chair, watching her with a guarded eye like an overprotective mother hovering around her firstborn.

"I baked sweet potato pies," Vera went on. "You want some sweet potato pie?"

"No, thank you. I'm fine." I offered a weary smile. Baking was one of the few scattered memories that time and illness allowed Vera to hold on to. She hadn't baked a pie in as many years as Martha Littlejohn had been dead. I missed one, but not the other.

"You seen Sammy? He ain't come by the house in I don't know when." Vera removed a handkerchief from her dress pocket and twisted the end with thin brown fingers. "I want him to put up my screens so I can open up the windows around here."

"I'll tell him to stop by."

"How about Ellie? You seen Ellie?"

Tears pricked at the corners of my eyes. "I'll tell her to stop by too." I rubbed Vera's arm, more for my comfort than hers. We sat in silence for a few minutes until the door swung open. A male attendant with two gold teeth symmetrically placed in the front of his mouth barreled inside holding a dinner tray.

"Time for dinner, Ms. Henderson," the attendant said in a loud cheery tone, baring his toothy golden wares.

Vera's smile dissipated into a grimace and I sensed trouble right away. I patted Vera's shoulder and clicked the Barcalounger into an upright position.

"Salisbury steak and mashed potatoes," he said, placing the tray on the table in front of her. Vera's eyes set squarely on the man, a lion on her prey.

The attendant gave a wary look at Vera, then at me and back at Vera. "We got you some sweet tea, just like you asked." The attendant smiled, lifting a white doily from the top of the tall glass.

I moved in and lifted the stainless-steel top from the entrée dish. "It looks good, Vee." The attendant waited quietly for a few seconds before I chimed up again. "Let me help you with your napkin." I shook loose the paper napkin and tucked it inside the collar of Vera's blouse.

"I'm not eatin' that shit!" Vera said, her

icy glare still locked on the attendant.

He gave a nervous laugh. "Aww . . . Ms. Henderson, the food around here isn't that bad, is it?"

"I said I'm not eatin' that shit."

"Okay . . . I'll just leave it here. You can eat later." The attendant cast a glance at me looking for rescue.

Vera glowered at the attendant, her eyes steeped with anger. The kind of countenance that I had only seen since moving her into the nursing home but was becoming more frequent with the progression of her illness.

The attendant leaned slightly in Vera's direction with a tentative smile. In an instant, Vera sliced her thin brown hands through the tray, sending Salisbury steak, mashed potatoes, and dishes careening against the wall and onto the floor in a loud crash. The attendant darted back to avoid the flying food.

Vera bent a pleading face to me. "Miss, please help me. They're trying to poison me in here. Please help me."

The attendant gave me a sympathetic nod before he knelt down to clear the food and broken glass strewn across the floor.

"Vera . . . listen to me. No one is trying to poison you." I grasped Vera's hands. "It's okay, sweetie."

"Get me outta here! I wanna go home!" Vera's pleas, demanding at first, soon swelled into the sort of hiccup-sobbing that always made me feel so guilty for doing this to her. She just wanted to be somewhere familiar. Two years and all my visits failed to make this place feel like home to her.

"I'll get a mop," the attendant said quietly as he carried out the remnants of Vera's meal.

"Thank you." I turned back to Vera. "Shh . . . Vee, it's okay. It's okay."

I stroked Vera's hands, fighting back my own tears. I missed her so much even though she was right here beside me. The heartache hits different when someone you love so deeply is physically present but mentally a hundred miles away. The attendant returned and cleaned up the mess. I still held on to Vera even after he left, until the hum of the heater lulled us both into subdued silence. I sat on the arm of the Barcalounger, holding her close and stroking her gray braids. This woman who had once been a dominant force in Chillicothe was like a small and fragile bird in my arms, her wings broken by the dementia. After a few minutes, Vera fell asleep in my arms. I used to think being here in the safety of this facility was better than her ambling around in that old farmhouse alone. Now, I didn't know what to think anymore.

A couple minutes later, my brother, Sam, strolled into the room wearing jeans, a windbreaker jacket, and a Nike baseball cap. Sam was the soft brown color of vanilla wafers and looked ten years younger than his actual age. Sam and I didn't look alike and knowing Martha Littlejohn, I'm pretty certain we have different fathers. The top of the blue crucifix tattoo on his neck peeked out from the top of his jacket. He looked like he was dressed for a fall football game instead of a cold January evening.

"Hey! There's my two favorite girls."

"Shh . . . she's asleep." I whispered. I eased Vera back into the chair before I met Sam at the foot of her bed. I was happy to see him here for a change. I knew he didn't stop by to visit Vera as often as I did.

"Oh, sorry." Sam lowered his voice. "Where you been hiding? I tried to call you a couple times." He leaned over, pecked me on the cheek, and finished up the greeting with a weak side hug. I knew what was coming. I've known my brother since he came into the world and there were only certain times he ever greeted me so heartily. "I just happened to drive by and I saw your car in the parking lot."

"Oh, you did, did you?"

Between the two of us, he was the extrovert. He was the one who chatted up the old lady in line behind him at Kroger's grocery store before letting her go ahead of him. Or he might buy a beer for some guy he met at a bar who was down on his luck, the two of them exchanging stories about their similar experiences in prison. He was a "people person."

"And as for calling me, I told you before, I can't talk to you while I'm at work," I said, ignoring the pinch of guilt behind that lie. "And speaking of work, did you put in an application at that hardware store I told you about? They're looking for people who have experience with electrical matters."

"Work, work, work. Do you think about anything besides work?"

"I'll take that as a no."

"Have you ever thought about getting a hobby, or a man, or something?" Sam said, giving me a boyish grin.

"Have you ever thought about getting a real, steady job?"

"I'm serious. Maybe you need to find yourself a man to chill that ice-queen image." He mocked a shiver and laughed.

"Shut up, Sam. You're not funny." I walked

to the window and closed the blinds.

Sam watched Vera sleep. "You know, she could stay with me if you're too busy to watch her."

"Ha! Right. And who would watch her when you disappear for days and weeks at a time?"

Sam gave a half smile. "She's tough, but everybody gets called up eventually."

"Don't talk like that."

"Where's the lie? We both know it's only a matter of time." Sam took my seat in the chair across from Vera, removed his cap, and ran his hand across the scruff of his Afro. "Anyway, while I'm here . . . um . . . can you let me hold a few bills?"

I glared at Sam. "So that's why you're here?"

"Nah. I told you. I just —"

"Geez, Sam. I'll make a deal with you. You can have all my money when I'm dead, okay? For now, why don't you let me keep a little for myself?"

"Just a couple thousand, Ellie. I promise I'll pay you back."

"No, you won't. You'll disappear with it, blow it on God knows what, and I won't hear from you until the next time you need a couple thousand or you need me as an alibi. Sam, I can't afford to take care of you

153

anymore." I hesitated. "What do you need the money for this time?"

Sam looked down at the floor. "I need to handle something. I've got some of it, but not the whole thing."

"Another gambling debt?" I was so sick of either bailing him out of jail or paying off one of his bookies.

"Are you gonna loan me the money or not?"

I folded my arms. "Not."

Sam stood from the chair. "Same old Ellie. Always looking out for herself. I'm family."

I rolled my eyes. "Stop being dramatic."

"I'm just being real. I'm about the closest thing you have to anything real in your life. But that's cool. Keep thinking the world revolves around you. I'll find the money from someplace else."

Vera grunted in her sleep. I glanced over at her, then lowered my voice. "Sam, you fall off the grid for weeks at a time — no calls, no contact. Usually after you've created some mess I have to clean up. And then when you do call, you're looking for a handout."

"Handout? HANDOUT?" Sam took a deep breath. "C'mon, Ellie . . . all we've got is each other at this point. We lost Vera. Let's not lose each other."

"I've told you, stop talking like that. We haven't lost Vera. She's still *very* much alive in that chair. In fact, she asked about you tonight. You might try stopping by to visit more often. Maybe when you're not trying to ambush me for money."

"You know something, Ellie, you're a real piece of work. You live your life like you're the only person that matters in it. It's like I don't exist to you. And you drag Vera from her house and lock her up in this place. All so you can play the big-shot lawyer. How about back when we were in Chillicothe? You weren't such a big shot back then, were you?"

I gritted my teeth. "I'd think you would be grateful for my big-shot status. Otherwise, who would you hit up for bail money?"

Sam glared at me for a beat and then put his cap back on. My heart plummeted. I'd gone too far. But before I could say another word, he was out the door.

"Sam, wait." *Shit!* I followed him, but he was already halfway down the stairs. "Sam!"

He was gone. I'd taken a cheap shot and I wanted to kick myself for it. His skill with electrical work had landed him in prison for his involvement in a burglary ring. I knew he was trying everything to avoid going back to jail.

Our relationship was always so complicated, a by-product of growing up in Chillicothe. I managed to escape. Sam didn't. After I left, he scuttled between living at Vera's house and living with our mother. Vera tried as best she could with him. But Sam was always conflicted between Vera's strict rules and his desire to save Martha from her own self-destructive behavior.

And Sam was right. Vera was slowly slipping away. Each day, she slid further into the recesses of her faulty mind and erratic behavior. Her disease was lessening her independence and selling her mind short of the here and now. And no matter how many times I visited, it wouldn't keep her here.

I returned to the room. "Vee." I gently tapped her shoulder. "Vee, I'm going to leave now. I'll be back tomorrow."

Vera grunted then opened her eyes. "All right, sugar. It sho' was nice of you to stop by. You tell Reverend Sampson I said hello and I'll be back in the choir stand next Sunday."

"I will." I put on my coat, then I stooped down in front of her, my face level with the old woman. I stared squarely into her eyes, hoping the close proximity might kick-start some recognition switch in Vera's brain. Maybe, if she got a real close look, she might see me. Ellie.

Vera smiled and patted my hand. Nothing.

"I love you," I whispered.

"I love you, too, sugar."

I released a deep breath and picked up a years-worn blue quilt with faded yellow daisies from the foot of the bed, unfolded it, and spread it across Vera's lap. The same quilt Vera had wrapped me in years ago after I showed up on her doorstep. Fourteen years old, scared, desperate, and pregnant.

Chillicothe, Georgia, June 1979

Martha counted the Kotex pads in the bathroom every month. Even though she spent half the day sprawled across the sofa drunk out of her mind, or just not at home at all, somehow she was always sober enough by the fifteenth of the month to take inventory of the feminine hygiene products like a pimply-faced stock clerk in a drugstore. The first month I missed my period, I took out my daily rations and tossed them into the garbage can in the girls' bathroom at school. But the following month, I was out of school for the summer and completely forgot. I didn't have some grand plan for what I would do. I guess I just tried to wish it all away.

I was sitting on the bed reading a book in the small bedroom I shared with Sam at Willie Jay's house. Sam was outside playing somewhere. It was hot inside the house, but with the roller shade pulled down, the room offered a little relief from the full brunt of the summer heat. A quiet spot where I could perch my nose inside a book and escape this house. His house.

I heard Martha's footsteps stomping toward my room. She burst through the door. "Are you pregnant?!"

Shock raced through me. "I . . . I . . ." I suddenly realized I had forgotten to take my napkin rations from the bathroom. I didn't know how to answer her. I was too scared.

"I asked you a question. *Answer me.*" Martha's voice was brittle, like she was on the brink of tears.

Before I could utter a word, Martha leapt across the small room and slapped me so hard it made my ears ring. "Answer me, you lil' bitch!" Then she started to cry. "Why would you do this to me?"

Martha raised her hand and brought it down in another burning sting across my face. I didn't flinch. She yanked my hair in a tight wad and dragged me out of the bed. The book flew in one direction and Martha dragged me in another. "Why would you do this to me?!"

Martha had a way of making me feel like I was the source of all our problems. Now I had given her a reason to justify every ugly thing she always told me I was. Her words finally made sense.

Willie Jay hustled into the bedroom and grabbed Martha before she swung again. "Martha, leave the girl alone." His concern caught me off guard. For the way he normally treated me and Sam, his effort to rescue me from Martha's venom was my second shock of the day.

"You ruined everything! You ruined everything," she screamed, as Willie Jay dragged her down the hall to the room they shared. I fell onto the edge of the bed and quietly stared at the chipped polish on my toenails. I heard the door slam, their voices muffled on the other side.

Martha was right. Everything would be ruined. All my hard work, the scholarship to Coventry Academy, my lifeline to escape Chillicothe, all of it slipping away from me. I wanted that scholarship so bad that I daydreamed about it all day long. It was the first thing I thought about when I woke up and the last thing on my mind before I drifted off to sleep. And I'd done everything I could to keep anyone from turning down my application once they looked at it. Stellar grades. *Check.* Impressive recommendations. *Check.* Financial need. *Check. Check. Check.*

My teacher, Mrs. Cook, sent the application materials home along with a note inviting Martha to come up to the school to discuss it all. I purposely waited for a day when Martha's "demons" were chasing her to talk about the scholarship. She even passed out while I was talking. So I took matters into my own hands. I filled out all the paperwork myself. I even drafted a note on some of Miss Vera's fancy paper she'd given me, apologizing for not being able to come to the school to discuss the scholarship and signing Martha's name. I wasn't sure whether my handwriting fooled Mrs. Cook. If it didn't, she never let on. Mrs. Cook probably knew what Martha was. Everybody in Chillicothe did.

I sat on the bed and tried to tuck my hair back into the ponytail where Martha had ripped it out. I thought about going to Miss Vera's house. The only saving grace about living at Willie Jay's was the fact that it was close enough to her house that Sam and I could go there as often as we liked. If Martha wasn't in a mood, she would let us spend the night there. Miss Vera's cousin Birdie would bring me Bonne Bell lip gloss or some musk oil. Miss Vera would make

Sam's favorite meal, macaroni and cheese and fried pork chops, and let me paint my nails in her bedroom. But if I went to her house now, she would ask me why I was so upset and I was too scared to tell her or anyone else.

I waited for a few minutes, then I ran through the kitchen and out the back door. The heat outside was stifling. The thick, humid air clung to my clothes, my skin, my lungs. This small miserable town was suffocating me, pulling its blanket of poverty over me, leaving me to wallow in its dust and heat. Being fourteen and pregnant was like a death sentence for a poor Black girl in a town like Chillicothe. I ran to the rugged edge of the riverbank that backed up against the house and fell to my knees in tears. What would I do now?

The day sat on the edge of dusk, just before the choir of crickets and night owls began. I listened to the soft tumble of water against the edge of the river, its murky, green-gray surface like a soft velvet coating. If you sat real still on a calm evening like this, you might spot the thick horny scales of an alligator head slowly floating through the river. I stared into the water until an alligator gently skimmed the surface. I watched it bob and slink across the river, peacefully passing me as if every good thing in my life floated away with it.

What would I do with a baby?

CHAPTER 11

Monday morning. In one week, everything in my professional life had been turned on its head. My God sense about this promotion settled in the back of my brain, niggling away at every thought I had about working in the executive suite. Everything about this promotion seemed unnerving. Too convenient. Too rushed, like the way you hustle inside of a building at the first claps of thunder just before a downpour. All running without thinking.

I sat in a custom Eames chair in Michael's old office — now *my* office — gazing at spindles of winter-bare trees in Piedmont Park. This office was at least ten times the size of my old one. Building Services completed the renovations in record time. Hardwood floors replaced the blood-soaked carpet from a week ago. Fifteen thousand dollars for a handwoven oriental rug. Ten-thousand-dollar Bernhardt white linen chairs — two of them! Only now, sitting in this office, as its full-fledged occupant, did I fully appreciate the vast divide that charted the us-versus-them landscape of the company. For all Houghton's talk about family, it was obvious that some members of the clan enjoyed far better perks than others.

And every other officer up here sat in the same kind of luxury. For a company that was swimming in red ink just a couple years ago, I'd think we would be better stewards of the company's resources. I couldn't understand how Houghton had made such a fast turnaround.

With this office, I'd traded my pedestrian view of Peachtree Street in the Legal Department for the tranquil vista of Piedmont Park. I could even see the playground area. I relished this sprawling view, although today the freezing temperatures and the metal-gray sky made the park a deserted island. On warmer days, the playground would be teeming with squealing kids. I'd convinced myself that I didn't want kids. Or maybe the choices I made convinced me that I didn't. Either way, I usually found myself staring at them with a quizzical eye, wondering what it would be like to have someone else to think about before myself, to make sacrifices for someone totally and completely dependent on me.

I rubbed the back of my neck and released a deep breath. Michael was murdered right here in this office. My first thought had been like Grace's — maybe his wife, Anna, did it. Maybe she'd found out about us. It might explain why she looked at me so weirdly at Michael's funeral. But why would she come into the office to stage his suicide? Maybe she was smarter than I gave her credit for. If she knew about us and she hired someone to do it, then perhaps I was supposed to be in the office too. Maybe . . . The thought made me shudder.

"Hey there!" Anita said, rolling into my office with a fistful of papers. She wore a pair of black slacks and a neon pink blouse that fit so snug it left the buttons in a precarious dance with the button-holes to keep everything under wraps. "Here's the Executive Committee agenda and the backup you need for the meeting. Also, bad news on Michael's emails. I've spent the past couple of days on the phone with IT getting the runaround about getting you access to Michael's email account."

"What do you mean?"

"IT said they deleted all his emails. They said it was company policy whenever somebody left the company."

"That's either a bald-faced lie or we've got a huge e-discovery problem if we're automatically deleting emails. I'll check with Jonathan. IT rolls up to him."

"I would have checked with Michael's assistant, but she quit. She said she's not working in any office where people get murdered."

"That's probably not a bad policy to follow."

Anita snickered. She set the documents on my desk, cupping the edges in a tight little stack. "By the way, I set up the meeting you wanted with Queen Willow to talk about minority hiring like you asked. You're all set for this Friday."

"*Queen* Willow?" I slid the documents across the desk and giggled. Anita's sense of humor was refreshing in an office where everyone took themselves so seriously.

"HR is a different world down there now that Joe Barton was kicked out and Queen Willow took over."

I grinned. "You're not following the corporate messaging — Willow Sommerville was promoted to replace Joe Barton after his retirement."

"Corporate messaging, my foot! She's a stuck-up little lightweight if you ask me."

My interest was officially piqued. "Why

do you say that?"

"One day, Joe was here. The next day, he's out. And all because Willow cuddles up to Jonathan."

"So you think Willow got promoted because she was having an affair with Jonathan?"

"Duh."

"You're funny." I swiveled my chair and stared out the window. I locked in on a runner down in the park, just as he approached the playground. Long and lean. His stride confident and even.

Anita kept talking. "By the way, Operations wants to set up a meeting out at the Conyers Operations Center to go over some shipping orders. And Mallory wants to know if she could get about thirty minutes on your calendar to talk about managing her team. It seems George's flatulence problem has reared its ugly head again and the folks in the nearby cubicles are convinced he's doing it on purpose. And a few of the attorneys are complaining about the memo you sent out this morning with the new deadlines for budget submissions. You know, you're the new boss so everybody wants to push ya buttons."

I sighed, still staring out the window. "A forty-five-minute drive out to Conyers each way?" I shook my head no. "Have Rudy go to the meeting with Operations," I said flatly to Anita over my shoulder. "And it's a no to Mallory. I don't have time to deal with George's particular brand of nonsense. She'll have to figure it out. As for the attorney complaints, I don't give a damn, but you don't have to share that with them."

Anita was right. Everyone in the Legal Department would take it upon themselves to try to test the new boss. Just a week ago, they were making small talk with me in the breakroom or stopping by my office to show me a picture of their kid kicking a soccer goal. Now, I was the enemy, the sellout.

I followed the runner down in the park as he cleared the slides, then the swings, before heading toward the pond. A cold day for a run, but the guy was making headway through the park. A steady, competent runner. Probably a marathoner. I suddenly felt like a fraud in this office, little shards of doubt cutting away at my confidence. How could I be expected to handle the morass of legal matters for a corporation like Houghton? Quarterly board meetings? Supervising a group of people, some of them almost half my age and the majority of whom I didn't even like? My next thought, *Maybe I shouldn't be in this office.* But I told myself it's just the grating and incessant voice of impostor syndrome. I have every right to be in this office.

"Pretty nice view, huh?" Anita said.

I'd nearly forgotten she was in the room with me. I finally swiveled back around in my chair and gave her a lukewarm smile. "Yeah, pretty nice if you like breathtaking vistas," I muttered with about as much enthusiasm as a teenager on test day.

Anita fancied herself the "Mama Bear" of the Legal Department. She walked around to the side of my desk and peered down at me like a disciplining parent. "Okay, spill it. What's the matter?"

"Nothing, really."

"That doesn't sound like nothing to me," Anita said, glancing down at her blouse to check on the button situation.

I leaned in toward a bright bouquet of yellow roses, blue hydrangeas, and lavender sitting on my desk. I closed my eyes for a second and inhaled the pleasant floral scent. "By the way, thanks for the flowers. Very nice, but you don't have to buy flowers for my office."

"Oh, it's no big deal . . . it's just a six-dollar garden medley from Kroger's. Besides, this office needs a personal touch. Something to show that a real live person works in here."

"You're full of jokes today."

"Can I ask you a personal question?"

"No," I replied as I fished through my desk drawer for an ink pen. People asking me personal questions was always off-limits, especially in the office.

"Why don't you have anything personal in your office? A picture? A plaque? Something."

"So you're asking anyway?" In all the years I'd worked in office settings, Anita was the first person to bring this up.

"I mean, this office is beautiful, but there's nothing in here that tells anyone *you* work in here. Even when we were downstairs in Legal. Nothing. I know you're not married or anything. But what about a vacation picture with your girlfriends? A picture of your dog or pet hamster?" she asked.

I rummaged through my pencil tray for a few seconds more, trying to think of something clever to say. It had never been my intention to create an emotionally sterile office environment. I guess it just came along with who I was — Martha Littlejohn's daughter. I had learned a long time ago to compartmentalize the different areas of my life — family, work, friendships — into various little boxes, standing side by side but never touching one another. It made it so much easier to grapple with all the pain and memories. It was my version of therapy without the two-hundred-fifty-dollar-per-hour price tag.

I grabbed a blue ink pen and clicked it a few times to make sure it worked, closed the drawer, then looked squarely at Anita. "To answer your question, this is an office, not my living room mantel. I don't line the walls of my kitchen with legal memos, and likewise, I don't particularly care to fill my office with mementos of my personal life. Work is work and home is home. Any other questions?"

"No, ma'am." Anita raised her eyebrows and gave a fragile smile. "That should do it."

Maybe I came off like a first-class bitch, but at least I had put the subject to bed permanently. A ping of guilt hit me. Anita was one of the few decent people around here. Nosy or not, she meant well, unlike some of the others in the Legal Department who were either clawing to get ahead or backstabbing and conniving to keep others from getting ahead.

"Well, anyway, I just hope we aren't going back to the eighteenth floor anytime soon," Anita said. "I love it up here. The chair at my desk feels like it was custom-made for my butt. And have you seen how the breakroom is stocked? I never have to buy another Diet Coke or Snickers again in my life."

I laughed and shook my head at Anita's silliness. At least one of us was comfortably settling into the executive suite. My taste for luxury had finally met its match in the extravagance of this office. Although I loved it, I still couldn't understand why it put me on edge.

A few minutes later, I headed down the hall to the ladies' room. For all my doubts, I had to admit, life on Twenty was 100 percent better. The HVAC system worked gloriously on this floor and the bathroom was much closer to my office for my navy-bean-size bladder. On my way to the restroom, I spotted Jonathan standing at his assistant's desk, laughing.

"Excuse me, Jonathan, can I speak with you for a minute?"

He glanced down at his Rolex. I ignored the gesture. If he had time to yuck it up with his assistant, he had time for a colleague's question. "Sure. What's on your mind?"

"I can't get access to any of Michael's emails. I know the IT Department rolls up to you, so I was hoping you could make a call for me."

"Emails? Why would you want Michael's emails? We use shared files up here on Twenty. Maybe have your assistant show you how it works. You should be able to find everything you need in the shared drives."

Goodness, this guy was a major prick. "I understand how shared files work. But I need access to some of his correspondence he might have had with outside counsel. Things like that. Can you make the call?"

"Sure. I'll call downstairs." He gave me a face full of annoyance, like I was a child who'd spilled milk he would have to clean up. "Anything else?"

His assistant darted a glance between the two of us before she went back to her monitor.

"Do you think I could get that access today?"

He sighed deeply. "Let me see what I can do." He turned his back to me and started up with his assistant again. I had the distinct feeling he wouldn't be in a rush to pick up the phone to call anyone on my behalf. He had obviously mistaken my civility for weakness.

Asshole.

■ ■ ■ ■

A little later, I sat at my desk thinking about Vera and Sam and the argument from the night before. I hated arguing with him. He was the only blood relative I had — that I knew of. Maybe he was still mad at me, but there was only one way to find out. I picked up my cell and hit the quick dial button for his number.

He picked up on the first ring. "Ellie?"

"Hey, did I catch you at a bad time?"

"Nah. On my way out, though." He sounded rushed, preoccupied. "Wait, I thought you couldn't talk when you're at work. Everything okay?"

"Yeah . . . yeah. I just . . . look, I'm sorry about last night at Vera's." Apologizing to Sam was never hard for me. I'd done a lifetime of things for which I was always asking for his forgiveness.

There was a long pause. I wanted to fill up the space, but I didn't know what to say. I was the queen of screwing up my personal relationships. I wouldn't blame him if he hung up on me. But he didn't.

"It's nothing. Forget it." Typical Sam. Never holding a grudge. Always ready to move on.

"No, you're right. I can be a bitch. I'm sorry. Stop by my place tonight. I can lend you the money."

"Nah. Don't worry about it."

"What do you mean?"

"You were right last night. I'm a grown-ass man. I need to do better. I been talking to Juice."

"Juice? Why?"

"He's got a buddy, friend of a friend, who hooked me up with some work and he's got some more."

"What does that mean?" I could sense another argument in the air, so I tried to soft-pedal things. "Sam, you're not getting into more trouble, are you?"

"No. It's all legit. It's all on the up-and-up."

"What kind of work?"

"I don't have all the details yet. Look, I gotta run. I'll call you later."

"Promise?"

"I promise. We're good."

My guilt eased. "Okay. Love you."

"Love you, too."

I clicked off the phone. I remember when Sam was little. He used to collect new pennies he found on the street or in Vera's sofa cushions. Always the bright new copper pennies. Never the old ones. What bright, new shiny thing was he chasing now?

CHAPTER 12

A couple hours later, I hustled inside Houghton's boardroom, a glass-enclosed structure on one end of the twentieth floor affectionately called the Fish Bowl. Not surprisingly, I was the first to arrive. I planned it that way. I always liked to know what goes on before a meeting. Decisions are made in the "premeeting," the off-site lunches, and the Saturday morning golf rounds.

More luxury. An antique credenza held a huge exotic floral arrangement and an assortment of beverages. A long mahogany conference table and high-back leather chairs stretched across the expanse of the room. Nate's executive management team was lean in number and wholly disproportionate to the size of this table. Even though I was bathed in all the external trappings of executive leadership, inside I felt like a freshman on the first day of high school.

This would be my first Executive Committee meeting. I was pretty sure there was a certain protocol and I didn't want to run afoul of it. Where should I sit? How did Nate conduct the meeting? I'd craved a place in the executive suite for so long. Now that I'd made it, I wasn't sure how to behave.

Willow strolled in shortly after me. "Hey, Ellice, honey," she said, southern drawl dripping. "Your hair sure looks pretty that way."

"Thanks." White women usually complimented me on my hair when I wore it straight and Black women complimented me when it was coiled. I'm sure there was a philosophical conversation in there waiting to be unpacked. Since my promotion to the executive suite, I just wore my hair flat-ironed. Another compromise and one less battle to fight. I tried wearing it coiled when I worked in the Legal Department. But it always stirred up an awkward comment, or heaven forbid someone asking to touch it. I envied other women who wore their hair unapologetically natural — coils, curls, kinks, locs — whatever. Women who dared their colleagues to judge them by their worth instead of their crown.

"So I guess we're it for now," I said.

Willow didn't acknowledge my comment.

She crossed the room and stood in front of me leaning against the conference table. "Ellice, honey, can I give you a little piece of advice I wish someone had given me when I started up here?"

"Sure."

"Dealing with these guys can be a delicate dance."

"What does that mean?" A few seconds later, we heard voices approaching.

She tapped my arm gently and whispered, "Let's just talk later."

Jonathan and Max strolled into the room. I noticed Jonathan tap Max's lapel pin. "Why so formal today, Maxie? Maybe you should take that off." Jonathan glanced at me and moved toward an empty chair without another word. Max rubbed the pin nervously and took a seat. I lingered near the credenza at the end of the room, fussing over a bottle of Voss and giving everyone else a chance to plant themselves in their usual spots around the conference table. With everyone seated, I slid into an empty chair next to Willow.

Jonathan piped up. "Hey, Ellice. Welcome to the heartbeat of Houghton."

I nodded in Jonathan's direction then turned to Max. "Good morning, Max," I said with a lilt in my voice. He nodded and turned away. I didn't care whether he liked me or not, but he would have to contend with the fact that I was his equal colleague now. Some people need to remember you long after you've left a room. Especially the people who didn't think you deserved to be there in the first place.

Nate was the last one to enter. He sat at the head of the table with the rest of us tucked around him, side by side, forming a tight little clump at one end of the conference table.

"Let's get started," Nate said. He nodded in my direction. "First, let's all welcome our newest member of the Executive Committee. We're so pleased that you're joinin' my team to keep us on the straight and narrow. When it comes to legal advice, we'll be sticking to you like a piece of hair on a grilled cheese sandwich." Someone, I wasn't exactly sure who, let out a quiet, impatient sigh. "We're gonna miss Michael, but I'm glad you're here. Welcome, Ellice."

I smiled. "Thank you."

"Now let's get after it." Nate peered down at his notes. "A couple follow-up items from the last meeting before we get into the agenda. First up, the protesters. The crowds have started to pick up again ever since the

181

news cameras showed up after Sayles's death. So what are we gonna to do about it?"

Max responded first. "Since our cracker-jack security team can't manage to think their way out of a paper bag, much less handle a bunch of thugs in front of the building, I suggest we call in a private security firm."

Thugs.

"That's a bit of overkill, Maxie," Jonathan said. Jonathan grinned then removed his horn-rimmed glasses and tapped one end against his chin like he was mulling through the solution for all Houghton's problems. "We should just wait them out. Maybe things will slow down like they did before the holidays."

Wait them out. Was he serious?

"Well, that might work. Ellice, what do you think?" Nate said.

I was still bristling from Max's *thug* comment, but I managed to take a deep breath before speaking. "The protesters have every right to be in front of the building. They have been peaceful and there is no need for security or law enforcement to get involved. My recommendation is that we look at those protests within the larger picture of what's happening at Houghton. Our numbers for minority hiring and promotions do not look stellar." I heard the sigh again — Max. I ignored him and powered forward. "My advice is that we get in front of this thing and negotiate an amicable settlement on the EEOC charges. We currently have six discrimination claims that the EEOC is actively investigating. From the way the charges are written, we believe the complainants have lawyers. I think we can expect a lawsuit any day now. Things will only get worse if we get a lawsuit and continue to ignore the protesters. Perhaps we should think about engaging with them. Find out what they're looking for and what it might take to make them use their time in other ways."

"Well, that's just ludicrous!" Max's twang thrummed across the room. "Now why would we negotiate with those people. They're troublemakers. That's all. And I for one don't think engaging troublemakers will lead to anything positive."

I didn't just hit a nerve with Max — I split it open. He opened one with me, too. What the hell? I was one of *those people.* My face went hot. As pissed as I was, I knew I would have to be the "adult" in the room. It was up to me to diffuse the situation if I didn't want to be labeled the angry Black woman.

Another deep breath. "Max, I think you're missing the larger picture here. Our track record for hiring and promotion is what brings the protesters out every day."

"Look, I'm sure you mean well, but you're way off base here. Those people are trying to take Houghton's good reputation hostage. And we won't negotiate with kidnappers."

I wanted to reach across the table and slap that poorly executed comb-over off his head. But I resisted the urge. "Until we show communities of color that we are serious about being inclusive and making Houghton look like what the real world looks like, you can expect protests for a very long time, along with the lawsuits that will come as a result."

Max shook his head before he leaned in toward Nate and pointed his finger at me. "You see, this kind of thinking. This is what I mean."

"Excuse me?" I said.

"I just mean . . . I think Michael would have taken a different approach."

"Well, Michael's not here. I'm the general counsel and my advice is that you take a more open-minded approach on issues of diversity and inclusion."

Max glowered at me before he turned to

184

Nate. "Nate?"

We all turned to Nate, who stared out the window without a word.

Jonathan cleared his throat. "It's certainly something to think about. Don't you agree, Nate?"

Nate broke his trance from the window. "Oh yes. Of course."

"So are we on the same page? We'll engage with the protesters?" I asked. Max sneered at me. I wondered what he would think if he knew his beloved Michael-white-like-me-Sayles had been sleeping with a Black woman.

Jonathan took the reins again. "Not just yet. Let's just take a wait-and-see approach for another week or so. Don't you agree, Nate?"

"Sure. That's fine," Nate said, his face molded in a blank stare. I thought he might be sick or something, but he shook it off. Nate looked back down at his notes. "Let's see . . . uh, Max, how are we coming on the new DOT regulations?"

"Fine, Nate. Everything checks out," Max responded. He avoided making eye contact with me.

"Did you get our new GC to have a look? We're talking safety here," said Nate.

"I'm happy to help," I chimed in.

"Not necessary," Max said as he glared at me, his lips in a tight little line of anger.

Nate paused, stroked his mustache, then moved on. "Next up . . . Libertad Excursiones." He drew out the last word, making it sound like "X-curse-e-onez." Nate gave a self-deprecating little chuckle. "My Spanish isn't great. I never learned a foreign language. Only the King's English for me." Everyone else laughed in unison, everyone except me. "I betta learn how to pronounce it since Libertad is gonna put us on the map for international deals, contracts with the bigger companies. This is the third deal we've done in the past twelve months. Each one pumping up the bottom line. Jonathan, are we all set to announce the deal?"

"The deal's all wrapped up. But I think we ought to keep this one confidential for a bit." Jonathan grinned broadly and nodded at Willow. "As we discussed before, I don't think we want to do a loud splash with this deal. It might be better to let this one slide under the business trade magazines without an announcement. Less hype. Less competition."

"All right. Good."

Libertad? Where had I heard that name before? *The party in Savannah.* Jonathan and Max had argued about something called

Libertad.

I could either sit quiet or I could find out what was so interesting it set the two men off against each other. I felt compelled to step in again. I cleared my throat and looked around the conference table. "Excuse me."

"Yes, Ellice?" Nate said.

"The Libertad deal. I'm not familiar with that one and I didn't see any background materials in the packet you sent out with today's agenda." I smiled and eyed Jonathan, hoping to appeal to him directly.

"Oh, sorry, Ellice. I should have mentioned it," Jonathan said, adjusting his glasses and flashing a grin at me. "Michael and I buttoned this one up already. There's not much for you to do. I might need you to draft a few contracts. I'll let you know what needs to be done later."

White male privilege was alive and kicking between Max's refusal to work with me and Jonathan's attempt to dismiss me.

"It seems to be a pretty big deal and I have zero information on —"

"I said I've got this covered." Jonathan brushed me off like he was flicking a piece of lint from his jacket. "Nothing to worry about on this one, Ellice. Michael and his outside lawyer went through this deal with a fine-tooth comb. Like Nate said, we don't make a move up here without Legal's blessing. Nate, I can get Ellice up to speed offline." Jonathan's smile melted into a tightened jaw as he stared back at me.

Nate raised a hand in Jonathan's direction, silencing him. "You good with that, Ellice?"

I scoped the room for a sympathetic face. Every eye was on me. But I was on my own. "Sure. That's fine. And, Jonathan, perhaps you can get me access to Michael's emails while you're getting me up to speed." I smiled at him to soften the dig.

Jonathan's nostrils flared and I thought I spotted a hint of a vein sprouting through the center of his forehead. "Uh . . . sure."

Nate offered me a wink and a slight smile. "All right then, let's move on."

At the end of the meeting, I spotted Max patting Jonathan on the back and smiling at him. Apparently, they'd patched things up since Nate's party. Or maybe they were congratulating each other on successfully shutting down the lone Black woman in the executive suite. Jonathan eased over to Willow and the two of them huddled together in a conversation. I began gathering my things.

Max walked around the conference table and stood beside me. "Ellice, can I speak with you for a minute?" he asked quietly.

I decided his banjo twang was a lot more palatable when he lowered his voice. "Sure."

"I just want you to know that I'm not the enemy here. I care about Houghton and most especially Nate. His little experiment to do things different is fine by me, but I hope it doesn't go awry."

"What do you mean 'his little experiment'?" I knew exactly what he meant, and his comment slithered under my skin, spiking my blood pressure and my ire. This was the second time for his racist nonsense.

"Just make sure you know what you're doing when you're advising folks up here. Michael was always careful to look at all sides of an issue."

"I think I'm far better equipped to give advice about the protesters. More so than Michael or anyone else on this floor. If you've got a problem with my advice, perhaps you should take that up with Nate."

He scowled. "Like I said, make sure you know what you're doing. Now that you're up here, you wouldn't want to do anything to mess that up, huh? It might be a pretty long and ugly drop back down to Eighteen."

I matched his scowl. "Is that a threat or are you genuinely concerned about my career?"

Max walked off without another word.

"Ellice, can I speak with you for a minute?" Nate asked.

Willow and Jonathan stopped chatting midsentence and stared at Nate.

"I'd like to take a look at your new office," Nate said as he smiled back at Jonathan and Willow.

Nate and I walked in silence down the hall. Neither of us uttered a word until we reached my office and he closed the door behind us.

"Looks like Building Services did a great job with your office. Did you select the furnishings?" Nate asked.

"Yes." Surely, we didn't amble over to my office to discuss the decor.

Nate strolled to the window, hands in his pockets. He jingled some coins or keys as he gazed onto the park below. "And of course the view . . . I love this view." He turned and beamed at me. "How do you like your new space?"

"It's very nice."

"It *is* very nice. I want you to have whatever you need to be successful in this role. You have a tough job handling all the legal issues a company like Houghton can throw at you." Then he cleared his voice in a "harumph-harumph" sort of way, like what he was about to say would be the most important thing since Churchill's Iron Curtain speech. I released a deep sigh before slumping into my chair. Nate hadn't come to my office to see anything. I could smell a lecture coming.

"I sensed a little tension in the room back there with Jonathan."

"Well, I wasn't happy with Jonathan. But I'm more troubled by the threat Max just made to me."

"Max is a cantankerous old goat. Look past him. Now as for Jonathan, he brought the Libertad deal to the table. This is his baby. Of course, I want you to bring your perspective and your particular talents to this team. But first . . . *first,* you need to get a sense for how things work up here, how we get things done, and how we support one another. If you're gonna be successful up here on Twenty, you've got to build yourself a circle of allies."

I nodded. He was right. I'd broken the first rule of corporate politics: protect your ass with allies. "It's just that I have zero information on the Libertad deal. I can't get access to Michael's emails. I just want to make sure I'm on top of all Houghton's legal matters."

191

"I can appreciate that. But people like Jonathan require a deft hand. Open confrontations with him aren't the wisest course."

I listened, but it pissed me off that I had to adjust my behavior to accommodate what was clearly sexist, probably racist, conduct on their part.

Nate raised an eyebrow and collected a deep breath before he spoke. "You know there's something my daddy once told me. An old proverb. 'When elephants fight, the only thing that suffers is the grass.' When the folks with all the power bicker, innocent folks get hurt in the process. You all try to work things out. Just remember, I'm squarely in your corner. But I want you to work on getting others on board." Nate sauntered back across the room and eased into one of the linen guest chairs. "You know, some folks weren't happy with my selection of you as GC. Some folks said they didn't know enough about you, that I'd plucked an unknown out of the Legal Department. But I know you're smart and you get things done. So why don't you work on making 'em see what I see in you. Okay?"

"Okay." I gave a fragile smile. "Thanks for the support."

"You're family, Ellice. All of us are. You know why I treat folks around here like family?" Nate asked. "It's 'cause this company was started by family. My granddaddy started this company with an old Ford Zephyr he drove around making deliveries down in Henry County. He built this company from nothing. And as long as I'm in charge, I'll do everything within my power to make sure this company is viable and competitive in the marketplace. I fight every single day for this company."

Nate shifted his gaze out at the rain thrashing against the window. "My son died when he was just sixteen. My only child. Drunk driver. His momma was never the same after." Nate gave a long wistful sigh. "I had it all planned out. I'd bring him in here. I'd teach him everything I know, and he'd take over when I stepped down." Nate went silent.

I stared down at my hands. It was almost like I was listening in on a secret conversation I shouldn't be privy to.

He finally piped up. "We're family here at Houghton. You know why I treat folks around here like family?" Nate asked. "It's 'cause this company was started by family. My granddaddy started this company with an old Ford Zephyr he drove around making deliveries down in Henry County. He built this company from nothing. And as

193

long as I'm in charge, I'll do everything within my power to make sure this company is viable and competitive in the marketplace. I fight every single day for this company."

What in the world? He'd just said that.

"Knock, knock!" Willow tapped on my door with a big smile. "I didn't mean to interrupt, but, Nate, we're scheduled to meet with Jonathan's team about the audit."

"Oh yes, that's right. Ellice, the office looks great! Keep up the good work. Let's go, Willow."

What the hell was that? Is he okay? And that whole play-nice-in-the-sandbox-with Max-and-Jonathan bit even though they try to treat me like crap? I was fuming mad. I really hate it when people piss on me and try to convince me it's raining.

My cell phone rang. I picked it up from the desk, then I nearly dropped it.

The caller ID: Michael Sayles.

CHAPTER 13

"Hello?" I whispered into the phone.

"Ellice, this is Anna Sayles. Michael's wife. I found your number on Michael's cell phone."

I froze.

"Is this a bad time?" she said.

My stomach churned. "Uh . . . no."

"I need to talk to you. It's about Michael and it's rather urgent. Can you come over?"

"Okay . . . sure. I can stop by after work." I said, trying to mask my panic.

"No. Like I said, it's urgent. Can you come now?"

"Well . . . I guess I could take an early lunch. Is everything okay?"

"Let's just talk when you get here."

Michael's house was in Buckhead, a lush, hilly old-white-money community that had sprawled across northwest Atlanta to include upscale shopping and a popular spot for celebrity sightings. The entire drive to his house was like some weird excursion into a mistress's nightmare. How was I supposed to handle the poor distraught widow who suddenly discovered her now dead husband had a side piece? I pulled into the circular drive of the huge French Colonial and cut the car engine. Even in the dormancy of the winter season, the home's pitched rooflines and lush grounds exuded understated wealth. And despite the size of this house and its tony Buckhead zip code, Michael and his family lived modestly compared to some of the other executives at Houghton.

The thought occurred to me again: *Maybe Anna killed Michael.* What scornful wife hasn't dreamed about killing her cheating husband and his mistress, too? I might be walking into some sort of trap. I couldn't tell whether it was the hammer pounding its way out of my head or the crush of a confrontation with an adulterer's wife, or maybe my own deplorable behavior in the wake of Michael's death, but I seriously contemplated starting the engine and getting the hell out of there. But I didn't. Instead, I planned to give the freshly minted Widow Sayles five minutes and then I'd leave and pretend she never existed.

I slipped out of my car and up the pave-stone walkway. A peek through the large bay window into the living room revealed no noticeable activity. I pressed the doorbell and launched a deep melody of chimes that reverberated through the house. A dog barked somewhere off in the distance before the soft pad of feet approached the door.

An elderly woman with small features, blue-gray hair, and a dress in the same shade opened the door. I recognized her from the funeral, sitting in the front row with Anna. "Hello. May I help you?"

"Hi. My name is Ellice Littlejohn. I work . . . uh, worked with Michael . . . at Houghton."

The woman's eyes narrowed as she scoped me. "I'm sorry, Anna's resting right now. I can —"

"I believe Anna's expecting me." I was polite but firm with the old woman.

"I'm sorry. She really needs to rest. Maybe you can come back another time."

"It's okay, Momma," Anna interrupted, walking up from the side of the open door. "Ellice, please come in." I smiled at the blue-gray woman, sliding past her small frame, as I stepped inside the house. The woman gave me a side-eye, a warning of sorts, before she closed the door and disappeared into the back of the house.

"Here, let me take your coat," Anna said as she closed the door behind me. I hadn't planned to stay long enough to be without my coat, but I removed it anyway.

"Thanks."

She hung it on a nearby hook. "You mentioned this was your lunch break, so I prepared a little something."

Her hospitality was unsettling. The model southern wife, even now as she was about to confront her dead husband's mistress. I followed Anna through the house. The kitchen was massive but inviting. The hard edges of the stainless-steel appliances were warmed by the cherrywood cabinetry, and the smell of fresh baked bread wafted through the room. The center island was covered in sandwiches and salads.

"Help yourself. Can I get you something to drink?"

"No, thank you. I'm fine." She looked disappointed. "I don't have much time. I have to get back for a meeting." I wasn't crazy enough to eat food from a woman whose husband I'd had an affair with. Martha Littlejohn wasn't a stellar parent, but she didn't raise a fool.

I sat in one of the soft-cushion barstools at the center island and watched Anna take a couple wine goblets from the cabinet. Her petite figure was draped in a gray silk shirt and wool slacks, her blond hair pulled back into a loose ponytail. She filled one glass with red wine and the second glass with sparkling water and smiled as she pushed the glass of water in my direction.

"Water for you since you have to get back to work." She raised her glass in a mock toast. "As for me, it's five o'clock somewhere in the world. Cheers."

I wondered how long she had been day-drinking. Probably since Michael's death. Maybe she knew nothing.

"How have you been?" I said. Awkward, but I didn't know what else to say. I wasn't in the habit of socializing with the wife of the dead man I'd been sleeping with. Out of nowhere, a flash of Michael's bloody body sliced through my mind. I took a deep breath and willed myself not to run out of this house.

"I don't know. Most days are tough. The kids went back to school." Anna took a sip of wine. "Anyway, how about you? I heard about the promotion. Congratulations." Anna's eyes brightened a bit.

"Thanks." I was uncomfortable as hell. I eyed the door. Surely, she hadn't summoned me to her home to pop the champagne cork on my promotion and provide a lunch spread. "You mentioned something urgent about Michael."

She gazed at me for a beat. "Ellice, I need to know something. And I want the truth, okay?"

"Sure . . . of course." *Oh God. Here it comes. Just be honest, apologize, and leave.*

"What was going on in that office?" Anna asked, her voice soft and low.

My mouth went dry. My hands moistened and trembled. "I . . . um . . . I don't know what you mean."

"I know something was going on at the office, Ellice."

"It's . . . well —" I stopped. I noticed something in her. Her demeanor changed. Her shoulders slumped and her faced flushed with worry. Not what I expected from a wife about to get into a dustup with her dead husband's mistress. My instincts kicked in. Just be quiet. Let her do the talking. Admit nothing.

"Ellice, I want to know what was going on in that place that would make Michael change."

"Change? Wait . . . what?" *Were we talking about the same thing?*

"He spent a lot of time working on some case. I didn't press him at first. I just figured

200

he'd resolve it at some point, that things would get back to normal. I know you lawyers have your confidentiality rules, but this time, whatever he was working on, it was different. It consumed him in a way I'd never seen before."

I picked through my brain, trying to recall the last few weeks between Michael and me. How had I missed what was apparently obvious to Anna? I remembered Hardy telling me the security guards noticed Michael working over the weekend before his murder.

"Did he tell you anything about it? A name or what the case was about?"

"No, he didn't, but I want to show you something." I followed her down the hall to Michael's study. "Last Friday, while we were at Michael's memorial service, we had a break-in, here at the house."

"A break-in?"

Anna flung open the door of the study and clicked on a light switch. Books and papers were scattered across the floor on one side of the study. On the other, a few picture frames and papers were stacked in short uneven piles on the desk.

"Pardon the mess. I haven't taken leave of my housekeeping skills," Anna said. "During the break-in, this room was ransacked

— the *only* room in the whole house. The police dusted for fingerprints but didn't find anything. I've tried to pick up in between everything else going on." Anna stood in the middle of the room, hands on her hips, shaking her head, perplexed, as if it had just happened.

"Oh, good Lord. Did they take anything?" I scanned the chaos across the room. From the looks of things, Michael had something someone was looking for.

"As far as I can tell, no. And that includes jewelry that was upstairs and china and silver in the dining room. Computers. TVs. Nothing stolen. They disabled the alarm system panel and everything. They knew what they were doing, a real professional job. The police think the break-in is tied to Michael's death. But they can't be sure. I can tell you for a fact, whoever came in here was looking for something in particular. But I happen to know they didn't find it."

"Why are you so sure?"

"I was going through Michael's things upstairs in our closet. I found a key and a lease document to a safe-deposit box at Wells Fargo." Anna lifted a large manila envelope from the desk. "This morning, I went to the bank. I found this in the safe-deposit box. I think this may be what they were looking for."

I opened the envelope and pulled out a small stack of papers. The first document on the top:

January 3
To: Nathaniel C. Ashe, CEO & Chairman
  Houghton Board of Directors
From: Michael Sayles, EVP & General
  Counsel

Effectively immediately, I resign from my position as Executive Vice President & General Counsel.

Short. Sparse. Thirteen words. The resignation letter was dated the same day Michael was killed. I peeled my eyes away from the paper and stared at Anna, speechless.

"Exactly! Did you know Michael was planning to resign?" she asked.

"No . . . no, I didn't."

"Well, I didn't either. Keep reading."

I flipped to the next page, a copy of an email thread between Michael and an outside lawyer named Geoffrey Gallagher. From what I could discern, Michael had enlisted Gallagher to review documents regarding a joint venture between Houghton and a company called Libertad Excursiones.

Libertad. There was that name again.

Gallagher's reply email to Michael came exactly seven minutes after the request: Call me ASAP!!! Written in the margin of the paper, a 614 area code phone number.

"Who is Geoffrey Gallagher?" I asked. He was not our usual mergers and acquisitions outside counsel.

"I looked him up. He's a lawyer who specializes in defending executives who get into criminal trouble. Some kind of collar or something. Do you know him?"

"White-collar defense?" I shook my head, confused. "No. I don't know him."

"Well, whoever he is, I think he and Michael may have found some trouble with that company . . . Libertad, is it? What is this all about?" Anna said, with impatience in her voice.

"I'm not sure. Were these the only documents in the envelope? Just this?"

"What kind of business deal is this?" Anna asked, more forceful this time.

I bit my bottom lip and gave Anna an I-wish-I-could-tell-you kind of look.

"Ellice, this is my husband we're talking about. Someone thought this business deal, or whatever it is, was worth more than my husband's life."

"Anna, I'm not even sure what all this means myself. Have you shown this to the police?"

"No." Anna shook her head. "No."

"You need to go to the police."

"NO!"

"Listen to me. Someone *murdered* Michael. You really need to turn this information over to them." For as much as I hated the police, even I knew this was big enough that Detective Bradford needed to be involved.

"*Absolutely not.* The media — everyone — tried to make Michael out to be some sort of suicidal nut job. And then when I finally convince that detective that Michael would never kill himself, she starts acting like I was involved in his murder. No" — she shook her head forcefully — "I will not have them drag my husband's good name through the mud again. If I take this to the police, they'll take it to Houghton and . . . the company will spin it in some way to make Michael look bad. And besides, that detective . . . Bradford. I don't like her. That's why I called you, Ellice. You were one of the few people in that place that he trusted."

"I don't know how I can help you, Anna."

"I think Michael was in some kind of trouble — maybe he did do something he shouldn't have. I don't know. I do know I can't live through that scrutiny again. News stations had trucks parked out front last week at all hours of the day. People calling here, saying all sorts of crazy stuff. Some people think my husband's murder had something to do with the protests against the company, like it was Michael's fault that Houghton didn't want to hire Black people. Ellice, ... I can't . . ." Anna's eyes welled as she cradled her arms across her chest.

"Everyone knows Michael was aboveboard. He'd never be involved in something bad," I said.

"I need you to help me, Ellice. Find out if Michael was in some sort of trouble. If he did something wrong, I want to know about it without the police smearing his good name."

"What?" I didn't know how to do what she was asking of me. "Listen, Anna, if Michael was in some sort of trouble, the police need to investigate it. That's the only way they'll find his killer."

"You don't understand. Michael had changed over the last few weeks and I think this is the reason why. It has to be pretty awful if he couldn't talk to me about it."

"That's exactly the reason you need to go to the police."

"Maybe you could just call that lawyer — Gallagher? Find out what all this is about."

"Anna —" I looked at the papers again. "I'm sorry, Anna. I don't think I can . . ." I tried to hand the documents back to her. "I'm sorry."

"You have to. Not for me." Anna composed herself and gazed at me with a sly, calm look. "Weren't you in his office the morning he was killed?"

"Wha—What are you talking about?"

"We *both* know what I'm talking about. I know you two had one of your *early* morning meetings." She bent over, lifted a few papers from the floor, and gently placed them on the desk. "I know all about your early morning meetings in the office, the legal conferences, Michael's Saturday morning golf outings, too . . . to your condo."

I shot a look at Anna. All my worst fears knotted up in the pit of my stomach. She knew. She had known all along.

"Anna . . ."

"I made peace with it a long time ago. I had no choice. From the first day you stepped foot inside Dillon & Beck, you were all he talked about. Do you know how hard it is to compete with the woman who has captured your husband because she's so smart, so hardworking, so . . . so perfect? Then it dawned on me. Michael's feelings about you had nothing to do with your looks, your education, any of that. It didn't even have anything to do with me. You made him feel something that I couldn't replicate. My husband was in love with you. And how do you tell a man to stop loving who he loves?"

I remembered Vera's saying, *A woman just knows.* I glanced at Anna then averted my eyes. A deep and painful sadness swept over me. "I have to go."

"Do the police know you were in his office that morning?"

I nearly dropped the papers. "What are you talking about?"

This time, Anna casually picked up a book from the floor as if she were doing her Saturday morning chores. She glanced at it before she placed it on the bookshelf. She walked closer to me, leaned against the side of the desk, and gave me a sympathetic look.

"I stayed in my marriage because I didn't want my kids to become a casualty of divorce. Why did *you* stay in my marriage all those years?"

Her question sliced like a steel blade, forcing me, yet again, to contend with the stupid

208

decision I made to get involved with Michael.

"And what do you have to show for those years? A few weekends and some dinners at a remote restaurant on the outskirts of town?" She raised an eyebrow. "What are you? Forty-one? Forty-two?"

She was off by a few years in my favor, but I didn't respond.

"Have you ever been married?" Anna asked.

"No."

"Then you might not realize every marriage is perfectly imperfect. It's just the way things are. Every couple has some pact. Some tacit agreement neither of them discusses but both fully understand the terms. I suspect if Michael had made his way to a marital bed with you, you would have struck your own pact with him too. Men don't change."

She inhaled deeply before she spoke again. "I know you didn't kill Michael. Maybe you thought you were in love with him. But the police might think otherwise if they knew what was really going on, don't you think? Listen, I just need you to help me find out if he was in some kind of trouble. You and I both know my husband was no Boy Scout. But I'm his wife, we have kids. And I don't want his legacy tarnished in some sort of scandal after he's dead and can't defend himself. Just help me."

I wasn't prepared for this type of appeal. I wished she had set off on a screaming match. I wished she had yelled and called me a home-wrecking bitch, slapped me. Anything but this. I couldn't look at her anymore. I just stared at the papers in my hands. Her request, the silence between us, the secrets — All of it dragged like lead weights around the collar of my conscience.

"Ellice, if you loved Michael, please help me find out if he was in any kind of trouble. I'd rather hear it from you. Maybe there's a way to help him, even now after his death, if he was in some sort of trouble. I know Michael wasn't the perfect man. But he was a good man. Please, help me."

If I loved Michael. Did I love him? If I did, who loved him more? His feckless mistress who left him dead in his office or the wife he cheated on who was still trying to protect his reputation as an upstanding pillar in the legal community? This woman stood in front of me, asking for *my* help for *her cheating husband.*

I closed my eyes for a moment. When I opened them, Anna was still there, eyes pleading, waiting for a reply. "Let me see what I can find out. I'll dig around a little, but after that . . . Anna, at some point, you need to share this information with the police, okay?"

"Yes, of course. I know I shouldn't ask you to do this but —"

"Like you said, he wasn't the perfect man, but he was a good man."

I pulled out of Anna's driveway and headed for the highway, mentally beating myself for ever getting involved with Michael. Now I was being dragged into his murder, too. I should have called the police the day I discovered his body. Whatever demons I struggled with, all the ghosts from my past, the truth remained clear: he deserved better. Maybe helping Anna in this small way was the least I could do to make up for my heinous behavior in leaving his body without calling for help.

Also, I didn't trust my new colleagues. Maybe I might find the answer to why Libertad kept rearing up in the middle of all this.

CHAPTER 14

I returned to work and sat at my desk pushing around the contents of a carton of Hunan shrimp. I'd passed on the spread at Anna's house and still my appetite was MIA. Between this morning's Executive Committee meeting and Anna's little bombshell, I was starting to realize I might be better off leaving Houghton. A place where I was promoted to be the general counsel among a group of people who didn't think they needed one. A place where Michael was murdered in this very office and some mysterious business deal was smack-dab in the middle of it. I needed to call a headhunter and find a new job before I got sucked into this mess any further.

I closed the lid on the food and was just about to pull out the documents Anna had given me when Detective Bradford strolled into my office with enough confidence and bravado that someone could have mistaken *her* for the general counsel. Now that Michael's death was ruled a homicide, I noticed more police presence in the building. I'd seen Detective Bradford in the lobby a few days ago talking to some of the security guards. My disdain for the police, and by extension her, was stupid and based on some long-ago events that had nothing to do with the detective. I had no logical reason to make assumptions about her based on the actions of some ignorant small-town deputy sheriff. Still, the last thing I needed now was Bradford in my office throwing around her swagger like Mardi Gras beads on Fat Tuesday.

She stopped short of sitting in one of the guest chairs before she gazed around the room. "So I guess congratulations really are in order," she said with an easy smile. "This is quite impressive." The charcoal wool pantsuit she wore wasn't bad, just about what you'd expect a midlevel civil servant could afford. Every inch of it accentuated her slim figure. I wasn't jealous. Once she hit forty, all that svelte body would turn on her and give her a midlife wake-up call.

"Good afternoon, Detective," I said in the cheeriest voice I could muster. "How can I help you?" The faster I answered her questions, the faster I could get her out of my office. I knew she was simply doing her job. But that didn't quell the overwhelming feeling I had that she was judging me, examining me for some slipup.

"This morning we looked at security footage from the lobby. Perhaps you could take a look at a couple of photos for me."

Just like Hardy said, no footage from the executive suite. I nodded toward the pricey linen chairs in front of my desk.

Bradford didn't sit. Instead, she spread two grainy photos on the desk in front of me. The pictures were taken from cameras in the lobby, one from a top angle near the security badge turnstile and another front facing near the elevator bank. The man in the photos was dressed casually. A baseball cap covered a portion of his face, but not enough to make him unrecognizable.

"Do you know this man?" Bradford asked.

I looked at the first photo. The knot in the pit of my stomach was instantaneous. I glanced at the second photo and then back to the first. "Who gave you these pictures?"

Detective Bradford glared at me with a furrowed brow. "Why don't we try this a different way? I'll ask the questions and you'll answer them. Do you know this man, Ms. Littlejohn?"

"It's hard to tell. These pictures aren't

very clear." The detective's stare was unnerving, and I tore my eyes away and focused on the pictures again.

"Look closely." Bradford's cool demeanor made me panic inside. How did she know?

"Well . . . with the baseball cap, it's hard to see his face. How is this man connected to Michael's death?" I asked.

"You tell me. This man was seen entering Houghton's lobby the day before your boss was murdered. And he used *your* ID badge to enter the building. So for the third time, Ms. Littlejohn, do you know this man?"

My eyes riveted on the grainy photos. I tried to slow my breathing, to gather my thoughts, to stay in control of the situation. *Breathe in. Breathe out.*

"Like I told you the last time you were here, I lost my ID badge a few days ago."

"Yes, you did mention that, didn't you?" Bradford said flatly. She shook her head. I could tell my explanation fell on disbelieving ears.

Don't get rattled. "I guess this guy must have found it and entered the building," I said coolly.

"You folks are awfully lax on security around here." She eyed me, waiting for a response. Another familiar pregnant pause between us. "So you're telling me you don't know who this man is?"

"No." It disturbed me just how easily the lie rolled off my tongue. I knew almost as soon as I said it that I'd made a huge mistake. Lying to the police was not a good look, especially as a lawyer. I glanced toward the door, hoping an interrupting colleague might stop by, or maybe I just wanted to run.

"Let me get this straight. You didn't meet with your boss as you normally do on the same day he's brutally murdered, and a man you claim you don't know used *your* security badge to enter the building." The detective shook her head slowly. "That is quite a co-incidence, don't you think?" Bradford gave me a suspicious stare.

I glanced at the photos again and released a long, deep breath. "I'm sorry, Detective. I wish I could help you."

"I wish you could too. I'd be happy if *anyone* in this company would help me with this investigation. Michael Sayles was killed right here in this very office and no one knows a thing." Bradford said, scooping up the photos. "I showed these pictures to a few people around here and no one seems to know who he is. Not even the person whose badge he used."

I gave a weak shrug. She glared at me

again. I knew she didn't believe me, but that was her problem since she couldn't prove I was lying.

She did a 360-degree turn and surveyed the room, sizing up my office again. "So how do you like being the new general counsel?" Bradford said.

"It's fine." If I was curt, maybe she would finally get the message and leave instead of standing around trying to trip me up in a lie.

"So now you work directly for the CEO, huh?"

"Yes."

"From the looks of things around here, it must be a pretty sweet gig." Bradford stroked a finger across the top of one of the linen guest chairs in front of my desk. "Beautiful view, expensive furniture, fresh flowers. Fine indeed. And how do you like working with your new colleagues?"

"They're fine."

"Your promotion happened pretty quickly, too." She leaned across the back of the guest chair in front of my desk and gave me a slight smile. "I've transferred departments before. In my experience, it always takes a little time for my new colleagues to get used to working with someone like us, the new woman in their midst. How's it going for you so far?"

I tried to tamp down my anxiety. Bradford was smart. Maybe even smarter than me. "Is there anything else I can do for you, Detective?" I asked calmly.

"You should probably replace that security badge, huh?"

"I will."

She cast another suspicious glance around the room and then stared at me for a beat before leaving. I watched her float out of my office for the second time, and for the second time, I had lied to her.

Shit. I tried to think. Why the hell didn't Hardy tell me he'd released the lobby footage to the police? I'd have to deal with Hardy later. I had more pressing problems now.

I gave the detective what I imagined was enough time to get off the twentieth floor before I grabbed my purse and coat and bolted through the office door.

"Anita," I blurted. "I have to leave."

"Okay, is everything all ri—"

"I may not be back today!" I yelled over my shoulder.

I knew exactly who the man in the photos was and I'd need the rest of the day to figure out why my *brother* was roaming the halls of Houghton with *my* security badge the day before Michael was murdered.

Chapter 15

I rolled up to the front of Geno's Convenience Mart, a small shabby-looking store located in a strip mall in the West End section of Atlanta. Sam was likely to be here in the middle of the day. This was the slice of town Atlanta's prosperity boom had forgotten. The area was littered with an array of storefronts offering nail salons, soul food restaurants, twenty-five-dollar hair weave bundles, and all things in between. It was only a matter of time before gentrification gurus and developers would find this gem in the raw.

The store's windows were cocooned in black iron security bars and bright neon signs advertising everything from Budweiser to the Georgia lottery. For every attempt I made to rise above Chillicothe and put places like this behind me, Sam's antics always dragged me back. And every time I had to chase after Sam into a place like this,

I vowed it would be my last. It always reminded me of the times I had to go into the Blackjack Tavern to pull Martha out when Sam and I were hungry and there was no food in the house. It made me feel guilty for having gone off to boarding school and leaving that awful task to him.

Whatever Sam was into, whatever the reason he showed up at my job, he had stepped too close to the line I drew between my personal and professional lives.

I parked my BMW next to a dingy white pickup truck at the front of the store. Two guys leaning against the building stared at me before they looked at each other and grinned. My shoulders tightened. I carefully placed the strap of my purse over my head and across my body. I hoped they were still watching. I wanted them to know that whatever they had planned, I wasn't giving up without a fight. I stepped out of the car.

"Hey, gorgeous," the heavier one said as I paced briskly toward the door.

"Gentlemen," I said without stopping. I learned a long time ago, with some men, it was better to respond and keep moving, lest I face being called a stuck-up bitch or come back later and find my car keyed or tires slashed.

Inside, the place barely resembled anything close to a convenience store. The shelves were nearly bare, but the beer and wine refrigerator cases held ample selections. Otherwise, this place was hardly a convenient stop for anything else. The store was empty except for the cashier, a slovenly guy with a long unkempt beard who sat behind bulletproof glass.

"Can I help you?" he asked.

"I'm looking for someone. I need to get in the back."

He gave me a deadpan stare. "I don't know what you're talking about."

"What's your name? Rolly?" I could tell by the quick jerk of his eyebrows that he was surprised I knew his name. "I know you're a friend of Sam's. I need to find him. Just let me take a quick look. I'll be in and out in two minutes."

"I don't know any Sam. I don't know what you're talking about." He peered over my shoulder like there might be another customer walking up behind me at any minute.

To hell with him. I didn't have time for his games. "Listen, I'm looking for Sam Littlejohn and so are the police." I nodded toward the door at the side of the cash register. "I suggest you unlock the door and let me back there before the police come up in here looking for him. They might not be as polite as I am."

"He's not here." He took a sip from a bottle of Peach Snapple.

"So let me see that for myself." I wasn't scared of him even though Sam once told me the owner kept a sawed-off shotgun behind the counter for would-be robbers. But I also knew the police posed a bigger threat to him than I did. "Look, just open the door. I'll be in and out. You never saw me."

The guy rubbed the end of his beard, calculating how much trouble Sam might bring to his doorstep. He lifted the bottle to his lips and took another sip. He stared at me for a beat before he hit the buzzer under the counter. I heard the lock click and I headed through the door.

I stepped inside what was supposed to be the stock room of the store — if they'd had any stock to sell. It was a pretty good size-room, dimly lit and humming with the low cha-ching of about a dozen slot machines. Every machine was occupied by some poor soul hoping to make a big win. Under state law, Georgia permits what they call "coin-operated skill redemption games" — slot machines where people can insert cash but can't get cash out. Instead, they can earn lottery tickets or store merchandise. But backroom gambling joints like this one offered real slot machines that were illegally slipped into the state and actually paid out cash. What the people slumped over these machines didn't realize was that the games were rigged to pay out wins small enough to keep them in the chair plugging more money in than they could ever recoup. Old Rolly out front and his partners were making a small fortune off the poor souls who made this place a regular stop, all without the knowledge of the Georgia state tax commissioner.

I strolled through the first row of machines looking for Sam. I kept an eye on the door, not sure what Rolly might pull now that I had forced him to let me in the back. No one flinched or even bothered to look up as I passed by. They all sat like zombies from some old black-and-white TV show staring, eyes glued to the screens. A young woman sat at one of the machines holding a baby and playing something called "Hold 'Em or Fold 'Em." For a nanosecond I wanted to snatch the child from her arms and drag them both out of this place.

The first time I pulled Sam away from this type of den was a few years ago, the night Martha died. Vera had called to tell me we needed to come back to Chillicothe right away because Martha had died in a fire. The authorities believed she fell asleep on the sofa while smoking. We drove out to Chillicothe that night, both of us crying the entire drive — Sam crying for Martha, and me crying for Sam because he had lost someone he loved.

I walked through the room twice, but Sam wasn't there. I paced back to the front of the store.

"Find what you were looking for?" Rolly asked with a snarky grin.

I ignored him.

Outside, thankfully, the two men were gone and my car was intact. I opened the car door and heard my name.

"Ellice!"

I spun around. Sam's friend "Juice," as he was known around the neighborhood, trotted up to me. Juice was the only friend of Sam's I knew. He was tall, the color of mahogany wood, and handsome to boot. His short locs framed his face like dancing little wands of soft brown hair. If he had a real job and less baggage, he might make some woman happy.

"Hey, beautiful. What are you doing over here?" His voice had a deep sultry quality, and I got irritated at myself for the butterflies that floated in my stomach whenever

I saw him.

"Juice, I'm looking for Sam. Have you seen him? I need to find him. It's urgent."

"Is everything okay?"

He didn't need details. "He hasn't answered my calls in a few days."

"You know Sam. He's probably met some pretty little thing and he doesn't want to be interrupted with his sister nagging him about whether he ate lunch." Juice laughed at his joke, but I wasn't amused. "Hang on," he said.

Juice pulled his cell phone from his back pocket and dialed. He leaned against my car, holding the phone and gazing at me. "Woman, when are you gonna stop breaking my heart and marry me?"

I rolled my eyes. "I don't date my little brother's friends."

"Ouch! You know, age ain't nothing but a number," he said with a wide grin. "Hmph." He looked down at his phone. "No answer. Just rings over to voice mail."

"Yeah, that's the same thing I got."

"For what it's worth, Sam don't hang around here no more. My boy is on the come up."

"What do you mean?"

"I saw him a couple days ago. He said he's done with these side hustles and places like

Geno's. He's going legit."

"He told me you had a buddy who was going to give him a job. Where is he working?"

"Not sure. I referred him to a friend of a friend. But it's all legit. I'm not trying to send my brothers back in the joint. That's not what I do."

"Look, if you see him, tell him to call me. It's really important."

"I will." Juice grinned at me again. "Hey, give me your number just in case . . . you know, if I see him."

"Nice try. Give me yours instead." Juice laughed and called out his number as I tapped it into my phone. I climbed inside my car and started the engine.

"On the serious tip, if you don't find Sam, let me know. He's like a brother to me."

"Thanks."

I pulled out of the parking lot. Sam's face flashed through my mind. The security footage of him strolling through Houghton's lobby before Michael was murdered, his burglary experience, and Anna's disabled home security system. I tried Sam's number again, but no answer. A nauseating wave of panic washed over me.

I made a U-turn and sped toward his house.

CHAPTER 16

Sam wasn't answering my calls, but he'd have a hard time running from me if I showed up on his front porch. I turned onto his street, located in a "transitional" East Atlanta neighborhood. Elderly Black people had once owned these small brick bungalows, had sat on the front porches and tended the small lawns in front of them. Now those owners were either dying off or selling out. Young white couples were moving in by the droves and spending their six-figure incomes and trust funds to renovate the small dwellings into a gentrified and much-sought-after neighborhood of thirty-five-hundred-square-foot Craftsman-style homes. And perched among the stunning refurbishments was Sam's little slice of the "American dream," a small redbrick bungalow. The house was neat and pleasant but lacked any personality. No flowers or planters. Blinds drawn.

The first thing I noticed as I pulled into Sam's driveway was the FOR SALE BY OWNER sign planted in the center of the neatly trimmed lawn, Sam's phone number scrawled in black marker. He hadn't mentioned he was selling the house. If he was serious about selling it, he could make triple the money he paid for it. Or I should say, the money I paid for it.

I jumped out of the car and hustled up the short steps to the front porch. I rang the doorbell. No answer. I peeked inside the mailbox located next to the front door. No mail. That meant he'd been home recently. I knocked a couple times. Still no answer. I located the spare key on my key chain and inserted it into the front door lock. It wouldn't budge. I tried shimmying it. Nothing. Had new owners already changed the locks? But that didn't make sense because the For Sale sign was still up.

I pounded on the door. "Sam . . . it's me, Ellie. Open the door. I need to talk to you."

Still nothing.

I leaned in toward the door, straining to hear any sounds coming from inside. Nothing. I peered across the landscape. A gray cat slinked across the street and underneath the house next door. The entire street was empty except for a black Escalade and a red

MINI Cooper parked nearby. A strong gust of wind blew, rustling the nearby trees and shrubbery. The streetlights blinked a couple times, signaling the approach of wintertime dusk. The lights finally glowed continuously, eerily illuminating the neighborhood.

Maybe he was off the grid again. *Or maybe something is wrong.*

I remembered whenever Sam stole Martha's cigarettes to cop a smoke in the bathroom, he always opened the window to clear the smoke, forgetting to lock it back after he closed it. I gave a cautious glance at the nearby houses. Sam's neighbors were either nonexistent or comfortably tucked inside their homes. I headed to the back of the house and trotted up the small wooden deck. The porch was empty except for an orange Home Depot paint bucket and two empty recycling bins.

Luckily, Sam's house backed up to a mass of pine and dogwood trees, but I scanned the yard anyway to make sure I was alone. I grabbed the paint bucket, flipped it upside down, and placed it under the small frosted-glass window at the end of the deck. I gave the window a good swift tug.

BINGO!

I hiked up my coat and dress, hoisted myself up to the window jamb, and started the most unladylike climb through Sam's bathroom window, silently cursing myself for not wearing pants more often. Heaven forbid that Sam's neighbors were watching the crazy woman in a $3,500 Prada cashmere coat climbing into his bathroom. But the neighbors would be nothing if the police showed up and discovered the chief legal officer of Houghton Transportation breaking into a house.

I swung my long legs inside the window and planted my foot on the top of the toilet tank. The tank top shook under my body weight before it slid off the back of the toilet. I lost my footing and fumbled, holding on to the windowsill before the tank cover crashed to the floor. I quickly regained my balance, straddling my feet atop the narrow rim of the toilet bowl.

"Damn it, Sam, put the toilet seat down," I whispered to myself. I closed the window, replaced the cover, and tried to smooth out my coat and dress.

The house was quiet. I peeked inside a nearby bedroom that housed a lonely but tightly made twin bed and oak dresser. The room looked like it hadn't been touched in days. A light layer of dust covered the furniture. I wondered how long it'd been since he'd slept here. And where was he now?

Walking through his house made me realize how little I knew about my own brother now that he was an adult. Except for Juice, I didn't know any of his friends. Did he entertain women here? Did he have a neighbor who dropped by to borrow a wrench or lend a hand with projects around the house? This house was a fixer-upper and Sam had always been handy around a toolbox, especially electrical things. He had just moved back to Atlanta after getting out of Dodge State Prison three years ago. Sam had fallen in with a burglary ring, using his particular talents to disable alarm systems. I felt so bad for him that I gave him $28,000 to buy this house. I figured the extra work needed to make it livable would be enough of a distraction that he might avoid a repeat stint in prison.

The hardwood floors creaked like wooden clarion calls as I crept up the hallway from the bedroom. The evening sunset cast a warm orange glow over the entire house, but I spotted a light coming from the kitchen. "Sam?"

In the living room, the decor was starker still. The only landmarks: a black faux leather sofa and matching chair and a small metal TV stand — no TV. Not a book, a picture, or a knickknack in any of the rooms. Like me, Sam didn't keep a lot of personal keepsakes around. Another progeny of Martha Littlejohn. Nothing about this place gushed home. It whispered shelter.

I walked through the living room into the kitchen. No Sam. I peeped out the window over the sink, hoping not to see a nosy neighbor or worse, a police officer, peering back at me. I opened the refrigerator and leaned over to glance inside. A bottle of mustard, a half pack of Oscar Mayer hot dogs, and three Budweisers from a six-pack, plastic ring still intact on the remaining beers. *What the hell? Doesn't this man eat?!*

I closed the refrigerator and scanned the kitchen table. Final notices and unopened bills — Georgia Power, Atlanta Watershed Management, Scana Gas — were scattered across the table alongside my Houghton ID badge. *What the hell was Sam doing with my ID badge?* And right beside the badge, a small black flip phone. Sam carried an iPhone. I knew because he was on my phone plan. But a lot of folks who engage in activities they shouldn't carry several phones, so maybe it wasn't so far off that he would have one.

I flipped it open. It still had a bit of charge left on it. No emails. Only one text from a 614 area code. It looked like the same phone number from the email Anna had given me! The text contained several photos, all of the same man. One was a professional headshot of a middle-aged man dressed in a dark suit and striped tie. The man's receding hairline and staged smile was like a thousand other white male faces I'd seen in legal journals and company org charts. There were other photos of the same man, one as he left the W Hotel in Midtown, another of him getting out of a town car.

I checked the phone log. Only one number there. The same 614 area code phone number. I decided to call, listen to whoever answered and then hang up. Maybe the person on the other end might say enough to lead me to Sam. I hit the redial button. The call took a few seconds to connect. An instant later, the phone rang — *behind me.*

A heavy knot of fear landed in my chest. Before I could turn around, I felt it.

Hard.

A sharp blow to the back of my head, landing so fast and severe that it knocked me onto the kitchen floor. The pain was quick, a hot pulsating throb rushing through my head. I heard footsteps race through the kitchen. I tried to lift my head, to follow the direction of the blow. The hard tread of a boot hit the side of my face and bashed my head into the floor again. The pain engulfed me.

"Sam!" I yelled.

Sparkles of light swirled around my head. I tried to get up, fighting against the dizzy spin of light. I couldn't see through the blur of pain in my head. But I could hear. The footsteps were behind me. On the move again. Racing from the kitchen to the living room. I tried to get up. My legs were failing me. A lock clicked, then the hard slam of the door against the wall. Footsteps barreled out the door and down the front porch. The last thing I heard, the squeal of rubber against the road.

After a moment, I finally managed to prop up on all fours and squinted toward the living room. The front door stood wide open. My head throbbed. I crawled to one of the kitchen chairs and bolstered myself upright. A putrid wave of nausea rushed over me as I stood and stumbled to the front door, searching the street. The black Escalade was gone. My attacker had vanished, leaving me with a colossal headache and a rapidly swelling knot on the back of my head. I rubbed the spot, sending a bolt of pain through my entire body. A dull ache settled over the side of my face. Who the hell was that? Sam would never hit a woman, especially me. Maybe someone he owed money to?

I fished my phone from my coat pocket to dial 911, but stopped short. How would I explain this to the police? I came looking for my brother — the same man they were looking for. The same man I lied about and said I didn't know. What if they asked me for a picture of Sam? *They could connect it to the surveillance photos from Houghton's lobby.*

If he had something to do with Michael's murder, I couldn't risk being linked to him. But more important, Sam had seen his fair share of trouble with the law. If he was involved in Michael's death, I needed to find him first and figure this whole thing out. I couldn't just send him back to prison.

I had to find Sam.

I slid the phone back inside my pocket and stumbled back into the kitchen. Every step I took, every time I moved, my head pulsed. I rubbed the back of my head again. The knot was more painful than the first time I touched it, and bigger, too.

I scanned the room and spotted it immediately — an empty space on the kitchen table where the small black phone had been just a couple minutes ago. The phone was gone. And so was my ID badge.

Outside, the last vestiges of natural light were ebbing away. I headed out, this time through the front door. The temperature was beginning to drop. I shivered against the cold prick of wind as I ran to my car. Inside, I locked the doors and dialed Sam's cell again. Still no answer. I couldn't even imagine what the hell Sam was into this time. Waves of panic and dread washed over me.

Could Sam have killed Michael?

Sam was a thief. He had a criminal record a couple inches thick. He had abominable judgment when it came to picking his friends. But Sam didn't kill people. I turned the engine and hit the seat warmer before I dialed his number again. This time I let the call roll into voice mail.

"Sam, it's Ellie. You really need to call me back. I need to know what's going on. Call me right away." I rubbed the huge knot on my head and looked back at the small dark house.

Sam. Where the hell are you and what have you done this time?

Charlotte, North Carolina, December 1981

The rolling green hills of Coventry Academy in Virginia were a stark contrast to the red clay dirt of my cloistered East Georgia upbringing. The kids at Coventry wore their wealth and privilege like a new set of clothes. They fell into little cliques divided by their background and family income: the kids who traveled to the Swiss Alps or Aspen for holiday skiing trips fell into one clique while the kids who attended exclusive tennis and equestrian camps landed in another. And then there were the scholarship kids like me, straddling and code-switching between two vastly different worlds: a school where I worked twice as hard, as Vera had advised; and a school where white boys quietly told me in class I was pretty "for a Black girl" but wouldn't ask me to dance at the school mixers. And as for those mixers, I liked Aerosmith, Elton John, and Queen just as much as they did. I just wished the DJ would round out the music and play some Michael Jackson, Luther Vandross, or a little bass line and horn section from Earth, Wind & Fire.

For months during my freshman year, I was stumped about where I would go for school holidays. Vera said I shouldn't return to Chillicothe. She said it was too soon and we needed to let things die down. Fortunately, Coventry stayed open for Thanksgiving, but the dormitories and cafeteria closed for Christmas and summer breaks. But, like everything else, Vera had a solution. She always had this endless network of cousins and extended family. Her solution: I would spend holidays at her cousin's house and she and Sam would catch the bus up from Chillicothe to join me. Everything at Coventry Academy paled in comparison to my excitement at seeing Sam and Vera on holiday breaks.

Benson Randolph Harris, or Uncle B as everybody called him, had a sprawling house in Raleigh, North Carolina. Thank God for Uncle B's house. He was my first introduction to the practice of law. Uncle B graduated from Howard University Law School with honors in 1957. He told me he had dreams of becoming a partner at one of

Raleigh's silk-stocking law firms. But after graduation, none of the white firms in town would hire him. He had a wife and two young daughters to feed. So he took a job at the post office sorting mail at night while he set up his own law firm. He handled anything Black folks brought his way — slip-and-falls, landlord-tenant issues — any kind of case that put food on the table for his family. He once told me a funny story from back in the day about a lady who came to him and asked if he could sue a numbers runner she claimed cheated her out of her money when she hit the number. By 1981, Uncle B owned the largest Black law firm in North Carolina. This was after the early days when his law office was torched and he suffered threats for taking away business from the white lawyers in town.

Myrtle, Uncle B's wife, was like a movie star to me. She had bronze skin and dyed her hair scarlet red. She wore the most beautiful dresses, read *Essence* and *Ebony* magazines, and always left the sensual jasmine scent of Shalimar perfume lingering in the room. Aunt Myrtle showed me how to apply makeup, style my hair, and gave me tips on how to clap back at the rich kids who tried to put me down.

At Christmas, Aunt Myrtle always made

sure there were presents for me and Sam under that old silver Christmas tree in the corner of the living room. Uncle B said the rotating color wheel for the tree stopped working back in the 1960s, but Aunt Myrtle said she loved that tree and would continue to put it up until the silver fell off it. Like Vera's house back in Chillicothe, on Christmas Eve the house would be filled with the loud cackle of a dozen or more people laughing while Sam and I drank Cheerwine, clinking our glasses together and pretending to toast like the adults. The smell of red velvet cakes and roasted turkey crawled through the entire house. And there was the ever-present thump-thumping beat of the Temptations or Ray Charles spilling from the record player — "good music" as Uncle B called it, not the "be-bop-de-bang" he called the R&B music Sam and I liked. Without fail, before I returned to school, Uncle B would slip some money in my bag, telling me I could do anything I wanted to do because God's hand was on me.

My senior year, I finished my exams early and headed to North Carolina. Aunt Myrtle picked me up from the bus station — a real bus station with indoor seating and a small concession stand in the lobby. I could hardly contain myself as we pulled up to the house.

I hadn't seen Vera or Sam since the summer.

I grabbed my suitcase from the back seat of the car and dashed inside the house. Vera came running out of the kitchen. "Baby girl!!"

"Aunt Vee!" I fell into her open arms.

"Ellie, baby, let me take a look at you." She backed up a step and gave me a tip-to-toe look. "Lord have mercy. I swear if you grow any prettier, I'ma have to take a baseball bat to all the boys sniffing after you. Come on and sit down with me on the sofa for a spell."

I peeped around the room. "Where's Sam?"

"Come on, baby girl. Sit." Vera was already on the sofa, patting the spot next to her.

"Okay, I just want to see Sam first. Is he upstairs? Sam!" I yelled.

"That's what I want to talk to you about. Sit down."

Aunt Myrtle walked through the front door and headed straight for the kitchen without stopping to joke with us like she usually did.

Something was wrong. "Is Sam okay?"

"He's fine, sugar." Vera patted the spot on the sofa again.

I eased onto the sofa beside her. "What's

going on?"

"Sam couldn't come this time. He —"

"Is everything okay. Is he sick?"

"No, Ellie, baby. Nothing like that. Seems Sammy got into a bit of trouble. He been running around with some older boys. They got caught in a stolen car in Augusta."

"What?! Sam's only thirteen."

"I know." Vera shook her head.

"So where is he? Is he with Martha?"

"They sent him to the juvenile detention center there in Augusta. Uncle B got a friend down that way. He's helping us out and we think we can get Sammy home by the new year."

I slumped back onto the sofa and leaned my head on Vera's shoulder. "How did this happen? I thought he was with you. I thought he was doing so good in school."

"He was with me, but then Martha . . . well, you know your momma. She said her demons were back. I think Sammy felt bad for her. He went back out to her place to stay. I couldn't convince him to stay with me. Anyway, the next thing I know, Sammy calling me from jail. He said he couldn't find Martha."

I began to cry, not so much because Sam was in trouble but because *I was the reason* he was in trouble. I'd left him behind to fish Martha out of the Blackjack Tavern, to argue with Vera and leave her house to tangle with Martha and her many moods. I'd left him and he needed me. The guilt consumed me. How could I enjoy private school and Christmas presents when Sam was locked up and alone?

Vera put her arms around me. "I know what you thinking, but you ain't got nothing to back that up. God give everybody a path and you can't walk Sammy's path no more'n he can walk yours. Just because he made a mistake don't mean he can't right himself up. Mistakes don't make nobody bad. It makes 'em human." She hugged me, her strong arms trying to reassure me everything would be okay. "We'll help him. He'll be okay."

As much as I wanted to believe Vera, I knew Sam's trouble was my fault. I had been selfish to leave him behind. I thought I had fixed things before I left Chillicothe, but I'd only made it worse. Why couldn't I ever get things right for me and Sam?

CHAPTER 17

Early Tuesday morning, I arrived at my office to the heady aromatic scent of Anita's garden medley bathing the entire office. *Bless you, Anita.* Maybe she was right. Maybe I did need something in this office to show the Houghton clan I was part of the family.

I flung my tote bag on the desk and hung my coat in the small closet near the office door. I had a full-out closet in my new office where I could hang my coat on a hanger like a civilized person, instead of on a hook on the back of the door. Since moving to the executive suite I'd developed some new habits too. The first, I no longer dumped my bags in the guest chairs like I'd done in the Legal Department. These chairs were too expensive, too pristine. They were like pricey white reminders that maybe I didn't really belong here.

My head still ached from last night's attack. Although the knot at the back of my head didn't hurt as much, the bruise on my face was vivid in all its black and blue and green glory despite forty-dollar Laura Mercier concealer and a hefty slather of foundation. I reached inside my desk drawer and pulled out a small bottle of Tylenol Extra Strength, dropped three of them in my mouth, and chased them with a can of Diet Coke sitting on my desk from the day before. I clicked on the computer and gobbled down a banana as I emptied the contents of my tote bag onto my desk. I started in on a cinnamon-raisin bagel and opened the manila envelope Anna had given me the day before. I read the email thread in the documents again. Geoffrey Gallagher's response in the email signaled some sort of problem with Libertad. Whatever the problem, it was big enough to make Michael not only keep it a secret from me, but to also resign over it. It ticked me off a little that he'd kept secrets from me.

As I perused the documents, I saw again in the margin of the email the same 614 area code as in the black flip phone from Sam's house. Why would this number appear in some random documents from my boss *and* a phone inside my brother's house? I typed the number into the computer — 614 was the area code for Columbus, Ohio — and I tried to do a reverse search. Nothing. I had the crushing urge to dial the number again. I was safe in this office. I dialed. It rang and rang. No answer.

I sat staring at the email thread and thinking. *Libertad.* What was going on with Libertad? I thought back to Nate's party in Savannah. Jonathan and Max arguing behind closed doors. Max's voice echoed in my head: *Can we talk about Libertad for a minute? I don't think Libertad should be part of this. It's too risky.* What was it that Max didn't want Libertad to be a part of? And why?

I took another bite of my bagel and googled Geoffrey Gallagher. He was a name partner at Gallagher, Grant & Knight. The firm's home page described it as a boutique white-collar criminal defense firm, specializing in defending executives and professionals who found themselves in hot water over things like insider trading and securities violations. What was Houghton doing? What the hell was *Michael* involved in? I scrolled through the alphabetized list of attorneys and clicked Gallagher's name. The cursor blinked for a few seconds before Gallagher's lengthy professional bio popped onto the screen alongside his picture.

I took one look at his photo and had to steady myself against the desk.

I slowly dropped the half-eaten bagel in the garbage can as I stared at the picture. The same dark suit and striped tie. The same receding hairline and stilted smile. The exact same picture I saw at Sam's house. The documents from Michael's safe-deposit box contained the name of a lawyer whose picture was on my brother's cell phone!

I tore through my purse until I landed on my phone. I hit the quick dial button for Sam's number. No answer. The call rang over to voice mail.

"Sam, it's Ellie. What the hell's going on? The police have footage of you in the lobby of my job and what's the deal with Geoffrey Gallagher? You need to call me back right away!"

I took three deep breaths. It didn't calm me one whit. I picked up the landline and dialed Gallagher's number at the firm. A polite woman answered in a singsongy voice.

"May I please speak to Geoffrey Gallagher? This is Ellice Littlejohn."

"I'm sorry. He's not available. Can I take a message for him?"

I paced the floor behind my desk. "When do you expect him in the office?"

"I'm not sure. I'm sorry, who did you say

you were with?"

"I'm the general counsel for Houghton Transportation. When do you expect him back?"

"Um . . . can I place you on a brief hold?" The woman didn't give me a chance to respond before she disappeared behind the riffs of jazz music.

The past twenty-four hours had been a sucker punch of surprises. Sam on security footage, me getting kicked in the head at his house, and now this. Sam and I ran in entirely different circles. He had no reason to know anyone I ever knew. And I preferred it that way.

A man returned to the phone. "Hello, Ms. Littlejohn. This is Chris Knight speaking. Can I help you with something?"

"Yes. I need to speak with Mr. Gallagher."

"I'm afraid Mr. Gallagher is out of the office. Can I be of assistance?"

"When do you expect him back?"

"I'm not sure."

I was losing patience with this runaround. "You're not sure? Listen, Mr. Gallagher provided some advice to my predecessor and it's rather important that I speak with him."

"What were they working on?" Knight asked.

"An acquisition or a joint venture maybe. Can you send me the Houghton files? Everything you have related to Houghton Transportation. Everything."

"Absolutely. I'll handle it personally right now. Give me a few minutes and I'll call you back."

"Thanks." I hung up the phone.

I looked at the documents again. Whatever was going on with the Libertad deal was bad enough to make Michael seek outside counsel from a white-collar defense firm and resign from the company. Why didn't he tell me? What other secrets had he been keeping from me? And Sam all in the middle of this was beyond bizarre. Sam had no reason to know Michael or Geoffrey Gallagher. I jotted down the phone number from the Gallagher email and tossed the documents back inside my tote bag before locking it inside my desk drawer.

I stormed out of my office to find Anita putting away her coat and purse in the hall closet.

"Anita, I have to go downstairs to Hardy's office. If someone named Chris Knight calls me, come find me."

"Of course. Hey, what happened to your face?" she asked.

I touched the spot where someone used

my face for a stepstool. "Just a bruise. I fell down some stairs last night. I'll be back in a few minutes."

CHAPTER 18

I marched downstairs to Hardy's office on the nineteenth floor. His assistant, a sixtyish woman with bleached blond hair, sat perched at her desk holding a small compact and tweezers and plucking hairs from her chin. *Classy.*

"Hey, is Hardy around?" I asked.

"Yeah, go on in." She never looked up from her compact.

I tapped lightly on his door. "Hardy, you got a minute?"

"Hey!" Hardy's thunderous greeting practically lifted him from his chair. "For the Legal Lady, absolutely." Although I was in no mood for it, I knew the drill and submitted to the requisite bear hug. One of these days, I was going to have a heart-to-heart with Hardy about his office etiquette. "Let me just move this stuff outta the way," he said.

Hardy's office looked like a four-walled

version of himself — cluttered, unorganized, and filled to capacity with information. His desk obligingly stood under the weight of papers, files, and miscellaneous binders and, by my count, two empty pizza boxes and three coffee mugs — two of them still half filled with black coffee. Hardy lifted a banker's box and an empty Houghton water bottle from the guest chair in front of his desk and extended his hand toward the empty seat like a magician showing off a rabbit he'd just pulled from a hat.

"I need some information," I said.

"I'm glad you stopped by. I wanted to talk to you, too." Hardy closed the door. "Just between me and you?"

I nodded.

"That Detective . . . uh, Bradford, she called me. She said she can't get Jonathan to return her calls."

"What? What do you mean?"

"She said she's called him, even dropped by his office a couple times, and she can't track him down. She didn't say as much, but I get the feeling Johnny Boy is avoiding her."

"Why?"

Hardy walked behind his desk and planted himself in his chair with a loud *whoosh*.

"Again, between us and these four walls, I

don't trust Jonathan."

"Why?"

Hardy leaned back in his chair and folded his hands across his protruding girth. "The guy wears a twenty-five-thousand-dollar watch, but he's trash. He walks around this building like he's God's gift to Houghton. Pisses me off, too, the way he tries to manipulate Nate. I suspect he's siphoning cash off Nate's family legacy. But I got nothing to back that up. Just an instinct, you know? I'm gonna put a couple feelers out. Try to find out why he's so cagey with the police."

"Sounds like you're not a card-carrying member of the Jonathan Everett fan club. Is that why you ran off so fast at Nate's party?"

"Remember the whole budget fiasco three years back?" Hardy asked with a smirk. "That asswipe cut my budget to the bone. I had to lay off some of my best guys. But his staff has been fat and happy for years. Anyways, you'd think the guy would be more helpful to the police considering one of his colleagues was killed."

"Speaking of helping the police, did you give the police security camera footage? Without telling me?"

"Yeah, about that . . . look, I'm sorry. One of my guys was tryin' to be a hotshot.

Passed the security footage without clearing it through me first. As a matter of course, we try to help the police whenever we can." Hardy ran a couple meaty fingers through his graying head. "I only found out about the badge thing after my guy released the footage. I woulda given you a heads-up. I just didn't know. That detective has been pressing me about the loopholes in security around the company. I'm sorry."

"Look, Hardy, tell your guys just don't release anything else outside the company unless we talk first, okay?"

Hardy lowered his head. "Of course. I'm really sorry."

"It's okay. I just mean, we ought to co-ordinate on this thing, okay?" It was like talking to a four-year-old.

"Nope, you're right. You're our new GC, I should have alerted you, even after I found out. I promise it won't happen again. So do you know him?"

"Know who?"

"The guy on the security footage? My guy told the detective the name on the badge was Littlejohn."

"Oh . . . well, I lost my ID badge. And I guess the guy must have found it."

"No worries. We'll get you a new one. I'll send it over to Anita." Hardy threw his hands up in front of him. "Aaah . . . there I go again, rambling on. You said you needed some information from me. What can I do for you?"

I decided to enlist Hardy's wide network of security contacts without going into detail. "I've got some crank calling my phone. I was wondering if I give you the number, maybe you could get me some details." I handed Hardy the slip of paper with the number I found in the documents, the same one on the phone at Sam's house.

He looked at the number. "Hmm . . . sure, no problem."

"Thanks, Hardy." I rose from the chair and tried to brush off the back of my dress without Hardy noticing.

"Hey, not that it's any of my business." He touched the side of his own face with a couple of fingers. "What happened there?"

"Took a nasty tumble on some stairs. It's fine."

Hardy gave me a long suspicious stare. "You sure everything's okay?"

"Everything's fine."

By the time I returned to my office, my landline was ringing and Anita was nowhere in sight. I hustled behind my desk and picked up the phone. "Ellice Littlejohn speaking."

"Ms. Littlejohn, Chris Knight again, from Gallagher, Grant & Knight. I checked our files and we don't have anything for Houghton. In fact, it looks like we've never done any work for your company."

"Are you sure?"

"I'm sure. I checked for Houghton and any holding and subsidiary companies. Nothing."

"Not even a miscellaneous memo to the general counsel . . . ? How about an email dated a couple weeks ago?" I asked as I sank into my chair.

"Absolutely nothing. I'm sorry."

This didn't make any sense. Gallagher's email to Michael was in my tote bag. "When do you expect Mr. Gallagher to return to the office?" I asked again.

"We're not sure."

I released a deep, impatient sigh. "Is there a number I can call to reach him? This is urgent."

"Ms. Littlejohn, I don't mean to be difficult. Hold on a second." I heard him close his office door before returning to the phone line. "We're not sure when to expect him back. His family has reported him missing." Knight's voice was softer, filled with concern.

Missing. "Oh . . . I'm sorry. Uh . . . How long has he been missing?"

"He didn't come home last night. What's the name of the company you guys are doing the joint venture with?"

"Libertad Excursiones."

"Hold on a minute." I could hear Knight typing on a keyboard in the background. "Hmm . . . we have no record of doing work for that company, either. Sorry."

"Yeah, I am too." Now I was confused and angry.

"Wait a minute. You said Geoff worked with your predecessor? Michael Sayles . . . the general counsel who was murdered?"

"Yes."

"I think we'd better call the police," he said.

"Um . . ." This mess was more complicated than I imagined. I had to find Sam fast. "Listen, thanks . . . thanks for checking." I hung up the phone.

Anita walked in my office to drop off some paperwork for me to sign. "Hey, do you want me to get you a cold compress for that bruise?"

I gently touched the side of my face. "No. I'm fine. Thanks."

Anita left. A few seconds later, my cell phone buzzed on the desk. I glanced down.

A text from Sam: U called. What's up?

I immediately dialed his number. It just rang. *Damn it, Sam. Pick up the phone.* He let it roll over to voice mail. "Sam, call me. I really need to talk to you. It's urgent."

A few seconds after I hung up, another text: Can't talk now. Call u later.

Something wasn't right about this entire thing. All these disjointed little pieces to a frightening puzzle floated around me. Max and Jonathan arguing about Libertad. My boss dead. Another attorney missing. And my brother connected to them both. I stared back at the door of my freshly renovated office, the same door someone had walked through just a week before and killed Michael. The only thing I knew for sure was that Sam didn't kill Michael. I felt it in the marrow of my bones.

But Sam was mixed up in this mess somehow, which meant I was mixed up in it too.

CHAPTER 19

An hour later, Rudy stepped inside my office with his shirtsleeves rolled up to the elbow and gave a long wolf whistle. "Now *this* is an office."

"Very funny. This place worries me sometimes."

"Why?"

I caught myself. There was no need to drag Rudy into my string of doubts. "Oh, nothing. What's up?"

"Well, I came upstairs to find out what horrible thing I did to deserve a meeting out at the Operations Center and to promise you, whatever I did, I won't do it again." Rudy shook his head like he was trying to shake off a cobweb he might have walked into. He planted himself in the chair in front of my desk.

Rudy's joke took the edge off and I smiled. "That's why Houghton pays you the big bucks. Besides, those trucking guys don't want to spend time with a skirt."

Rudy laughed. "They are pretty old-school."

"I think this whole company is old-school. No women or people of color on the board of directors. Only me and Willow on the Executive Committee, and I'm the token splash of color in the upper ranks of this place. There's nobody who looks like me anywhere above the fifteenth floor."

"I feel you. There's nobody who attends temple with me above the fifteenth floor, either."

"Anyway, what came out of the meeting?" I asked.

"Not much. One of the managers in Operations left the company a couple weeks ago. The interim manager came across some shipping orders that looked weird. I told him I'd take a look at the contract and get back to him. Nothing earth-shattering. And certainly nothing worthy of a ninety-minute drive in Atlanta traffic."

"Hey, let me ask you something," I said.

"Sure. What's on your mind?"

"You seem to have your finger on the pulse of the company gossip —"

"I told you, I don't gossip." He laughed. "People tell me things and I share them with you."

"Oh yeah, right!" I rolled my eyes and snickered. "What have people told you about Max Lumpkin?"

"He's either a true southern gentleman *or* a misogynistic, xenophobic racist. Depends on who you talk to."

"I tend to believe the latter. Yesterday, he told me my promotion was Nate's 'little experiment in diversity.' "

"What?"

"Yeah."

"Well, if it's any consolation, people tell me he's also not partial to anyone's religion outside of conservative Baptists. As one of only seven Jewish people at Houghton, that's a strike against me, too. I heard he's on his third marriage. His wife is thirty-eight and teaches yoga." Rudy raised an eyebrow. "I can only imagine the imbalance in that little marital setup."

I shook my head and smiled. "I would have pegged him for a long-term marriage with *Mother* since they met at teen Bible camp back in the sixties." We both laughed.

"Most people steer clear of him," Rudy said. "Too unpleasant. Always seems to have a chip on his shoulder."

"What about Willow?"

"From what I hear, she's a nice person, but most people think she's in over her head running HR for the whole company. Makes you think there might be something to those rumors about her and Jonathan, huh?"

"And speaking of Jonathan, what's his deal?"

"You mean Mr. Fantastic? Half the women around here think he's Houghton's version of George Clooney." Rudy smirked. "He puts on a good show. Smiling. Friendly. From what I hear he has a lot of influence with Nate."

"Yeah, that's the same thing I heard from Hardy."

"I also heard he grew up dirt poor in Kentucky. Made it out on a basketball scholarship. I guess that explains the Rolex and the fancy car he parks downstairs in the garage."

"Oh God, he spends half the day looking down at that damn Rolex! New money has no class." We both laughed again. "Speaking of watches." I looked down at mine and stood from my chair. "Sorry, I don't mean to give you the bum's rush, but I've got a conference call in thirty minutes. I need to look over a few things beforehand. Thanks for the gossip — I mean the *information* you shared with me."

Rudy chuckled and nearly bumped into Hardy as he walked into my office.

"Hey, Rudy!" Hardy grabbed Rudy's hand and pumped it a couple times before leaning in for a man hug. I smiled at Rudy's awkward expression. "How are the twins?"

"Great! Two teething babies. Nothing but paradise." The men laughed before Rudy excused himself.

Hardy lumbered in. "Hey, Legal Lady, you got a minute?"

Thankfully, no hug since I was standing behind my desk. "Well, I'm just about to get on an important call. What's up?"

"I'll make it fast." Hardy closed the door and lowered his voice. "Remember I told you I was putting out some feelers on Jonathan? Well, I think I found something and it's not good."

"Okay."

"I'm not even sure we can release what I'm about to show you to the police. But I think you need to know." Hardy walked over to the side of my desk. I pretended not to notice the coffee stains down the front of his shirt. "Please promise me you won't tell anybody I gave this to you."

"What is it, Hardy?" I tried not to sound exasperated.

"Remember I told you Mikey and Jonathan had their heads together working on some big confidential deal? Well, I found out what it was." Hardy slid a folder from under his arm. "I went over to Finance and had a chat with another friend of mine." He thumbed through the folder. "There's some sort of a deal with a company called Libertad Excursiones. Here, take a look." He handed me a spreadsheet.

I gleaned the piece of paper. "Okay, a log of bank accounts."

"Those are Houghton's bank accounts. Quite a few of 'em too. Offshore accounts in Bermuda and the Caymans with lots of money. Take a look, fifth line down."

"Appalachian Bank & Trust . . ." I read the line and reread it again, pulling a finger across the paper to make sure I read it correctly. "There's almost a quarter billion dollars in this account."

"It's a small bank in the middle of Kentucky."

"I don't get it."

"I didn't get it, either. But here's the crazy part. My buddy tells me money is regularly wired out of Appalachian Bank & Trust to several other banks in San Diego, California. Take a look at this." Hardy pulled another sheet from his folder, a listing for wire transfers to various vendors, and, nestled in the middle of them, transfers to several California banks. There were at least two dozen during the month of December. And all of them to an account titled LXL Enterprises.

"Wait. What?! This company was swimming in red ink almost two years ago. Where is Houghton getting this money and why is the company sending it to California banks? What is LXL?"

"Not sure. But offshore accounts? And money flowing like water in and out of a small Kentucky bank in the middle of nowhere? Deposits and transfers, usually a couple hundred thousand at a time, all of them from Houghton. It's been a long time since I was a cop, but it looks like dirty money. Maybe some sort of money laundering or something? Here's the thing, the deposits slowed a few months ago, around the time the Libertad deal popped up."

"Where did you get this from?"

"One of the analysts in Finance. Seems like she's not enamored with her boss. I promised her I wouldn't get her involved."

Someone around this place was always willing to sell out a coworker for some untoward remark or a supervisor for being passed over for a promotion. It didn't surprise me that Hardy had found a willing benefactor of information in Jonathan's department.

"Looks like something the police need to know about, but I wasn't sure if I could turn this stuff over to them," Hardy said.

"These documents are confidential records of the company. We can't turn them over without a subpoena. Do you have any other information that backs up your theory? Something Jonathan said or did?"

"Nope. Just this and I'm not supposed to have this, either."

I whirled my chair around to face my computer. Hardy walked around my desk and stood behind me as I pulled up the search engine and typed in the words *Libertad Excursiones.* Libertad, part of a conglomerate of companies, was owned by a guy named Juan Bernardo Ortiz. Another quick search of Libertad yielded its parent company as LXL Enterprises, a holding company that included hotels and restaurants in addition to Libertad. I clicked on an image of Ortiz: tanned, muscular, and draped over some Hollywood actress I recognized but whose name I couldn't recall. I followed the trail of articles about him, most containing pictures of Ortiz on a yacht surrounded by bikini-clad girls or dressed in a tuxedo surrounded by the same type of young women.

"Humph . . . not a bad life, huh?" Hardy said.

I gave him an ugly side-eye.

"Sorry."

"Why would an international big shot like Ortiz want to get involved with a middling, family-owned delivery company like Houghton?" I signed into the LexisNexis database and followed another thread of articles about Libertad's parent company, LXL. No lawsuits against the company popped up.

"Look, it just seems to me that Jonathan is awfully tight-lipped for a man whose colleague was murdered right down the hall from him. The guy is hiding something. I just thought you ought to know."

"Of course. Thanks for bringing this to my attention."

"Also, I checked into that phone number you gave me. It's a cheap burner phone. We can't trace it. When was the last time the creep called you?"

I rubbed the back of my head. The knot from Sam's house was nearly gone. "You know what? Don't worry about it."

"You want me to put one of my guys on you. In case someone is following you or something?"

I shook my head. "No, that's not necessary."

"Listen, I know you're a big girl and all, but just be careful up here. This stuff doesn't look good. Dirty money, crank calls."

"Thanks. I'd better get on that call now."

"Oh, sure. Sure."

Hardy left. I pulled up Houghton's board minutes. No mention of the Libertad deal or any other deals. Just perfunctory notes about the company's operations and financial status, which had been on an upswing for the last eighteen months.

Jonathan was definitely hiding something about this deal. Nate said this deal was Jonathan's baby. But any acquisitions would have involved Michael, especially in the early stages of the deal. If Libertad was a huge boon for the company, where was the paper trail? And Michael would have needed outside legal help. Especially with a foreign company involved. He should have been consulting a mergers and acquisitions law firm.

I picked up the phone and called Richie Melcher at Kilgore Findley, the law firm Houghton used for all its mergers and acquisitions. He picked up on the first ring.

"Hi. This is Richie."

"Richie, this is Ellice Littlejohn at Houghton."

"Hello, Ellice. Did you get my email? I'm really sorry about Michael. Is there anything we can do for you folks over here at the firm?"

"Right now, I need some information. I need to know what's going on with the Libertad deal."

"Libertad? You mean the company down in Monterrey, Mexico?"

"Yes."

"Well, nothing as far as I know. Michael called me a few weeks ago and told me that Houghton was considering doing something with the company like a joint venture. He told me he would send over some information for me to look at, but I never heard back from him. With his murder and all, I just assumed the deal was off or you all were postponing it."

"Did he tell you what kind of information he was sending over?"

"No. He just said the company was based in Mexico and that he was working with your chief financial officer to sort out the details."

"Nothing else?"

"No. Is something wrong?"

"No. Thanks."

I hung up. Another dead end.

CHAPTER 20

The smoky aroma of grilled steak floated from the doorway of the executive dining room, a room on the twentieth floor flanked by floor-to-ceiling windows on three sides. White linen tablecloths, the soft tinkle of crystal glasses, and Wedgewood china gave the room a light airy atmosphere despite the cold wind and rain that battered the Atlanta skyline. The hostess, a thick, well-dressed woman with an accent that reminded me of steel drums and warm, white sand greeted me at the door.

"Good afternoon, pretty lady. May I help you?"

"Hi. I'm scheduled to have lunch with Mr. Ashe."

"Ah yes . . . Mr. Ashe's table is just this way. And congratulations on your promotion." She gave me a wink. "Very nice to see someone who looks like me on this floor."

My tribe. "Thank you." I smiled and

winked back.

I followed the woman as she meandered through a sea of tables. I recognized most of the managers sitting in this room. Several of them turned and watched me walk through the dining room with leering eyes. No smiles. The same vibe from Nate's party. I ignored them.

I had asked Nate if we could have lunch. The information from Hardy, coupled with the fact that I couldn't find a scrap of paper related to Libertad, gave me a lot of concern. The American Bar Association rules on attorney ethics required me to raise any concerns with the CEO. Maybe if I could talk to Nate alone, I could get to the bottom of this Libertad mess, maybe even launch an independent investigation.

We finally came to a stop at Nate's table in the far corner of the dining room. He was checking emails on his phone but promptly jumped up from his seat. "Hey! There's my favorite lawyer!"

"Today's special is southern-style chicken and dumplings," the woman said in her lilting accent as I took the seat across from Nate.

"That sounds great. Ellice, you're okay with chicken and dumplings, right?" Nate asked.

"*No.* Actually, just a garden salad with grilled chicken, please."

Nate gave me a quizzical smile. "Bring the lady what she wants. I'll have the chicken and dumplings and heavy on the dumplings."

"Of course, Mr. Ashe."

"Not a fan of chicken and dumplings, huh?" Nate chuckled.

I gave a weak smile, suddenly embarrassed by my overreaction. "Never liked them, even as a kid."

"So how are things coming along in Legal?" Nate popped a chunk of corn muffin in his mouth.

"Nate, I asked to have lunch together because I wanted to talk to you privately about the Libertad deal."

"Libertad?"

"Yes. The deal Jonathan was working on with Michael before he was killed?"

Nate stared down at his corn muffin for a beat. "Oh yes. Now I remember. Is something wrong?"

"Well, I'm not sure. I can't find any information on the deal and, if it's as big a deal as you say, there should be a paper trail. A memorandum or MOU, a contract, something." Nate set the half-eaten muffin down and swabbed at the corners of his mouth with his napkin.

"I don't understand," he said. The waiter came over to our table. We sat in silence, allowing him to serve our plates and leave.

I leaned in to whisper. "I have some concerns about —"

"There you are!" I looked up and Willow was standing behind me with a big toothy grin. "Sarah told me I could find you two here. Okay if I join you?"

"Absolutely," Nate said.

What the hell? Why was she always around whenever I talked to Nate?

The waiter approached. "What's the special today?" Willow asked.

"Chicken and dumplings."

"Oh God, no. Too many carbs. I'll have what she's having," Willow said, pointing a French-manicured fingernail at my salad. "So what do you two have your heads together about?"

Nate smiled and gave me a pleading look seeking rescue.

Ethically speaking, Willow had no business in a conversation where I was giving legal advice, but I decided to let her interruption slide. And discussing my concerns about the Libertad matter with Jonathan's mistress at the table probably wasn't the wisest course.

I feigned a smile. "We were just discussing some ongoing legal matters."

"So, Ellice, how are you getting settled in as department head?" she asked with an impish grin.

"Fine."

"You know employee surveys go out in March. I'm sure everyone in Legal will have good things to say."

"I'm sure they will," I said.

Nate smiled. "Now, that's *exactly* what I told Willow. You're smart and you're gonna do a great job. You're family."

I pushed around the lettuce in my salad bowl.

"You know why I treat folks around here like family?" Nate asked. "It's 'cause this company was started by family. My grand-daddy started this company with an old Ford Zephyr he drove around making deliveries down in Henry County. He built this company from nothing. And as long as I'm in charge, I will do everything within my power to make sure this company is viable and competitive in the marketplace. I fight every single day for this company. Make sense?"

This was the same canned speech he'd given yesterday in my office. Twice. Verbatim. If I was a betting woman, I'd think

Nate was in the early stages of dementia. The constant midsentence forgetfulness, the repetition of his stories. It suddenly dawned on me that I was wasting my time trying to appeal to Nate directly.

Nate stabbed his fork into a thick dumpling and swirled it inside the bowl to sop up the gravy. "So, Willow, what's going on in HR?"

She jabbered on incessantly about the employee surveys and benefits consultants. Not a word about hiring anyone who looked like me or the protesters in front of the building. I stopped pretending to eat and simply sat my fork on the side of the salad bowl. I stopped listening, too.

"Don't you agree, Ellice?" Nate said.

I realized I hadn't been paying attention. "I'm sorry. What's that?"

"I said, you're gonna show all the naysayers that I was right to promote you to head up the Legal Department. You just do everything I tell you and you're gonna find a lot of success in this company. Just remember, I'm in your corner. Something goes sideways, you see me. Deal?" Nate asked.

I forced another smile. "Deal." Since he was so generous with his support, I decided to take advantage of his offer right there on the spot and get him on board with my plans to do something more about the protesters. "Nate, did Willow tell you about our upcoming meeting this Friday?" I watched every muscle in her face go slack with disbelief. "Willow and I are going to meet to discuss some hiring initiatives to bring more people of color into the company. I think it could go a long way with making peace with the protesters outside and also ensure Houghton looks like a twenty-first-century organization."

Nate muffled a soft belch. "Well . . . no . . . this is the first I've heard of it."

"Nate, I was planning to wait until *after* Ellice and I met, so I'd have something to report out." She scowled at me. "Ellice, honey, maybe we can discuss things with Nate after we've met, so we have something more substantive to share."

I grinned as I watched her squirm. The idea of bringing more Black and brown people into the company would send her running for the playbook on "quality hiring" and finding "the right fit" for a job. The three of us sat in silence for a moment. I was content to sit and watch them both find some moral high ground for their denial that Houghton's hiring and promotion practices were antiquated at best and discriminatory at worst. With the exception of hiring the Black figurehead — read: me — they had no plans to change business as usual.

The hostess walked over to our table. "Mr. Ashe, your assistant just called and told me to remind you of your one o'clock meeting."

"Yes. Thank you." Nate took a sip from his coffee cup before he quietly folded his napkin and tossed it on the table. "Listen, I've got to get back to my office. Remember, we're family around here and I've got your back." Nate left the table.

"So it's just us gals again," Willow said with a tight smile.

I hated the word *gal*. I spent too much time answering to it in Chillicothe. The waiter brought a salad identical to mine and set it in front of Willow. "Ellice, what was that all about? A repeat performance of yesterday morning in the Executive Committee meeting? These things take time, they take some socialization. We'll talk to Nate about our little meeting when the time is right."

Little meeting? Oh God. Getting more folks of color inside the doors of Houghton was going to take some kind of Herculean strength.

"Can I ask you something?"

"Of course." Willow cut into the lettuce wedges of her salad. "Anything."

"You seem to spend an awful lot of time with Nate. Everywhere he goes, you go. What's going on?"

"You noticed." Willow smiled, ate a forkful of salad, and then lowered her voice. "It's for his protection."

I didn't respond. She needed to keep talking if she wanted me to believe her.

"Well, you're the lawyer, honey. This is a family-owned business that Nate doesn't want in the hands of someone who's not family. The company could become the target of a hostile takeover or acquisition by an equity firm if word got out that Nate is not one hundred percent himself."

"What does that mean exactly?"

"About two years ago, he got a diagnosis of early-onset Alzheimer's. I just stay close to make sure Houghton's interests are protected."

"And why you?"

"Why not? The guys are so busy with running the company for Nate. I can spare the time to run to a few extra meetings."

"Who else knows?"

"Now? Everyone on the Executive Committee."

I pushed my salad away from me. "Wait.

The board of directors doesn't know?"

"No." She gave me a pained expression. "They might not have Nate's best interests in mind if they did."

"And how long do you plan to keep up this charade?"

"As long as necessary."

I was incredulous. "This is a family-owned business. Is there a succession plan in place?"

Willow shrugged. "Nate doesn't have any family interested in the business. He lost his only child." She shook her head sadly.

"But who runs the day-to-day matters?"

"Jonathan and Max have things under control," she said.

"Willow, this can't be a long-term solution. You can't expect to run a company like this. I mean, what are you thinking? Did Michael know about this?"

"It was Michael's idea, honey." Willow grinned and ate another forkful of salad.

"*Michael* approved of this?! Are you sure? I mean, we have an obligation to bring this to the board's attention. I'm sure something can be worked out."

"Leave it be, Ellice. Yesterday, before the Executive Committee meeting, I was going to give you a bit of advice. Specifically, let the guys handle things. That buzz saw you walked into yesterday with Max and Jonathan is just the sort of thing you can avoid in the future. I told Nate you were the best choice to replace Michael because this company needs someone like you."

"You mean someone Black to shoo away the protesters?"

"I'm in HR. I don't see race. I only see people." She turned and scanned the room.

I rolled my eyes in frustration. If people didn't see race, they wouldn't have to go around saying they don't see race. No wonder there were protesters at the front door of this place.

Willow let out a dainty sigh, like a petulant little girl. "What I mean is that we need someone who can use an artful hand in working with the guys. The way Michael did."

I leaned back in my chair. "Sorry, but yesterday's meeting was about as artful as I can get without turning into a doormat." So Willow had chosen her path for survival in the executive suite, working as a second-class, deferential lieutenant to the men. That wouldn't work for me. I would leave first.

"Trust me, Ellice, you don't want to make waves. Jonathan's got the company operating at a profit. Max has all our trucks at full capacity. Things are fine."

"If things were fine, we wouldn't have protesters out front and a murdered executive inside."

Willow stared at me for a beat, then closed her eyes briefly and shook her head in exasperation. "Honey, you won't last long up on Twenty with such a negative perspective. Do you want to be right or do you want to be successful up here?"

"Are you serious?"

"Trust me, it won't help matters much if you bump up against folks around here. You're new. Get a lay of the land first. Let Jonathan and Max run things for Nate. I think this is the way he would want it."

"Are you guys nuts?!"

"And on that note, I'd better go check on what Nate's up to." Willow tossed her napkin on the table and sashayed toward the exit.

CHAPTER 21

I settled in on a park bench in the playground section of Piedmont Park, waiting for Rudy and watching my warm breath hit the cold air. The chilly temperature forced me to button my coat and I wished I'd brought gloves. The park was empty except for a couple of millennial moms pushing their kids on the swings and a squat older woman chasing a curly-haired blond boy, tightly bundled in a red barn jacket but no hat or gloves. Such a cold day and she hadn't bothered to at least put a hat on him.

Watching kids play was like a guilty pleasure for me. I was a sophomore at Coventry Academy before I finally understood that giggling or singing loud and off-key was actually a part of childhood, that parents encouraged it. Once at Coventry, a girl who lived in my dormitory fell doing some silly pratfall and fractured her arm. Her father drove down to Virginia from New York City to check on her. I was studying in the common space and I eyed her as she explained to him how it all happened. He watched in amusement as she demonstrated her silliness. I was awestruck. That someone loved her enough to make such an effort and then encouraged her silliness hit me in a way I hadn't expected. I never really cared for the girl, but from that day on, I hung out with her just so I could be close by whenever her parents visited campus.

I glanced down at an old keloid scar on the back of my hand. The skin, a slightly lighter shade of brown, puffed and twisted over itself like kneaded bread. A searing brand that reminded me of my days growing up in Chillicothe. Now, here I was — never married, no kids. With such imperfect role models for parents, I was afraid that raising one of my own would be another exercise in dysfunctional child-rearing. All the better to let my scars and wounds serve as the last remnants of the Littlejohn family imprint. Anyway, my life was fine without the traditional trappings. I have Vera, and Sam when he wasn't off the grid. I have my law degree and my job. I'm the executive vice president and general counsel for Houghton Transportation.

I have a life, at least.

"So what's with all the cloak-and-dagger stuff?" Rudy asked as he strolled up to the park bench. "It's like thirty-five degrees out here. Couldn't we meet in a warmer venue like . . . uh, I don't know. Maybe that big fancy office of yours?" He snickered and blew a quick puff of warm air into his hands before he rubbed them together like a praying mantis.

I reached into my bag and pulled out the manila envelope. "There's something really weird going on up on Twenty. Michael's wife, Anna, found this in a safe-deposit box he secretly kept. Houghton is supposed to do a joint venture with a Mexican company called Libertad. Here, take a look." I handed Rudy the envelope. "The day of Michael's memorial service, someone broke into his house. They ransacked his study. I assume whoever killed Michael was looking for these documents." I sat quietly, allowing Rudy time to read through the papers.

"Michael was going to resign?!"

"Looks like it. I think he found out Houghton is laundering dirty money for that Libertad company. Hardy looked into it and found a list of Houghton's bank accounts. Houghton has a quarter billion dollars in a small bank in the middle of nowhere."

"What the hell?"

"Yeah. And there's no record or paper trail for this deal." I recounted my phone conversation with Richie Melcher, the outside attorney. "Michael should have been talking to Richie about a deal like this. Instead, he was consulting a white-collar defense firm."

"Oh shit."

"But that's not even the best part. Nate has Alzheimer's and my esteemed colleagues on the Executive Committee are covering for him."

"I don't understand."

"Willow plays nursemaid and attends all his meetings with him, and Jonathan and Max are acting as de facto CEO. And just to round things out, Max made a veiled threat. It's like a corporate freak show up on Twenty."

"What the hell? You *have* to go to the police. Show them this stuff. Tell them what Max said."

"No. I can't disclose the email thread or the bank information because they're privileged and confidential company records. Although, if the police are smart, they'll figure out a way to get their hands on them soon enough."

"But there's criminal activity involved . . . somebody murdered Michael. All bets off.

That's a *clear* exception to the privilege rule," Rudy said. "Besides, if Anna has already seen these documents, the privilege is broken anyway, right? You can take the documents to the police."

Lawyers inside corporations are bound by the same ethical canons as lawyers in law firms. If a lawyer discovered illegal activity going on inside the company, ethical rules required the lawyer to report it up the chain of command, to the CEO and/or the board of directors. It was essentially "see something, say something" for lawyers, with a few exceptions. If you have an iota of a moral compass, a lot of practicing law is a matter of doing what's right, making commonsense choices. Admittedly, since I discovered my *own brother* was mixed up in this mess, I hadn't tried very hard to justify taking the documents up the chain of command or to the police. Doing what's right in this case meant protecting my brother. I think the only reason I was telling Rudy about all this was to vent and have someone tell me I wasn't crazy. Deep down, I knew I needed to give this information to the authorities. But doing so would be like handing Sam over to the police too.

I sighed. "I haven't brushed up on the ethics rules lately, but I think there has to be some threat of imminent harm or danger before I can go to the police without breaching my ethical duty. And as for Anna seeing them, the privilege might stand if it was Michael's intent to keep them under lock and key away from her. Anyway, I don't have any proof that these documents got him killed. A resignation letter and an email thread to schedule a phone call isn't much motivation for a murder. And Anna made me promise that I'd find out what's behind all this, just in case Michael was tangled up in some sort of trouble."

"That's not your job, Ell. Who are you? Nancy Drew?! This isn't just Houghton's confidential information. It's possibly evidence in a murder investigation. Maybe somebody killed him because he threatened to blow the cover on Nate's dementia."

"That's what I thought, too. But Willow said the cover-up was Michael's idea."

"What the hell? The guy was having an affair with some woman. Now he's involved in a fraud and cover-up. He sure fooled me."

I ignored Rudy's comment about the affair. But he was onto something. Michael must have been involved in something pretty bad to get him killed. This entire situation was a complicated knot of moral and ethical issues I wasn't quite sure how to fix.

"Rudy, listen to me. I'm stuck. I can either lose my license to practice law for releasing privileged company information or get hemmed up in an obstruction charge in a murder case."

"So you're gonna sit on top of information that could help the police find Michael's killer?" Rudy shook his head.

"I told Anna I would look into it a bit, but then she'd have to go to the police."

Rudy looked at me with a knitted brow then stared out into the distance. "I don't understand. Why wouldn't Michael's wife immediately go to the police to give them info to find her husband's killer? Why would she call you? Humph . . . sounds suspicious."

Rudy's armchair detective work was making me both uncomfortable and frightened. Maybe he was right. Maybe I was being gullible, and Anna was setting me up. Lord knows she had every reason to. I was sleeping with her husband and she knew it. But according to Anna, it was *because* I was sleeping with her husband that she called me. Me and Anna, the defenders of Michael's spotless reputation.

This whole thing was beyond bizarre. Here I was helping people I shouldn't be in alliance with and chasing after my brother, who was knee-deep in the middle of a murder and disappearance of lawyers he shouldn't even know.

The cold gusts picked up. An eddy of dry leaves skittered near my feet. The women began packing up their young charges.

"Maybe I'll go to the police." I hated cops and Detective Bradford hadn't changed my mind either. I closed my eyes briefly to break Rudy's stare. "Listen, I'd better get back to the office."

Rudy handed me the documents and shook his head again. "Be careful up there, Ell. I know you're the boss and all, but it seems to me that you're completely justified in going to the police under these circumstances."

I glanced at Rudy. This was the second time in one day I'd been warned to be careful on Twenty. But it wasn't as easy as Rudy made it seem. I had let Sam down so many times before. Good, bad, or otherwise, he was still my brother. And I wouldn't send him back to prison for something I knew he didn't do.

Rudy and I headed back to the office, in lockstep silence, before my cell phone rang. I fished it from my pocket and checked the caller ID.

"Uh . . . why don't you go on ahead. I

need to take this call."

Rudy's eyes narrowed in confusion.

"It's personal."

CHAPTER 22

I retreated back to the park to answer the call. "Sam! Where are you?"

Sam's tone was cheery and upbeat. "Hey, Ellie, what's up?"

I eased back onto the bench in the playground. "Where have you been? I've been calling you! Why haven't you called me back?"

"I guess I've been busy." Sam chuckled into the phone.

I gave an exasperated sigh. "Sam, I don't have time for games. Why were you at my office last week?"

"I stopped by to meet with a guy I'm working for."

"You're working for somebody at Houghton?!"

"You're not the only one who gets to work for the big shots. I was over there last Monday to meet the guy."

Sam knew people at my job?! I shot up

from the bench. "Why didn't you tell me? What guy? Who?"

"Jonathan Everett . . . you know him?"

"Jonathan Everett?! Of course, I know him. What kind of work are you doing for *him*?"

Sam chuckled. "The kind of stuff that pays better than working in a hardware store."

"This isn't funny, Sam. What the hell are you doing for him?" I yelled into the phone.

"Look, the guy just needed some help —"

"Needed some help with what?!"

"Why are you yelling? And why are you so interested in my business all of a sudden?"

"The police have you on security tape walking into the lobby of Houghton the day before my boss was killed."

"What?"

"Sam, listen to me. My boss was killed last week, and the police probably think you did it."

"What the hell are you talking about?!"

"Geez, don't you watch the news? An executive was murdered at Houghton last week."

"I didn't kill anybody! The Everett guy hired me to do some insurance surveillance work. Just tail someone for a few days. That's all. If the police are investigating a murder, maybe they're looking at the wrong Littlejohn, huh?"

My stomach gave a flutter at Sam's dig. "Sam, I don't have time to get into it with you today. How did you get my ID badge to get in the building?"

"Again, I don't know what you're talking about. The Everett guy gave me a badge to get in."

A young couple jogged past me. I lowered my voice. "Jonathan gave you *my* security badge?"

"I don't know. He gave me a badge with the name 'Littlejohn' on it."

"How do you even know Jonathan?" I could feel my heart start to speed up.

"We have some mutual friends."

"One of your gambling buddies?"

"I told you, Juice hooked me up, a friend of a friend. Hey, you're the one who told me to get a real job," Sam pointed out.

I wanted to reach through the phone and throttle him. "Who's the guy you're tailing? Was it the guy in the pictures on your cell phone? You know the man in that picture was working with my boss and now —"

"Wait a minute. So you were in my house? Going through my phone. I knew someone had been in there! What the hell, Ellie? You're too damn tight to lend me a few bucks, but you feel entitled to go rifling through my house? By the way, you left my door unlocked. And where's my cell phone?"

I took a deep breath and tried to speak slowly, trying to de-escalate things between us. "Sam, I didn't take your phone. Someone else was in your house when I was there. Whoever it was took your phone. And before they left, they cracked me over the head, too."

"What? Somebody hurt you?"

"I'm fine. Listen to me, the police are looking for you. We have to figure this thing out. We can go to the police together and clear this up. I can tell them —"

"Are you nuts?!" Sam hesitated for a beat. "I'm still on probation. I can't just go waltzing into a police station to tell them I work for a guy who's involved in a murder. Besides, I didn't do anything. And I'm surprised at your sudden interest in helping the police."

Crap! I'd forgotten about his probation. "Okay. Let me think. Maybe we —"

"Oh, wait a minute. I see. Did you have something to do with your boss getting killed? You want me to clear things up for *you.* Now I see what's going on."

"Sam, this is not a game."

"Here we go again. Let's figure out what's best for Ellie first. Everybody else line up in the rear. It's Chillicothe all over again, huh?"

I was floored. Here I was trying to protect him this entire time and now he was turning on me? "Sam, this has nothing to do with *me* and everything to do with *you*. I told you the police have you on security footage entering the building."

"That doesn't mean I killed anybody," Sam stated calmly.

"That guy in the picture, on *your* phone, is a lawyer. His family has reported him missing."

Sam was quiet for a moment. "Missing?"

"That's what I've been trying to tell you. You've been trailing him. Where is he?" I stopped pacing. "Sam, stop and think for a minute. One of your sketch friends introduces you to a corporate executive who hires you to trail someone. We have an entire security department who could do that. That guy he hired you to trail is a lawyer that my boss was working with. Now my boss is dead and the man you've been following is missing. Maybe Jonathan is trying to frame you. Have you thought about that?"

"The last time I saw that guy was yesterday and he was fine. I didn't kill anybody,

Ellie." His voice was softer and, for a minute, I detected a bit of fear in it, too.

The phone went silent.

"I know you didn't. Trust me. Let's just figure this thing out. Maybe we can go to the police and explain everything. Okay? Sam . . . you there?"

"Yeah. Look I gotta go."

"Wait." I paused for a beat, remorseful that I'd started another argument with him. "I noticed you're selling the house? And you changed the locks on your door."

"Yeah, I'm trying to keep the bad element out. So much for that, huh?"

I ignored Sam's second dig. "Your fridge looked pretty bare and the TV is gone . . . Did you pawn it?"

"Whatever."

"I'm sorry. Let me help." The hard sting of tears pricked at the corner of my eyes. "Let me give you the money. Come by my house. I'll give you the money and we can go to the police station together."

"Nah. Forget about it now. I'm good. I gotta go."

The phone went silent.

"Sam? Sam?"

It was almost eight o'clock at night when I sized up the mountain of work still piled across my desk. Budgets to review, executive summaries to read, and a couple briefs I needed to look at because I couldn't trust the judgment of some of the lawyers who worked for me. All of it would be here in the morning. I was spent so I decided to call it a day. As I packed up my things to leave, my cell phone buzzed. Grace.

"Hey!" Grace said. "What you doing?"

"Getting ready to leave work." I heard the sounds of a crowd in the background and the thump-thump of a ball hitting the floor. "Where are you?"

"At my son's basketball game and it's not pretty. Lord, they need to fire this coach and the students, too! And that includes my son. Thank God he's making straight A's in chemistry. I don't think the NBA will be calling anytime soon."

I laughed. "Your maternal support is inspiring."

"Hey, I know this kid's strengths. I'm just leaning into it. Why are you working so late? By late, I mean later than normal."

"That's the story of my life these days." I flipped the light switch and headed for the elevators.

"So how is the new job? Let me live vicariously through you."

I stepped inside an empty elevator.

"Ugh . . . I don't know. There's something strange going on around this place. Something about this place I can't shake."

"Strange how?"

"I don't know. It's something about my new colleagues. You know that weird vibe I told you I was getting at the party in Savannah? Well, it's still there. More so. And then something fishy is going on with some of the work. Like a cover-up or something."

"A cover-up? What are they covering up?"

"Some sort of business deal and maybe Michael's murder."

"Are you serious? Ellice, are you in some sort of danger?"

"No, I seriously doubt it. I'm their token Black person in the C-suite. Nobody will touch me, at least not until they can get rid of those protesters. I'm safe. But still the whole place gives me the creeps."

"Like how?"

"I don't know. Vera used to call it a God sense — it's a feeling I get. It's like they all operate on some secret wavelength or frequency I can't quite catch."

"Then you need to listen to that. Hang on, I think my kid just scored a basket." I heard the crowd roar in the background. "Well, I'll be damned! Okay, I'm back."

"Listen, get back to the basketball game. I

don't want you to miss his next shot."

"From your lips to God's ears."

"I'm almost at my car anyway. I can talk to you later."

"Okay, I'll call you when I get home."

"Please, don't. I'm so tired tonight, I plan on taking a hot shower and going straight to bed. If I'm lucky, by 9:30, I should be tucked in like a baby after a breastfeeding."

We laughed. "Okay, talk to you later."

I crossed the lobby and stepped into the frigid night air in the garage. I approached my car and squawked the key fob. The headlights blinked and the door lock clicked, echoing across the cavernous space. Most people had cleared out hours ago. I opened the door and tossed my tote bag and purse onto the passenger's seat. I climbed inside and closed the door. Just as I hit the start button for the engine, I noticed it. A white envelope propped against my dashboard. An unsteady lump of terror rose up in my chest. *Someone's been inside my car!* My doors were locked. I always locked my doors. I scrambled around and looked in the back seat. Empty. I looked around the garage. No one else. Only a smattering of cars at this late hour. I stared back at the envelope.

Typed across the front of the envelope:

Some secrets are worth keeping.

I ripped it open. Inside, a photocopy of a 1979 newspaper article from the *Tolliver County Register.* The headline:

LOCAL INVESTIGATORS SEARCH FOR
MISSING SHERIFF'S DEPUTY

Chillicothe, Georgia, November 1978

As far as I know, Martha and Willie Jay never officially married. At least they didn't have a wedding ceremony or anything. Just a month after Willie Jay roughed up Mario Jackson, Martha packed up the few things we owned from the house on Periwinkle Lane and moved all three of us into his house like some happy little family. And it was the talk of Chillicothe, too — both in the white section of town and the Black section too. Some Black people wondered out loud how Martha and Willie Jay came to be a couple. A blond, blue-eyed monster living with an alcoholic Black woman and her two bastard kids kept people talking for months. White people who lived in the other section of Chillicothe said Willie Jay was trash and had done about the best he could do when it came to marriage material.

I never imagined I could hate any place

more than that old shotgun house we lived in on Periwinkle Lane until we moved into Willie Jay's house on Red Creek Road. According to Martha, his house was supposed to be so much better, but it wasn't. It was just a bland depressing side of the same coin as the old Periwinkle house. There were only a couple more white people in this neighborhood, and they were just as poor and hardscrabble as the rest of the Black folks who lived there. Inside, the house wasn't much better. Willie Jay didn't like anything hanging on the walls. He wouldn't allow us to hang pictures or posters. He said he didn't like to look at his walls and have them look back at him. Vera used to say that the devil didn't like mirrors or prying eyes either. But the lack of pictures and knickknacks in his house was nothing compared with the stench. The raw fungal odor of sweating feet usually competed with the heavy burnt smell of Dutch Masters cigars. Life in his house was a living hell that no one openly talked about. And the couple times I complained to Martha about him, her only response was a lecture about how she was moved from one relative to another and we were lucky to have a house to live in.

Sam and I shared a bedroom at the back of the house. Our twin beds, rock-hard mattresses and frames only — no headboard — were separated by a narrow table and cheap wood lamp in the shape of a ship's wheel. I lay in my bed facing Sam. He always fell asleep before me, winded from a day of running and chasing other little boys throughout the day. Tonight, moonlight poured into the small bedroom and drenched his sleeping face in an autumn glow. His skin radiated under the cool starry night. Weird as it was, the soft wheezing snore of a ten-year-old boy could be really calming. Watching Sam sleep like this was a peaceful sight. He seemed shuttered from everything ugly in the world, the choices and consequences life would force on him when he got to be Mario Jackson's age.

I remembered the day Martha brought him home from the hospital and laid him in my little arms. Even though I was only four years old, Martha showed me how to change his diaper and make a bottle for him. It was like Martha had given me a real live baby doll. In the quiet of that back bedroom, I could watch my little baby doll sleep. But now I worried about who would watch out for Sam. As I waited to hear back on my scholarship application to Coventry, I worried about what would happen to him if I moved away to boarding school.

I lay in bed, trying to force myself to sleep in between worrying about Sam and listening for the sound that haunted me at night.

Footsteps.

Willie Jay's footsteps. The ones that used to come in our room on nights when Martha was out of the house. Then, encouraged by her ignorance, his footsteps came after she fell asleep at night. One time, he came into the room when he had mistakenly thought she was asleep. She wasn't and she showed up in the doorway asking why he was in the kids' room.

And every time was like the time before. First came the close of their bedroom door, then the hard, flat smack of his bare feet against the pine boards on the floor. Five steps before a floorboard creaked, eight steps more and another board creaked. And finally, the turn of the rusty metal doorknob to our bedroom. A few seconds later, he'd softly whisper my name, nudge me even if I pretended to be asleep.

The walk outside to the shed took less than two minutes. But it was enough time for me to slip away in my mind to another place. Two minutes was more than enough time to mentally slip from his grip and imagine all the places that I'd read about in books or to dream about the life I would live one day, the places I would travel to. Being in that shed forced me to think about all the things I could do — good and bad.

I finally drifted off to the sound of Sam quietly snoring beside me. I didn't hear a thing until Willie Jay's silhouette appeared above me.

"Ellie, wake up," he whispered. "Let's go out to the shed."

CHAPTER 23

Shit! Who the hell had been inside my car? How did they find this article?

Fifteen minutes after I sped out of the Houghton garage, I pulled up to Sam's bungalow. The light in the living room window was on. I rang the doorbell and waited. A few seconds later, Sam peeped through the blinds before he opened the door.

"Hey, Ellie." Sam stood in front of me, barefoot, dressed in sweatpants and an Atlanta Falcons sweatshirt. I didn't respond but my face must have said it all. "Oh God, what's the matter? Come on in out of the cold." He closed the door behind me. "Are you okay?"

It was only after I stepped inside his house that I realized I'd been crying. I couldn't speak. I handed Sam the news article.

"What's this?" He read the paper and then looked back at me, his mouth dropped open

307

in shock. "Where did this come from?"

I finally gathered myself together. "Some-one left this *inside* my car at work."

"In your car? Wait . . . What?"

I cradled myself. "It gives me chills to think he was in my car."

"Who?"

"The only person I can think of is Jona-than. Did you tell Jonathan about this?"

"No! Of course not."

"This isn't a coincidence. He knows we're related, and it looks like he knows about Chillicothe. Sam, why the hell are you work-ing for him?"

Sam slumped into a chair in front of me. "Because I'm tired of begging you for money." Sam slowly ran the palm of his hand down the front of his face in exaspera-tion before he looked back up at me. "This house, the car I drive, all of it's yours. I just wanna go somewhere, ask for a job, and not be second-guessed about who I am or the choices I've made. I'm tired of living this way. I'm tired of living on handouts and hustles. Can you understand that? Look, Ellie, I don't want another argument, okay? Let's leave it alone."

"We can't leave it alone. Sam, don't do this! I think he's trying to frame you for something you didn't do. I think he's involved with some kind of money-laundering scheme. We need to go to the police."

"No. I told you, I'm still on probation."

"I can help you find another job. This guy Jonathan is bad news. Trust me."

"Ellie, I can take care of myself! Let's drop it. You want something to drink? I was just about to make myself a hot dog. You want one?"

"Sam, listen to me. The last time I was here at your house —"

"Drop it, Ellie!" He released a long deep breath. "I'm tired of arguing with you. I'm not perfect. We already know that. Let's just hang out and be a family for a change." He got up from the chair and strolled into the kitchen.

He was right. I was tired of arguing too. And God knows, it had been a long time since we had just hung out like two normal siblings. Whatever that meant. I knew I needed to be more patient, more understanding. I needed to be his sister, not his probation officer. I looked around the room. Everything was neat and tidy. The TV was back on the stand. I took off my coat and tossed it on the sofa along with my purse. I followed him into the kitchen.

"Mustard and onions. No ketchup," I said as I slipped into a chair at the kitchen table.

Sam stood at the stove and glanced a smile at me. "What did ketchup ever do to you? How's Vee?"

"Same."

We both went quiet for a minute.

"I love that old chick. Remember that time she caught me smoking cigarettes out behind her house?"

"Oh my God. She chased you straight across the field."

"What was I . . . nine, ten? I thought I could outrun her." Sam leaned against the stove. "She was built like a tank, but damn she was light on her feet. She caught up to me and snatched me up by the back of my pants. My undershorts were wedged so far up my ass I had a hard time sitting down the next day."

"After that whipping she gave you, that wasn't the only reason you had a hard time sitting down." We both cracked up. His laugh filled the entire room and the space seemed lighter because of it.

"To this day, I can't stand the smell of cigarette smoke." Sam served up two hot dogs, a beer for himself, and sweet tea for me. We quietly started in on the hot dogs.

"I did like you said," Sam said.

"You did what?"

"I went by to see Vee. She said she wants

to go home." Sam slathered his hot dog in more ketchup before he bit into it.

"I know. I feel awful about that, too. But you see how she is. She can't be out there on that farm by herself."

We both went quiet. Vera had stepped into the gap and loved us when Martha couldn't. And leaving her in a nursing home, when all she wanted was to wake up in her own bed, on her own farm, was tugging at all three of us.

"I've been thinking," Sam said. "I might move back to Chillicothe. I could move into the farmhouse and be with her."

I set my hot dog back on the plate and stared at Sam. "Are you serious?"

"I'm tired of Atlanta. The streets. All of it. I just want a simple, uncomplicated life. I wanna wake up, move through my life like everybody else. Not have to spend the day looking over my shoulder." He stared down into his plate for a moment. He looked back at me with a weak smile. "And, hey, with the sales market, you could make a small fortune if we sold this place. I know you don't like to hear it, but Vera won't be around forever. She ought to be in her own house."

I was shocked and moved by Sam's plan. "Well . . ."

"And you could save all that money you're dropping on that nursing home, too."

"All right, let me think about it." I hesitated for a moment, picking at my hot dog bun. "I really don't mind helping you out until you get back on your feet."

"Let it go, Ellie. I'm good." Sam took a long sip of his beer, then nudged my arm. "Oh, by the way, I ran into Juice."

"Oh God."

Sam let out another huge laugh. "My man is crushing on you big-time."

"Very funny. I'm not interested in your little buddies." I took another bite of my hot dog. "Y'all met at Dodge State, right?"

"He's decent people, though. He might not wear a suit and tie like the brothers you work with but he's genuine. I've never seen him hurt a soul."

I bit into my hot dog and reached for a napkin from the counter. "Nope. I make enough bad decisions on my own. Remember, I'm Martha Littlejohn's daughter. Us Littlejohn women specialize in bad decisions when it comes to men."

Sam scrutinized me for a moment. "You know, maybe it was a matter of options."

"What?"

"Maybe she made bad decisions because she had bad options. And the alcohol didn't help. Remember how she used to tell us about how she had to live in all those different places when she was growing up?"

"Yeah."

"I just think she wanted some place, a real home."

"Sam, there's some stuff about Martha you don't know. And it's not worth going into now."

"Who knows everything about anybody? All I know is most folks are trying to do the best they can with what they got. Martha didn't have much, so she couldn't do much."

"Hmm . . ."

"It's not like some curse or something. You have better options. You can make better choices."

I stared back at Sam and his wisdom shook me. His insight made sense. A small town like Chillicothe had not been kind to Black women back when we were growing up. "Humph. You might be right. Anyway, I've decided to put my dating life on hold for right now. Pickings are slim for the over-forty crowd like me."

"That's not true. Good brothers are always looking for a good woman."

I noticed a bit of ketchup on the side of Sam's face. I passed him a napkin. "But what about you? Who are you keeping company with these days, as Vee would say?"

Sam snickered. "Hey, Juice ain't the only one looking for a good woman."

I smiled and shook my head. I glanced down at my watch. "I'd better get going. I have an early meeting tomorrow."

I picked up my plate and glass and sat them in the sink. "Sam, I'll just say this and then I'll leave it alone. I think Jonathan is involved in some dangerous stuff. My boss is dead, and the man you've been trailing for him is missing. I think he's involved in both, which makes you involved. I don't know what he's up to. I can't go to the police with that news article floating around. And I know you can't go, either, because of your probation. I think the best thing for both of us is for you to stay away from him."

I headed to the sofa and retrieved my coat and purse. Sam followed. I reached inside my wallet and pulled out two hundred dollars. "Here, take this. It's all I have on me."

Sam pushed my hand away. "No, Ellie. Seriously, I'm good. Let me stand on my own."

We stood there, face-to-face like some kind of sibling standoff. Silent. The little boy I adored had become the brother I was proud of. A good man with a kind heart who'd made some mistakes. I'd made my share of mistakes too. But Vera used to say mistakes didn't make you a bad person. They made you human.

I finally broke the impasse and reached over and hugged him. "I love you, Sammy Littlejohn."

"I love you, too, Ellie."

■ ■ ■ ■

PART 2
THE GRASS

■ ■ ■ ■

CHAPTER 24

Sam Littlejohn was out in the middle of nowhere in the middle of the night.

The navy-blue Camry jerked and sputtered along Anders Creek Road. He managed to maneuver the car to the shoulder of the desolate road. The slow crackle of rock and gravel pinged the undercarriage of the car before it gave a final spasm, a long, slow hiss, and then stopped completely.

"Aww . . . Shit." Sam looked through the rearview mirror into an ink-black hole, having passed the last vestiges of life over a mile back. Streetlights didn't exist out here in this part of Georgia. He turned the ignition key a couple of times, desperate to restart the car.

This job was supposed to be easy, although it gnawed at him from the moment he agreed to take it. But it paid more money than he'd ever seen in his life. Enough money to stop begging Ellice and give him a fresh start in Chillicothe. Maybe hire a couple people to get the farm going again. *But what if she's right and that Jonathan Everett guy is trying to frame me for some murder?* He thought back to their last meeting. *Just drop the car off at the cabin, pick up the last installment of my money, enjoy the cabin.* Jonathan said he'd pick him up in the morning. But Sam decided he would collect his money and be gone before daybreak. He didn't need a ride. Just the rest of his money.

Everett even gave him a 9 mm Glock just in case of an unforeseen emergency. They had prepared for everything except the part about the car being a piece of crap that wouldn't make it the entire trip.

Sam opened the glove box and groped around, looking for a flashlight, but came up empty. Maybe there was a flashlight in the trunk. He took a deep breath, flexed his gloved fingers, pulled down the brim of his baseball cap, and slid out of the car.

The wintry night air blustered about, forcing Sam to hunch over against its chilly bite. Now he regretted not wearing a real coat. The thin black leather jacket he wore was a piss-poor match for the freezing temperature. He hated winters in Georgia. And he hated being in the woods, ever since he was a kid.

A plume of breath encircled his head when he exhaled. The cold wind was unrelenting against the tall Georgia pines. Dry brittle foliage rustled beneath the trees and a coyote howled off in the distance. These were the kinds of noises he grew up with back in Chillicothe, but now, here alone on a deserted rural county road, the sounds were almost deafening. Sam tried to convince himself that all he had to worry about out here was a loose deer or an itinerant bear, both of which he could comfortably handle with the Glock packed firmly in the waistband of his blue jeans.

Within the first few steps, tentacles of fear moved in, laying claim and burrowing underneath his skin. *Something isn't right.* Vera would have called it his God sense warning him. He hustled to the back of the car and popped open the trunk. The small beam from the upper side of the trunk provided the only illumination on the body inside.

Shit!

The shock sent Sam stumbling backward, tripping over a large chunk of gravel before falling flat on the ground. He jumped up, brushed off his pants, and glanced around as if this were some cruel joke at his expense.

Sam took a couple of timid steps toward the trunk, nervous curiosity and unbridled fear jumbled together inside of him. He recognized the man: it was the same guy he'd been hired to trail for Jonathan, the same guy Ellice said was missing. The man's body, crumpled on top of some newspapers and a toolbox, was neatly dressed in a pin-striped suit and tie and black coat. But how'd he wind up in the back of this car?

Sam didn't want to touch him at first. But he did. Cold. Hard. *Dead.*

He nervously lifted the man's jacket and retrieved a slim brown wallet from the breast pocket. The driver's license confirmed him as Geoffrey J. Gallagher and showed a Johns Creek address.

Ellie was right. The Everett guy really is trying to frame me for murder. Yeah, I'll call Ellie as soon as I get back into the city. She can help me figure this mess out.

Sam left everything in place, including one hundred eighty-seven dollars inside the wallet, along with credit cards and the man's titanium wedding band. He slipped the wallet back into the man's pocket.

I'm not a monster.

Sam zipped up his jacket and stared into

the black hole of night around him. Nothing about this job had felt right and now he knew why. Behind him, the roar of a car engine and the sudden shimmer of headlights barreled over the crest of the road. Sam stiffened for an instant before peering over his shoulder into the oncoming lights. He quickly closed the trunk and lurched into the middle of the road flailing his arms for the driver to stop.

Sam mustered up a weak smile, ready to enlist a stranger's help. The black Escalade pulled to a full stop beside him. He peered in the cab as the window slowly slid down. A streak of panic slid through him when he recognized the man behind the wheel.

"What are you doing out here on the side of the road? I thought we were meeting at the cabin?"

"Uh . . . yeah . . . the car broke down," Sam said nervously.

"No worries. Get in the car. I'll give you a lift back to the city."

Sam started to back away from the car. His first thought: *Just run.*

"C'mon. Get in. I'll pay you and drop you back off in the city."

Sam anxiously scanned the dense woods again. He needed to get out of this mess. He wanted nothing to do with this job or these people. When he turned back to the car, the hot flash of a .45-caliber pistol powered a single blast right between his eyes.

The black Escalade peeled off into the frigid night air, leaving Sam Littlejohn and Geoffrey Gallagher out in the middle of nowhere.

CHAPTER 25

I rolled over, for what seemed like the hundredth time, and stared into the soft red glow on the digital alarm clock: Wednesday, 6:45 A.M. Another fifteen minutes before the alarm was set to blare me out of bed. These days, sleep was a fleeting commodity I could only gather in small fragments between bouts of worry and dread. My life had become too complicated for sleep. I was working for a company that was operating under a sham leadership structure. My brother was somehow involved in my boss's murder. And I was hopelessly stuck between turning my brother over to the police or turning over confidential documents that could be a breach of my ethical duty as a lawyer and get me disbarred.

I lay in bed staring at the ceiling fan and lining up all the problematic little pegs. Michael was murdered and a white-collar defense lawyer he hired was missing. Both of them were concerned about a deal that Jonathan brought into the company, a deal that Jonathan said was all buttoned up. But why would Jonathan hire *my* brother to trail Gallagher? Could Jonathan have killed Michael and was setting my brother up to take the fall? Jonathan had to know Sam and I were related. Littlejohn is not a common name. And somehow Jonathan had found out about Chillicothe. Was all this some sort of threat directed at me?

I just needed to figure out a way to go to the police and sort this whole thing out with Sam. Maybe I could tell them that Sam was inside Houghton looking for me the day the security cameras caught him in the lobby. I could tell the detective the security photos were grainy, that I'd made a mistake when I said I didn't recognize Sam in the pictures. I could make up some logical explanation for Sam being in those photos. No matter what it took, I'd find a way to get Sam out of this mess.

I pulled back a tangle of Italian bed linens, swung my legs over the side of the bed, and sat staring at nothing. My head throbbed. Maybe I was still suffering from the kick in the head at Sam's house a couple nights ago. Was Jonathan the man in the Escalade who hit me?

I picked up the remote control and pointed it at the flat-screen television on the wall in the corner of the bedroom. A perky young blonde jabbered on about a 50 percent chance of snow with the kind of glee in her voice usually reserved for a kindergartner's visit to see Santa. After, she turned it over to an equally enthusiastic guy interviewing some official from the Georgia Department of Transportation as he enlightened Atlanta on the effectiveness of brine solutions and the road crews standing at the ready to ensure safe roads for morning motorists. I knew it wouldn't snow. It rarely snows in Atlanta. The north Georgia mountains could usually garner a few inches. But Atlanta? Hardly. And if it did snow, it was either an all-out "snowmageddon" or a whimper of snow dust that melted as soon as it hit the ground. Either way, the local news media made an elaborate production over nothing.

I ambled into the closet, yawned and stretched, and started the daily ritual that had been the same since I was a college freshman with the epic question, What do I wear today? Who would I have to impress? Who would I have to disguise myself for?

Ever since earning my first paycheck waiting tables at IHOP in college, shopping was my one vice, and dresses were my particular drug of choice. Maybe it was Aunt Myrtle's influence. The more money I made, the more money I poured into my addiction. I walked to the middle of the closet and gazed into a sea of designer clothing that rivaled the racks of any upscale boutique in the city. Unfortunately, half the clothes in this closet didn't fit anymore. Still, I couldn't part with them, always holding on to the thought that I'd lose a few pounds and slip right back into them. Too bad that salesclerk at the Port showed her ass. Otherwise, I might be wearing that sky-blue Alexander McQueen dress.

I pulled out a black suit, then decided against it while half listening to the local news coming from the television in the bedroom. This time, a serious-sounding male anchor: *"As we reported earlier in this broadcast, a road crew laying brine solution along an icy road . . ."*

Maybe the gray dress? Nope, I wore gray yesterday. Maybe the winter-white Escada sheath to lift my spirits.

"The Habersham County sheriff stated that two bodies have been discovered along Anders Creek Road . . ."

I sauntered over to the floor-to-ceiling shoe rack. Now what to do about my feet? I was partial to heels but wavered between the black leather boots and the blue suede Louboutin pumps.

"One of the bodies has been identified as Atlanta attorney Geoffrey Gallagher. Mr. Gallagher was found in the trunk of a stolen car."

It took all of a nanosecond for Gallagher's name to reach me in the closet. I scrambled back into the bedroom, just in time to catch the tail end of the report.

"The second body found along the road nearby has not yet been identified. Both were shot . . ."

Perched over the anchor's shoulder was Gallagher's picture, the same picture that appeared in his firm bio. The same man who appeared in Sam's phone at his house. I grabbed my cell phone from the docking station on the bedside table and dialed Sam's number.

No answer.

Pacing the floor, I hung up and dialed his number again. Still no answer. This time, I waited for the call to roll over to voice mail.

"Sam, where are you? The police found the lawyer's body. I *really* need you to call me back."

I hung up the phone and continued to pace the floor. Why the hell was he involved in the murder of two people he shouldn't even know? I dialed Juice's number. Maybe he knew where Sam was. Juice didn't answer either. I left a voice mail. "It's Ellice, Sam's sister. Can you call me back? It's urgent."

The desperate energy inside me bubbled and expanded. *Think. Think. Find Sam.* I'd call in sick at work and post myself outside Sam's house until he showed up. No more pushing me away like last night. He'd have to talk to me. I would go with him to the police station. I could help him figure this mess out without getting my name or Houghton's associated with it all. The last thing I needed was more media attention on this.

My cell phone rang: *Michael Sayles — Home.*

"Hey, Anna." I tried to mask the panic in my voice.

"Oh my God, have you seen the news this morning? Geoffrey Gallagher is dead. That's the name of that lawyer in those emails."

"I know . . . I just saw it."

"Ellice, whoever killed Michael must have killed Gallagher, too. It's the stuff in those documents. What was Michael involved in?"

"I don't know. I haven't figured out what's going on yet."

"Oh, dear Lord, maybe we *should* get the

police involved like you said. I was wrong to ask you to look into this alone."

"It's not quite that simple. Those documents contain confidential information about the company. I have an ethical duty not to disclose that information without going through some channels first." I wasn't being completely honest, but Anna wasn't a lawyer, and I needed to buy some time to figure out how deep my kid brother was involved.

"You sound like Michael with all your legal rules. I can't just stand by and watch more people get killed because of some damn attorney rules. You could be next. You've got to get out of that place."

"I'll be okay." My doorbell rang. "Listen, someone's at the door. I have to go. I'll call you back." I hung up the phone, grabbed my bathrobe, and dashed to the front door. Maybe it was Sam. *I'll kill him for dragging me into this nightmare.*

I opened the door. Two uniformed cops stood there. One male, big and burly. The other a female, petite and probably no more than twenty-five or twenty-six years old.

"Ellice Littlejohn?" the male officer guessed.

"Yes."

"You're related to Samuel Littlejohn?"

"What's this about?" My heart raced. Had the police found some link between Sam and Gallagher? Were they putting on the pressure to find him now that Gallagher was dead? Had Jonathan framed my brother for two murders? I glanced over the female officer's head and caught Mr. Foster, from across the hall, peeking through a crack in his door.

"It's about Mr. Littlejohn. May we come in?" the officer said; his face was grim. The female officer gave me a sad look of concern.

I replayed the news anchor's words in my head. *The second body found along the road nearby has not yet been identified.*

I suddenly felt dizzy, the dots now connecting between the police officers standing at my door and the news report on television. It was then that I heard the alarm clock from the bedroom, blaring a long and loud wake-up call.

Chapter 26

An attendant ushered me inside a small room at the back of the Habersham County Coroner's Office, a bland brick building, to identify my only blood relative. My legs were like gelatin, loose and barely capable of holding me up. The jackhammer pounding inside my head was relentless.

She flipped a switch and a monitor on the wall popped on with Sam's lifeless face resting against a metal table, covered up to his shoulders by a white sheet. For the second time in as many weeks, I gazed into the rough remnant of a bullet hole to a man's head. This one on my baby brother. His face was paler, and his small Afro still bore the imprint of his baseball cap. The blue crucifix tattoo on his neck seemed less pronounced, almost blending into the muted brown-gray shade of his skin. He didn't look peaceful. He just looked quiet, still, like I could nudge him awake, to tell him I'm sorry and beg him to forgive me.

It took a few seconds for my brain to catch up with the picture on the monitor. And when it did, everything changed, much like the way a flag unfurls to reveal all its colors and symbolism. *Sam was dead. I was alone.*

Everything inside me went numb, and a crushing ache engulfed me. All at once, I heard this awful earsplitting sound. A low guttural wail that rose into a high-pitched scream blasting off the walls of the room and piercing my eardrums. In the same moment, I raised my hands to my face and realized that awful horrible wail of grief was coming from me.

I felt someone behind me holding me up as I collapsed toward the floor, the screams still ringing in my ears, the heartache still ripping me apart. Someone guided me to a waiting room.

The attendant returned and handed me a box of tissues. "Take as much time as you need, Ms. Littlejohn."

I sat in the small waiting area. The dreary blue walls seemed like they were wading in toward me, creating a claustrophobic little box I had neither the energy nor desire to leave. Even though he was dead, all I wanted to do was stay close to Sam now. I was entering the bewitching season Vera used to talk about. I had finally become everything I told people I was, an orphaned only child. All the paper-thin lies I told and the secrets I tried to squash had brought me and Sam to this cold, sterile building. And like everything else that happened between us, this, too, was my fault. Every time I tried to help Sam, I only made matters worse. Why hadn't I ever been able to get things right for me and Sam?

For decades, I'd rejected everything that connected me to Chillicothe, embracing some ridiculous idea that successful lawyers didn't come from backwoods towns with jailbird siblings and dark secrets. I was stupid. Someone had left a news article in my car about Willie Jay. And now, Sam was dead. Somebody was lurking in my life, creeping through my carpetbag of secrets, and they now had stolen the one person I loved more than anything. I once read somewhere that the things we regret the most are the things we *didn't* do, the choices we didn't make, the path we didn't take. I've regretted so many things for so long. But nothing hurt more than the regret of not taking better care of my brother, of not fully acknowledging him in my life. Now Sam's death was one more regret to tuck in my carpetbag of secrets.

"Ms. Littlejohn?"

I didn't look up. I didn't have to. I'd expected her to show up at some point, surprised even that it had taken this long.

"I'm sorry about your brother. I know this isn't the most convenient time, but do you mind answering a few questions?" Detective Bradford inquired.

I didn't answer her. I didn't have the emotional stamina to deal with her right now.

"Do you know an attorney by the name of Geoffrey Gallagher?" she probed.

I still didn't look at her. "No."

"Are you sure about that? Chris Knight, Mr. Gallagher's partner, told us you called his office. You were pretty adamant about speaking with Mr. Gallagher. Why?"

I wiped my eyes and blew my nose and fought back another round of tears. "I didn't know him. I was just trying to get some files."

"I see. What kind of files?"

I just stared at the brightly colored tissue box in my lap. "I thought he'd worked on some company matters but I was wrong. Chris Knight told me the firm didn't have any company files."

"Mr. Knight told us when he suggested the two of you call the police, you hesitated.

Why is that?"

I remembered that exact conversation. I was trying to find Sam at the time, to protect him.

She took a few steps and stood over me. "When was the last time you spoke with your brother?"

"Last night." I fiddled with the tissues.

"Did he seem unusual to you?"

"No."

"So how did your brother know Mr. Gallagher?"

"Why are you asking?" I didn't trust any cop. Willie Jay Groover had sucked up that commodity years ago.

"Mr. Gallagher was found dead in the trunk of a car and your brother's body was found nearby."

I finally looked at the detective for the first time since she'd entered the room. She was in her usual outfit of expensive pantsuit and professional demeanor. She looked so put together. I found myself wondering whether she had any brothers. Was she raised by a loving mother and a doting dad? She sat down in the chair beside me and for a moment, I thought she was going to reach for my hand or pat my arm in some display of concern. She didn't and I appreciated her professionalism.

I blew my nose again. "So you think whoever killed Gallagher killed my brother?"

"Not exactly." Bradford hesitated for a few seconds. "The gun found on your brother's body was used to kill Mr. Gallagher. Your brother was killed with a different gun."

"What? Are you trying to say my brother killed Gallagher and stuffed him in the trunk of a car?" I knew Sam better than anyone, and while he had an impressive rap sheet for low-level crimes, he was as likely to murder someone as a parish priest on Sunday. "You're wrong. Sam wouldn't do something like that."

"Can you tell me why you lied to me when I showed you pictures of your brother the other day?"

"I didn't lie. The photos were grainy. I wasn't sure." I snapped away from the detective's glare. Maybe she'd known all along that it was Sam in those surveillance photos.

"Your brother is dead. Why are you being so evasive?"

She was right. Sam was gone. I couldn't protect him anymore. No more lies. No more dances around the fringes of truth. "I don't know what's going on myself. I stopped by my brother's house last night.

I found out that someone from my company hired him to trail Gallagher."

"Who?"

I hesitated for a beat, not knowing what the implications would be on my new status in the executive suite. "Jonathan Everett."

"The CFO? Why would Mr. Everett hire your brother to trail Gallagher?"

"I honestly don't know. I *do* know that my brother would never kill anyone."

"How does Mr. Everett know your brother? Did you introduce them?"

"Of course not! I have no idea how he knows Jonathan. Sam told me a friend of his got him the job working for Jonathan."

"What else did your brother tell you?"

"He told me the last time he saw Gallagher was Monday and Gallagher was alive. I'm telling you, I know my brother. He's never hurt anyone in his life."

"Why would your brother be inside Houghton's lobby the day before Mr. Sayles was murdered? Did you give him your badge to enter the building?"

"I told you before, I lost my badge. I didn't give my brother my badge. He said Jonathan gave him the badge. I told you everything I know. Detective, please!" I slammed the box of tissues in the chair beside me. "Can we do this another time? I just saw my kid brother dead on a metal table. I can't do this right now." I jumped up and headed for the door.

Detective Bradford stood as well, taking a couple of power strides in the same direction, blocking my exit from the waiting area. "I understand this is a difficult time, Ms. Littlejohn. I'm sure answering questions can't be easy right now. But it will help us find his killer." Her voice was calm and caught me off guard. "Trust me, I know the line between loyalty and a lie is razor thin, but right now, we have three dead men and all of them are connected to Houghton. I really need your help."

"Detective, I told you everything I know. I can't do this right now. I'm sorry." I stormed past the detective and out of the building.

Inside my car, my cell phone rang.

"Ellice, it's Juice. I got your message. Is everything okay?"

"It's Sam!" I cried into the phone.

It took me nearly ten minutes to compose myself before I could say another word.

CHAPTER 27

I left the coroner's office and ran back to the one person I could find solace and comfort in: Vera.

I entered the lobby, surprised to find it completely empty, the front desk unoccupied. Strange for a late afternoon. I signed in anyway and headed for Vera's room. I tapped lightly on the door before entering. Vera was sound asleep in the chair, her head tilted back, the TV off. The entire room was a quiet oasis.

I gently kissed Vera on top of her head and stood over her. She looked so peaceful. She'd never know the pain of losing Sam. And that was a good thing. I waited for a minute, debating whether to wake her or just let her rest. The selfish part of me opted for the solitude and calm of just being near her. I slung my coat across the foot of her bed and spotted a vase with two dozen long-stemmed yellow roses on her bedside table.

Who sent Vera flowers?

I walked closer and lifted the envelope leaning against the vase. I read the words typed across the front of the envelope: *Some secrets are worth keeping.* The same words from last night's envelope.

My heart gave a thud as I ripped it open. Inside, a 1967 black-and-white mug shot of Vera. Her almond eyes cold, her long wavy hair sweeping against her shoulders. Even the scowl she wore couldn't hide her red-bone beauty. I'd never seen this picture before.

Every muscle inside me tightened. Someone had killed Sam and now they'd been close enough to Vera to harm her, too. Who was playing this sick game?

I rustled Vera awake. "Vee . . . Vee, wake up." Vera stirred a bit before opening her eyes. "Vee, it's me . . . Ellie. Did somebody come by to visit you today? Who left these flowers honey?"

Vera smiled. "Hey, Ellie, baby. I must have fell asleep. What time is it?"

"Vee! Who left these flowers?"

Vera craned her fragile frame in the direction of the bedside table. "Oooh . . . how pretty. Did you pick 'em?"

"I'll be right back." I shot from the room, my heels racing up the hall so fast that a young aide at the nurses' station stood from her chair.

"Is everything okay, Ms. Littlejohn?" the aide asked.

"Someone's been in Vera's room — they left roses. Who's been here to see her?"

"I haven't seen anyone. Is she okay?"

I ran off without answering. I raced down the staircase to the front desk in the lobby.

"Hey, Ms. Littlejohn," Quineisha said.

"I need to see the visitors' log."

"Is everything okay?"

"Did Vera have any visitors today?"

"I'm not sure. I just came on duty. Is everything okay with Ms. Henderson?"

I didn't answer. I scanned the log from the bottom up. Only one visitor. Me. What was Jonathan's deal?! Why was he doing this?

I ran back to Vera's room. I was both terrified and livid. Jonathan's little games were beyond the pale. Why was he threatening me with secrets from my past? How did he know about Willie Jay? And how did he get a mug shot of Vera that I didn't even know about?

By the time I got back inside Vera's room she was wide awake and eating a cup of fruit cocktail from her lunch tray.

"Hey, Ellie, baby. Did you bring me those

flowers? They so beautiful."

I gave a weary smile at Vera. Her smooth brown face lit up with pleasure. A stark contrast to the mug shot I held in my hand.

"Those flowers smell so good. Did Sammy pick 'em?"

"Yeah, Vee . . . they smell really good," I said before falling into a chair, rubbing my left temple.

"Where is he?" Vera said.

"Who?"

"Sammy."

I gazed at Vera and shook my head. I couldn't explain to Vera that Sam was dead. It would only upset her, and it would be forgotten fifteen minutes after that.

"Sammy's not here right now, Vee. He . . . he had to go away."

He had to go away.

I started to cry as I gazed down at the crumpled picture in my hand. Vera was all I had left. I wouldn't put another person I loved in harm's way. Vera had saved me so many times before. Now, I had to save her.

Chillicothe, Georgia, July 1979

Martha had left the house earlier in the day, off to the Blackjack Tavern or wherever she spent her days when she didn't want to spend them with us. Sam and I sat on the front porch steps. We'd just finished eating fish sticks and pork 'n' beans I'd made for the two of us. I was just weeks away from leaving Chillicothe for boarding school. All I had to do now was survive the last few summer days and then I would be free of this town. I heard the putter of a car engine and glanced up from the book I was reading. A police cruiser pulled up to Willie Jay's ranch house in the cul-de-sac. Every time I saw a police car, it rattled me and set my stomach churning.

Sheriff Coogler stepped out of the car, coughed up a big fat wad of spit onto the ground, and hiked his pants up. The day's heat had plastered his comb-over against the thick red skin of his scalp. He waddled up to the porch and rested a thick flat foot on the third step just beneath mine.

"Willie Jay ain't showed up for work in two days. Either of you monkeys know anything about that?"

Sam and I both shook our heads no.

"Where's your momma?"

"She's not here," I said.

Coogler stared at me. "Well, where is she?"

I shrugged. I really was telling the truth.

"What about it, boy? Where yo' daddy?"

Sam scowled up at Coogler. "Willie Jay ain't my daddy."

Coogler sneered at me then gazed up at the porch, trying to see through the screen door. "So you won't mind if I take a look around?"

"Martha said we can't let nobody in the house when she's not home," I said.

Coogler spat again, off to the side of the porch. "This is official police business, gal."

He removed his foot and climbed the stairs to the front door. I whispered to Sam, "Go next door and call Miss Vee. Hurry!"

As soon as Coogler walked inside the house, Sam took off like a shot.

I tried to go back to my book like everything was normal.

Coogler's heavy boots slowly moved from

room to room. I didn't flinch. But I knew if Sam didn't make it back before Coogler returned to the front porch, he might consider it suspicious enough to put us both in the back seat of the cruiser and off to the police station. I remembered Mario Jackson. I wouldn't let that happen. I knew the only chance we stood of staying alive was to avoid getting into that cruiser in the first place.

Hurry, Sam.

My edginess turned to panic when I heard the screen door from the kitchen open with a long, slow squeak and quickly slam against the doorjamb. Coogler was looking out in the back now. Was he looking in the utility shed? All I could think about was Willie Jay's rule that kids should be seen and not heard. A rule he reinforced by locking us in that shed out back, cigar burns, and threats to throw us into the alligator-laden swamp out behind his house.

Sam, please hurry.

It was quiet now. Coogler was probably headed across the backyard for the shed. I was too scared to leave the porch and peep in the backyard. He would be back inside the house at any minute and there was no sign of Sam. I didn't want to be alone with Coogler, especially in the police cruiser.

Come on, Sam.

Finally, I saw a small ball of chugging arms and legs. Sam came sprinting across the cul-de-sac from next door. He ran so fast, his legs reminded me of the spinning limbs of one of those cartoon characters on TV. Only a few seconds more until he made it back to the front porch beside me. I blew a sigh of relief. Sam jumped the small hedges at the edge of the driveway, his eyes full of excitement at having made it back. He crossed the lawn just as Coogler rounded the side of the house.

"Hey, boy! Stop!"

Sam froze in his tracks. Coogler hustled in and snatched Sam up by the back of his collar, his feet barely touching the ground. I had visions of Mario Jackson and my instincts kicked in.

"Leave him alone!" I dropped my book and raced over to Sam. "Get your hands off him," I yelled. I yanked at Coogler's arm trying to free Sam.

"Where you run off to, boy?" Coogler asked.

"I just went to look for my ball, that's all." Sam struggled against the man's thick paunch.

I pulled at Sam's arm, trying to wrestle him away. A few seconds later, Coogler's thick, hard palm slapped me across the face. The hot, stinging force sent me flying backward to the ground. "Stay out of this, gal. This between me and the boy. Now tell me where you ran off to."

Sam was still squirming. Coogler's strong grip unyielding. I shook the burn from my face and watched as Coogler grabbed a billy club from his waistband.

"NOOO!" I screamed.

Coogler threw Sam to the ground. He raised his arm and brought down the club in a quick hard crack against Sam's head. This time, I jumped to my feet and lunged for the billy club from behind as Coogler pulled back his arm to swing at Sam again. Although I didn't weigh much, I was tall, as tall as Coogler. The surprise of my body on top of his caught him off guard. Coogler stumbled. I straddled his back. One hand around his neck and the other trying to keep him from hitting Sam again. He almost had the upper hand. He flung his stick behind his head, narrowly missing my head.

He still held a tight grip on Sam. I fought with everything inside me to keep Sam alive. Coogler zigzagged trying to shake me from his back. I held on, digging my nails into the flabby flesh of his neck. Sam twisted and contorted himself, trying to get free of

Coogler's grip. The tables were turning and now the fat cop was struggling against two squirming bodies instead of one. Sweat poured off Coogler's head, but I ducked his billy club again and leaned in toward him. This time, I bit down on his ear so hard I could taste blood and the salt of his sweat.

"*Aaaaah!*" he screamed. Coogler staggered backward and I nearly fell off his back.

Suddenly, I heard the sound of tires screeching behind me and then the rusty scrape of a car door swinging open. "Hey!" a booming voice called out behind us. "Coogler! Turn them kids loose."

Vera.

For a second, it felt like the earth was moving beneath us as Vera stormed in. We all froze, me still straddling Coogler's back and Sam on the ground caught up in the knot of the man's fist. Vera barreled in, first helping Sam from the ground. I jumped off Coogler's back. She pushed the two of us behind her.

"Have you lost your goddamn mind?! What are you doing?" she yelled. Vera, dressed to the nines in a fire-engine-red dress, pearls, and heels, looked like she was going out for a gala celebration instead of rescuing a couple kids from a backwoods sheriff.

"This ain't got nothing to do with you, Miss Vera. I'm aiming to find out what they know about Willie Jay. He ain't been seen for two days and I think them kids might know something about it."

"With all the people around this town that hate that mean-ass son of a bitch, you may as well arrest half of Chillicothe."

"I told you," Coogler barked through panting breaths. "This here ain't none of yo' business."

"These kids *are* my business."

Coogler swiped a hairy arm across his forehead and placed the stick back inside the holster on his belt. He tugged at his ear where I left teeth marks and blood. "Like I said, Miss Vera, this don't concern you. Now step aside, I'm gon' take them young'uns in for questioning."

"Like hell you will. These kids staying right here."

Vera and Coogler stood facing each other. She looked like she could take him out and never get a single wrinkle in her red dress. But Coogler carried a gun and a billy club to make up for the lost inches. Two giants.

Vera broke the impasse. "Your wife at home, Coogler? Maybe she might like to hear about that young girl you brought over to my place a couple months ago. What was she . . . two, three months pregnant?"

Coogler slowly backed away from Vera. He blinked a few times before he looked over at me and Sam. "You ain't heard the last of me. I'll be back and I'll bring help with me next time." He shuffled back to his patrol car and threw his weight inside before speeding off on screeching tires.

CHAPTER 28

I'm a big girl. I can handle this by myself. I left the nursing home, went back to work, and sat in my office behind closed doors, making more false promises to myself. *I can handle this. I can handle this. But how?* Juice had offered to come by, to help me in any way he could. I thanked him but declined his offer. I didn't call Grace, either.

I rubbed my temples, trying to massage away the same dull headache I'd had since I'd looked at Sam's lifeless body earlier that morning. Then I remembered the Libertad deal. Both Michael and Gallagher were concerned about it. No paper trail. No files or emails. The voluminous bank account in Kentucky. The Libertad deal was a fraud and Michael and Gallagher knew it. Did Jonathan kill them, too, to keep them quiet?

"Ellice, we need to talk." I looked up. Jonathan stood in the doorway of my office, his face flushed and angry. "We need to talk right now."

My heart seemed to stop, then roar back again with the rush of blood pounding through my ears. Every fiber inside of me wanted to kill him. If I owned a gun, I couldn't trust myself to show restraint. "Get the hell out of my office! I'm calling the police!" I turned my back and reached for the telephone. I heard the door slam behind me.

I whirled my chair back around to face him. "What are you doing? I said get out!"

"I had a conversation with Detective Bradford. So you told her that I'm working with your brother, that I've got him trailing lawyers. Are you sure you want to play this game with me?"

"I know you killed my brother and now the police do, too. Get out of my office. I won't tell you again!"

Jonathan's eyes narrowed. Something dark rose up in him and swept across his face. He quietly strolled across the room. Another rush of panic flooded through me. I immediately stood up, trying to think two steps ahead of him. How would I get out of this office if he was blocking the door? Could I get to the phone and call security or 911? Where was Anita? He proceeded around my desk. Slowly. Deliberately. I could feel my heart rise up to meet my throat. I didn't flinch. We stood face-to-face, so close that I could smell the sharp bite of garlic on his breath.

"Let me make this as plain as I can." His voice sizzled in my ears like hot grease across a cast-iron skillet. "I didn't kill your brother, but if I get another visit from the police, I'm going to point them in the direction of a murder they might be more interested in."

"Excuse me?" I backed up a couple steps, still thinking through my exit from this office if he tried to grab me. "Get out! *Now!*"

I paced toward the door. Jonathan hung on my heels. We reached the door at the same time. I grabbed the doorknob just as Jonathan placed his weight against the door and grinned at me.

His eyes locked with mine. "You know, I can appreciate you decided to fuck your way into the executive suite. But you need to be more careful now that you're up here."

I felt my eyes grow wide with disbelief.

"Come on. You're a smart gal. You know we can't go around making such lavish offers of promotion to the executive suite without doing our . . . what do you lawyers call it? Due diligence. I use a little firm out of Savannah. They put together all the glorious highlights of your climb out of that shithole called Chillicothe. They're pretty good, too. Do you know they even managed to tell me you got a B in high school chemistry? The only B in your entire four years at that swanky boarding school. You're smart. Very smart."

My skin prickled. "What did you say?" I stared into Jonathan's eyes. Two black holes of evil stared back at me.

"That's right. I know all your dirty little secrets." He chuckled. "So the police said your brother ran into the wrong end of a gun. I didn't know you had a brother. Most of the folks around here didn't know it either. But you know what? My friends down in Savannah knew about him though. You know what else they told me? They said your brother's not the only black sheep of the family."

My knees buckled. Jonathan's words landed like a hard jab to the chest.

"Tell me something. How did you manage to get out unscathed and leave your poor brother behind to waffle in and out of jail?" Jonathan leaned in closer. "You decided to leave all those secrets behind for the big bright lights of Atlanta, huh? By the way, you been back to Chillicothe lately?"

I slowly released my hand from the door-knob.

"Seems you're not exactly the self-righteous do-gooder you make everyone around here believe you are. All your talk about legal ethics and doing the right thing. Yeah, right! A little piece of advice since you're new around here. If you want to continue to keep your little family secrets undercover, I suggest you waltz your uppity Black ass into Nate's office, tell him we talked and you're good with the Libertad deal and any other deal I bring into this company to make money. And since we're on the subject of Nate, Willow tells me you have a problem with the way we do things around here. I suggest you keep that little nugget under your hair weave, too." He laughed again, louder this time.

"Fuck you!"

"Nice. Just about what I expected from someone like you. If I hear you've uttered a word to a board member about our little business operation, I'll destroy you."

I stood cemented to the floor like Lot's wife from the Bible, turning into a pillar of fear instead of salt.

"And as for the police, it's probably not a good idea to direct them to me again. You might not like what I have to tell them." He placed an index finger to his lips. "Remember . . . *shhh.* All this is our little secret. If you don't tell, I won't tell." He glanced down at his watch and gave a sly grin before he opened the door and strolled out of my office.

And for the first time in my entire professional life I did something I'd never done. I cried in my office.

CHAPTER 29

Every lie you tell, every secret you keep, is a fragile little thing that must be protected and accounted for. One misstep, one miscalculation, and your safe little treasures can topple the perfect life you've built around them. This became all too real to me after Jonathan's threat. Everything I had worked so hard to protect — my career, my reputation, my secrets — were on the brink of being exposed. I hated Jonathan. I finally understood why Michael was consulting a white-collar defense attorney. He knew Jonathan was laundering dirty money. But if Jonathan thought he could kill my brother and threaten me without paying for it, he was sadly mistaken.

Killing Sam would be the worst mistake he ever made.

Jonathan left. A few minutes later, my landline rang. I jumped. I didn't recognize the number, so I decided to let it roll over.

Anita could answer and take a message. Moments later, Anita eased in the door of my office, her face sad and filled with concern. I dabbed at the corner of my eyes, trying to wipe away the tears without her seeing.

"What is it, Anita?"

"Ellice?"

I spun my chair away from her, talking to her over my shoulder. "Now is not a good time. What do you need?"

"Detective Bradford is on the line for you. I tried to take a message, but she said it had something to do with your *brother*?" I spun back around. Anita stood in front of me, wringing her hands. "Is everything okay?"

"Yes, thanks. Close the door behind you." *Shit!* Why the hell did Bradford say that? Now it would be all over the office that I had a brother no one knew about.

I took a deep breath and picked up the receiver. "Detective, you talked to Jonathan. Are you going to arrest him for killing my brother?"

"That's why I'm calling. We've spoken to Mr. Everett. It would really help me out if you could come down to the station to give me some additional information. Just a few questions."

"Of course." I hung up the phone, slightly relieved that the police might finally be doing their job.

I was surprised when I walked into the Atlanta Police Department. I'd foolishly imagined the place would look like it did on the television show *Law & Order* — a large open room buzzing with police officers going to and fro, handing off files containing all sorts of incriminating evidence, telephones ringing off the hook with callers in distress. Instead, I found a typical-looking open space with half-wall cubicles, most of them empty.

I stepped up to a sleepy-looking gentleman reading a newspaper at his desk — sixties, threadbare corduroy jacket, and ill-fitting brown pants. I could tell he hadn't put any real effort into his appearance since the Clinton administration. His whole drab demeanor made me think he was simply biding his time until the paperwork approvals for his retirement came in.

He peered over the top of his newspaper with a couple of jaundiced eyes. "May I help you?"

"Yes. I'm looking for Detective Shelly Bradford."

"And you are?"

"I'm Ellice Littlejohn from Houghton Transportation."

The officer raised his eyebrows before he folded the newspaper and stood. I wasn't surprised by his reaction. Everyone in here probably buzzed about the hotshot detective investigating the murderous enclave at Houghton Transportation. My showing up was likely the highlight of this guy's day.

"Why don't you have a seat?" He pointed to a row of dingy upholstered chairs against the wall and then disappeared down a hallway.

I didn't budge. God only knows *what* had sat in those stained and ratty old chairs over the years. He couldn't make me sit there, even under threat of arrest. I canvassed the room again. This whole place made my skin crawl. I scanned the old man's desk. Aside from his folded newspaper and a half-eaten cheese Danish, nothing was particularly enlightening. I was bored just looking around this station.

"Hello, Ms. Littlejohn. Thanks for coming in to speak with us," Detective Bradford said as she approached. "You remember my partner, Detective Burke." My stomach did a somersault. I'd forgotten about her partner. I fought mightily against the panic creeping in.

Detective Burke was casually dressed in a blue button-down shirt, sleeves rolled to the elbow, and slacks. His brown bald head glistened. Detective Bradford, in a break with her usual formality, had removed her suit jacket to reveal a silk white blouse and wool pants.

She led our little trio into a small box posing as an "interview room." The fluorescent lights and the government-green walls produced a dull yellowish tint to the space, giving all three of us a sickly, unnatural appearance. A narrow window in the corner tendered a sliver of light that reflected off the metal table in the center of the room, but hardly enough to invigorate the tight space. Bradford and Burke took the two chairs that sat side by side, leaving me the lone chair across from them.

"Can I get you something? Water, Coke?" Bradford asked.

"I'm fine."

"Let me say first, I am very sorry for your loss."

"Thank you."

She nodded. "Were you and your brother close?"

I stared at the detective for a beat. "Yes. Why?"

"I'm just wondering if you knew any of his friends *or enemies*. Anyone you could think of that might want to kill him."

"I thought you said you spoke to Jonathan. He's involved in Sam's death, right?"

Bradford glanced at her partner. "We're narrowing in on a suspect. We're just trying to gather more information. When was the last time you spoke to your brother?"

"I told you, last night."

"And what did the two of you talk about?"

"I told you. He said Jonathan hired him to trail Gallagher. But he didn't kill him. Jonathan set him up."

Detective Bradford nodded as if she understood.

"What did your brother do for a living?"

"As of yesterday, he was doing surveillance work for Jonathan Everett. We've covered all this." I stared at the window, a small ration of sunlight forcing its way through the slim frame. I knew the police had already collected the highlights of Sam's long and sordid criminal record. They didn't need me for that information. "Who is this suspect you're narrowing in on?"

Detective Burke cleared his throat and opened a folder in front of him. He scrutinized the papers inside. "Let's go back to the day Mr. Sayles was murdered. You said you arrived around seven a.m., but not to meet with Mr. Sayles. Is that correct?"

I clasped my hands together underneath

the table. "Yes."

Burke cleared his throat again, but the rasp was still there. "His assistant told us you and Mr. Sayles typically met around seven A.M. His wife also told us you usually had early morning meetings with her husband. Were you in Mr. Sayles's office the morning he was murdered?"

I could feel the air leave my lungs like a balloon slowly deflating and shrinking. The lights in this small box of a room seemed to dim around me. It finally dawned on me who they were closing in on as a suspect and it wasn't Jonathan. I started calculating the damage I'd done by lying to Bradford previously and now, coming in to speak with the police without a lawyer. I couldn't leave now without looking like I had something to hide.

Bradford and Burke continued to stare across the table at me; neither of them blinked.

"Look, I did go to Michael's office that morning but when I arrived, he was already dead. I got scared and just left."

The two of them gazed at each other. Bradford shook her head in her typical judgmental way. "Let me understand this. You *discovered* Mr. Sayles *dead* and you *didn't* call for help?" she stressed.

I sat silent. They could think whatever they wanted. I'd spent the better part of a week kicking myself over my atrocious behavior.

"Why not?" she said.

"I told you. I was in shock. I was scared. Leaving a dead body is not a crime."

The two of them stared at me for a beat before glancing at each other again. Doubt and skepticism loomed across their faces.

"So how long have you known Mr. Sayles?" Detective Burke said, leaning forward into the table.

"Almost ten years."

"And you've always worked for him during those years?"

"Mostly."

"First at the law firm Dillon & Beck and then at Houghton?" Burke said.

"Yes. But what does that have to do with my brother's death?"

"How would you describe your relationship with Mr. Sayles?" Burke asked.

I gave a deep sigh but no answer as I looked across the table at him. I gazed at his gold wedding band before I lowered my eyes to the table.

They knew.

"What happened at the law firm, Ms. Littlejohn?" Burke asked.

"What do you mean?"

"Why did you both leave the firm?"

"I don't see what this has to do with anything." But I was a lawyer. I knew this line of questioning was all fair game.

"We talked to Mrs. Sayles. She said you were sleeping with her husband. She told us your affair had become a distraction at the law firm where you worked. You two were asked to leave the law firm and you followed him over to Houghton."

"It wasn't like that . . ." I began, my eyes still glued to Detective Burke. What did he think of me? Now I was ashamed and embarrassed. They were making it sound so sordid and one-sided.

Detective Bradford perked up. "Were you two still sleeping together before he was murdered?"

I turned away from their prying eyes. They'd delved into my personal life and came out swinging. They were trying to force me to discuss an area of my life that was painful and stupid, but it had nothing to do with Sam's or Michael's murders. I didn't utter a word.

Detective Burke stepped in again. "Ms. Littlejohn, we recovered your brother's cell phone. It appears you left several voice mails for your brother. You sounded rather irritated. Why is that?"

"What are you talking about?"

"There was an iPhone on your brother's body. We were able to open it using his thumbprint. You left him several voice mails over the past few days," he said.

"I hadn't heard from him . . . I was just worried, I guess." I tried to remember all the messages I left for Sam. The night I broke into his house, the day after, when I discovered who Geoffrey Gallagher was, the day Sam's and Gallagher's bodies were discovered. On every single message I left for him, I must have sounded like some shrieking banshee bellowing for him to return my calls.

"How about the message you left a few days ago? You said: 'What the hell's going on? The police have footage of you in the lobby of my job and what's the deal with Geoffrey Gallagher?' That's the message you left for your brother."

I sat still as a stone.

Detective Burke continued, "Early this morning, you left the following voice mail, 'Sam, where are you? The police found the lawyer's body.' Let me ask you, Ms. Littlejohn, would that lawyer have been Geoffrey Gallagher?"

I felt faint, like the lights were dimming

around me. I didn't say a word.

Burke and Bradford exchanged glances again. Burke continued, "Let's move on. Your brother had a gun tucked in the waistband of his pants. Mr. Gallagher was killed with that same gun."

"So what are you saying?" As far as I was concerned, they weren't the only ones who could ask questions about my brother.

"Do you know why your brother would want to kill Mr. Gallagher?"

"My God! How many times do I have to tell you — my brother didn't kill anyone. Why are you hammering me with questions? Did you bring Jonathan in and grill him like this? What about some of the other people on Twenty? You were at Michael's funeral. Wasn't it strange to you that none of his colleagues attended, including Jonathan?"

"We did speak with Mr. Everett. He told us that the executive team was out of town for a business meeting the day of Mr. Sayles's funeral."

The party in Savannah. I was the only one who didn't fly down the day before.

"Mr. Everett also told us that you told people at Houghton that you didn't have any siblings. Is that true?" Burke asked.

I couldn't speak. Every stupid lie I ever told was here, haunting me.

"He seems to think you're trying to implicate him in this matter because of a workplace disagreement. He says that he was against your promotion, that the company needed someone with more experience in the executive suite. He thinks you're trying to sully his reputation among your colleagues."

"What?!" My pulse pumped. "And you just accepted that? That doesn't make any sense! I told you, he lured my brother into this mess to frame him for a murder he didn't commit. Probably to get back at me because —"

"Because what?"

"Attorney-client privilege prevents me from going into it." As a lawyer for the company, I couldn't discuss Houghton's bank records or deals without clearing it through the CEO or the board of directors first. "But Jonathan is the person you should be pressing. He's not what he appears to be."

"Do you have any evidence that would point up a relationship between your brother and Mr. Everett?"

I threw my hands up in exasperation. "I don't. Isn't that *your* job to find the evidence? All I know is that my brother said Jonathan hired him to trail Gallagher.

Maybe Jonathan needed to know where Gallagher was so he could kill him after he killed Michael."

"Okay. Did he ever do any work for Houghton?" Burke asked.

I folded my arms across my chest. "Who?"

Burke pushed his shirtsleeves up a bit and gave me an irritated look. "Mr. Gallagher."

"To my knowledge, Houghton never engaged him or his firm." Across the table, Burke and Bradford looked at each other yet again, this time with the kind of familiar glance that signaled they knew something I didn't.

"Are you sure about that? Gallagher's partner Christopher Knight tells us you called the firm and asked him to send over Houghton's files. Why is that?" Bradford probed.

I didn't respond. I simply stared at her. I was in here voluntarily. I wasn't obligated to answer their questions.

Detective Bradford pulled a document from the folder in front of her and slid it across the table toward me. "Ms. Littlejohn, have you ever seen this before?"

I read the one-page document:

Law Offices of Gallagher, Grant & Knight

PRIVILEGED AND CONFIDENTIAL —
ATTORNEY WORK PRODUCT

EXECUTIVE SUMMARY OF
MEMORANDUM OF OPINION

December 28
To: Michael Sayles, Executive Vice
President & General Counsel
Houghton Transportation Company
From: Geoffrey J. Gallagher

You have asked me to opine on the consequences of your status as an executive officer at Houghton and the company's involvement in a joint venture with Libertad Excursiones, a company headquartered in Monterrey, Mexico. As I understand the facts, Libertad has recently become the target of an investigation by the Mexican government for financial improprieties involving its hotel businesses. As we delved deeper into Libertad's organizational structure, we learned that the company's CEO, Bernardo Ortiz, has come under fire for his association with individuals alleged to have ties to criminal activities, including human trafficking, gun trafficking, and illegal drug distribution. This information has been confirmed through our local counsel and contacts in Mexico.

I **strongly caution** Houghton against engaging in any transactions with Libertad Excursiones or any of its subsidiaries or holding companies. More importantly, your status as a member of the executive management team involved in an organization tied to illegal activities can subject you to personal and criminal liability. The law has evolved over the last few years to eliminate the corporate veil and hold directors and executives criminally liable for bad acts of the company.

The factual research supporting this opinion is attached herewith.

The dizziness that rollicked my head earlier in the day was back again. I'd never seen this document before. Hardy was right. Houghton was laundering dirty money for Libertad. My mind raced as I tried to think clearly, struggling to figure out where the document had come from. Gallagher's partner told me that they didn't have any Houghton files. Anna hadn't included this document in the envelope she gave me. I slowly peeled my eyes away from the paper on the table, the gravity of it all now settling in on me.

Had Anna set me up?

"Ms. Littlejohn?" Bradford asked again. "Have you seen this document before?"

I stared back down at the paper, not bothering to answer her.

"Let me help you out here, Ms. Littlejohn," Detective Bradford teased. "Geoffrey Gallagher is giving his legal opinion about a joint venture that Houghton is planning with a company called Libertad Excursiones, a company he states has been engaging in money laundering, drugs, and guns." Detective Bradford let her words hang in the air, while watching me. "Geoffrey Gallagher's wife gave us this document. Mrs. Gallagher found it in his briefcase at home. She heard about Mr. Sayles's death on the news and thought this document might have something to do with her husband's murder. It would appear that he *has* done some work for your company in some capacity."

"This is what I'm talking about. You guys should be investigating Jonathan, not me. He's the CFO. He's in charge of deals like this."

Detective Bradford ran her hand across the back of her pixie cut. "Ms. Littlejohn, your boss was killed on a day that you lied and said you didn't meet with him as you normally do. Your brother uses *your* ID badge to roam through the building. And a lawyer your boss hired is found dead after he gave a legal opinion about an illegal transaction your company is involved in. That lawyer is killed with a gun that your brother had on him. And your brother is dead as well, killed by someone he knew. That's three dead bodies all connected to you. Tell me, Ms. Littlejohn, why is it that so many people around you have managed to wind up dead?"

I stared at her, then at Detective Burke. The slow throb in my temple gave way to a full-blown pounder battering the inside of my head. I was sitting in the middle of a police station under suspicion of murder, without an explanation or a lawyer, my personal life and my professional life now converging in a death-spiraling nose dive. *Why didn't I just give Sam the money like I always did? Why did I ever agree to help Anna? Why did I accept the promotion?* Now it made sense why Nate and Willow were so anxious to promote me. They were setting me up to take the fall for a couple of murders.

"Did you know someone broke into the Sayles home after Mr. Sayles's death?"

"Yes . . . Anna told me."

"Did your brother break into the Sayles's home and ransack it looking for this document for you?"

"For *me*? What are you talking about?"

"Perhaps to help you," Detective Bradford responded.

"To *help* me?! Help me do what?"

"According to Mr. Everett, you've wanted a promotion for some time. You were sleeping with the boss, but you still weren't promoted. Perhaps you needed some assistance getting into the executive suite and you enlisted your brother for a little help. The two of you devise a scheme to kill Mr. Sayles and Mr. Gallagher. From the looks of this document, it appears that Houghton may be involved in something it ought not be. If the old general counsel and his outside attorney were against the deal, maybe the new general counsel might be more amenable to breaking the law, huh? Anything to get ahead."

"What?! Are you insane? Jonathan's the one who brought this deal to the company. He's the one who's in bed with a bunch of criminals. Subpoena the company's financial records. This was all Jonathan's scheme."

"We plan to do just that," said Bradford.

"So after your brother helped you get promoted, what happened? Did the two of you argue or did you just decide you didn't need him around anymore risking the details of your secret climb up the corporate ladder? If he disappeared, no one would be the wiser since you told people you didn't have a brother."

Her insinuation that I might have killed Sam was the final straw. We squared off, eye to eye. I didn't care about her badge or her hotshot reputation.

Detective Bradford finally released her stare and moved on. "Mrs. Sayles said she gave you some documents she found in her safe-deposit box, some documents she said pertained to Houghton's business deal with Libertad. Why didn't you bring those documents to our attention?"

"Did Anna tell you *why* she gave me those documents?"

"She did. But you're a lawyer, an officer of the court. We're wondering why you didn't refuse to help her and encourage her to come to the police. Maybe because you knew the documents might incriminate you in your boss's murder?"

"That's ridiculous! Anna asked me to find out what was going on inside Houghton without dragging Michael's name through the mud. She didn't think *you guys* were taking her concerns seriously and insinuated she killed Michael. At the time, I didn't know that Michael's and Gallagher's murders had something to do with what she'd given me. And I certainly didn't think my brother was involved."

"But once you found out your brother was involved, you made the decision not to involve the police?"

I stared back at the sliver of daylight forcing its way through the small window and wondered why my life always seemed to go in vicious circles of pain and death. What lesson was I not learning? It was Chillicothe all over again except this time I wasn't fourteen and Vera couldn't save me.

"Your company's engaged in some sort of transaction that may have led to the deaths of three people — one of them your own brother — but you don't bother to go to the police with information that might help find the killer."

Detective Bradford wasn't asking a question and I had no answers even if she had asked.

She continued, "Did you ever think that maybe you might have prevented your brother's death if you had brought this information to our attention?"

I shot a look at the detective. Did she not know that would become the biggest regret of my life? With everything we'd survived, it was finally my own selfishness in trying to hide the past that had caused Sam's death. I'd mangled this whole affair so badly that even I was starting to question my involvement in it. I should have insisted more forcefully that Anna take the documents to the police. I tried to protect Sam like I always had and instead, I got him killed.

"Where are the documents now?" Detective Bradford asked flatly.

"At my house."

"We'll need those documents, too." Bradford and Burke looked at each other again, this time like they'd run the end of their course. "Ms. Littlejohn, you are the single thread through all these murders. Trust me, we'll figure this out. Better that you come clean now," Detective Burke insisted.

Come clean. There was nothing else I could say. I took a deep breath, backed my chair from the table, and stood. "I have to get back to work."

I turned on my heels and headed out the door.

CHAPTER 30

If the police considered me a real suspect, they would have arrested me while I was sitting in front of them. They had nothing. But that didn't mean I was out of the woods yet. I had lied so much that my credibility was shot with the police. And if they continued to eye me, I was facing two options: going to jail for a murder I didn't commit or climbing into bed with a group of executives who were knee-deep in corporate fraud and crime, including the murder of my brother. I hated both those options, which meant I needed a third one. My hope for getting out of this mess was somewhere up on the twentieth floor. I just had to find it.

I pulled into my reserved parking space inside Houghton's garage a little after four o'clock. I sat in the car and parsed through everything that had happened. My life had spun out of control almost since the day I accepted the general counsel position. The speed at promoting me to the executive suite. The odd vibe at Nate's party. The argument between Max and Jonathan. What was it that Max didn't want connected to Libertad? What was too risky?

Max's veiled threat: *It might be a pretty long and ugly drop back down to Eighteen.*

A few minutes later, I stormed inside my office suite. Anita stared up at me in disbelief. "Ellice, what's going on? Please tell me."

"Get Willow on the phone. Tell her it's urgent. Better yet, tell her I *desperately* need her help." I knew she'd respond to the latter plea. If she was so willing to give me sisterly advice about how to handle "the guys," maybe she could do it on my terms.

"Sure." Anita picked up the phone, cautiously looking at me as she dialed Willow's extension.

I rushed into my office and slammed the door behind me. I sat at my desk. Waiting. Simmering. A few minutes later, I heard a light tap at my door before Willow walked in.

"Hey, Ellice, honey, Anita told me you need my help on something urgent?" She eased into the chair in front of me with a sympathetic expression, like she was really concerned. "Is everything okay?"

381

"Why the rush to promote me to this office? And don't bullshit me this time."

Willow's eyes widened in surprise. "I . . . I don't . . ."

"Everyone on this floor used the party in Savannah as a convenient excuse to skip Michael's funeral. You and Nate hustled me into this job so fast, I barely had time to think about it. And neither Jonathan nor Max wanted Nate to promote me. Why?"

"What?"

My entire body was fueled by rage. "In one of Nate's *lucid* moments, he told me some people on the Executive Committee didn't think he should promote me. I happen to know through a couple of sources that Jonathan is not my biggest fan. Neither is Max. So why? And tell me the truth because if you don't and I go down, I'm dragging everybody on this *goddamn* floor down with me. So tell me what the *fuck* is going on!"

Willow stiffened. "I'm not sure myself. A couple weeks before your promotion, Jonathan and Michael got into a big row about something. I don't know what it was. But Jonathan said he thought Michael wasn't cutting it around here and that maybe we should look into finding a replacement for him. Maybe it was time to force him into an early retirement or something." She looked down at the huge sapphire on her finger, avoiding my gaze. I never took my eyes off her. When she looked up again, she gave a deep sigh. "Ellice, honey, what does that matter now? You're here. You're in this beautiful office and Nate is pleased with his decision."

"So why are Jonathan and Max out to get me?"

"I don't know what you're talking about."

"My promotion was discussed in that boardroom right down the hall. I'd have a hard time believing the vice president of HR didn't participate in those discussions."

Willow blew an exasperated sigh. "Actually, you got it all wrong. It was Jonathan's idea to promote you. He said you'd be perfect, that you had things in your background that would make you perfect for working on the kind of deals he brings into the company."

"Oh, he did, huh?"

"Yeah. He said he had a feeling you two would see eye to eye."

If Jonathan said that, I knew he wasn't referring to my résumé. He'd dug up all my secrets to threaten me, blackmail me into going along with him. "So who was Nate referring to when he said someone didn't want me promoted? Max?"

"Max's thinking hasn't evolved since the Ice Age. He's a dinosaur."

"I know that, but why was he trying to thwart my promotion?"

"Same thing he thought about me. He seems to think anyone who doesn't have an appendage hanging between their legs is a second-class citizen."

"So he's not fond of strong women." I tossed Willow a bone with my comment and she snapped it up with a grin. "But I'm sure he's never threatened you."

"Threatened you?! What do you mean?"

"A little side conversation we had. Don't worry about it. What did he say about me during the meeting to discuss my promotion?"

"Ellice —"

"What did he say?"

"He thought you'd fail, that you couldn't bring what Michael brought to the table. He said he didn't want to sit on the Executive Committee with a —" Willow stopped.

"With a Black person? Or did he freely express himself in the meeting and use the N-word?" Had Max's hatred for having to work beside me driven him to kill my brother? Black people had been killed for less.

"I'm telling you, he's from the Dark Ages. But it all worked out. The folks who count supported you. And now you're up here in this lovely office. Let's just move forward, okay?"

"Yeah. Thanks for the information."

Willow stood from her chair and lightly tapped a manicured finger on my desk. "So what are you gonna do now, honey?"

"Prove Max wrong."

Willow left and I sat in my office. I didn't move a muscle. I waited. At some point, Anita peeked inside my door to say good night. I never moved. I sat at my desk and waited some more. The lights went out across the floor. I still waited. I'd wait until midnight if I had to. When I was sure everyone on the floor was gone for the day, I walked the entire twentieth floor. Twice. The office was bathed in the dusk-dark lights of the reserve lighting system. I needed to be sure I was alone. On my last walkabout, I hit the override switch at the elevator bank.

I paced down the hall to Max's office suite, quietly opened the door to his office, and flipped on his lights. Willow was right. Walking into his office was like stepping back in time. Every executive on this floor selected the decor for their office. From the looks of it, Maxwell Lumpkin had selected Early Antebellum as his decor theme. Lots of heavy dark wood and boys' club atmosphere, from the beadboard paneling to the heavy mahogany desk, lamps fashioned to look like replicas of hurricane lanterns and the huge bald eagle bust lodged on top of it. Anchored on the wall behind his desk, an oversize American flag. It nearly covered the entire wall. I bet if I peeked under it, there was a Confederate flag there too.

On the credenza behind his desk was a photo of Max shaking hands with David Duke, another of him posed in between two American flags shaking hands with Donald Trump, and a third of him holding a bible, smiling broadly into the camera. In the corner of the credenza, a neat stack of *National Review* magazines. This guy didn't hide who he was.

I pulled away the huge leather chair and searched through a couple files on top of his desk, looking for anything related to Sam or my secrets. Nothing. Everything was quiet, except for the soft hum of the computer. *His computer was still on.* I peeped toward the office door before clicking the escape key on his keyboard. The screensaver, a picture of the emblem from his lapel pin — the two intersecting gold flags and the red heart — popped up on the screen. His club again. I hit the Outlook icon and his email sprung up on the monitor. He didn't even lock his computer.

Idiot.

I glanced toward the door again before I started scrolling through his in-box. The first few emails yielded a lot of traffic between Max and other employees in Operations. Nothing unusual. I tried to keep my eye on the door as I continued clicking through the emails. Nothing. I did a search for *Michael Sayles.* Several emails popped up. I scrolled through them and then opened the one with the subject line: Our Discussion.

December 28
6:39 pm
To: MaxwellLumpkin@Houghton.com
From: MichaelSayles@Houghton.com
Re: Our Discussion

Perhaps you should focus more on the protesters in front of the building instead of things like this! I'm not interested!! But maybe the authorities will be!!

I scrolled down further . . .

December 28
5:55 pm
To: MichaelSayles@Houghton.com
From: MaxwellLumpkin@Houghton.com
Re: Our Discussion

Michael,
I hope you've reconsidered. Our organization could benefit from your broad experience and the wide reach of your business network.
   I think you could be a very useful general in our efforts to restore order where others have sown chaos.
   The fight continues.

Max

General? The fight continues? What did any of this mean? Why was Max trying to recruit Michael for some fight?

I searched for a few minutes more, but there was nothing else related to Sam or Michael or me. I scanned the desk again. This time, I spotted the edge of a document peeking out from underneath the blotter on top. I slipped the paper out. A flyer for the Tri-County Outfitters gun shop. The exact same flyer I found in Michael's duffel bag at my house. Why would Max and Michael have the same flyer for a local gun shop? I lifted the blotter but there was nothing else underneath. I slipped the paper back under the blotter.

I moved on to the drawers in his credenza. More dead ends. I slipped open the pencil tray on his desk. A slew of business cards, pens, and other minutiae were scattered about. And I almost missed it. But sitting there within the desk clutter was a silver-and-black thumb drive. Along the side was a single name: Ellice Littlejohn. My stomach tumbled. I placed it in my pocket and left.

I hustled back to my office, grabbed my belongings, and headed for my car. Working beside me would be the least of Maxwell Lumpkin's problems when I was done with him.

I wound through late-evening traffic in Midtown. A cold, icy rain pelted the hood of my car. Every time I thought about Max, my head shook with fury. I had only given him credit for being a racist. His being a murderer had never occurred to me. I turned off Peachtree Street onto Collier Road, barely making it through a yellow light. A silver sedan and a black Escalade followed me right through the light. Atlanta traffic.

I drove for a bit when I noticed the

Escalade was still on my tail. Suddenly, I remembered the black Escalade that had been parked in front of Sam's house the night I was attacked. My pulse quickened. It was nightfall and the dark tint of the windows and the glare from the headlights made it impossible for me to make out the driver. I made a right turn onto Northside Drive. I slowed down, waiting for the car to pass me. It didn't. I sped up. The Escalade sped up. I drove faster, weaving in between a minivan and a Range Rover. I blew through another yellow light. The car never let up on my tail. Who was in the car behind me? Sam's killer?

If Max or Jonathan wanted to play games, then I could play games too. Slick currents of rage and fear ran through my entire body. I gripped the steering wheel and floored the gas. The car hummed with the steady climb in speed as I raced through traffic. The Escalade never lost pace. I raced past the Atlanta Girls' School and through the intersection of West Paces Ferry Road. I sped through another light before I suddenly hit the brakes. Tires screeched behind me and I watched in my rearview mirror as the Escalade swerved to the right to avoid rear-ending my car. A few seconds later, the hulking SUV backed up before speeding around to the side of my car.

"Hey! What the hell are you doing?" A young blond guy stuck his head out the driver's-side window of the Escalade. The guy sped off but not without a parting good-bye. "Crazy bitch!"

A couple drivers honked their horns now that I was blocking traffic. I dropped my head onto my steering wheel.

I was becoming unhinged.

CHAPTER 31

My heart was still pummeling by the time I arrived inside my condo. The first thing I did when I stepped inside was to slip off my coat and heels in the foyer and pull out my laptop at the kitchen table. I inserted the thumb drive from Max's office. Two files popped up on the screen. One titled "The Brethren" and the other titled "Ellice Little-john."

My stomach was a knotted mess. I clicked on the file with my name and there it was. The sordid and shameful past that I had spent nearly my entire life running from. This was the Savannah dossier that Jonathan was talking about. Newspaper articles in the *Tolliver County Register* about Willie Jay's disappearance and his fourteen-year-old stepdaughter as a person of interest, along with the sheriff's investigation report with police photos from that shack on Red Creek Road. Just like he said, Jonathan's investigators had even collected my school transcripts going back as far as Coventry Academy, along with my transcripts from Georgetown and Yale. Birth certificates for me and Sam. A death certificate for Martha. Sam's assorted arrest records and a tax assessment on his house. They'd even collected my medical records for an appendectomy ten years back. All the peaks and valleys of my entire life.

And Jonathan's Savannah friends were thorough too. They'd collected information I'd never seen before. There were mug shots of my mother before her life with Willie Jay, a myriad assortment of solicitation and DUI arrests. And scattered in the midst of all this, a 1967 black-and-white mug shot and arrest record for Violet Richards — or as I knew her, Vera Henderson — from Monmouth Parish in Louisiana. Manslaughter. I studied the mug shot for a minute — the same picture left in the envelope in Vera's room at Beachwood — then clicked on the arrest record. Vera had been arrested for killing a man whom she reported as her rapist. She'd obviously skipped bail and made a run to Georgia.

Everybody has a secret.

My entire life was corralled onto this small digital device. Every secret I ever kept, every lie I ever told, every shame I tried to bury was stored here. The violation was obscene. Jonathan and Max, working together, peeping through all the cracks in my perfect little lawyer life. The two of them working in concert to bring me to my knees and make me a part of their criminal enclave. It wouldn't work.

I closed the file on my sordid life and clicked on the file marked "The Brethren." A Word document sprang to life. The first thing that caught my eye, an emblem of two waving flags and a red heart between them. Max's lapel pin, the same pin worn by the board members, the senators, and the Fox News commentator at Nate's party. The rest of the document nearly took my breath away:

Brethren of the Elite Order

The Brethren are a select group of executives and leaders in upper echelons of business and politics. Our mission is simple — to recruit pure race executives and leaders like you to assist us as we work to eliminate all impure races and religions and restore the prominence of the white race as the superior and dominant human force on the face of the earth.

Your inclusion as a general in the Brethren will ensure that you are not exposed to the threat of lawsuits or blackmail because of our exclusivity and covert requirements. We also have our own legal and financial teams that support our efforts.

Our silent crusade to restore conservative values and order is conducted under the following strict guidelines:

- Keep the generals free of controversy so that they may establish conditions ripe for creating a pure society.
- Arm the foot soldiers with weapons for the fight and provide logistical support.
- Connect pure pastors and religious leaders with conservative politicians who will push forward the mission of the Brethren.
- Avoid the use of racial slurs, swastikas, Confederate flags, KKK symbols, and other images that may be sympathetic to our cause, as our fight is more strategic.
- Destroy the fake liberal Jew media by giving them misinformation or avoiding them altogether.
- Females in the pure race may be helpful but must be kept in servient roles to

ensure they do not become sympathetic to the plights of the enemy.

- Infiltrate the enemy races by befriending them, hiring and promoting them in very limited quantities, to avoid arousing curiosity or attention to our cause.

The Brethren are growing in numbers and power. We sit in meetings and boardrooms right beside you. Join us in this important endeavor for the continued purity of our race.

The fight continues.

I went numb. The Brethren? The Elite Order? Max was recruiting for a white supremacy group. And not just any white people. He was seeking business leaders. Men with money and power. The generals.

I typed in "Brethren of the Elite Order." Nothing popped up. I tried several other iterations of the words, but it only produced a string of event planners and caterers. I typed in "Tri-County Outfitters," the name from the gun shop flyer. The store, located in the Atlanta suburb of Shelton, sold guns and hunting equipment. Was this place tied to Libertad's gun-trafficking operation?

My God. I stood from my chair. I thought I was going to be sick, so I sat back down again, still staring at the manifesto. All this time, I'd been played by the likes of Jonathan Everett and Maxwell Lumpkin. Men who had power and money to do extraordinary damage in this country.

Now, it became clear why Michael was killed. He threatened to expose Jonathan's money-laundering scheme. And he refused Max's invitation to join a racist hate group and threatened to go to the authorities. What had I gotten myself involved in? Max was against the protesters in front of Houghton. Hell, Max was against me sitting across from him in the boardroom. Did Max kill Sam to get back at me?

What to do now? *Think Ellice. Think.*

This thumb drive wasn't privileged or confidential company information. I could turn it over to the police. Should I delete the Littlejohn folder first? Detective Bradford didn't need to know my secrets, or Vera's. The officer could piece the breadcrumbs together the best way she could. I was just about to hit the delete key on my laptop when I thought about everything I'd been through in my life, all the things collected on this device.

I had to believe that I was more than my worst mistake. Every one of my secrets had been a painful lesson that I should have been learning from instead of running from.

Until I stood up and owned them, they would continue to hold me in this impossible grip of fear.

I pulled up Vera's mug shot again: her eyes glowering at the camera; her beautiful face etched with a stoic frown; random numbers emblazoned across her chest. She was arrested for serving justice by her own hand against a man who violated her. I had done the same thing, too. Jonathan and Max weren't the only "bad guys." Vera and I had our issues too. Each one of us a killer. Each of us capable of doing the unthinkable for reasons we believed were right. But were any one of us less culpable than the other? Was it Vera's place to determine the justice for her rapist? Was Willie Jay's life any less valuable than Sam's or Michael's? Were my actions any less despicable than Jonathan's?

Still, the fact remained, in the midst of wrangling with these racists, my brother was murdered. Anger crawled up my spine like a copperhead snake seeking its next meal. How dare they try to blackmail and beat me into submission to commit a crime.

The last time I'd felt this angry was decades ago, when Willie Jay Groover went missing.

The Brethren kept me awake the entire

night. Somewhere around four o'clock in the morning, I finally dozed off, having decided the only way I could end this nightmare was to explain everything to Detective Bradford, including their blackmail scheme of me. I would turn over the jump drive, the "Ellice Littlejohn" folder included. Sam was dead and my keeping secrets hadn't served either of us well thus far. I was prepared to deal with the consequences if it meant Jonathan and Max would go to prison for Sam's death. The only thing that still troubled me — why did they kill Sam?

I woke to the sound of my cell phone ringing at 6:30 A.M. I rolled over and tried to clear the frog from my throat. "Hello?"

"Hey, Ellice, it's me, Rudy. Did I wake you? I'm sorry."

"Rudy?" I sat up in the bed. "What's going on?"

"I know you get busy and I wanted to catch you first thing this morning. I've found something I think you need to see right away."

CHAPTER 32

I was a frazzled mess by daylight. I didn't remember getting dressed or driving into the office. In fact, I was halfway into work before I realized I hadn't even combed my hair. Luckily, I found a headband on the back seat of my car that I used to pull my hair back on the few occasions I ventured out to exercise. I snapped it across the front of my head and tried to finger-comb my hair before I walked inside the building. When I arrived at my office suite, Rudy was standing at Anita's desk talking, folder in hand. They both looked at me in astonishment.

Anita asked, "Ellice, is everything okay with you?"

"Yes." I knew I looked like hell.

"You look a little rough around the gills, girl." Anita said.

I ignored her comment and proceeded into my office. "Come on in, Rudy."

He followed me inside. "Are you sure

you're all right? I mean, you just look . . ."

"You said you had something urgent?" Maybe Anita had told him about Detective Bradford's call about my brother. I decided not to address it. That was my personal business.

"Yeah, right. You remember that meeting you sent me to out in East Hell — oops, I mean the Operations Center in Conyers?"

"Yes." I didn't have it in me to laugh at Rudy's joke. I took off my coat and hung it in the closet. My mind wandered. As soon as Rudy left my office, I would call the detective, meet her, and give her the flash drive. Next, I needed to resign. Maybe I should ask Rudy about the Brethren. But I would have heard about it a long time ago if he knew anything. Besides, he was Jewish and not likely to know about their hate-filled bigotry. I'd just take the stuff to the police and let them figure it all out.

". . . so that new manager is right. Something screwy is going on with the orders. There's no contract for the account and the manager can't reach the company that placed the order," Rudy said.

"I'm sorry. I've got a lot on my mind. What did you say?" I took a seat behind my desk and motioned for Rudy to sit down.

"There's no contract for an account we're

handling, and we can't trace the source. Apparently, we pick up a monthly shipment of fifteen boxes out in Shelton. Five are shipped to an address in southern Ohio, five to southern Illinois, and five to an address in Upstate New York."

"Okay?"

"The shipments started about four months ago. But they started increasing in frequency over the last two months."

I shrugged. "So a business has picked up some extra orders."

"I don't think a business is involved. They're shipped using a PO box address in Shelton."

"A post office box? We don't pick up without a physical street address."

"Exactly."

"Who's shipping?"

"Something called Cavanaugh Industries. But that's not the best part. We can't find any such company in Shelton or anywhere else in the state of Georgia. And the shipments are paid through a PayPal account. But here's the part I think you'll be most interested in. Two months ago, a shipment of ten boxes went to San Diego, California. An address right on the US-Mexico border. That shipment was addressed to *Libertad Excursiones.*"

"What?!"

"Yep. I can't find any corporate address for Libertad in San Diego. The boxes are delivered to a warehouse address there."

"What the hell? What's in the shipments?"

"Don't know. The next shipments are slated for Tuesday. They're headed up north to Ohio and Illinois."

"Who are the shipments addressed to up north?"

"Same company. Cavanaugh Industries."

I carefully studied the documents Rudy spread across my desk and zeroed in on the recent shipment addressed to Libertad in San Diego. Could this be the drugs or guns Gallagher had referenced in the memo from the police station? Was Jonathan hiding drugs or guns in Houghton trucks and shipping them to Libertad?

"I agree with you. This looks suspicious. Let's get Hardy and his team involved. Have them run down these addresses up north. Then, let's intercept those shipments up to Ohio and Illinois on Tuesday."

Anita walked into the office. "Ellice, I'm sorry to interrupt." She looked like someone had died. I assumed she was going to ask me for permission to go home early or something.

"What is it?"

"Can we go into your conference room?"

"Can it wait?" I asked.

She shook her head. "I don't think so."

Rudy and I looked at each other. Butterflies tangled in my stomach. The three of us walked into the adjoining conference room. Anita clicked the remote for the flat-screen television on the wall and turned to WSB-TV.

"What's going on?" I asked. Anita hit the volume control as the serious-looking brunette rattled on about the protesters in front of Houghton and their increase in numbers over the past few days. I froze when I read the tag line below the anchor:

BREAKING NEWS: POLICE QUESTION HOUGHTON EXECUTIVE IN THE MURDER OF TWO ATLANTA ATTORNEYS

I stood in front of the television, like a petrified deer staring into the barrel of a hunter's rifle, staring at the words beneath the woman and hoping they would melt away. I had tried to will this entire nightmare away, but it just kept getting worse.

"Ellice, they mentioned your name. What's going on?" Anita asked softly.

Rudy walked past Anita and stood beside me. "Ell, what's going on? Anita told me you showed up earlier this week with a bruise on your face. She said the police called about *your brother*? I didn't even know you had a brother." Rudy placed his hand on my shoulder. "Just tell me what's going on. Let me help. I told you Kelly's brother is a police officer. I can see if he knows anything."

"I'm sorry. I have to go." I bolted from the conference room, grabbed my coat and purse, and headed straight for my car.

I drove toward the entrance of my condo building. Sitting out front, in the semicircle drive, was a WSB-TV news truck. *Oh God.* They had already found out where I lived. Now they were circling me, like lions creeping and shifting into position on slow young prey. I drove past the front of the building, turned at the next corner, and entered the building through the service entrance.

I felt like I was falling into Dante's ninth circle of hell. My lattice-work of lies and pretense was starting to crumble around me. I was always so sure of myself, so convinced that I could do everything by myself. Because I always had. Now, I sat in my car, scared and alone. I pulled out my cell phone and dialed the one person who wouldn't judge me.

"Grace, it's me. I'm in trouble."

CHAPTER 33

Inside my house, I felt safe. I couldn't see the news trucks from the vantage point of my condo, so I pretended they weren't there. I undressed and headed straight for the shower. I had this overwhelming need to bathe and wash away the hard crust of lies and guilt. And as if on cue, sepia-brown memories of Chillicothe crept back in — the heavy pungent smell of Dutch Masters cigars, a broken casserole dish, a gray plastic tarp. The hot water could wash my body, but it couldn't cleanse my soul.

Dressed in a pair of sweats and a T-shirt, I was back at the kitchen table. I opened my laptop and pulled up the search engine. If I was going to figure my way out of this mess, I needed to know how bad it was first. I typed in the home page for WSB-TV. The website carried a few paragraphs detailing Michael's murder and describing me as the recently promoted chief legal officer and my being questioned about the deaths of Michael Sayles and Geoffrey Gallagher. And there at the end of the article, it mentioned that *my brother* was found dead with Gallagher; the police were investigating a link between the three deaths. The way the article was written, people would either feel sorry for me or be convinced that I had killed all three of them.

The article didn't carry a picture of me or a statement from Houghton. I searched inside CNN's website. No mention of me and nothing about Houghton since the day Michael was killed. I surmised either the national media outlets hadn't picked up the story or they were sitting on it until there was some bigger development. Maybe if things remained quiet, the story might have a twenty-four-hour cycle at best.

I grabbed a sleeve of Oreos from the pantry. I mowed through half of them as I jumped between the news article on the computer screen, the Tri-County Outfitters flyer from Michael's duffel bag, and the Brethren manifesto on the thumb drive. All of it was coming together, like a marching band on a football field, all the band members walking into place, the people fitting neatly together to form a bigger picture. Houghton was a bunch of racist bigots who had killed three innocent people and set me up to take the fall.

From what I could piece together, Michael discovered Jonathan was laundering money and brought in Gallagher, a white-collar defense lawyer. Michael also found out about the Brethren after Max invited him to join. He threatened to go to the authorities. Why didn't he tell me all this? But then how could he tell his Black mistress that his white executive colleagues wanted to cleanse the country of "impure races"? *Did Jonathan kill Michael to keep him quiet about the money laundering or did Max kill him to keep him quiet about the Brethren?*

And still, the question that obsessed me: Which one of them killed Sam?

My doorbell rang. I opened it and Grace stood in front of me in a navy-blue suit and Burberry trench coat. Her long ponytail was wrapped in a neat little bun at the back of her head.

"Girl, I got here as fast as I could," she said. "Who do I need to fight?"

I leaned into her petite frame and hugged her. "You're dressed up. What's going on?"

"Job interview. Don't tell Jarrett." Her husband was in an uphill battle to keep her as the stay-at-home, doting arm candy to an ex-basketball player. "Enough about me.

What's going on? You said you were in trouble."

I gave her a weak smile and closed the door. "Have you heard the news?"

"No, why? Is it something to do with your boss's murder?"

I didn't answer. I walked back through the living room into the kitchen and Grace followed me. I slid the laptop toward her. She eased into a chair and began reading the news article. When she finished, she stared up at me with her mouth agape.

"Close your mouth before something flies in there," I told her flatly.

Grace swallowed hard. "Ell, the police think you had something to do with the murders. The hell?"

"Grace, I didn't kill them."

"I know you didn't, but why do the police think you did?"

"Let me take your coat." Grace eased out of her coat and I walked it back to the foyer. I took my time hanging it in the closet, trying to figure out what to tell her or *how much* to tell her. When I got back to the kitchen, she looked up at me with sad pitiful eyes.

"Ell, why didn't you ever tell me you had a brother?"

Okay, so I would have to start with Sam. I

never imagined telling the truth, after so many years of lying, could be so hard. Although with Sam, it was more like lying by omission. And telling her that she should believe me now because I was in trouble seemed like the start of an arduous journey that might leave our friendship in tatters. But I slipped into the chair beside Grace.

"I know I should have told you. I guess it was easier to not talk about him, to keep him under wraps, than to tell everyone how often I was bailing him out of jail or paying off his bookies to keep him alive. He had really poor judgment and made some stupid decisions."

"Haven't we all?" Grace said.

I wasn't quite sure what that meant, but I suspect it had something to do with her and Jarrett's marriage.

"Anyway, Sam . . . my brother . . . got involved with the CFO at my company. The CFO has threatened to expose some stuff from my past. I think he set me up to take the fall for these murders."

"Wait, I don't understand. What is he threatening to expose?"

I bit my bottom lip and gazed at my red painted toenails. "Some stuff happened . . . a long time ago in Chillicothe. It's a really small town in east Georgia where I grew up. I did some stuff that I'm not proud of. Things this man could use against me. I could lose my license to practice law. He hired a firm to put together a dossier on me and now he's threatening to go to the police if I don't go along with some illegal stuff he's doing at the company."

"Oh, Ellice, I'm so sorry." Grace hugged me. "I'm not gonna press you. Just tell me what you need me to do. How can I help?"

"That's just it. I don't know if anybody can help me at this point."

"Okay, so what did your lawyer think about the police questioning?"

I shook my head. "I don't have an attorney."

"What do you mean you don't have an attorney? You spoke to the police without having an attorney present?"

"I know, it was stupid. They said they had a few questions, that I could come in and help them clear things up regarding my brother's killer. I was just so desperate for answers. It was only after they started questioning me that I realized who they suspected."

"So what did you tell them?"

I scarfed down another Oreo cookie and shrugged. "The truth for a change. But they seem to have some crazy theory that I put my brother up to killing Michael and an attorney he was working with so that I could become the general counsel. Then I killed my brother when he didn't want to cooperate or something. It's all lunacy."

"Okay, we need to get you lawyered up. We can take care of that —"

"Um . . . Grace, it's pretty bad. You know when you asked me about my boss? You asked whether I was sleeping with him?"

"Yes."

I didn't respond. I just stared back at my feet.

"Girl, I knew you were sleeping with him. But how does that factor into all this?"

I gave a long deep sigh. "Because I discovered his body the day he was murdered, and I didn't call the police."

Grace stared at me for a beat before she patted my hands. "It's gonna be okay. Let's just figure out a way to get you out of this mess." Grace shook her head. I think she was starting to see what a dumpster fire my life really was. "Girl, I always knew you were an overachiever, even when you step in a pile of it, huh?"

We laughed and it took the edge off.

"So, this Jonathan guy, what's his deal?"

"Jonathan Everett. He has a freaking dossier on me. He tracked down my brother and hired him to trail the lawyer that was found dead with my brother."

She removed her suit jacket and slung it across the back of the chair, like she was about to get down to work. "Okay, we have to fight fire with a flood. You got any dirt on this Jonathan guy?"

"He's laundering dirty money for a company in Mexico. They're into all sorts of illegal stuff — drugs, human trafficking, and gun running — and Jonathan was the one who set up the scheme inside the company."

"Drugs? Guns? Damn, girl! When we get you out of this mess, I'm going to write a book about it!"

I smiled. Grace was doing what any good friend would do. She was trying to keep me from falling into a bottomless hole of despair over how bad things were. But she would need to be more than Chuckles the Clown to help me see my way out of this mess.

"Grace, it gets worse."

"Please don't tell me that." Grace leaned back in her chair and placed her palms flat on the table, like she was steadying herself. "It can't get worse."

I leaned over to the laptop, clicked a couple times, and pulled up the Brethren manifesto. I slid the computer back to face her. I picked up another Oreo and ate the entire cookie, no bites. I watched her read it, her mouth open, her eyes widened in shock. She finished and stared up at me with a look of horror, like she'd just discovered a badly decomposed body.

I handed her the gun shop flyer. "What's this?" she asked.

"Michael left this in a duffel bag here a few nights ago. I just thought it was the place where he bought a gun when we all thought he committed suicide. But I think it's part of the gunrunning the company is involved in. The CEO has Alzheimer's, and I think Max and Jonathan have run amok. The two of them are behind all this."

"Who's Max?"

"Maxwell Lumpkin. He heads up Operations. Max was trying to recruit Michael to join the Brethren. I think Max made arrangements to ship the guns on the company's trucks to the Libertad company, the criminals down in Mexico. A month ago, they started shipping guns south of the border. And by the way, Max also threatened me."

Grace tilted her head and folded her arms. "Let me get this straight. You work with a group of white supremacists who are involved in money laundering and all manner of criminal activity. And they promoted a Black woman to join their executive ranks. And one of them even threatened you. And they promoted you because . . . ? I would think they wouldn't even want to sit in the same room with you."

"They promoted me because they could prop me up as the figurehead Black employee to the protesters and the people suing Houghton for race discrimination. With that dossier, I guess they thought my secrets were bad enough to blackmail me into going along with all the criminal crap they're doing."

"Ell, how are you still working in this place?"

"What do you mean?"

"You refuse to spend your money where you're not valued. You've told me before that there are hardly any other Black people or people of color who work at that company. There are Black protesters in front of the building every day. Why do you work at a place that doesn't value what you value? A company that doesn't value *you*!"

"Because I need a job. I have bills to pay. I don't have a wealthy husband and an invitation-only Black American Express Card."

"I know you need a job. But you don't

need this one."

I leaned forward on the kitchen table and rubbed my temples. Grace was right. Years ago, I used to worry about where my next meal would come from. Even after graduating from law school, I still harbored quiet, back-of-the-brain fears that I was just a stone's throw away from the poverty of Chillicothe. Now I was collecting a huge paycheck from a company where people despised me and were responsible for my brother's death. How did I get here? How many pieces of myself had I tossed away on my climb for corporate career success?

"You are working with some extremely dangerous people, Ellice. A dangerous group of lunatics. You can't continue to work for these people. You have to get out of that place."

"I know. I plan to resign tomorrow."

"*Thank you!* Now in the meantime, you have to tell the police what's going on and give them this stuff."

"They don't believe me. Jonathan convinced them I'm lying. And it didn't help my case after the police realized I lied about my brother and about being in Michael's office the day he died."

"They'll believe you after you give them

this stuff."

"Let's hope so."

CHAPTER 34

The next morning, I strutted inside the lobby of Houghton Transportation Company. I would be done with this hellhole and the ignorant bigots that inhabited it in less than an hour. My hair was a large, luscious coily mane encircling my head and I wore my best navy-blue power suit. It was incredible what a fresh twistout and a quality power suit can do for your confidence.

From the moment I stepped inside the building, it was apparent the Houghton clan was turning on one of their own. Everyone watched the news just like Anita did and everyone had decided I was the she-beast killer of Houghton Transportation. When I stepped into the lobby, Jimmy, the guard, stood at the security desk. His face went loose with shock, as if I had just stepped up to the urinal beside him in the men's room. I rode up the elevator with two lawyers from the Legal Department. Both mumbled,

"Good morning," but none of the usual ingratiating ass-kissing comments about how hard they were working lately. The homely-looking guy even raised his eyebrows at the female lawyer as they stepped off the elevator on Eighteen.

I arrived at my office and spoke to Anita. She gave me a sympathetic smile before I closed my office door. It had been less than ten days since I'd discovered, *and left,* Michael's lifeless body in this office. I stood at the window, watching a light dusting of snow fall across the park below. Everything about my life now seemed unreal. It was like walking around in someone else's life, sitting in someone else's office, and facing someone else's future. I'd already left a message with a local headhunter, well known for placing executive talent. I could easily find another position with a company that respected me and valued what I value — human life and decency.

My landline rang, startling me. My body was in the office, but my mind was light-years away. At last, I was beginning to see daylight at the end of this harrowing tunnel. "Hey, it's Sarah. Nate's ready to see you."

"Tell him I'll be right there."

I fully expected Willow to be in Nate's office with him. Fine. She could babysit Nate during my resignation the same way she did during my promotion. I calmly reached into the top desk drawer and pulled out a blue folder. Inside, a single sheet of paper. My resignation letter. For whatever reason, Michael decided to stick his resignation letter in a safe-deposit box instead of Nate's hands. But I wouldn't follow in Michael's footsteps or suffer the same fate.

The walk down the hall to Nate's office was like a death march to the execution chamber, a series of humiliating steps toward the demise of my corporate legal career. Not even a full two weeks as general counsel and here I was resigning in the midst of a police investigation.

At least I was leaving on my own terms.

Sarah was away from her desk by the time I reached Nate's office. His door stood open, but I tapped lightly anyway.

"Come in and shut the door behind you," Nate commanded.

I stepped inside. Just as I thought, Nate was not alone. But it wasn't Willow. Sitting in the chair across from Nate was *Jonathan*. I felt a small ping of trepidation. Jonathan sat in one of Nate's guest chairs, legs crossed, wearing a pin-striped suit and the smug demeanor of a pompous jerk. He slid a thumb and forefinger along the crease of his pants. "Good morning, Ellice," he said. "Did you do something different with your hair?"

Asshole.

Nate nodded toward the chair beside Jonathan. I chose to stand. "Ellice, Jonathan tells me you've been too busy to meet with him about the Libertad matter. Something about not preparing some paperwork." Jonathan had left two messages for me yesterday, telling me I needed to draft some contracts for him. I ignored both messages.

"I have some very serious concerns about this deal." I was talking to Nate, but I stared at Jonathan. "I believe Libertad is involved in laundering dirty money. That's a violation of federal law. As a lawyer, I can't ethically stand behind whatever deal you may be planning with Libertad."

"I see." Nate gave me a long unblinking stare. Jonathan didn't say a word.

I thumbed the side of the folder. "Nate, I know that having me on your team . . . that the circumstances of my brother's death . . . are . . . it can send the wrong message. The focus should be on running Houghton, not my personal problems. I'm resigning. I don't want to bring any unnecessary attention to the company. Here's my resignation." I removed the paper and slid it across

Nate's desk.

Nate never looked at the paper; instead, he looked at Jonathan, then back at me with a sad plea in his eyes. "I'd rather you didn't. Darlin', that's not what this is about."

For a moment, I assumed he would try to convince me to stay on board. "I appreciate the support, Nate, but I think it's best that I leave the company. I need some time to sort —"

"I'm sorry, but *no.* You can't resign." His voice was firm, but not harsh. This went beyond a supportive gesture. He was *ordering* me not to resign; I didn't have a say in the matter. This would *not* be a repeat of my promotion to the executive suite. I was free to leave if I wanted.

"What do you mean I *can't* resign?"

Nate stared back at me in confusion, then turned to Jonathan, eyes pleading again. He'd gotten himself lost in the conversation and was looking to Jonathan to rescue him. Nate needed medical attention, not corporate babysitters.

"What Nate is trying to say is that we need a top lawyer in place. And right now, that's you. There's a lot going on. So you need to go back to your office and draft several documents. We need an agreement that outlines —"

"You don't get it, do you, Jonathan?" I turned to Nate, hoping to make a direct plea. "Nate, I'm sorry. I can't do that. I would be complicit in illegal activity. I could get disbarred. All of us — me, you, and Jonathan — could go to jail. I can't do that. So you really need to accept my resignation." I pushed the paper a bit closer toward Nate. I glared at Jonathan, his expression still smug and confident.

Nate leaned forward and scratched his head.

Jonathan looked down at his Rolex, then piped up. "Take a seat, Ellice. You might want to hear us out for a minute."

"I'm done here! You two can go to jail without me." I headed for the door.

Jonathan cleared his throat before he spoke. "I was just telling Nate, there've been some developments in Sayles's murder investigation. I understand the police have questioned you a couple of times about Sayles's murder. They seem to think you might be involved in this thing with your brother and that other lawyer they found dead. What's his name . . . Gallagher?"

I stopped and turned around. Tendrils of fear slithered through me.

Nate chimed in. "I know you couldn't have done these heinous things. Jonathan tells me you may go to prison for murder?"

"Nate, I had nothing to do with any of this." I marched back toward Jonathan. "You did this! You set me up."

Jonathan gave me a sly smile and threw his hands up in a gesture of surrender. It was when I looked at his raised hands that I saw it. The small little symbol of hate in the form of a lapel pin. The Brethren lapel pin. "Ellice, think about it. Losing your law license is going to be the least of your worries if this thing plays out the way the police have it down. Right now, your best option is to work with me on this."

"And if I don't?" A line of sweat trickled down the center of my back.

"Hmm . . . that wouldn't be in your best interest. We talked about this before. My friends down in Savannah have given me a fulsome report. I don't think it would bode well for you if details from that report were to land in the hands of the police or the media." I watched an ugly grin slick across Jonathan's face.

My eyes darted between the two men. I could feel a small, slow throb nibble at my left temple, my chest rising and falling with the mounting anxiety that Jonathan's statement elicited. I wanted to bolt from this office, from this building, to run as fast and as far as I could from anything having to do with Houghton Transportation.

"So what exactly happened out there in . . . Chillicothe, is it?" Jonathan asked.

I blinked a few times, willing myself not to cry in this office. I turned to Nate.

He gave me a sympathetic smile. "Jonathan thinks this is best for the company."

"So why didn't you go to jail back then?" Jonathan prodded with a crooked smile. "That hobgoblin band of thugs and misfits you call a family manage to save you? Or maybe that lady — Violet Richards . . . I mean Vera Henderson. Did she help you cover things up? Tough childhood, huh?"

I wanted to lunge over and throttle Jonathan with my bare hands. "Keep her name out of your mouth."

"I think she's had some legal troubles of her own. How's she doin' these days?" Jonathan winked. "Now do you really think the Atlanta police will be as gullible as some small-town redneck sheriff after they find out about the things that happened in Chillicothe?"

My knees buckled.

"I'll bet the Disciplinary Committee of the State Bar of Georgia will want to launch an investigation too. Between the police, the state bar, and the media, you'll be up to your ass in investigations. You'll never practice law again — in Georgia or anywhere else," Jonathan declared.

My intricate scaffold of deception and false persona was now falling into so many pieces around me. Everything was falling apart. I glared at Nate. "Like I said, Jonathan thinks this is best for the company," Nate said weakly. "You don't have to go to jail. No one does if we just work this thing out the way Jonathan says." Nate gave me a fragile little smile. "You're a part of the Houghton family now. We take care of each other. We just need ya help."

Jonathan's little plan was on the spectrum of genius: pluck the loner attorney from the Legal Department to replace the murdered general counsel, dig up all her dirty little secrets, and use them to keep her in line while the company engaged in a panoply of corporate fraud and criminal activity. Absolute genius.

Jonathan slid my resignation letter back across Nate's desk to me. "You're pretty smart. Michael's hiring you was probably the best thing he's ever done for this company. You don't know this, but we have some friends in very high places. You stick with us and I'll bet we can pull the police off your coattail." He grinned as he adjusted the wristband of his Rolex.

Nate stared out the window, either too much of a coward or too cognitively incapacitated to understand the full picture of what Jonathan was doing. I couldn't tell which and it didn't matter anyway.

I lifted the paper. The tightly written paragraph lauding the opportunity to work and grow with such a dynamic company. My neatly curled signature. Just an hour ago, this piece of paper represented my escape from this whole hellish nightmare. I placed it back into the folder. And for the first time since I'd left Chillicothe, I felt like a shackled animal without the ability to run.

"Thanks, Ellice," Jonathan beamed.

I headed to the door, resignation in hand. Thankfully, I managed to make it out of the office just before the first hot tear rolled down my cheek.

CHAPTER 35

I hustled back to my office and told Anita I had an outside appointment. I grabbed my coat and bag and I pulled out of Houghton's garage, driving aimlessly through the streets of Atlanta trying to figure out how to put my life back together. All I'd ever wanted to be was a lawyer, ever since those Christmas and summer breaks I spent at Uncle B's house, listening to his stories of helping to bring order and civility to the world through the law. And now the thought of never working as a lawyer was looming large. But I could never work for those racists at Houghton, people who'd killed my brother. And I'd probably never work anywhere else if Jonathan carried through with his threats.

I wove my way through the streets of downtown Atlanta and somehow wound up on Auburn Avenue. "Sweet Auburn" as it is affectionately called. At one time, this street was the economic, social justice, and religious spine of the Black community in Atlanta. Historical landmarks of the civil rights movement still towered along the street. Places like Ebenezer Baptist Church, where Dr. Martin Luther King Jr. preached. A 1960s-era storefront that housed the Southern Christian Leadership Conference, and, right around the corner, a six-stories-tall mural of civil rights icon John Lewis, all looming in the shadow of Atlanta's gleaming skyline. How darkly fitting I should drive down this street on this particular day, the same day I ran from a couple of racist bigots who threatened to destroy me.

I pulled into a Texaco station. As I pumped gas into my car, I remembered Grace's advice to give the police the things I found in Max's office and Michael's duffel bag. I should have gone to the police sooner instead of trying to protect Sam. As it all worked out, I hadn't protected him at all. My stupidity caused his death. I topped off the tank, then quickly climbed back inside the car. The sky was heavy with the threat of snow, as the weatherman had predicted. I pulled out of the gas station and headed straight for the police station.

A few minutes later, my cell phone rang: Rudy. I thought about not answering but I did anyway.

"Look, Rudy, this isn't a good time."

"Anita told me you left the office. We didn't finish talking yesterday."

"I'm headed to the police station. We can talk after I'm done."

"That's what I wanted to talk to you about. Maybe we should talk before you go there. Let's talk in person. You know where to meet me."

By the time I arrived at the playground in Piedmont Park, Rudy had staked out a bench. The temperature was barely above freezing now and largely accounted for the near empty playground. With the exception of the occasional beast runner, all of Piedmont Park was empty too.

"Aren't you cold? Where's your coat?" I asked.

Rudy cast a serious look at me before he tugged at his ear and stared back across the empty playground. Rudy always tugged at his ear when he was nervous. Something else was wrong. "C'mon, Rudy, what's up?"

He leaned forward, elbows on his knees, staring into the playground. I could tell he was hesitant to speak at first. "You know I told you Kelly's brother is a police officer? He told me something."

431

"Yeah, okay."

"I . . . he didn't want to tell me at first but —" Rudy looked at me, full of fear and sympathy.

"Wha-what is it?"

"Ellice, the police are going to issue a warrant for your arrest. I thought you should know before you go." He lowered his voice. "You know, in case you need to take an attorney with you."

I stared at Rudy, trying to grasp the words. *A warrant. Your arrest.*

Hearing my name associated with a criminal process was like an out-of-body experience. It was as if Rudy were gossiping to me about someone else we both knew. Ever since I'd left the police station, I knew I was being framed, but Rudy's words somehow made it real.

"It's time to come clean with the police," Rudy concluded.

Rudy sounded like Detective Bradford. "Arrest me for what?"

"Murder . . . your brother."

"What?! That makes absolutely no sense. Rudy, I didn't kill my brother. What are they thinking?"

"I don't know, but you have about twenty-four hours to convince them otherwise. My brother-in-law said something about your brother walking around Houghton before Michael was killed. Ell, I've known you for years. Until a few days ago, I didn't even know you *had* a brother."

I didn't know what to say, so I didn't say anything. Between Grace and Rudy, I'd told so many lies that my friendship with them might not survive.

Rudy tugged at his ear again and looked away from me.

"What is it, Rudy?"

His voice was quiet, solemn. "My brother-in-law . . . he told me something else. Something about you and Michael."

I stiffened. The lump in my throat was a rock. I just stared at Rudy. This could not be happening. I tried so hard to be so much — the consummate professional, upstanding attorney, the "good one" — and now it had come to this. One of the few close friends I had thought I was a liar and a whore. Why wouldn't he make the next logical leap and believe I was a murderer, too? My world was slowly falling apart. The successful, well-crafted lie that used to be my life was now sitting in shambles around my feet. I thought about the Brethren and the Littlejohn dossier. Then, I thought about Sam. Why did they have to kill him? Sam's murder was the one link in this horrific chain of events that I could not figure out.

"I saw you there, in the office early that morning. The morning Michael was killed. You have a brother nobody knows about, you show up at work with a black eye, and now this? Ell, why are you all caught up in this thing?"

I jumped up from the bench. "I gotta go."

"Ell! Ell!" Rudy called behind me. I never looked back.

I might be arrested and charged with murder, and this time, I didn't do it.

CHAPTER 36

Large fluffy snowflakes hit my windshield then melted before the wipers swooped across the glass and erased their watery residue. The swish-swish sound was like a mechanical lullaby as I mentally compiled a checklist of all the ways I'd been so stupid and naïve. Sam was dead and it was largely my fault. I should have trusted my instincts, my God sense, and never accepted the promotion to the executive suite. And now there was no way in hell I'd stay at Houghton and continue to work with the same people who killed Sam and threatened Vera. But if I left, they'd ruin my career. I'd never work as a lawyer in Atlanta or anywhere else. And even if I didn't leave the company, I might be arrested depending on whether the Brethren reached the top of the Atlanta Police Department. If I were arrested, who would care for Vera? I was all she had.

Thinking of Vera made me think of Sam.

Of course, it was hard not to. I'd been crying off and on ever since the police showed up at my door. Every time I thought about our last conversation at his house, it broke my heart. His talk of being tired of Atlanta and moving back to Chillicothe prompted me to honor his last wishes of sorts by having his services there. Besides, funeral services for Sam back in Atlanta might stir up the media or, worse, make Rudy and Grace feel compelled to attend. I could hardly afford to add pity to the already heavy baggage I dragged around with me. I'd only been back to Chillicothe a handful of times since I left for boarding school. The last time was to move Vera to Atlanta and the time before that was to attend Martha's funeral.

Another wave of sadness engulfed me as I cruised into Chillicothe, Georgia. Things had changed since the last time I'd been here, nearly two years ago. The main strip was still anchored by the Tolliver County Courthouse on one end of Church Street and the VFW Hall at the other end. But in between them, little shops and cafés had sprung up, replacing the old country diners and dilapidated storefronts. And the hallmark of civilized convenience — a spanking brand-new Starbucks. The Piggly Wiggly, with a storefront refresh, still stood across from the VFW Hall, but the Greyhound bus now picked up and dropped off passengers at a small station a quarter mile past the grocery store. It was as if someone had given the town elders permission to dust off the grime of Chillicothe's past and join everyone else in the twenty-first century.

Still standing just beyond the VFW Hall were the remnants of an old abandoned gazebo, a seventy-five-year-old fixture in the middle of Chillicothe's Town Circle. The southern bars and stars of the Confederate flag had hung alongside the American flag from the gazebo arch until 1998 when a young Black woman, driving through town, spotted the flag. Witnesses say she pulled it down from the gazebo, set it on fire, and got back in her car yelling, "That's what I think of your fucking white heritage!" No one knew who she was, and the Confederate flag was never replaced.

I rounded the circle, past the gazebo, before turning onto Pulliam Avenue, a narrow cobblestone street dotted with modest frame houses. I parked my car in front of the blue three-story Victorian house perched neatly behind a short black iron fence. The black-and-white sign in the yard read GRESHAM & SONS MORTUARY. For as small as the town was, Chillicothe had two funeral homes — one for white people and one for Black people. One of the last vestiges of the segregated South. Gresham & Sons handled all the Black funerals in town.

The solitude inside the funeral home was deafening. The heavy scent of floral sprays made me feel both calm and queasy. It creeped me out to stand in this building, ghoulishly filled with lifeless bodies. But Vera used to say, *Don't waste your time worrying about dead folks; it's the crazy-ass living ones you need to worry about.* I waited patiently, reading the plaques above the various viewing rooms off the foyer. The Slumber Room, the Rest Well Sanctuary, the Heavenly View Chapel, and the Cherubs Corner.

"Ms. Littlejohn?" A petite Black woman in her seventies wearing a conservative blue suit and sensible shoes extended her right hand. "I'm Lila Gresham. I'm very sorry for your loss. I'll be assisting you with the arrangements for your brother."

"Thank you."

"Why don't we go in here." I followed Mrs. Gresham to a room with the misnomer "The Comfort Suite," like someone could ever be comfortable in a funeral home. Surprisingly, the room was pleasant enough with its large windows, a smattering of soft upholstered love seats angled about, and a respectable-looking desk in the corner. Still, the pleasant surroundings and the flood of sunlight could not erase the cool feel of death that permeated the building.

Mrs. Gresham directed me to a love seat. She sat beside me with her efficient-looking clipboard and papers resting in her lap. "We received your brother's remains this morning. I know this is a difficult time, but have you decided on the type of arrangements you'd like to have for your brother?"

I hadn't really. Who would I invite to his funeral? Besides Juice, I knew absolutely none of Sam's friends. We had no blood relatives left. And I would cut off my own arm before even thinking about bringing Vera out here for his funeral. Then I thought, *What would Sam want?*

"Nothing extravagant." I said. "Just a plain coffin, one simple floral spray, and a private cemetery service."

I drove back through the town and cruised to a red light, crying and lost in my head. I had screwed up Sam's life by always leaving him when he needed me the most. For all the years between us, I had never learned to allay my guilt over being the beneficiary of

439

life's good fortune when Sam was not. And always niggling in the back of my brain was the unforgivable thought that I had set all this in motion decades ago with my own plans.

Suddenly, the truck driver behind me blasted his horn. I jumped. The light was green. Rattled by the loud sound, I sped off, making a sharp turn onto Periwinkle Lane, the street where we lived before moving in with Willie Jay Groover. The street was littered with the same cornucopia of dilapidated shotgun houses. I was surprised they were still standing. The front yards were full of trucks and cars in some sort of disrepair, road-worn tires and other remnants left behind by shade tree mechanics. Unkempt little kids happily played in dirt and mud that should have been grass. One porch held an old lumpy sofa that doubled as outdoor seating, yellow foam stuffing sprouting from its cushions.

I stopped the car in front of a single-story shotgun house near the end of Periwinkle Lane, the windows now boarded up with wood planks and painted over with fading hues of red and black graffiti. Looking at this house was like looking into the cracked mirror of my psyche. There weren't enough $2,000 dresses or Bernhardt linen office chairs in the world to erase where I came from. But driving through this town, I caught a glimpse of what I'd forgotten since entering the executive suite. I realized who I really was. *I was a fighter.* Black girls — big-boned and thick-skinned — fight all the time. We fight to be heard, to be recognized, to stay alive. We fight even when we don't know we're fighting. And now, despite all the labels society tried to place on me, I knew I wasn't an *angry* Black woman. I was a *fighting* Black woman and I'd trained hard right here in this town.

I shook myself from the memory and drove off. A few minutes later, I was driving along the outskirts of town, finally pulling onto Red Creek Road. Not much had changed on this street either since the days when Martha, Sam, and I lived in Willie Jay's house. The same squat ranch houses dotted the street, weathering the changes in seasons and occupants, every house the same as when I'd left back in August 1979. All but one. Willie Jay's house was gone.

The view from the street where Willie Jay's house stood stretched clear across to the river swamp that ran behind it. After his disappearance, Martha discovered he didn't own the house. In fact, Sheriff Coogler did. He kicked Martha out and she was back to living off the generosity of friends around town. Coogler eventually died of a heart attack and the house was torn down for whatever reason. And I wasn't mad about that, either. That house of horrors was gone along with all the gruesome memories it held. People in town eventually forgot about Willie Jay Groover and Martha Littlejohn and her two bastard kids.

A few minutes later, I drove up the gravel path leading to Vera's farmhouse. I hadn't been to this house since I moved Vera out of it two years before. The dull patina of time and weather covered the entire structure. Everything about the house was dismal and gray. The roof, the faded yellow clapboards, the bare pecan trees that framed it — all of it, gray. Back in the 1960s and 1970s, Vera's house had been a lifesaving way station for a lot of women in Chillicothe and neighboring towns, too. Vera considered herself a public servant of sorts. She used to say she gave women something men would never give them: control.

I stepped out of the car and could almost hear Aretha Franklin's powerhouse vocals spelling out the letters to "Respect" from the radio Vera used to keep on the open windowsill at the front of the house. The smell of collard greens and pound cakes would float outside from the kitchen, Vera's friends like Miss Toney and Bankrobber and her cousin Birdie all sitting on the porch laughing and chatting as most people do when times are good. Bankrobber, whose real name was Roscoe Wilkins, was rumored to have actually robbed a bank somewhere up north and his relatives sent him south to hide out for a while. Bankrobber used to tell stories about all the money he'd stashed in various spots around the city of Chicago. He made promises to buy Miss Toney a candy-apple-red Cadillac and threatened to slather Birdie in so much Chanel No. 5 perfume that he'd be forced to marry her because she smelled so good — all those promises, when he spent the better part of the day bumming cigarettes or waiting on someone to invite him in and offer him what generally became his only meal of the day.

Sometimes, when their conversations turned serious, Vera would shoo Sam and me away. Sam would get distracted by one thing or another. But me, I'd always sneak back along the side of the house and eavesdrop. The adults talked in low voices about how nothing good ever came out of Chillicothe. How this town sucked the life out of Black folks and anyone who missed the opportunity to escape was doomed to die here the same way they lived here: poor and miserable. And Vera always talked about "saving the babies." She said she'd spend the rest of her life saving little babies, even if that meant preventing them from coming into a waiting world full of abuse and people who didn't want them or, worse, wouldn't love them.

Miss Toney and Birdie were dead now. Bankrobber, too, having never returned North.

And now, everything was quiet. Gray.

Chillicothe, Georgia, June 1979

Martha and I stepped inside Vera's big yellow farmhouse. To me, she was like a golden-colored angel. A beacon in a dark sea of neglect and abuse, and I swam to her as if my life depended on it. She stared at me without saying a word. Ever since Martha discovered an inventory overage of sanitary napkins in the bathroom, she and Willie Jay argued about what to do about my *situation*. Willie Jay, being the force to reckon with, overruled Martha's plan that I should have the baby and sent us both to Vera's. I wondered whether Martha knew why Willie Jay would be so concerned about *my* future or if he confessed his fear of my bringing a child into the world whose skin tone would point an accusatory finger announcing to the world that he was a monstrous pedophile.

After a moment, Vera ambled over to the

door and pulled me into a warm soft hug. I think I must have cried for five minutes straight and Vera never let go.

"She's young, Martha. Why you let this happen?" Vera asked as she pulled out of the hug.

Martha stood mute, wringing her hands.

"You'll be fine, sugar," Vera said to me.

I stared at the cracks between the boards of the dull hardwood floor, full of shame and fear. Vera shook her head as she stomped into the kitchen and returned a few minutes later with a cup of tea. She handed it to me. "Drink this. All of it."

I winced at the first sip, a heavy mint taste that faded into a strong burning sensation at the back of my tongue and crept down my throat, stinging my nose and ears in the process. I'd never tasted liquor before but figured Vera had placed some into my tea. I couldn't understand how Martha could drown herself in something so disgusting. Vera tapped the cup when I refused to drink more. I sipped the tea again. By the third sip, the burn eased, the taste was smoother, and I began to feel calmer. But my head felt like lead and any quick moves sent the room into a revolution.

"This might be a while, Martha. Why don't you go on home?" Vera said to my mother. "There's nothing for you to do here."

"No, I wanna stay."

"I can bring her on back home. You don't need to stay none," Vera said.

"No." Martha reached into the back pocket of her jeans. She pulled out a small wad of bills and handed them to Vera. "He told me I had to stay."

Vera shook her head again in disgust. "You know womenfolk gotta count for something on this earth 'cause we the ones responsible for bringing other people in the world. But it oughta be our decision when we wanna do so or who we wanna do it with." She shook her head and rolled her eyes at Martha. "You stay right here, and I don't want to hear a mumblin' word outta you."

By now, I was completely buzzed and rising higher with every sip of tea. Vera guided me to a back bedroom. I stumbled a bit before gaining my legs. The room swirled then stopped, then swirled again. I closed my eyes to quell a wave of nausea that washed over me.

I stepped inside the room and thought Vera had the biggest bed I'd ever seen in my life. The large ornately carved bed took up the bulk of the space in the room. A picture of a blond, blue-eyed Jesus hung above the headboard, next to a picture of Martin Luther King Jr. The bedside table held a small lamp, a well-worn bible, and a basket of brightly colored yarn with slim blue metallic knitting needles. I didn't know whether it was the tea or Vera's protective presence, but the room had a cozy soft glow that made me feel safe, like I had arrived at some sort of refuge. Vera's farmhouse was the closest thing to women's health care anyone could expect or afford in a poor rural town in east Georgia.

Vera eased me into a chair. She pulled a long folding table from under the bed, snapped open the legs, and stood the table upright at the foot of her bed. I watched her, my head lolling about like a large stone as she moved around the room, fussing with towels and covering the table in a yellow plastic tablecloth.

"Drink every lick of that tea, baby. It'll help things along."

I did, growing foggier with each sip, until the room became a swaying kaleidoscope of furniture and pictures. The room was filled with music coming from somewhere, distant and muffled.

"Will it hurt?" I whispered.

Vera stopped her preparations and stood in front of me.

"Yeah, baby, it'll hurt." She moved in closer. "It's gonna hurt a lot. But I can look at you and tell, you a strong girl. Real strong. Strong girls are brave girls. Always remember that. No matter what nobody tells you. So I'ma need you to be brave tonight, okay?" She gently rubbed my back. "Now I need you to slide your panties off."

Again, I did as she told me. Vera went back to the busyness of table preparations. The table complete, she carefully lifted my thin limp frame to a standing position and led me to the folding table. My legs felt like thin twigs and I grew scared all of a sudden that they would break. All I could think was that my legs would break, and I'd never be able to walk again. Ever. I wanted to run, but the same legs I feared would break wouldn't move now.

"Stay strong, baby. Remember what I told you. Be brave." Vera held me close before carefully laying me on top of the smooth hard table.

I heard the music again, garbled sounds of a song that I couldn't comprehend. The music was hypnotizing. My head spun as Vera gently bent my legs at the knees and spread them apart.

"My God . . ." she uttered softly as she rubbed her fingertips across the cigar burn scars on my thighs. "Lay real still, baby."

I strained to make out the tune of the song. It was something slow, a male group harmonizing words, something about love and rainbows. The song didn't make any sense. Everything seemed hazy, moving in slow motion. Vera carefully removed a slim blue metallic knitting needle from the basket of yarn. She wiped it gingerly with a washcloth before swirling it inside a bottle of alcohol. After, she swiped it through the air a few times like a conductor waving her baton. I turned my head toward the dresser. I found it. The source of the music — a wooden radio, the old-fashioned kind, with gold knobs and lines demarking the stations. The radio sat like a big brown guard in the center of the dresser, spilling music and lyrics of love. I focused everything I had inside of me on the huge gold knob — the perfect circle, the smooth, round orb.

I winced as Vera laid her hand against my thigh. I could feel the cool hard metal as she slid the pointed end of the knitting needle inside me. A few seconds later, a pain ripped intense and searing, like fire slashing through my body. I grabbed the sides of the table. The music grew faint as the pain ran hot and fast. The gold radio knob blurred through a rush of silent tears.

I didn't scream. Not a sound. Not a whimper. Vera told me I was strong and brave, and I believed her. But more than anything, I didn't scream because I was afraid Vera might stop and I would be forced to have a baby I didn't want by a man I hated.

Everything was over just a few minutes after it began. Vera helped me get cleaned up before she wrapped a heavy blue quilt with bright yellow daisies around my shoulders.

Before we left the bedroom, she took my hand. "Did Willie Jay do this to you?" Vera whispered. "Tell me the truth."

I nodded yes.

"Humph." She gently rubbed the cigar burn scar and squeezed my hand. "Okay, we'll take care of all that later. Don't you worry none. You go on home with your momma. I'll check on you tomorrow."

She kissed me on top of my head and wrapped me in another soft warm hug. We walked back to the living room where Martha sat on the sofa in the same spot we'd left her. She jumped to her feet as we entered the room.

"You okay, baby?" Martha asked, trying to sound upbeat. I couldn't even look at her.

The two women held me up, one on either side of me, as they piled me into Martha's beat-up '67 blue Mustang. The pain was excruciating when I tried to sit upright, so the two of them laid me across the back seat and Vera placed a blanket over me.

I didn't think I'd make the car ride back home. And it would have been okay with me if I didn't. I silently prayed for God to let me die. No one would care. Black girls go missing every single day and I could be one of them. Another young face full of promise that melts away with time and memory. No one would miss me and all the pain and heartache that crawled through me would vanish, too.

I didn't die. But something inside me did. I didn't speak for an entire week. It was like all the pain and nausea from that night washed over me, sealing my lips as well as my emotions. I tucked away that entire experience in my carpetbag of secrets. What Vera called "grave secrets." The kind I'd never share with another soul on Earth. What I didn't know was just how heavy my carpetbag of secrets would become.

I've heard some women say having a baby changes you. Not having one can change you, too.

■ ■ ■ ■

PART 3
THE FIGHT

■ ■ ■ ■

Chillicothe, Georgia, July 1979

I almost never hung out with the kids from school. Mostly because I was always too afraid they'd ask me something personal like why my mother drank all the time or why she married Willie Jay or what it was like to live with someone so mean.

But a group of girls from my grade were getting together one Saturday afternoon. One of them lived down the street from Willie Jay's house and she insisted I come over. They were going to "jam" and listen to records. I decided to go only because it was so hot outside, and I knew she had air conditioning in her house. I had planned to stay for an hour, then make up an excuse and leave. But somehow, while I was there, I was actually having a good time. We giggled and danced, and nobody asked me about Willie Jay or Martha. Nobody made me feel bad for not wearing Gloria Vanderbilt jeans or the latest Reeboks. Before I knew it, I'd spent nearly the entire afternoon there. When I realized it, I raced back to Willie Jay's house to make sure Martha and Sam were okay.

Willie Jay's car was nowhere in sight and I was glad. I stepped inside the hot, empty house and called out for Sam. No answer. Maybe he was out playing with some of the neighborhood kids. I went to the kitchen to make myself a jelly sandwich and noticed Martha sitting on the back-porch steps, rocking back and forth and staring off. I watched her from the back door for a moment. Maybe she had been drinking again and her demons were back.

"Martha?" She didn't answer me.

I slipped out the screen door and back into the brutal heat. As I walked up beside her, I saw tears rolling down her face and the ugly remnant of Willie Jay's anger, a purple-red knot on the side of her forehead. Willie Jay had beaten her again.

"Martha?" She still didn't respond. What was there to say?

I sat down on the porch step beside her. Her body rocked, tears quietly streaking her cheeks.

I gently touched her shoulder. "You okay? Where's Sam?"

It was like she was in some sort of shock or something. She shook her leg and cradled herself, her stare focused on the faded red shed across the yard. I followed her line of sight and that's when I heard the soft faint cries. My heart kicked inside my chest. It only took me seconds to realize what was going on.

I jumped off the back porch and ran straight to the shed. I pulled the rusty latch open. Sam tumbled out, crying and drenched in sweat. His face was bright red and his hands were raw and scraped. I lifted his small soaked body and gathered him to his feet. I couldn't tell where his tears ended and the sweat began. He cried in my arms as we crossed the backyard. I looked at Martha, still on the back stoop, crying and rocking. By the time we reached her on the back porch, I was so angry I wanted to slap her.

"He told me Sam stole something and needed disciplining," Martha blurted out through tears. "He told me as long as he was making noise in there, he was fine."

"What's wrong with you?! It's the middle of July! Come on, Sam, let's get you inside and get some cold water."

"He told me he would be fine in there," Martha whimpered. And still, she didn't move from the porch.

I ignored her as I helped Sam to a kitchen chair. I raced to the sink and poured him a glass of water. I watched him drink it all in one long swallow. I refilled the glass and handed it to him again.

I was supposed to leave for boarding school in a month. But Sam wouldn't be safe with Willie Jay *or Martha.* I grabbed Sam by the hand. "Come on, let's go."

We stepped onto Vera's big wraparound porch, a place that always seemed to beckon people to come inside to laugh, to rest, and to drop their troubles at the door. And no matter what time of day, the smell of something good always floated through the house.

Vera was in the kitchen baking when Sam and I arrived. The old box fan was perched on the counter and blew hot air all over the room, failing miserably to cool things down. The only thing that made the space comfortable was Vera's dimpled smile when we stepped inside.

"Hey! There's my little honey bunnies."

Sam sat down in one of the brown cane chairs and started to spin the Lazy Susan Vera kept on her kitchen table filled with condiments.

I stood beside Sam. "Hi, Miss Vee."

"Y'all hungry? I got some ham left over. I can make you a couple sandwiches."

"No, thank you," I said.

Vera gazed down at Sam before she flitted a glance at me. He continued spinning the condiments without a word. His eyes were starting to swell from crying, and a few mosquito bites were starting to welt on his face and arms.

"Sammy, baby, I think I might be able to scrounge up a couple pork chops. What you think?"

No answer. The Lazy Susan spun slowly.

Vera eyed me again. I bit my bottom lip.

"Sammy, you wanna go watch some TV?" she asked.

Sam eased from the chair and sulked into the living room. Vera and I stared at each other and waited until we heard the laugh track of a TV show come alive in the other room.

"I've never known Sammy to turn down my pork chops," Vera said as she returned to the counter. She began sifting flour. "Ellie, come help me with this here pound cake."

I walked over and stood beside her.

"Crack me six eggs."

I pulled a bowl from the cabinet and opened the carton of eggs.

"What happened?"

"I was only gone for a few hours —"

"Uh-uh. This ain't about you. You can't stand guard twenty-four hours a day. Just tell me what happened."

"He locked him in the shed out back and told Martha to only open it if Sam stopped making noise."

Vera rested the sifter on the counter and stared out the window. "Heavenly Father."

"Miss Vee, I don't understand how he can be so mean if he's supposed to be a police officer." I finished cracking the eggs.

"Sweetie, if I lived a thousand years, I'd never understand some folks." She went back to her mixing bowl.

"Sometimes I think Martha hates me and Sam. She's been saying she's not gonna let me go away to school." My voice started to crack as I fought back tears. "She said she needs me to help her around the house and she doesn't have the money to send me to Virginia, so I can't go."

"I already told you, I got that all taken care of. I'll talk to her."

Vera's voice of authority soothed me.

"Why would she marry a man like Willie Jay? Why would she stay with someone who treats us the way he do — all of us. I hate him."

"I don't know, sugar. Only the good Lord knows why some folks make the decisions they do. And don't say hate."

"It seems wrong that someone who's supposed to enforce the law doesn't follow the law. What kind of justice is that?"

Vera lifted the sifter and started preparing the flour. "There's different kinds of justice in the world. Willie Jay Groover sees justice one way. Some folks see it another."

I stared at Vera for a moment. Just long enough for the kernel of an idea to sprout. An idea I'd been cradling and nursing in my mind since the first time Willie Jay touched me. An idea too big and evil for me to utter in words. "How can I go to Virginia and leave Sam? I don't think I could concentrate on my schoolwork knowing Sam had to live alone in that house with Martha and Willie Jay."

Vera finished off the flour and clapped the dust from her hands. She turned to face me with one hand on her hip. "Listen to me, you getting that scholarship to school is the best thing to come out of Chillicothe since I've been here. And that's a heap of years. If you don't go, you'll let a lot of people down, and most especially you'll let yourself down. You go on to school. I'll look after Sammy."

We both went quiet. The laugh track from

the television roared up again through the silence.

I finally wrangled up enough courage to ask her about my idea. I edged a bit closer to Vera. "Can I ask you something?"

"Sure." Vera picked up the sugar canister and started to measure out another ingredient for the cake.

"What do you think would happen to Martha and Sam if Willie Jay wasn't around while I was gone?"

I noticed a small tick of hesitation in Vera before she poured the last cup of sugar in the bowl with the flour. "I suspect Martha and Sammy would get along just fine. What you think?"

"I think they would too."

Vera never looked up from the mixing bowl. "It might take a lot to get Willie Jay out that house though."

I threw out the eggshells and returned to Vera's side at the counter. "I guess it wouldn't be so hard if I had some help."

Vera pursed her lips together. "I imagine it wouldn't. Hand me that vanilla extract."

I handed her the small brown bottle. We both went quiet again.

Vera measured out the liquid into a separate bowl, tapped the measuring spoon against it, and handed the bottle back to me. "I suppose everybody could do with a little help now and then."

Sam and I stayed at Vera's until nightfall. She made pork chops with macaroni and cheese for Sam, and my favorite, grape Kool-Aid with lemons. I had two slices of cake after dinner. I'd never had cake that tasted so good.

CHAPTER 37

The drive back to Atlanta from Chillicothe gave me time to think, but it provided no clarity. It was after five o'clock and I'd been gone from the office all day. I finally pulled up my voice mails, all the calls I'd ignored during the day:

Juice: *"Hey, Ellice. It's Juice again. I want to make sure you're okay. You need to call me. It's the only way I'll stop calling you."*

Anita: *"Hi Ellice. It's me, Anita. Jonathan's looking for you. I told him you had an appointment outside the office. He wanted to know what time you'd be back. Just call me back when you can."*

Grace: *"Hey, Ell. How'd the resignation go this morning. Are you outta that racist hellhole? Let's go get a drink after work. I wanna hear how it all went. Call me. Bye."*

Willow: *"Hey, Ellice, honey. This is Willow. Is everything okay? Jonathan just stormed out of my office. He said you left the office, and no one can reach you. I'm not sure what's going on but call me. It's urgent."*

Juice: *"You know it's me. Call because I'm persistent."*

Hardy: *"Hey, Legal Lady, Rudy just told me about those shipments to Libertad. I'll take care of it. In the meantime, give me a call when you can."*

Anita: *"Ellice, it's me again. Can you call me back? Both Jonathan and Nate are looking for you. Jonathan said something about he needed to hear from you by the close of business and you would know what it was about. Are you all right? Call me, okay? Bye."*

Anita: *"Hey, Ellice, I'm leaving for the day. Jonathan came by again . . . for the third time. He said he still hadn't heard from you and that he would just talk to Detective Bradford. He said you would know what they were going to discuss. Ellice, I hope everything's okay. I'm worried. Okay. Bye."*

I clicked off the phone. And just like that, everyone wanted to make sure I was okay.

Everyone wanted to talk to me. A week ago, I sat in a cold, cramped office with all my secrets. And now, I was locked in this hellish quagmire of blackmail and murder.

I had to get to Vera. I needed to see her, to just touch her, so that I would know everything was fine, that the world still made sense somehow. It was nearly six o'clock when I pulled up to the empty parking lot at the nursing home.

I opened the door to Vera's room and was surprised to find her awake and sitting up in the Barcalounger.

"Ellie, baby, this is a pleasant surprise." Her gray braids were wrapped and pinned across the top of her head. A golden-brown queen wearing her silver crown.

I breathed a sigh of relief. I was lost, but Vera was lucid. "I just wanted to see you, Vee."

"Sit down, baby."

I didn't take off my coat or grab a nearby chair. Instead, I fell to my knees, dropped my head on Vera's lap, and started to cry. Tears gushed from some deep pit of panic and dread inside me. And all of it rumbled out onto Vera's fragile knees.

"Baby, you okay?" Vera gently stroked my hair, twirling my coils between her thin brown fingers. The old woman's gentle touch unleashed more tears and a flood of guilt and regret I didn't have the willpower to stop.

"Ellie, tell me now, did he bother you again? I done told your momma she can't let no man mess over her kids. Did he hurt you again?"

Oh God. She recognized me but her mind was lodged somewhere back in Chillicothe. I was too emotionally spent to fast-forward Vera decades into the present.

"No, Vee, I just wanted to be with you."

"That's fine, baby." Vera began to hum a low throaty tune. A gospel song that I recognized immediately. "His Eye Is on the Sparrow." The choir sang it the very first time I had ever stepped foot inside a church, right after Sam and I moved in with Vera. After everything fell apart. *After Vera saved the babies.* Vera bought us some clothes and it was the first time I had ever worn a brand-new dress. It was the color of fresh green apples with pink flowers embroidered along the neckline and hem. I was afraid to sit in that dress because it was so pretty. I remember rubbing my fingers along the embroidery over and over, amazed that anything could be so beautiful and belong to me.

Vera stroked my face lightly before removing a soft white handkerchief from her pocket. She dabbed it across my face. "Shhh . . . Hush now, honey bunny, you don't need to cry none."

It was like I was back on her front porch in Chillicothe.

"Ellie baby, you got to remember, family is important. But some family is good and some family ain't so good. Some family downright rotten." She was right about family. Unfortunate for me, I'd landed in the Manson family when I joined Houghton!

Vera continued toying with my hair. "And Willie Jay, well, he 'bout rotten as they come. He use his job and all the law behind it to do whatever he wanna do. You might not be as powerful as he is, but you a hell-ava lot smarter."

I closed my eyes, listening to the old woman.

"I learned a long time ago, family is who you love and trust, not who the law say you supposed to love. That no-count scoundrel. Ain't nobody on God's green earth he love except hisself." Vera started to hum again.

After a couple minutes, Vera broke from the song.

"Now, Ellie, did you do what I told you to do?" Vera asked firmly. I didn't answer. I didn't have a clue what she was talking about, but it didn't matter. I was here with the one person in the world who loved me. Nothing else mattered right now. I just wanted her to go back to humming. I wanted nothing but her and that little sparrow that God watches over.

"What'd you do with dem chicken and dumplings I made?"

My eyes shot open.

Now, I knew exactly where Vera was mentally benched. A nervous panic coursed through me. The secret I'd spent nearly all my life running from came bubbling from Vera's debilitated mind. A deadly, criminal secret surfacing like a body rising from its watery grave. I raised my eyes in time to catch a stern glare from Vera.

"Answer me, child. Did you do like I told you?"

"Vee, everything's okay. I did what you told me." In an instant, my mind scrambled with memories of murder and the fear of what Vera might have released out into the world.

Vera and I had barely spoken of that night since it happened. Then it dawned on me. How many times had she mistaken a nurse or an attendant for me and shared this very same memory? Maybe some random stranger like Jonathan or Max when they left her flowers.

Vera leaned forward. "You did *exactly* like I told you?"

I nodded solemnly.

"Good. That's good. Then there ain't nothing to worry about now."

I gave a weak smile and Vera smiled, too, before she sank back into the Barcalounger.

"Now you dry dem tears, baby. You ain't got no time for tears. You fightin' for ya life. Like I always told you, you use your heart to love but you use your head to fight."

Chillicothe, Georgia, July 1979

Living in Chillicothe in July is like living inside a gas stove set at broil. It was after eleven o'clock at night. Even at this late hour, the house was so hot that the linoleum felt warm and sticky under my bare feet. I trembled standing at the kitchen sink washing dishes. I had to make sure the kitchen was clean before Willie Jay got home. Sam was at Vera's house and Martha had passed out in the bedroom an hour earlier. Her "demons" were back, and I heard her crying in the bedroom right before she passed out.

Now I waited.

A few minutes later, I heard Willie Jay's car muffler rattle to a stop in the driveway. He always demanded his dinner be served on the table piping hot when he walked in the house. I rinsed the soap off my hands and scurried to the stove. I grabbed a dish towel and lifted the warm casserole dish from the oven. My hands were shaking so bad I nearly dropped it. I pulled a plate from the cupboard and a fork and serving spoon from the drawer. The car door slammed, and I peeked out the window over the sink. I quickly scooped up the chicken and dumplings from the casserole dish and heaped them on the plate. I managed to set the plate on the table at the precise moment Willie Jay walked through the back door.

He barreled into the kitchen without a word, still dressed in his blue police uniform. He never washed his hands before eating and I eyed the small slivers of dirt underneath his nails in disgust. It was his rule that he sit at the table alone and eat dinner first. Me, Sam, and Martha would eat whatever was left.

Willie Jay looked at the plate, inspecting it like something was wrong. The pounding of my heart nearly took my breath away.

"Looks like your cooking skills are coming along, gal."

I was too scared to say a word. I simply nodded.

Then he eyeballed me from head to toe and licked his lips with a nasty grin, "After dinner, maybe I'll have you for dessert." He

472

gave a loud, ugly laugh, and I backed away and watched as he said a blessing over his food. After the first bite, he laughed out loud. "This is really good. You and Sammy gon' hafta eat jelly sandwiches for dinner."

By the third bite, sweat beads lined his forehead. He wiped his brow, but he never stopped eating. "God, it's hot in here," he huffed. "Open the window!"

I scrambled to the window over the sink and slipped it up just a crack. He took several more bites, then he stopped. He wiped his brow with the back of his hand before he slumped in his chair. He gazed at me with a blank stare, like he was staring straight through me. I backed up against the cupboard, into a plastic tumbler that fell to the floor in a hollow clunk. His stare still locked on me. I wasn't sure if he had figured out what was going on. Suddenly his right hand dropped to the table; his fork clinked against his plate before tumbling onto the linoleum. A few seconds later, he was gasping for air before he finally fell to the kitchen floor.

I quietly watched as Willie Jay roiled in convulsions for what seemed an eternity, his body moving in fits and spasms. I left him there a couple times to dart between the kitchen and the hallway, peeking in Martha's bedroom to make sure she was still out. The last time I returned to the kitchen I glowered down at him. He reached his arm toward me, as if pleading for my help. I didn't budge. I just focused on the slivers of dirt under his nails until he dropped his arm.

Finally, Willie Jay stopped moving. His mouth gaped, the last bite of dumplings still inside. His eyes were two slits, just barely apart. I stared at him lying on the floor.

Dead.

I couldn't really explain it but something inside me lifted — a weight of relief or perhaps an odd joy knowing Willie Jay was never going to smoke another cigar or burn another piece of human flesh. He would never lock up another innocent person in jail or another helpless child in a backyard shed.

I lifted the telephone receiver on the wall and dialed. "It's me. I'm done."

Then I eased into a kitchen chair and sat for another five minutes with him on that kitchen floor, relieved it was all over.

I heard another car pull up in the driveway. My heart pounded so loud and fast. I raced to the living room and peeked out the window before I opened the door and fell into Vera's arms in tears.

"Shh . . . it's okay, sugar. Everything's okay now. Where is he?"

"In the kitchen."

"Where's Martha?"

"She passed out in the bedroom. She was in a really bad way tonight."

We both hustled into the kitchen and got to work.

"Get his feet. I'll take care of his pockets," Vera said.

As much as I hated to go near his feet, I removed his shoes and socks while Vera emptied everything from his pockets. She said these things could fall away from him, so it was really important to remove them first. I placed his socks inside his shoes and put them under the sink, along with the things Vera removed from his pockets, including his gun and holster.

"C'mon, let's get him out of here," Vera said. I reached under the cupboard and pulled out a gray tarp. I scooted around the table and placed the tarp on the floor next to the body; together Vera and I rolled Willie Jay onto it and pulled it up and over him. "Go prop open the back door."

I did as she said and then joined her back at the table. We stood over the blanketed lump for a moment.

475

"Remember, you're a brave girl. You ready?"

I nodded. "Ready."

Vera grabbed the top end of the tarp and I carried the bottom. Together, we dragged his body out the kitchen door, down the back steps, and to the edge of the river. He was so heavy we had to stop a few times just to catch our breath or adjust the tarp around his body. Sweat poured off me. My arms ached. A couple minutes later, we stood at the edge of the riverbank with Willie Jay at our feet.

The backwoods were quiet, as if bird and beast alike held their breath, waiting witnesses to what we were about to do. The slight rush of water hit the riverbank. I pulled back the tarp. I wedged my foot underneath Willie Jay's body and gave it a rough push toward the river embankment. I watched him slowly slink into the water as I stepped away from the river's edge. A minute later, I heard a hard snap and then a flurry of water splashing and moving about. Then it stopped. Dead silence, again.

Back inside the kitchen, we wrapped Willie Jay's belongings in the gray tarp, along with the plate, fork, serving spoon, and casserole dish with the remaining chicken and dumplings — laced with strychnine. Vera tucked it under her arm.

"I'll take care of his car now. If anybody comes looking for me, tell 'em I went around the corner. Don't let nobody in the house before I get back, you hear me?"

"Yes, ma'am."

"Now, what happened here tonight is what we call a grave secret. You take it on to glory with you. Nobody ever has to know. You understand?"

"Yes, ma'am." I hugged Vera tightly, the two of us locked in a grip of love and vengeance. She finally released the hug, patted my back, and left the house.

And none of us — me, Sam, or Vera — ever uttered the name Willie Jay Groover again.

CHAPTER 38

Love with your heart. Fight with your head. It was as if Vera had declared a rallying cry directly into my ear. I tried to imagine Vera cowering to Sheriff Coogler or Willie Jay or her rapist. She never did. She was a woman who had traveled a jagged road of poverty and racism and sexism. And she maneuvered it all while helping other women. She'd be ashamed if she knew I was sitting in my house crying about a threat from men like Jonathan and Max. She wouldn't have it.

I changed clothes. A black turtleneck sweater, jeans, and a pair of Sperry boots. I called Detective Bradford. She didn't answer so I left a message. I retrieved Max's thumb drive and the flyer from my kitchen table. I stuffed them into the pocket of my parka. I grabbed my cell phone, wallet, and keys.

Jonathan and Max were trying to box me

in. They had me down, but I wasn't out. I'd been naïve to think they wouldn't kill me because I was the lone Black person in the executive suite. True, they wouldn't kill me, but they'd decided to do something much worse. They were out to destroy me. They'd decided to hurt the people who meant something to me. Sam. Vera. Rudy.

Rudy.

Before I left the house, I dialed Rudy's cell number. "Hey, it's me. Are you still in the office?"

"Yeah. Why are you calling me on my cell phone? Aren't you upstairs on Twenty?"

"No. Listen to me. It's really important. I need you to do exactly as I tell you. Get the shipping documents we discussed this morning from my desk. Take them to Detective Bradford at the Atlanta Police Department as fast as you can. Tell her I have more evidence. After you do, go straight home. Whatever you do, do *not* go back into the office."

"Evidence? What?"

"Just do as I say. Get out of that office."

"Ellice —"

"It's too much to explain right now, but you're in danger. It has to do with the Libertad deal. Just trust me. Go get the documents right now. Get them to Bradford and go home to your wife and kids. I'll call you later."

Next, I called Beachwood and had them patch me through to the third-floor nurses' station. I confirmed that Vera was okay and that she was to have no visitors whatsoever.

I placed one more call. "Juice, it's Ellice. I need your help. Can you meet me somewhere?"

"Absolutely." He didn't even hesitate. We agreed on a meeting place.

I hung up and hustled to my car in the garage. As I pulled out onto the street, I noticed a black Escalade parked across the street from my building. My stomach did a flip. I convinced myself that I was just freaking out, again.

Thirty minutes later, I sat across a table from Juice at the Varsity on North Avenue, an iconic fast-food fixture in Atlanta since the 1920s. Juice had picked this place, and for this, he reminded me of Sam. He was dressed in a leather bomber jacket and jeans. His locs bounced every time he moved his head. His easy smile was front and center.

"You sure you don't want something to eat? My treat," Juice said. "I feel bad eating in front of you when you're not eating."

"Thanks. I'm good."

Juice took a big bite out of his chili cheese dog and wiped his mouth with a napkin. "I guess you finally figured out I wouldn't stop calling until you talked to me, huh?"

I tried to smile.

He nodded. "I like your hair."

"Thanks." I pawed at a few coils at the nape of my neck. I was awkward and scared around Juice for the first time since I'd met him. Not in bad way. Just a level of uncomfortability with having to ask a stranger for help. But I remembered Sam's words: *He's decent people . . . he's genuine.*

"I saw the news. About you. You okay?"

I didn't respond immediately. Was it safe to trust him? Did I have any other choice? He polished off another bite and watched me without a word.

"I need to find your friend, the one you said got Sam the job."

"Why?" Juice asked.

"The guy who hired Sam also killed him."

Juice's brows furrowed. "How do you know that?"

"Because I work with the guy. But the police don't believe me."

"You know the guy who popped Sam? The hell?" Juice put his hot dog back on the tray and wiped his hands. He gave me a long

481

unblinking stare, like I needed to keep talking or else he wouldn't believe me either.

"I think the guy intentionally set out to hire Sam so that he could get me to go along with some illegal stuff he's doing in the company where I work. When I started looking into the illegal stuff, the guy killed Sam and is trying to frame me for the murders. I think he also killed two other innocent people connected with the company."

Juice gave me the same shocked expression Grace had given me in the kitchen of my condo. "And you work with these people?!"

"Look, I know it's crazy, but I need to find someone who can corroborate my story. And your friend might be the only one who can. I just need to ask him a few questions."

"Listen, beautiful, I gotta be honest with you. I'm sure people will appreciate what you're dealing with right now — Sam's death and all. But actually, going to the police to corroborate a suspect's story is not where my friends want to be. I'm just sayin'."

"You said Sam was like a brother to you. Are you going to help me or not?"

Juice stared at me, his mouth turned up in a lopsided smirk, like he was internally debating with himself.

"You know what? Never mind." I stood from the table.

"Wait."

Juice wiped his hands again, then pulled out his cell phone. He dialed a number. He stared at me as he talked into the phone. "Yo, Mack. What's up? Hey, I need some info. You remember Sammy Littlejohn . . . Yeah, I know it's messed up. Do you know who set him up with that surveillance gig?"

I eased back into my seat and anxiously listened.

"Oh yeah. Is he still out at the same place? Uh-huh . . . Perfect! I owe you one, man. Later."

Juice hung up and stuffed his phone back in his pocket. He smiled at me. "Let me finish this hot dog, then we can take a ride."

Things were going along fine until we got to the parking lot.

"Just leave your car here. I'll drop you back off to pick it up," Juice said.

I stopped in my tracks. I'd only seen Juice a handful of times. The only thing I knew about him was that he served a stint in prison with Sam, where they met, for what crime I didn't know. I didn't know anything about the man who was about to take me

God knows where. I didn't even know his *real name*!

Juice spun around when he realized I wasn't walking beside him. "What?" He gawked for a beat. Then he realized the reason for my hesitation. He stretched his arms out in a gesture of innocence. "Ellice, you're Sam's sister. I would never hurt you. Cut the drama. Let's go find the bastard who killed Sam." He walked off. I hesitated for a moment. *Please God keep me safe.* With that little prayer sent up, I followed Juice across the parking lot.

We finally stopped in front of an older-model Audi A6. He squawked the door locks with his key fob and opened the passenger door for me. I slumped my shoulders in surrender and climbed inside the car.

Juice started the ignition and the engine purred. The air freshener clipped to the vent released the clean crisp smell of pine.

"This is nice," I said as I buckled my seat belt.

"You mean, this car is nice *for me.*"

"I didn't say that!" I snapped, offended that he thought I was making some stereotypical assumptions about him. But he was Sam's friend . . . maybe I was.

"Don't get all rattled. Truth be told, I'm amazed how blessed I am. God's been good to me, even when I didn't deserve it."

Juice pulled out of the parking lot and headed south on Interstate 75/85. Friday evening rush hour in downtown Atlanta meant we might be in this car for a while. I suddenly felt compelled to make small talk.

"So why do people call you Juice?"

He chuckled. "Hmm . . . you sure you want to know?"

"You don't want to tell me?"

"That's not it. It's just that I don't tell a lot of people this story." He glanced over at me with a playful smile. "Some folks can't handle it. They either think I'm lying or scratch their head in confusion."

"Try me."

"Well, I was living with a woman. She was an office manager for a law firm downtown. I didn't know it at the time, but she was embezzling money from the firm. When they discovered it, they wanted me to testify against her. You know, spill everything I knew about the expensive clothes, jewelry, and stuff. They figured I must have known what she was doing. Anyway, I wouldn't do it."

"Why not?"

"She had a young son from a previous relationship. I didn't want to play a part in helping the state separate a mother from her kid. Little Black boys — and Black girls, for that matter — have it hard enough in this world without being shuttled through the foster care system or shoved on relatives that abuse them. Anyway, the district attorney tried to put pressure on me to testify against her. He brought charges against me for aiding and abetting a felon. I guess they figured I'd plead out and testify against her. I didn't."

Juice skirted around a fender bender on the side of the road and headed west on Interstate 20.

"So what happened?"

"I took up residence at Dodge State. A lot of people told me I was a fool to go to prison over a woman. Anyway, that's where I met your brother. When I told him why I was there, Sam started calling me 'No Juice' because he said the state tried to squeeze me and got *no juice.*" He laughed. "It stuck."

I snickered. "You just made that story up."

"Trust me, I did not. Your brother was something else."

The image of Sam coming up with a silly nickname for him made me laugh too. A wedge of guilt moved in as I gazed out the window at the landscape whizzing by.

"Enough about me. Let's talk about the

chucklehead you're dating. I can tell he's doing a lousy job of making you happy."

I rolled my eyes and continued watching the trees zip by like a blurring forest.

"Cut him loose, whoever he is. You look like you haven't been happy in a long time."

"If you tell me I should smile more, I'll scream. I hate it when men tell me I should smile more."

Juice laughed. "I'd never tell you to do that."

"And besides, you don't know me. How do you know whether I'm happy or not?"

"Well, you're right, I don't know you, but the few times I've seen you . . . there's something about you. A kind of heavy sadness. It's in your eyes."

"Oh brother. Another guy trying to 'mansplain' the finer points of my feelings."

"I'm serious. A smile doesn't show how you feel. Your eyes do. What's that line about the eyes being the window to the soul? If you want to learn a lot about a person, watch what they do with their eyes. Do they look straight into yours? Do they gaze off when you talk to them? Do they dart around, looking for trouble? Do they constantly fight back tears?"

He glanced over at me and smiled again. I quickly looked away to the speeding traffic on the highway.

"Or do their eyes avoid you?" Juice asked with a chuckle.

I decided to change the subject. "So whatever happened to the woman?"

"She went to prison too. And after . . . well, it was never gonna be the same. We went our separate ways. After I got out, I scraped together what little money I had, borrowed some more, and started my foundation."

"You have a foundation?!"

Juice shook his head slowly. "There you go again."

I was suddenly embarrassed. He was right. I had made a lot of assumptions before I climbed inside this car.

"I help men get on their feet after they get out of prison. The probation system, halfway houses, they're all rigged against a man who had nothing before he went inside the prison walls and he damn sho' ain't got nothing after he comes out. I help them find jobs, get a decent roof over their heads. I got a couple grants a few months ago, so I started some after-school programs for young boys, too. That's why I spend so much time in West End, Vine City, or over on Bankhead Highway. Maybe I can put myself out of business one day if I can reach the young heads and keep them from going in the joint in the first place."

"That's pretty cool."

"I know how tough it can be to find a job after you've served time. A lot of folks like to decide your future based on your past. I believe if you keep your head on straight, one shouldn't have anything to do with the other. That's why I kept after Sam. He was smart, just made some bad decisions. And now, after he finally listened to me, this happens. Sammy was a good man. He didn't deserve this."

"I know. He was."

We rode in silence for the next ten minutes.

Juice finally exited the highway and we drove through a main thoroughfare dotted with restaurants and antique shops. A few minutes later, we turned into the Douglas County Plaza parking lot and parked in front of a store.

I nearly fainted when I read the sign above the store entrance.

TRI-COUNTY OUTFITTERS

CHAPTER 39

"Ellice, you getting out?" Juice asked.

My head spun. Tri-County Outfitters. The flyer from Michael's duffel bag and underneath Max's desk blotter. All I could think about was the fact that two men — Sam and Michael — from two very different parts of my life were tied to this place in front of me. And now, both of them were dead.

"Ellice . . . you okay?" Juice asked again.

I finally looked up at him as he stood holding the car door open for me. "Oh. Yeah, I'm sorry."

I'd never been inside a gun shop before. The place was huge and buzzed with customers, and more than a few of them wore "Make America Great Again" caps. One customer wore a red T-shirt emblazoned with a Confederate flag and the words IT'S NOT HATE. IT'S HERITAGE. Some of them watched us with suspicious glances as we walked inside. This seemed like exactly the kind of place Max Lumpkin would frequent.

I turned to Juice. "I don't get a good feeling about this place."

"Trust me. It's no different than a lot of other places in Atlanta. They think we're here to buy something. They'll take our cash. They just won't invite us to their house for Sunday dinner." He gave my arm a light squeeze and smiled. "It'll be okay."

A husky guy with a goatee and buzz cut approached us at the counter. "Can I help you folks with something?"

"Yes, sir. How do you do? I'm looking for Robert. He was helping me a few days ago."

"Sure thing. I'll go grab him," the man said.

"Thank you, sir." Juice looked at me and grinned after the man walked off. "I had to switch things up there for a minute."

"No problem. A brother has to do what a brother has to do." I smiled.

"Listen, while we're here, you're my girlfriend —"

"What?!"

"The guy we're gonna talk to owes me a favor, but I don't want him to lose his job. Just play along." Juice narrowed his eyes and looked at me.

"Now what?"

"I'm checking your eyes to see what they tell me since I called you my girlfriend." I rolled my eyes and he gave me a wink. "I'm just trying to take the edge off." He rubbed my arm. "Come on, you look like you're about to boost a couple guns outta here. Relax."

I glanced around the store. The only gun I'd ever seen was Willie Jay's when he came home and placed it on the top shelf of the closet. Guns were like a foreign, scary object to me. I'd never seen so many guns in one place. Guns on the wall, in glass cases, on shelves. They were everywhere. If this were just one store, how massive this industry must be and how violent our society had become.

A young white guy wearing chinos and a button-down shirt appeared behind the counter. If I'd seen him anywhere else, I might have mistaken him for a computer programmer in Midtown.

"Thaddeus Johnson! Good to see you again."

Thaddeus?

"Rob. How you been? Maybe you could show me something small but powerful for my girlfriend here. Atlanta's not the friendly little city it used to be." I cringed when he called me his girlfriend again. I knew this was just his little game. I doubt it made a bit of difference to the guy behind the counter.

"Absolutely. Let's go down to the end case."

The guy led us to the far end of the store, where the three of us stood alone. Both Juice and the sales guy casually browsed the guns in the case. I kept looking across the store, wondering how many times Sam had been inside this place. Sam was an extrovert, but this hardly seemed like the kind of venue he'd frequent. Had he been so desperate for a job that he'd come in here?

Juice lowered his voice. "Rob, I need some info. You hooked up a friend of mine. A Black guy by the name of Sammy Littlejohn." Juice pointed to a gun inside the case.

The guy's eyes darted quickly around the store. He bent over and lifted the gun from the case and handed it to Juice.

"Yeah. I know him." The guy's voice matched Juice's.

"I heard you introduced him to someone who hired him." Juice inspected the gun like an interested customer. "Maybe to work for a company in Midtown?"

"I didn't, but my boss knows a guy. The guy was looking to add someone to his security team, to do some surveillance work.

He said he was specifically looking to help guys like us . . . you know, give a guy a break."

Juice handed the gun back and browsed the case again. My stomach did a couple nervous flips. Standing in this store, in front of this guy, it was like I was retracing Sam's steps and I wanted to cry.

"How about that one?" Juice pointed to a small black gun in the case. "What was his name?"

The guy pulled another gun from the case and handed it to Juice to inspect. "His name? Jonathan Everett. He's one of our best customers. Real friendly guy. The guy hugs everybody."

I stopped cold. *Hugs everybody?*

I quickly pulled my phone from my pocket and searched for Houghton's website. My hands started trembling. I clicked on a picture of Houghton's leadership. I slid the phone across the counter to the guy.

"Is this the guy? Jonathan Everett?" I said as I surreptitiously pointed to Jonathan's picture.

The guy looked down at the phone. His brows pinched. He looked back at me. "There's some mistake. This isn't Jonathan."

I scrolled down farther. "What about this guy?"

"Yeah, that's the guy. That's him." He pointed to the picture of *Hardy King.*

"I think you got the names mixed up on these pictures. The name says Hardy King, but that's our customer. That's the guy who comes in and places the orders."

Hardy was posing as Jonathan to purchase guns.

I went cold, my head light and dizzy. "Are you sure?"

"Hey, are you a cop or something?" The guy gave me a suspicious look. I was blowing Juice's cover.

"No," Juice said, before he lowered his voice even further. "She's not a cop. She's Sammy's sister."

The guy looked at me again, his suspicion barely lessened by Juice's explanation. "I'm sorry. I haven't seen Sammy since I hooked him up with Jonathan. All I know is my boss said this guy needed someone to help out his security team. He wanted someone who had served time at Dodge State."

"He specifically said someone from Dodge State?" I asked.

The guy hesitated, as if wondering whether he should say anything else. "Yeah." I was angry at myself for having interjected in the conversation and raising his suspicions.

Juice chimed in. "We're just looking for information. Nobody'll know it came from you. You have my word. You said this guy is one of your best customers. What does he purchase?"

The guy nervously looked in the case. He raised his voice again. "Oh, how about this one? It's a Smith & Wesson Shield 9 mm. It's pretty slim, makes it easy for purses and bags."

The husky man with the buzz cut popped over again, giving us all a suspicious look. "You folks doing okay? Rob helping you out all right?"

"Yes, sir, he sure is. My girlfriend is having a hard time deciding," Juice said with a broad smile. The sales guy smiled back.

Someone behind us yelled, "Chuck, over here. I need your help." The husky guy excused himself and moved on to a gun rack and a waiting customer.

The salesclerk handed a small black gun to me this time. I almost dropped it. I'd never held a gun before. "That was my boss. I'm sorry, Juice, but you guys gotta buy something or leave."

"I'm sorry, but how many guns does he buy?" I asked.

"Look, the guy said he heads up security for some company . . . Cavern . . ."

I remembered the shipping documents Rudy showed me. "Cavanaugh?"

"Yeah, Cavanaugh Industries. He comes in, makes the purchases, and we send them out to his security teams across the country. The delivery truck picks up the shipment every month. That's all I know."

"A Houghton delivery truck?"

"Yeah."

Before I could ask another question, Juice piped up. "Where is he sending the purchases?"

"That, I don't know. My boss puts the packages together."

Juice looked at me. "You good?" I nodded yes. "Thanks, man. I really appreciate it."

Juice and I walked to the car in silence. He opened the car door for me, and I slid inside. I could feel the first inkling of tears. A few seconds later, he climbed inside the car. "Talk to me. What's the deal with the pictures?"

"The guy he pointed out, his name is Hardy King. He's the head of security for the company I work for. I thought he was a friend."

"You think this Hardy guy killed Sam?"

"Yeah." *Jonathan* didn't kill Sam. *Hardy* did.

It all seemed to make sense. Hardy would have access to the security badging system for making a duplicate for Sam. His showing me the bank logs and pretending to help me. He wanted me to think it was Jonathan who killed Michael and my brother. He must have hired Sam, posing as Jonathan. He knew Sam would tell me who he was working for. Hardy must have left the note in my car, the flowers in Vera's room. But why?

Juice started up the car. "So your company needs enough firepower that the head of security has to ship out guns monthly? What does your company do?"

"It's a trucking delivery company and we don't need guns for what the company does."

"My guess is this Hardy guy must be making straw purchases for folks who can't make them."

"Wait. What?"

"Yeah. It's a big business down here. Somebody has a criminal record and can't pass a background check, so they get someone who's clean to make the purchase for them. People do it all the time here in Georgia, buy guns and send them to other states with strict gun laws. Georgia is one of the easiest places in the country to buy a gun. My guess is that the Hardy guy must be making some money on the side or hooked up with some kind of gun club fanatics or something."

I leaned my head against the glass of the car door thinking about what Juice said. The shipping orders to Ohio and Illinois. And the recent shipments to San Diego. Hardy must have set up the phony Cavanaugh company to ship the guns on Houghton trucks. Michael had a copy of the flyer for the gun shop. He found out what Hardy was doing and that's why he was killed. Hardy didn't realize Michael hated guns, so he'd staged the suicide all wrong. Then I remembered Max's words from Nate's party, his southern twang singing in my ear: *I don't think Libertad should be part of this. It's too risky.*

I shot straight up in the passenger seat. "Oh my God!"

"Ellice, you okay?"

It all started to come together, like a camera lens sharpening its focus on a face. The Brethren. The fight. The foot soldiers. The guns.

Hardy was arming the Brethren's foot soldiers!

CHAPTER 40

By the time Juice and I arrived back at the Varsity to pick up my car, another kernel of an idea started to form, much like the one that formed back in Chillicothe when I applied for the scholarship to Coventry. I nurtured that small kernel of an idea until it bloomed into a plan back in the summer of 1979.

And tonight, I had another plan.

I thanked Juice for his help and assured him I didn't need an escort home. He had done as much as I was willing to let him. The rest I had to do for myself. Despite my protests against his following me home, he did it anyway, right up to the entrance to my garage. I waved and watched him drive off. After he left, I made a U-turn inside my garage. I left too. Anyone who hurt Sam had no explanation I wanted to hear, and they got no second chances with me either.

■ ■ ■ ■

It was almost nine o'clock by the time I pulled into Houghton's garage. The lobby was empty. Quiet. I strolled through the security gate with my new replacement ID badge from Hardy as if it were bright and early on a Monday morning. I gave a friendly nod to the young security guard. *One of Hardy's minions.*

"Ms. Littlejohn, is everything okay?" the guard questioned.

"Just fine. Hardy left some paperwork on his desk for me. He told me I could just stop by his office and pick it up." I decided a little chitchat and friendliness might go a long way tonight. "I see that fourth elevator is still out, huh? They ought to just chuck the whole thing and start all over," I said jokingly.

He laughed. "I think you're right."

I climbed into the elevator and faked a smile at the guard as the doors closed. I hit the button for Twenty instead of Nineteen, where Hardy worked. Moments later, I slipped into the dim menacing ambiance of the reserve lighting system in the executive suite. I didn't flip the override switch. I needed the darkness to work. Before I left

501

the twentieth floor, I grabbed a miniflashlight from my desk and headed for Hardy's office on the nineteenth floor. Maybe I was taking a huge risk baiting him here like this. But it was a risk worth taking.

Sam was dead. Hardy was mine now.

I arrived on the nineteenth floor. The layout was exactly the same as the Legal Department, offices along the outer walls, a maze of cubicles in the center. I knew it like the back of my hand. I headed straight for Hardy's office. I pulled the flashlight from my coat pocket. As usual, his office was a hot mess, papers strewn about and the same two half-empty coffee mugs still sitting on his desk. I was surprised he didn't have a bug problem in this place. I hustled behind Hardy's desk and quietly began searching through the drawers. I figured the first drawer must have been his junk drawer until I opened another drawer that was more cluttered than the first.

I pulled open the pencil tray drawer. Inside, an old greeting card. *For My Loving Husband on Valentine's Day.* The card, yellowed and frayed along the edges, sported a big red heart on the front. Inside, a small obituary: *A Celebration of the Life of June Cavanaugh King.* The obituary was adorned with a border of small flowers and a picture of June in the center — a short bob, pearls, and a polite smile. I flipped through it. June and Hardy were childhood sweethearts, no kids, loved traveling, bridge, and fishing. And down at the bottom, a list of the pallbearers included Nate Ashe.

I slipped the obit back inside the card and placed it all back in the drawer. As I did, I noticed the bright glint of metal. I did a double take. There inside Hardy's desk drawer was the double-flag lapel pin. Hardy was one of the Brethren. But was I really surprised?

I searched through the credenza. Another colossal mess. There was no rhyme or reason to Hardy's filing system. I quickly flipped through any files marked with the word *security* in the tab. I was about to move on when I spotted an envelope lying flat in the bottom of the drawer. I shifted a mass of folders and managed to lift the envelope from the drawer. Across the front: "Libertad." I swept open the envelope. Inside, three burner phones and an ID badge with the name "Littlejohn" on it, probably the same one he'd given to Sam to enter the building. I placed it all back inside the envelope and shoved it in my coat pocket.

A few seconds later, the elevator chimed.

My God sense kicked in. I stopped to lean into the sound of footsteps. Slow, heavy, clunky footsteps. I clicked off the flashlight. I left the drawer open and jumped from behind Hardy's desk and darted across the room, banging my shin against a pile of papers and boxes stacked near his desk. The pain shot up through my leg like a torpedo. I managed to stifle a scream and scrunch behind the office door. Suddenly, the footsteps stopped.

"Ellice, you up here?"

Hardy.

CHAPTER 41

He'd gotten here faster than I thought he would, but that was okay. There was no need to rush things. I heard his footsteps. Hardy was heading to his office. Every step hitting the floor like a giant drumbeat.

Let's go, Hardy.

Sweat beaded up along my hairline. He ambled to his office door just as I expected. I heard the elevator chime again. Then, another set of footsteps.

A man's voice: "Mr. King?"

"Yeah, down here," Hardy said.

"Mr. King, is everything okay?"

"Are you sure she said she was coming to *my* office? On Nineteen?"

"That's what she said. She said you left some paperwork for her and told her to pick it up. And I called you as soon as she showed up in the building, just like you asked me to."

"Good work, son."

"Do you want me to flip the override switch and turn on the lights?"

"No. Maybe she went to the Legal Department downstairs. Check Rudy Clifton's office," Hardy said.

"Yes, sir." I could hear the chunky guard from the lobby scamper down the hall, his utility belt with flashlight and keys jangling against the flab of his waistline. I peeped through the crack between the door and the wall. Hardy's hulking silhouette stood just outside the door. He rolled inside his office and gave a quick scan across the room. He was just a few feet away from me now. Only a couple inches of wood stood between me and the man who had murdered my brother.

Just be patient.

Sweat rolled down the middle of my back underneath the parka and turtleneck. My head was fuzzy, like I would pass out. I held my breath. I tried not to move.

He was unusually quiet. I peeked again. Hardy stood in the center of the office this time.

Even in the dim lighting, I could see the quizzical expression on his face as he studied the mass of clutter across the room. And then, he spotted the open drawer.

He lumbered over to the credenza and plopped down in his chair with a thud. He flipped on a desk lamp and twisted his bulky frame toward the open drawer. He peered inside and spied the gap left by the missing envelope. I watched as he rifled through the files, desperately searching.

What was his next move? I watched and waited, sweat dripping off the tip end of my nose now. My mouth was bone dry. I could barely think through the whip of fear and anxiety coursing through me.

Just wait, Ellice. Calm down and wait.

The room was stifling, my sweater soaked and sticky. My shin started to hurt from banging it on Hardy's clutter. I closed my eyes. I fought past my fear and pain and focused on my *small kernel of an idea.* When I looked again, Hardy sat scratching his gray buzz cut.

I quietly eased from behind the door. "Hey, Hardy. You looking for me?" I whispered.

He jumped. I'd startled him. "Hey, Ellice, I need to talk to you."

"About what? The Brethren?" I watched his fragile smile slowly melt into shock. "Or maybe you'd like to talk to me about why you killed my brother."

Hardy stood from his chair. "Ellice . . ." He started to move around the desk.

I shot from his office and down the dimly

lit hallway. I wasn't much of a runner, but I knew I could outrun Hardy.

"Ellice, wait!" His heavy footsteps trailed in my wake, the girth of his body slowing him. "Ellice! Stop! Let's talk for a minute."

That's right, Hardy. Let's go.

Panic rushed through me like a bullet train. My heartbeat booming in my ears.

I raced inside the maze of cubicles.

"Ellice, c'mon. Let's talk about this, huh? It's not the way it looks. Where are you?"

I found an empty cubicle and crawled underneath its desk. Every sound on this empty floor was a roar. The footfalls of his rubber-soled boots, squeaking under his weight. The rustle of his jacket flapping against his pants. All of it crushing me with terror. I held my breath. His steps slowly crept past me.

"Ellice? Come on out. Let's . . . just . . . talk. Ellice?"

His boots stopped. He was just a few feet away from me. His breathing was labored. Heaving. Sighing. The chase was beginning to take its toll. I crawled from underneath the cubicle desk on all fours, waiting for my next opportunity. A minute later, I slipped out from the cubicle. "Hardy!"

He realized I was behind him this time. He turned around and started another chase. I made a straight line for the staircase.

"Ellice!"

I raced past more cubicles, heading to the farthest end of the floor, the pounding inside my head in rhythmic lockstep with the thudding beast in my chest. I was drenched in sweat and fear.

Just keep up, Hardy.

I made it to the staircase door. Hardy still on my tail, I hustled through the door. It slammed behind me with a loud hard clang. A few seconds later, I heard him enter the staircase. I rushed up the stairs to the twentieth floor. I barely felt my feet beneath me.

"Ellice. Ellice!" His voice echoed off the staircase walls.

Hardy's heavy footsteps still trailed me, the girth of his body slowing him once again.

I dashed inside the twentieth floor. The floor was dark. Only the dim spotlights overhead every few feet. Now it was my turn. I slowed down a bit waiting for Hardy to catch up. He panted, heavy like a race-worn horse.

"Ellice, this was all Jonathan's fault. He messed up everything."

Just be patient, Ellice.

I glanced over my shoulder. He was still

509

behind me and moving much slower now. The air from his lungs was nearly gone, his body fighting to breathe through the sweat and exhaustion.

Just a few feet more, Hardy.

"Let's just talk. I spoke to Rudy about the shipments. You weren't supposed to find out about that." I slowed, giving Hardy time to catch up. But I still kept a brisk pace. And then Hardy finally caught up to me. He pulled a gun from his waistband. He pressed it into my back. "Legal Lady, please don't force me to use this. Let's just take a walk out to your car. We can go for a little ride and talk."

Like hell we will.

Hardy could hold ten guns to my back, and he couldn't make me cower. I was still fighting for Sam the same way I had done all my life. And like Willie Jay and Butch Coogler and anyone else who hurt Sam, Hardy would lose.

"Move!"

I started walking toward the elevator bank. Slowly. Taking the longer route past the Fish Bowl conference room.

Hardy's breathing was hot on my neck. "I think you have some things that belong to me," he said.

"You lured my brother over to Houghton

the day before you killed Michael to get him on security footage. But why did you have to kill him?"

"I'm sorry about that, Legal Lady. All you had to do was sit tight. I gave you the bank logs, everything we needed to get rid of Jonathan. I would have fixed everything. Sorry, I had to get rid of your brother to make everything work out."

Stay calm. "And that was you at my brother's house? You tried to bash in my skull?"

"I couldn't have you turn around when that phone rang. It woulda screwed up everything. Like I told you from the start, Jonathan is trash. He was bringing trash into the company, too, squandering Nate's legacy with all those foreigners. I just needed to get rid of him."

"So you pose as Jonathan to ship the guns and kill my brother?"

"I figured he told you he was working for Jonathan. I thought the police would think Jonathan did it. I just didn't count on the police fingering you. Lady, you got a lot of secrets."

"Why pose as Jonathan to ship the guns?"

"Anybody finds out, Jonathan's toast."

"And why kill Michael and Gallagher?"

"Now that was Jonathan's idea," Hardy

revealed between catching his breath. "Michael was gonna expose him and those foreigners he was in bed with." Hardy snickered. "Remember, I just do what they tell me to do."

I remembered Jonathan's words from Nate's party: *I gave him one fucking job to do and he screwed that up!*

"And apparently you got that all wrong, huh? You didn't know Michael hated guns."

"Keep walking."

"Hardy, you've done all this for nothing. Max is never going to promote you. Shipping guns, killing people. None of it will ever be enough. They don't respect you. Max, Jonathan, they're just using you."

"*Shut up.* Walk."

"You don't want to do this, Hardy. That organization, the Brethren? Trust me, you all won't get away with whatever you're planning."

"I was prepared to make an exception for you. You had a rough childhood. But I can't now. You understand, right, Legal Lady?"

Stay calm, Ellice. Stay calm.

"I actually like you even though you're —" He caught himself. "Let's just say I don't paint with as broad a brush as Max. I would make an exception for you, but I can't now. You could ruin everything and

512

bring Nate's legacy down. I can't let that happen."

Just a few feet more.

We approached the elevators. I stopped just shy of the small elevator vestibule. The dim spotlights from the ceiling reflected off the sweat pouring from Hardy's forehead.

"Push the call button," he commanded.

"I'm not going anywhere with you." I said calmly.

"Push the call button!"

"No," I said quietly.

He stared at me for a beat before he shook his head in frustration. The chase I'd given Hardy made him tired, weak, off his game. His breathing was still shallow. He took a couple steps inside the vestibule. He tripped on the stack of wood scaffolding boards that had surrounded the broken elevator. The gun fell to the floor. "Shit!"

Hardy spun in the direction of the gun and bent over to pick it up. I grabbed a pipe from the elevator scaffolding and brought it down across the back of his head with a dull thud. He stumbled again, this time in front of the open elevator shaft. I brought the pipe down again. But Hardy grabbed the other end of it. I held on to it as tight as I could. But Hardy was stronger. He gave the pipe a good swift tug.

But I let it go.

When I did, it was as if everything were in slow motion. I let go. Hardy lurched. The force of his tug, the bulk of his body sent him falling backward. His eyes widened in horror at the realization that there was no floor beneath him. No wall to break his fall. Nothing behind him except a long dark elevator shaft and the echo of his own screams.

And because of Nate's strict rule, there were no security cameras on the twentieth floor.

No security footage or video to show me as I arrived in the executive suite a few minutes earlier and put on my gloves. No cameras to catch me as I pulled apart the wooden scaffolding surrounding the fourth elevator. Or when I stacked the boards in a pile near the entrance to the elevator bank. No one to see me when I used one of the wooden boards to wedge between the doors of the broken elevator, giving me enough leverage to pull the doors apart. There were no security cameras to catch me as I prepared Hardy's grave — a long black hole twenty stories deep.

Detective Bradford's words slipped into my head. *Why is it that so many people around you have managed to wind up dead?*

■ ■ ■ ■

The static of the police radios and the bustle of the EMT echoed through Houghton's cavernous lobby. The strobe effect of the red and blue lights from all the police cars reflected through the tall glass windows and made my eyes hurt. I sat in a leather chair in the lobby, staring up at Detective Bradford.

"Hardy King has been shipping guns up north," I explained. "It seems that he, Jonathan, and Max are all part of some executive-level white supremacy group called the Brethren. A few weeks ago, he started shipping them down near the border, part of that Libertad deal mentioned in Gallagher's memo. You'd have to talk to Jonathan Everett about that. You might want to talk to him about the money he's laundering for Libertad, too." I stood, reached inside my coat pocket and pulled out the flyer, Max's thumb drive, and the envelope from Hardy's office. I handed it all to the detective. "There's a shipment of guns scheduled to go out Tuesday from a gun shop in Shelton called Tri-County Outfitters. I don't know what the Brethren are planning, maybe some sort of race war.

Whatever it is, it can't be good. You should be able to piece it together from this stuff."

Bradford took the items and stared at me, stunned. "Why didn't you tell us about this before?"

"Because I didn't know about it before." I rubbed the back of my neck and stared at the detective. "They were trying to blackmail me into going along with all this. That's on the thumb drive inside there, too."

"What do you mean? Blackmailing you how?"

I didn't answer her question directly. "I'm going home now. I didn't kill my brother, Detective. But Hardy King did, and it still doesn't make any sense to me. It was like my brother was some loose piece of trash they could discard as part of their racist criminal plans. I'll have to live with that for the rest of my life. I have to live with the fact that I worked beside people who killed my brother. I sat in meetings with them and ate lunch with them. And they smiled at me, the whole time. Men who wanted to see people like you and me dead simply because of the color of our skin. I'm just hoping you can stop whatever these cretins are planning to do. Don't let them kill anyone else."

CHAPTER 42

Four days later, Anita walked into my office, eyes bloodshot and her cheeks flushed.

"Stop it, Anita. You're gonna make me start and I'm an ugly crier," I said.

"I can't believe it. I just can't believe it. I don't want to work here either. Who will I buy flowers for?"

I shook my head and giggled. "You'll be just fine." I hugged her, then released the hug and squeezed both her hands. "And not too many Snickers bars from the breakroom, okay?"

"Okay, but you have to promise me you'll hang up a picture or two the next place you go."

"I promise."

She laughed and hugged me again before she left the office.

I didn't really need to return to my office. Frankly, I was surprised I did. I was surprised at how well I handled the imbecilic stares and awkward greetings when I walked through the building. I could have avoided it all and left everything as is in here. Like Anita said, I didn't have a single thing of sentimental value in my office. But maybe I came back to make real the fact that I was actually leaving Houghton. Or maybe I returned because my work ethic compelled me to at least organize things for the hapless soul who had to sort through the legal mess Jonathan, Max, and Nate had created. I paused for a moment and gazed on the playground in the park below. I would really miss this view.

"Hello, Ms. Littlejohn. May I speak with you?"

Detective Bradford strolled into my office in a navy-blue wool coat that looked like something I might wear. Nice cut. Quality material. She really was pretty.

"Detective, come in." I stiffened, steadying myself for what was inevitable. There's no statute of limitations on murder. And Detective Bradford was a lot smarter than Sheriff Butch Coogler. By handing over that thumb drive, I'd opened wide the entryway into all my darkest secrets.

"I wanted to thank you personally." She took a seat in one of the white linen chairs. "The information you provided was extremely helpful. We turned it over to the FBI and the ATF. Apparently, the Brethren was aligned with several other white supremacy groups, including one particularly dangerous organization called the Heritage Brothers. The Brethren funneled guns and money to the Heritage Brothers. Together, they were planning an attack on MLK parades and events in Columbus, Ohio, and Chicago. You kept a lot of people from getting hurt."

"So everyone on the executive team was part of the Brethren?"

"We know for sure Jonathan Everett, Maxwell Lumpkin, and Hardy King were all involved. Because of Mr. Ashe's cognitive state, it's hard to say. We're also unclear about how much Mr. Ashe knew about the guns. Apparently, there were more than a few other vice presidents around Houghton involved in the Brethren. We're tracking the group down in at least six other companies across the country. You're lucky. Seems Mr. King really liked you and talked Max Lumpkin out of killing you."

"Oh, right. Lucky me."

"As you said, Mr. Everett was laundering money for Libertad. Apparently, Mr. Everett set up the scheme nearly a year ago. Houghton trucks were used to smuggle dirty money across the United States border, where it was deposited into several American banks. Houghton would wire the money back to Ortiz and the Libertad folks as part of their *joint venture.* When the Mexican government started poking around in Libertad's financial affairs, the deposits slowed until they could get some documentation in place to prove the legitimacy of their so-called deal. Apparently, Mr. Sayles, advised by Mr. Gallagher, refused to go along. Mr. King was instructed to murder them in exchange for an executive promotion to the twentieth floor." In some twisted way they all thought they were saving Mr. Ashe's family legacy.

"Why were they sending guns to the border?"

"When your CFO discovered the arrangement that Mr. Lumpkin and Mr. Hardy had established for the Brethren to ship guns on the trucks, he wanted in on the action. He had Hardy ship guns to San Diego, where his contact transported them across the border into Mexico as part of his arrangements with Libertad. After killing Mr. Sayles, you were their next best hope for continuing their scheme."

"What about Willow Sommerville, the HR VP? Was she part of this, too?"

"From what we can tell, no."

I was glad. Willow was another woman trying to survive in a toxic culture. She had chosen her method for survival, different from mine, but she was surviving, nonetheless. Bravo to her for her fortitude to keep going in a place like Houghton.

"So they tried to blackmail me into going along with them." I released a deep breath and girded myself for my next question. "Did you look at the files on that thumb drive?"

"I did."

"Everything?"

Bradford shrugged. "You mean some old newspaper clippings and a poorly written report by the Tolliver County Sheriff's office about an investigation decades ago? An investigation that was inconclusive with no dead body? And as for Violet Richards, I have no clue who she is, nor do I care."

My eyes widened at the detective's comment. "But . . ."

"Ms. Littlejohn, can I be candid? The first day I walked into this building, I counted six Black people. Four of them worked downstairs in Security. The other two were you and me. Maybe you've got a few more around here, but my instincts tell me there can't be many more. Maybe the protesters

521

had it right all along. Perhaps you should spend some time focusing on your future. I'm not sure what's going to happen to this company. The FBI is down the hall right now carting out evidence from several offices up here. Mr. Everett, Mr. Lumpkin, and Mr. Ashe are in custody. You saved a lot of innocent people. Take that as your parting gift from the Houghton Transportation Company." She stood from the chair. "Thanks again for your help."

The detective strolled out of my office. I turned to the window for one last look at the park.

When I was younger, I used to pretend that I was born in New York City or Chicago, like Chillicothe, Georgia, never existed. When Vera and Birdie packed me up and shipped me off to boarding school, I stepped into my new life. I stepped out of one little box in my life and into another. But my cardboard life of elite schools and professional success never really eased the haunting ache of growing up poor, Black, and female in rural Georgia. And all the rage and anger that I was fully entitled to was tamped down by a chorus of voices telling me to forgive, to turn the other cheek, to look the other way. So that rage and anger sat bottled up, simmering on the inside. All the while, I spent an entire lifetime calmly trying to explain to people why I needed to be in a certain classroom or worthy of a certain job. Even after my rise, I was still explaining why I needed to be in the room, with a seat at the table, and a voice in the decisions.

I removed my resignation letter from the desk drawer and placed it in the center of my desk. Now I could shut down this little compartment of my life.

Juice was right. I hadn't been happy, truly happy, in a very long time. It was because I was so tired, too weary from juggling all the cardboard pieces of my life, fighting all the -isms of being Black and female in America. Now, all I wanted to do was take off my boxing gloves and rest.

CHAPTER 43

On a cold, snow-damp day, I drove along the winding gravel path of a cemetery. Gray and black headstones stood at attention across the landscape as I cruised up alongside a large magnolia tree that would offer eternal shade and cover for Sam's final resting place. Two men stood off in the distance near a backhoe. One of them gazed into his cell phone, while the other stared in my direction cleaning his teeth with a toothpick. Both of them waited their turn to toss dirt over my little brother. A small blue tent with the words *Chillicothe Memorial Gardens* emblazoned in white letters stood over Sam's casket and provided a thin shelter from the light dusting of snow just beginning to fall. His casket, gunmetal gray and covered by a huge spray of white roses, sat like a lonely soldier in repose under the tent. And standing beside Sam's coffin were Rudy, Grace, and Juice.

I was stunned as I walked up to the gravesite. "What are you . . . how did you all know?"

"Did you think we wouldn't be here for you?" Grace asked as she hugged me.

Rudy smiled and hugged me, too. "I keep telling you, you're both my boss and my buddy. Just because I work for you doesn't mean I can't care about you, too."

Juice grabbed my hand and squeezed it.

"Are we waiting for others, dear?" Mrs. Gresham asked.

"No."

"I can say a bible verse if you like."

"Sure, that would be fine," I said.

Grace and Juice stood on either side of me, all three of us holding hands.

Mrs. Gresham's voice was soft and gentle as she began. " *'Who shall separate us from the love of Christ? Shall trouble or hardship or persecution . . .'* "

I was so sure I could keep it together. And I probably would have, too, until I remembered how stupid I'd been for trying to keep Sam and every other thing in my life that originated out of Chillicothe a secret, a secret that was no longer secret. A secret that was never worth keeping in the first place.

" *'. . . No, in all these things we are more*

than conquerors through him who loved us . . .' "

Tears rushed to the surface, a powder keg of emotion that exploded.

" '. . . for I am convinced that neither death nor life . . .' "

I wept for all the lost innocence between me and Sam. I cried for leaving him behind and heading off to find a future without him. I cried for the kid brother who never really got to be a kid at all. But mostly, I cried for all the pain I'd caused him.

" '. . . neither height nor depth, nor anything else in all creation, will be able to separate us from the love of God.' "

She finished and everyone eased away to give me a private moment of grief. I slipped a white rose from the spray covering Sam's casket. It was the loneliest moment of my entire life. I only hoped he knew how much I loved him and how far I'd go to protect him and fight for him.

A few minutes later, Mrs. Gresham gently touched my arm and handed me a small packet of tissues. "Will you be okay, dear?"

"Yes. Thank you." I patted my eyes.

Rudy walked over to me. "So the rumor machine has been buzzing again. And I don't like what I'm hearing," Rudy said, half joking.

"I'm sorry, but there's no place for me there."

"I heard there was a place for you at the top of the organization," he said. "You know people *tell me things* and they told me the board wanted you to take over as CEO. Maybe help give the company a fresh start."

"You mean another figurehead position to gloss over the mess they created?" I shook my head at the thought. "Besides, half that board is filled with racists and bigots. Nope. I'm good. Trust me, they don't want people like you and me in there. Those protesters out in front of the building knew it all along."

"I don't disagree, which is why I've dusted off my résumé. By the way, thanks for the save. It scares me to think we worked with people like that, huh?" Rudy and I stood in silence for a beat. "So what are you going to do?" he asked.

"I'm gonna take some time off. Attend to some things I've been neglecting. I'll stay in touch." I hugged him before he headed to his car.

Grace stepped up and hugged me. "I'm here for you, girl. I'll swing by your place later today." Then she leaned in and whispered, "What's up with the cutie with the locs?"

She made me smile. "Good-bye, Grace. I'll see you later."

I looked around for Juice, but I didn't see him so I headed to my car.

"Hey, beautiful! Wait up."

I glanced over my shoulder. "Thaddeus." He was dressed in a sports jacket, jeans, and an open-collar shirt. The nervous butterflies were back.

He gave me a gentle smile. "Please don't call me that. You sound like my mother and I don't want images of my mother popping up when I look at you. Thad or Juice is just fine."

I smiled. He was funny and that reminded me of Sam too. He walked me to my car.

"So, let's get together again," he said. "Maybe a nice restaurant this time instead of a gun shop backed by white supremacists."

I bit my bottom lip. "Not right now. I need to sort out some things."

Juice nodded understandingly. "Well, you have my number . . . and now I have yours, too." He winked. "I'm persistent."

I leaned over and kissed him on the cheek. "Thank you for everything."

Now I had one last thing to do to put my life in order.

■ ■ ■ ■

One week later, I sat inside the office of Miriam Beazer, director at the Beachwood Assisted Care Facility. A bulletin board hung on a side wall containing sundry notes and flyers and a drawing with the words *I love Nana* scrawled by a child's hand. Miriam sat across from me trying to make small talk and laughing nervously.

"You'll sign in all the highlighted areas." Miriam opened a folder and removed a small stack of papers before passing them across her desk to me. "Are you sure about all this, Ms. Littlejohn? This is a huge responsibility and with your career —"

"I'm very sure." I began signing the paperwork. Somehow this decision felt right and long overdue. A lot had happened over the past couple of weeks and taking a chance on Vera felt better than anything else I'd done in a long time.

"Ms. Littlejohn, I assure you Ms. Henderson was never in any danger here at Beachwood. Safety is our —"

"I'd just prefer to take her home." I said, never looking up from the documents as I signed them. "I think Vera will be more comfortable in familiar surroundings."

"But who will care for her?" The concern in the woman's voice was enough to press me to look at her.

"I will. She's family and who better to take care of her than family?" I smiled and slid the papers back across the desk. "I've hired a private nurse to help me. I think Vera ought to spend these precious days on her farm, sleeping in her own bed. A place she knows and loves."

I finished up the paperwork and left her office. In the lobby, Vera sat in a wheelchair in a flowered dress and jacket, her hair in a soft gray ponytail. She looked like a little kid on Christmas morning. Smiling. Excited. Happy.

I kissed the top of her head. "Let's go home, Vee." An aide pushed Vera's wheelchair and helped me get her buckled inside the car.

People say you can't go home again. I wouldn't know. I've never considered Chillicothe home, at least not until now. I'd always been so eager to live somewhere else. To be someone else. Only now did I realize I had been on a fool's errand. I was wounded and bound up in the crippling vise of secrets and lies. Everyone has a secret. And no matter how old the secret, it always seems to sit right on the surface of our consciousness, buoyed by all the effort we put into suppressing it. But it's a rare secret kept in the dark that never comes into the light.

Eventually they all do.

Mine did.

The day I accepted the promotion in Nate's office, it was as if fate struck a match and imparted a small glow onto my deadly cache. But perhaps it was all supposed to happen the way it did. My secrets slowly tumbling out into the light of day was what I needed all along to finally realize what was important. Family. Home.

Spring was still over two months away. Whether it was global warming or the fickle nature of Atlanta weather, somehow there was a pleasant rise in the air temperature and a clear blue sky to go along with it. The balmy breeze whipped around the edge of my skirt as I hopped inside the car beside Vera. I started the engine and headed for Interstate 20 East, toward Vera's farmhouse in Chillicothe.

I opened the sunroof and let all the windows down. The fresh air rushed inside the car, sweeping across my face and blowing my coils about.

"That air feels good, Ellie."

It did feel good.

It felt like freedom.

ACKNOWLEDGMENTS

First and foremost, I thank God, whose divine hand is all over this book you hold in yours.

I set out to write a story about family and all the ways we are connected to and nurtured by one another. To that end, there is much family to thank for helping me on this journey.

To my new family: My enormously talented editor, Asanté Simons, for believing in this book from her first read and all the reads thereafter. Thank you for listening and for making me believe no question was too small or too stupid. To my incredible team at HarperCollins William Morrow, including Lucia Macro, Lainey Mays, Virginia Stanley, Chris Connolly, Liate Stehlik, Jennifer Hart, Kaitlin Harri, Christina Joell, Ploy Siripant, Diahann Sturge, Rachel Weinick, the entire Lead Read committee, and the sales team. To the woman who made all my writing dreams come true, my fierce and fantastic agent, Lori Galvin. Thank you for your wisdom, grace, and ever the right amount of honesty to rein me in or let me run free! You are an angel on earth. And a huge thanks to Allison Warren, Shenel Ekici-Moling, Erin Files, and the entire Aevitas Creative Management team. Thank you for holding my hand and guiding me through this crazy, exciting ride. To Paul Monnin for helping me get the legal ethics details right. And to moukies (your insight and wisdom are pure gold!).

To my found family: The Yale Writers Workshop, most especially Jotham Burello, Lori Rader-Day, Hallie Ephron, and Sergio Troncosco. To Brandi Wilson, Julia Dahl, and Richard Krevolin for your unflinching candor and support when reading the early pages of this book. The Association of Corporate Counsel–Atlanta Chapter Women's Initiative, Kellye Garrett, Wendy Heard, my Pitch Wars family, and Crime Writers of Color. And to my "sister" squad: Cheryl Haynes, Angela Cox, Michonne Fitzpatrick, Cheri Reid, Juli Harkins, Rachel Gervin, Key Wynn, and Melloney Douce.

To the family I'm lucky enough to have gained by my birth and marriage certificates: Myra, Herman Jr. ("Red"), Carolyn, and everyone else in the Morris crew, and to Linda, Bertha, Paul, Michael, Sandra, and the rest of the Hightower clan. Your love and support are without limits.

To the family I gave birth to: Alexandra, Mitchell, and Ashton, my precious sweet peas. Thank you for being the greatest gifts of my life. You make me proud every single day. And without a doubt, you three are the best cheering squad ever!

And lastly, to the family I was blessed to meet and marry: Anthony Hightower, my rock and the wind beneath my wings. Your quintessential humor, quiet strength, and unwavering support have lifted me ever since our blind date all those years ago.

ABOUT THE AUTHOR

Wanda M. Morris is a corporate attorney who has worked in the legal departments for several Fortune 100 companies. An accomplished presenter and leader, Morris has previously served as President of the Georgia Chapter of the Association of Corporate Counsel and is the founder of its Women's Initiative, an empowerment program for female in-house lawyers. An alumnus of the Yale Writers Workshop, member of the Sisters in Crime and Mystery Writers of America, and Claymore Award finalist, Morris lives in Atlanta, Georgia, with her husband and children. *All Her Little Secrets* is her debut novel.

The employees of Thorndike Press hope you have enjoyed this Large Print book. All our Thorndike, Wheeler, and Kennebec Large Print titles are designed for easy reading, and all our books are made to last. Other Thorndike Press Large Print books are available at your library, through selected bookstores, or directly from us.

For information about titles, please call:
(800) 223-1244

or visit our website at:
gale.com/thorndike

To share your comments, please write:

Publisher
Thorndike Press
10 Water St., Suite 310
Waterville, ME 04901